About the Author

Scott Beynon writes fiction for children and young adults. *Dumb Martians* is his second novel. Prior to writing his first novel, *Princess Sahaar*, he worked as a teacher and business analyst. Now semi-retired (meaning mostly unemployed), he writes novels and dabbles in creating 3D digital art for video games and films. He is currently working on his third novel, *Small Monsters*, to be published in 2025, and can be found online at www.scottbeynon.com.

DUMB MARTIANS

Scott Beynon

First published 2023

2 4 6 8 10 9 7 5 3

National Library of Australia Cataloguing-in-Publication data:
Beynon, Scott 1964-
Dumb Martians / Scott Beynon

ISBN 978-0-6488370-4-6

BOOK ONE

Chapter One

A hand gave Holly a gentle push towards the shore. Holly responded by kicking and paddling like crazy. She didn't get far and started to sink again. But she needn't have worried — a hand came up beneath her tummy and held her up. She laughed and sputtered water, and pulled herself back into the woman's safe arms.

Holly tried again, frowning in concentration. She was sure that if she windmilled her arms fast enough, she'd race across the water like a motorboat. This time she made it to the shallows and as her legs dropped, her toes raked pebbles.

She stood up and wiped the water from her eyes. She was among the tinkerbells that lined the canal. Their tulip-shaped heads were opening to the morning sun, their stalks waving in a tiny breeze. For a moment the stalks parted, and Holly glimpsed a flash of gold. Curious, she waded ashore and climbed the embankment, her swimming lesson forgotten.

The pebbles gave way to sand, and the tinkerbells to a field of grain. People with greenish-bronze skin were cutting the crop with scythes, and beyond them a golden city of spires and domes shimmered on the horizon.

In wonder, she pointed at the city and turned around to show the woman, but the tinkerbells blocked her view. Quickly, Holly returned to the water's edge – no one was there. The water was still as glass.

Alarmed, but not frightened – not yet – she called out. 'Mum?'

The only reply was the rustle of the tinkerbells along the shore.

Holly woke and rubbed her sore cheek. She had fallen asleep against the wooden railing of the motorboat. The dream again: swimming lessons with her mother when she was . . . what, six? She was having it more and more. It didn't disturb her – she just wished she could see her mother's face.

She leaned over the side and trailed her hand in the water. Tiny silver fish that had been surfing the wake at the bow paused to nibble her fingers.

'Holly, wake up. This is it.'

In the wheelhouse, her dad spun the helm, and the boat turned sluggishly towards the shore. It beached with a scrunch on a shelf of pebbles. Holly leapt from the prow and ran up the embankment. The sand gave way to . . . more sand, and to the outskirts of a ruined city so worn down it looked like a rumpled orange-brown rug.

Holly plodded back to the boat where her dad was untying the ropes that held down a tarpaulin.

'What's it look like?'

'A pile of rubble.'

Her dad shrugged good-naturedly. 'Well, we're archae-
ologists. We live for piles of rubble! C'mon, give me a
hand.'

Her father pulled the tarp away to reveal a small buggy
with fat balloon tires. Holly grabbed her bum bag, scarf
and goggles from the wheelhouse, and her father stashed
his backpack and camera in the boot. Automatically, they
both paused to read the oxygen levels in the slim cylinders
attached to their thighs. The bioengineered tinkerbells
converted carbon dioxide and water into oxygen at a rate
many times greater than normal plants, but they mainly
grew along the banks of the Martian canals; further inland
you had to be careful. Her dad checked her O2 reading
too and nodded in satisfaction.

The boat had a blunt nose like a landing craft and a
ramp that swung down. Holly hit a green button on the
railing and the ramp swung into the water.

'Can I drive?'

'You're fourteen.'

Holly made a face. 'You taught me to drive the quad
bike when I was seven!'

Her dad gave her a sideways glance. 'Valid point. But
the buggy's tricky. Maybe on the way back.'

Holly scowled but climbed into the passenger seat. Her
dad drove the buggy down the ramp and up the embankment. Soon they were bouncing over the dunes, spurting
sand behind them.

The site was even less impressive up close. Broken

columns and toppled walls, none of them more than waist height, stretched for several kilometres to the west. The only relief to the drab brown stonework were the yellow poppies that seemed to sprout from every crack. Mars had been terraformed over many decades, and seeded with hardy plants and animals from Earth that could handle the arid conditions. The poppies appeared to love it.

Her father parked the buggy beside a wall and got to work taking photos and tracing the glyphs carved into the columns.

'Hmm, judging by the style of writing, I'd say third Martian dynasty. Interesting to note how the endpoints are more decisive . . .'

He was talking to himself. Holly wandered off into the ruins, bored.

Climbing a shallow rise, she found the remains of a small amphitheatre, with broken, stony steps leading down to a pool of sand. At one end, two pillars had fallen towards one another, creating a dark triangular gap. A lizard was sitting on top of one of the columns, watching her. As she approached, it scampered down and disappeared into the gap.

Holly knelt in front and scooped away some sand. A hole extended down into the shallow hillside. If she squinted, she could just make out a corridor with intact stone pillars. She caught a golden glint in the lizard's eye before it disappeared into the darkness.

'Dad!'

Her father's voice drifted back, '. . . remarkably well

preserved.'

'Dad. Over here.'

'What? What's that?'

'Over here!'

'Where are you?' Her father scrabbled over the rocks and down into the amphitheatre. 'Don't go running off like that,' he scolded, but the reprimand belied his interest. 'What is it? What have you found?'

Holly shuffled back to reveal the hole. Her father got down on his hands and knees and stuck his head in.

'Huh.'

He stood and examined the glyphs carved into the columns. Holly was getting excited.

'It's a tomb, isn't it?'

Her father gave her a funny look. 'You've got a real nose for this stuff. Wait here, I'll get the flashlights.' He ran off, pausing at the top of the hollow. 'And don't move. We've got to scan to make sure the structure's stable first.'

'Yeah, of course.' Holly waved him away impatiently, before turning around again and smiling into the hole.

Her dad took forever to scan the structure. Holly jumped up and down on tiptoes waiting for him to finish.

'All clear,' he announced finally. He got down on his hands and knees, crawled into the hole and disappeared. Holly followed, sliding down a sand 'chute' and landing in the passageway in a cloud of sand dust. Her dad had wandered ahead to examine the reliefs of ancient life carved into the walls. She switched her flashlight on and played it over the pictures. Spindly, human-shaped beings with elongated animal heads danced around her. These were the gods of ancient Mars – creepy amalgams of Martian and beast.

Her dad pointed out a hieroglyph painted in red ochre on a ledge above the passageway. 'What does it say?'

He was testing her. He loved doing this. Ernest Henry McGuire PhD (Cambridge) was a professor of Martian Antiquities in Port Clarke and had taught there for many years. Out here he had only one student – who couldn't escape.

'It's a prayer,' said Holly. 'That all who enter will pass safely through the Well of Souls into the underworld.'

The professor grinned. 'We'll make an archaeologist of you yet.'

Holly directed her flashlight down the passage. 'Look, it opens up.'

The passageway led to a large, domed chamber. Beams of light pierced the space from holes drilled in the curved ceiling. Statues of the gods twice human height encircled a room full of sarcophagi arranged in neat rows. The stillness tingled on Holly's skin. She might be the first visitor in thousands of years. But then she noticed the lids had been pushed aside and broken. She ran to the nearest sarcophagus and looked inside.

'Holly, wait!' called her father.

A pile of dust – not even a bone. Her father came up behind and put his hand on her shoulder.

'Robbed. Long before we got here,' he said sadly. The

casket was empty except for a simple stone sphere, about the size of a baseball, half-buried in the dust at the foot of the sarcophagus. Puzzled, he lifted and examined it a moment before putting it back.

There was an inscription on the underside of the lid. He lifted the lid higher to get a better look. Brushing the encrusted dust away revealed a symbol: several S-shaped curves surrounded by a series of dots and flourishes. A stylised picture of a flame or a river?

'Interesting,' he murmured. He took a photo of the inscription and printed a copy, tucking it into his shirt pocket with his notebook.

It wasn't interesting to Holly, but she lived in hope. She made her way around the other sarcophagi, peering inside each one. Watching her go, her father sighed. He put down his backpack and got to work.

Holly soon finished the circuit. Except for one. In an alcove at the top of some broken steps there was a stone block. It was in deep shadow from the lights that her dad had set up at the entrance, and she only saw it because she tripped over the bottom step. After a quick glance at her father, she scrambled up. This was promising: the sarcophagus was ornate, and the lid was intact, inscribed with the face of some long-dead beast with open jaws. She peered closer. Inside the mouth was an inset stone. Holly reached out . . .

'Holly!' warned her father from across the chamber.

. . . and touched it.

The tomb rumbled. From somewhere below the chamber floor, ancient mechanisms groaned and churned. A lever on the side of the sarcophagus turned as the lid rose in a screech of rusted hinges and tiny explosions of dust.

'Holly!' Professor McGuire ran across the floor of the chamber but stumbled on the broken steps.

The lid creaked to a halt only half-open. The rumbling subsided. Holly peered inside – nothing but a ridge of dust in the rough shape of a body. She stuck her arm in and shovelled up a handful. It flowed through her fingers like water.

The professor crawled up the steps into the alcove. 'Holly, are you okay? How many times have I told you not to touch—'

'Dust,' Holly muttered. She couldn't hide her disappointment. 'That's all we do. Gather dust.'

Her father looked pained. 'Holly, don't be like that. We're doing important work for the museum. This is an excellent find. These pictures, the writing – we'll add it to the database.' He nudged her shoulder. 'C'mon, it's all part of the great mystery of discovery!'

Exasperated, Holly stared at him and then stomped off. She scrambled down the steps and walked towards the exit. 'Oh, and rocks. Don't forget the rocks!' she yelled as she went. 'Rocks *and* dust!'

'Now, young lady, don't make me have to talk to you – you know, have a serious talk with you about your attitude. Seriously.'

'Rocks!' Holly climbed into the passageway and

switched her flashlight on.

'Hey, this is an excellent find. Now, go and get the sample bags, please? . . . Holly? . . . Holly!'

Her father's voice receded with every step Holly took, the shapes on the wall seeming to leer and laugh at her.

Scowling, she crawled out of the opening covered in sand, and brushed herself down. What a stupid waste of time! Why did she let her father drag her on these expeditions? She could have stayed in Port Clarke and gone to school. Maybe even made a friend. What a concept! And yet, every time, she let him talk her into it, stirring her up with stories of golden treasure and ancient mysteries.

She walked up the side of the hollow – and stopped dead. In the near distance, maybe half a kilometre away, an airship floated above the ruins. It was majestic: an advanced helium airship with a sleek aerofoil shape and a tail with pointy fins. Jet engines stuck out from either side, and tucked under its belly were a collection of cranes and manipulating arms. Majestic and menacing – like a killer whale with retractable claws.

Holly fumbled in her bum bag for a pair of small binoculars and trained them on the ship. Details came into focus: silvery fabric skin, cables, struts, the smudges of oil leaks. As Holly scanned the hull, an elevator platform, a kind of cage attached to the underbelly by chains and pulleys, slid into view and descended to the ground. It hit with a clang that rang out across the ruins. A gate opened and out stepped five people: a woman, three men and a boy about Holly's age. The woman wore a leather jacket;

the men's clothes were stained with sweat and dirt. It was difficult to make out much more – they were too far away – but one thing jumped out: all except the boy had guns. The men carried rifles, and the woman had a pistol strapped to her thigh.

Instinctively, Holly dropped to the ground. She glanced back at the entrance to the burial chamber. She must tell her father. But before she left, she couldn't help taking another look through the binoculars.

The group scratched around at the edge of the ruins and poked at foot-sized divots in the sand. Panning to the left, Holly saw the boat's buggy, hidden from the newcomers' view behind a wall. She swept back to the group. They were deep in conversation. The woman spoke into a radio attached to her shirt collar and waited for an answer. The boy stood to one side with his arms crossed. A man went to him and slapped him on the back.

The woman shaded her face with one hand and studied the ruins. She turned in Holly's direction. Holly froze. Could she be seen from there? The woman's gaze seemed to move on. Unnerved, Holly scuttled back down into the hollow and crawled into the hole.

'Dad! Dad!' She raced down the passageway and into the burial chamber. Professor McGuire was sitting on a block of stone, studying the photo he had taken earlier and comparing it to other pictures in his notebook.

'What's wrong?'

Holly gasped for breath. 'Someone's here.'

'What? Who?'

'I don't know. An airship. People. They have guns.'

The professor looked confused. 'Guns?'

'Guns! I think they've found our footprints.'

'Um, okay.' He paused to tuck the photo of the symbol into the lining of his vest. 'Show me.'

Crouching below the lip of the hollow, Professor McGuire tracked the newcomers with Holly's binoculars. More people had joined the first group, and several buggies were lowered to the sand. The buggies powered up and started making their way towards the ruins. One stopped to pick up the woman.

'What do they want? Are they pirates?'

'For God's sake, Holly, keep your head down.'

The men and women fanned out into a rough line and methodically made their way through the ruins, the vehicles patrolling alongside. It wasn't long before they neared the parked buggy.

'They'll see it,' the professor murmured. He glanced at his daughter. She was peeking over the edge again. 'Stay here.'

'What? Why?'

'Keep your head down and don't move, no matter what happens.' Handing the binoculars to Holly, he crossed to the other side of the amphitheatre.

'Dad?'

'Do as you're told and stay here!' he said fiercely. He climbed over the lip of the hollow and vanished.

Minutes passed. The red sun was at its zenith. Holly covered her head with her scarf. The lizard had popped up again and was sunning itself on a rock nearby. For the hundredth time, Holly checked the binoculars.

The first rank of pirates was closer, only a hundred metres away. Holly hunkered down further.

There was a furtive movement among the ruins. Holly swung the binoculars towards it. Her father, looking ridiculous in khaki shorts with his skinny white legs, tiptoed from one hiding spot to the next. He disappeared behind a wall. Holly strained to locate him again.

Suddenly the buggy was off and racing, her father at the wheel. It swirled away in a loose arc into empty desert – away from the airship, from the boat, from the ruins. And from Holly.

The pirates saw it and raised the alarm. Their buggies turned about and pursued. Holly stood just as one man raised his rifle. There was a sharp crack of thunder. Holly flinched. More shots followed.

The chasing buggies bounced and careened over the sand. They were bigger and faster and soon closed on their quarry, cutting the professor off and forcing him to swing back towards the airship. Soon he was almost underneath, wedged between two converging lines of vehicles. The cracks of gunfire increased.

Whooomp! A balloon tire exploded and the rear end of the buggy launched into the air. The vehicle cartwheeled several times over the sand and came to rest upside down in a tangle of plastic and metal.

Holly screamed, 'Dad!'

Incredibly, no one noticed. Everyone was heading in the other direction.

Holly started to move too, but one of the pirates emerged from the rocks to her right – the same man that had slapped the boy on the back. He turned towards her. Terrified, she flattened herself against a column, inching her way behind it. Soon she heard footsteps. Holly ducked down, tucked her knees to her chest and held her breath.

The footsteps grew louder, and a shadow swept across her hiding place. Holly was shaking. She could hear him breathing.

There was a rattle of tyres on stones.

'Patrice. We've got the professor. Get in.'

'Claudia, wait. I thought I saw—'

'*Get in.*'

'Yeah. Comin'.'

The shadow disappeared. Holly let her breath out in a whoosh.

Summoning all her courage, she crawled back to the lip of the hollow and found the binoculars. She watched as the pirates assembled around the crashed buggy and dragged her father from the wreckage. Groggy, with blood flowing from a gash in his temple, he tried to stand, but a pirate pushed him back down to his knees.

Claudia and Patrice pulled up alongside, and Claudia jumped out with practised ease. Hands on hips, she stood in front of the professor and said something. He shook his head. The woman leaned forward and spoke again.

The professor didn't seem to reply; instead, he hung his head and stared at the ground. The woman motioned to another pirate. He came forward and struck Holly's father in the back of the head with his rifle.

'Dad!' Holly cried as he collapsed forward onto the sand. She wanted to move, but her feet were welded to the ground.

The pirates separated into groups. Some sorted through the remains of the vehicle, throwing some bits away and stashing the rest into bags. A crane lifted their buggies back into the belly of the airship, and most of the pirates rode up with them. The remaining pirates dragged the limp form of the professor towards the elevator.

With a shock, Holly realised they were leaving. She started to run.

The cage opened, and the woman and the pirates carrying her father stepped inside.

Holly sprinted through the ruins. She tripped on a stone, fell forward, grazed her knee. Barely breaking her stride, she ran on.

The jet engines on either side of the airship spun up, the noise increasing to a high-pitched scream. A storm was stirred underneath, sending billows of sand over the dunes. The elevator reached the underbelly of the airship and disappeared inside.

Holly ran as fast as she could.

The airship ascended at first slowly and then swiftly in a graceful arc.

Holly ran into the sandstorm. The massive bulk of the

airship blocked out the sun. Overwhelmed with distress, she staggered to a halt and fell to her knees.

And screamed, '*Daaad!*'

Chapter Two

Pursuit

Holly ran over the dunes, the sand sucking at her feet. She stopped and bent over, clawing at the pain in her side. She forced herself to straighten up, gulped a few breaths from the oxygen cylinder and started running again.

She topped the embankment to the canal, ran down into the shallow water and scrambled up the ramp of the boat, hitting the button to retract the ramp as she rushed past.

Holly ran into the wheelhouse and punched a button on the instrument panel. The motor started straight away with an electric hum. She grabbed the throttle and rammed it into reverse. The boat clunked and shuddered. She took the wheel and waited. Nothing happened.

She pulled the throttle up and forced it down again, harder. The engine whined and the boat shook, but it didn't move.

Holly ran to the prow and looked over the side. The boat was beached on the shingles. She leapt over the rail and landed on all fours in the shallow water. Getting up, she leaned against the prow and pushed. And pushed and pushed. The boat didn't budge. She leaned into it at a greater angle, digging her feet into the pebbles, and tried again, straining with all her might. Tears ran down her face; disgusted she wiped them away. The boat inched backwards, and after a final push it floated free – and Holly fell headfirst into the water. She scrambled to her feet and chased after it, grabbing the railing to vault back in. Returning to the wheelhouse she spun the wheel, and the boat curved backwards into deeper water. Before it had straightened up, Holly slammed the throttle into full forward and the little boat moved off down the canal, gradually picking up speed.

Holly grabbed the binoculars from her bum bag and checked the sky. The airship was an almond-shaped sliver of metal to starboard. She was heading in the same direction, but the airship was faster and moving away to the south-west.

The boat approached a junction in the canal where a separate ribbon of water led away to the right. Holly turned into the new canal, startling a pair of purple flamingos canoodling along the shore. They flew away, carping angrily.

The sun set. The little moon Phobos rose in the west and moved steadily across the sky. Soon Deimos would join it from the east. The sky had shifted from pale blue to dusty pink. In all the immensity the only sound was the murmur of the tinkerbells disturbed by the boat's wake.

Holly travelled with one hand on the wheel and the

other holding the binoculars. Her mind was blank. The tracks of tears on her face had dried, encrusted with granules of sand. Every few minutes, she robotically checked the sky. The airship had receded and was now only a shiny speck on the horizon.

Night. The sky was a blaze of icy stars. Holly sat on a stool, leaning against the wheel, the binoculars discarded beside her. Briefly, her eyes closed, and she fell forward and hit her head. The knock woke her up and she rubbed her eyes, forcing them to focus. She shivered – it had gotten cold – and tried to wrap her scarf around her shoulders.

Somewhere a child laughed, and there was a splash of water. Holly woke with a start and for a second forgot where she was. The boat sat motionless among the tinkerbells on the side of the canal. A light frost lay across the dunes, sparkling as the sun rose. She had fallen asleep against the wheel; her cheek pressed awkwardly up against a spoke.

'Mum?'

Then she remembered where she was. She ran out of the wheelhouse with the binoculars and pressed up against the railing. Frantically, she searched the sky. Empty. Wherever she looked.

'No. No. No!'

Holly climbed on top of the wheelhouse and did a slow turnaround. Nothing but sand in all directions.

It was too much. She collapsed onto the roof of the wheelhouse and cried – great wracking sobs that continued until she was too tired even to cry, and just lay there panting.

At last, numb, she wiped her face with the dirty scarf, climbed down from the roof and entered the cabin below the wheelhouse.

Holly got a glass of water from the sink, drank it and poured herself another one. The tiny kitchen table was covered in papers, maps, a laptop and assorted junk. She sat down and flicked the screen of the laptop. A pulsing symbol appeared and dissolved to show a topographic map of Mars. She took a stylus from a collection sitting in a mug and thought a moment, sweeping her fingers over the surface of the pad, moving the map around.

A blue dot sitting on a narrow straight line was the boat. Holly marked it with a red circle. She drew lines and arcs over the map, pausing to scribble calculations alongside. She plotted the direction the airship was heading in, based on her last sighting.

Now for its destination. Holly did some more calculations, extended the lines and connected them with an arc. She sat back to survey her handiwork: a red outline in the shape of an ice cream cone.

Holly leaned over the map and searched inside the cone, scrolling around, zooming in and out. The area was devoid of features other than craters and bluffs of rock. She flicked the image to satellite. Red hills and ochre sand materialised. Holly zoomed in on some purplish-brown smudges. Rocks. More rocks.

Except – one had an unnaturally smooth curve between

two sharp angles. She zoomed in; it became a pixelated blur. It might be a compound or a station of some kind. Maybe.

Holly zoomed out. A canal passed within a couple of kilometres of the purple smudge. She traced the route to get there. It was worth a try. What else could she do? This wasn't Earth. You couldn't radio for help and expect a rescue service. She was 3000 kilometres from the nearest settlement (that she knew of). The total population of Mars was only a few million, and most of them lived in towns halfway around the planet. Holly and her father had been exploring an area called Noachis Terra in the Southern Highlands. The only signs of civilisation were the ubiquitous canals the Martians had left behind, and lots of ruins. Which probably explained the pirates. One could make a good living raiding the ancient cities and tombs for gold and silver and rare artefacts prized by collectors on Earth.

Enough. She had to keep moving. The longer she sat here, the less chance she had of finding her father. Sore and tired, she went back up to the wheelhouse and pressed the engine button. The motor hummed to life and the little boat moved off down the canal.

Holly crouched among the tinkerbells at the top of the embankment. She had beached the boat a few hundred metres further back and waded to this spot through the shallow water. Keeping low, she looked through the binoculars. Four hundred metres away was a multistorey

structure with a dome on top, a helipad and several bolt-
ed-on cubicles and platforms. A collection of sheds, some
as big as hangars, surrounded it. Even from this distance
the place looked abandoned: broken windows, sand piled
up against the superstructure, tarpaulins flapping listlessly
in the breeze.

Holly took a canister of water from her backpack and
gulped some down. She put it back and moved off towards
the compound.

Deserted, apparently. Dust devils swirled about the
sheds. The doors were open as if the previous occupants
had left in a hurry. Holly stood in an open space outside
the primary structure and looked around. It reminded her
of the tiny settlements that had sprung up around Port
Clarke. Lots of simple, easily constructed domes and sheds,
erected by settlers from Earth looking for a better life, or
at least one where they didn't have to follow any laws but
their own. But out here? If they wanted to be left alone,
they had picked a great spot.

'Hello?' she said, too softly for anyone to really hear.

A clanging noise was coming from somewhere. Holly
followed the sound. It was a door to a shed, hanging ajar,
banging against a rock. She kicked the rock aside and
stuck her head in. It was dark . . .

'Anybody home?'

. . . and empty, apart from some broken crates and litter
on the floor.

Holly walked back to the centre of the open space
and considered the main structure. There was a flurry of

movement past an open doorway. Spooked, Holly swung in that direction.

'What? Who's there?'

Senses thrilling, she stood rigid. The wind? Sure, why not?

She approached the open door. The space inside looked dark and cavernous, but she could see vague shapes outlined against the far wall. She covered her eyes for a few seconds, preparing them for the dim interior, then took a breath and stepped through, stopping a metre inside the doorway. She made out barrels, boxes, a couple of gutted buggies and assorted rubbish. Above her, chains and pulleys and a single broken light hung from a ceiling up in the gloom.

'Anybody home?'

A table towards the centre of the space drew her attention. A shaft of light passing through a ragged hole in the wall illuminated a book sitting on the table. She walked closer. It was a copy of the Bible, with a leather strap as a placeholder. She picked it up and opened it at the placeholder. A handwritten note contained a single word: *Gotcha!*

Chains rattled and something big loomed fast overhead. *Bang!* It crashed to the floor around her, the impact knocking her off her feet. The chains rumbled to a halt and silence descended again.

Stunned but unhurt, Holly staggered to her feet. And immediately bumped her forehead against a steel bar. She was inside a cage, like a crate for transporting live animals or something. She grabbed the bars and shook them. As solid as – well, steel. Bewildered, she stuck her face up against the bars and peered into the settling cloud of sand and dust.

Two figures stood in front of the light from the open doorway. One was a small girl, about ten or eleven years old, with long dark hair, a snub nose and twinkling eyes. She was wearing desert boots that were too large for her and a floral dress with a cardigan. The other one was an older boy, with freckles and a thatch of unruly hair. He was wearing roomy trousers, suspenders and a vest, like he was going to a barn dance. They were both exceedingly, sordidly, grubby.

'It worked!' said the girl.

'Course it worked,' the boy replied.

'Well, it might not 'ave.'

That annoyed the boy. 'It was always going to work. I rigged it myself.'

'Alright, alright, I'm just saying.'

Holly listened to this exchange with increasing frustration. 'What? Who are you?' She shook the bars again. 'Let me out of here.'

'You're the prisoner,' the boy said. 'We ask the questions.'

'Yeah!' the girl added emphatically.

'Now . . . um, who are you? And what are you doing here?'

'What is wrong with you? Let me out of here *now*.'

'You have to answer our questions first,' said the boy.

Holly looked the two of them up and down. They were

both shorter than her and not at all intimidating. Despite her earlier fright, Holly was completely underwhelmed.

'What are you? Ten?' she asked the boy.

He sounded hurt. 'I'm thirteen.'

'I'm eleven,' the girl said helpfully.

'Let me out or I'll beat you both with a stick until you're purple all over,' she said with a menace that surprised even her.

The kids recoiled.

'Don't be like that,' the girl said. 'And anyway, you can't. I mean, you're in *there*.'

Holly glared, but the girl had a point. She sighed. Time for a different tack.

'Look, I came here in a boat. My father is a professor at the Museum of Martian Antiquities. Pirates kidnapped him yesterday and took him away in an airship. I'm trying to find him.'

The girl whispered loudly to the boy, 'Was that the airship we saw?'

Holly clenched the bars. 'You saw the airship?'

'Yeah. A big silvery one with—'

'Where was it heading?'

The girl pointed to the west. 'That way, kinda.'

'What's that way?'

'Dunno, probably Urbe Sicaria. It's the last stop before—'

'Stop. Stop!' the boy shouted. 'We're asking the questions, remember?'

'I was just trying to help,' the girl said.

'Help *us*. Us! Not her!'

The girl sulked and played with her hair. The boy took a deep breath and adjusted his suspenders.

'We've been watching the canal. There's no boat. You're lying. How did you really get here?'

'Are you brain dead? I pulled up two hours ago. I bet if you climbed to the top of the tower, you could see it.'

The boy looked uncertainly at the girl. 'Well?' he whispered loudly.

'I dunno,' she whispered back.

'What do you mean? You're supposed to watch the canal.'

'But I can't watch it all the time.'

'But that's your one job. You have *one* job! I do everything else. You watch the canal. That's it. That's—'

The girl defended herself angrily. 'I saw her approaching the compound, didn't I?'

'That's all you have to—'

'And I do plenty of other stuff.'

Holly tried to jump in. 'Guys?'

'Like what? What do you do?'

'Like . . . *other* stuff.'

'No, you don't. You never used to do your chores, either.'

'Guys?'

'I did too!'

'You did not. Mum always had to—'

'That's not fair!'

'*Guys!*' Holly screamed.

Scolded, the kids fell quiet, glowering at each other. The girl wiped her wet nose on the sleeve of her cardigan.

The boy was sniffling a bit too.

Holly rattled the bars in frustration. 'This is just. So. Stupid!'

'Well, watch her now while I check out this boat,' the boy said grumpily. 'She might have food or something to sell.' He stomped off. The girl stuck her tongue out at him as he walked out the door.

Holly paced up and down in the cage. The girl was sitting on a crate, scratching patterns in the sand with a stick, moping.

'Do you have a brother?' the girl asked.

'No.'

'Lucky. He's such a pain.' The girl looked up. 'What's your name?'

'Holly.'

'I like that. It's pretty. We're the Hendriksens. I'm Sophie, and my stupid brother is Toby.'

Holly nodded, distracted by an object on the ground. The cage had clipped a side of the table when it fell and smashed it, but one intact table leg lay in the sand.

'He always thinks he's in charge. *Do this, do that . . .*'

Holly noticed a tangle of chains on the back wall, just out of her reach. One looped up to the pulley overhead that was holding the cage.

'. . . always giving orders, bossing me around . . .'

Holly picked up the stick and glanced over her shoulder at Sophie. The girl was still scratching in the sand. Holly moved casually to the back of the cage, which was in shadow.

'. . . but nobody put *him* in charge.'

'What about your parents?'

'They did not!' Sophie looked up. 'What are you doing?'

'I, ah, need to go.'

'Go where?'

'I need to pee!'

'Oh.' Sophie turned away.

'No, I mean, where are your parents?' Holly continued, as she reached through the bars with the table leg and snagged the chain. It rattled a little. She quickly glanced at Sophie. The girl was absorbed in her complaining.

'Dunno. Gone.'

'Oh . . . kay. And the other adults?'

'Gone too. When the prophecy didn't work, they left.'

'The prophecy?'

'Oh yeah, we're the Order of the Saints of the Blessed Design. We had a prophecy. Davidus, our leader, said that Jesus would return on Mars and anybody who was there to greet him would be taken up to heaven.'

This was the silliest thing Holly had ever heard, but she had to keep Sophie talking while she worked the cable. 'What happened?'

'He didn't show.'

Holly wrangled the tip of the table leg through a link in the chain.

'Then there was a storm that broke the solar panels. Then the water pumps failed. And the crops died. People kinda lost faith after that and started to leave, first in drib-drabs and then . . . woke up one morning and all the hovercrafts and airships were gone. Everybody run off overnight.'

Holly lifted the chain off the hook and guided it into her other hand.

'Well, not Mum and Dad, of course. They were like, *really* faithful. And Davidus, he was somewhere. But then we ran out of food and got hungry. I mean *reeaally* hungry.' Sophie paused in her scribbling. 'Flip, I shouldn't have said that. Now I'm hungry too. I was trying not to think about it, but—'

Holly pulled on the chain. The cage rose a fraction. The noise attracted Sophie's attention.

'What are you doing?'

Sophie got off the crate and came forward, squinting into the gloom. It became clear. Despite the righteousness of her cause, Holly felt a little guilty, caught in the act.

'Hey, stop that!' Sophie said.

Holly pulled the chain through her hands. The cage rose several centimetres at a time.

'Stop. Help! Toby, she's escaping. Help!'

When the cage was a metre off the floor, Holly manoeuvred herself close to the bars. She paused, settled, ducked and rolled under the bottom bar, releasing the chain at the same time. The cage crashed to the floor, but Holly was now on the outside.

'That's not fair. You let me talk while you were getting out!'

'Well, yes,' replied Holly.

Sophie raised the stick that she was using to draw and pointed it at Holly. 'I warn you!'

Holly stepped smartly forward, twisted the stick out of the girl's hand and threw it away.

Sophie felt her wrist. 'Ow! That hurt.'

From outside came Toby's voice, getting closer. 'Sophie! You should see it. She has food and computers and all kinds of stuff we can sell. And fuel cells! We'll be able to power Ship and get outa here. Sophie?' His jaw dropped as he entered. Angrily, he turned to his sister.

'She's, like, really strong,' said Sophie, massaging her wrist.

Toby looked around and found a piece of copper pipe lying against the wall. He brandished it in front of him like a sword. Holly walked leisurely to the side of the cage and picked up the table leg. She returned and stood in front of Toby with her feet wide apart and both hands around the 'hilt'.

Toby licked his lips and lunged. Holly deftly parried his thrust, skipped to the side and whacked him. He yelped and held his stung shoulder. Holly stepped past, turned around and took up her stance again.

'Kenjutsu,' she said. 'Second kyu, blue belt.'

'Wow, that sounds really good,' said Sophie.

Toby shot his sister a withering look. He positioned himself for another round, this time mirroring Holly's stance. More sword fighting ensued. Toby was seriously outmatched, and then some. He absorbed a dozen more blows, his cries getting louder each time, but bravely returned for more. At last, in pain and desperation, he raised his sword for a big chop and charged. Holly ducked aside and tripped him. He fell flat on his face. He rolled over and tried to scramble to his feet, but Holly held the pointy end of the table leg to his throat. There was no escape.

'You said you had a ship?' said Holly.

'Maybe,' muttered Toby.

'It needs fuel cells?'

'Maybe.'

Holly lowered the point of her sword and stepped back. 'I'll give you two fuel cells if you take me to Urbe Sicaria.'

Toby got to his feet, wincing and feeling his sore spots. Sophie came forward and stood next to him, looking up at Holly as if she was a dangerous but alluring animal.

Toby thought furiously. 'Five. Five fuel cells!'

'Two,' Holly replied.

'Four,' he said.

'Two,' she said.

'Three!' he said.

'Two,' said Holly, eyes of steel.

Toby opened his mouth to make another bid, but he'd been beaten again. 'And the maglev.' He glanced at Sophie. 'We can sell it for food.'

Sophie nodded vigorously in agreement.

Holly considered it for a second before sticking out her hand. Toby flinched, thinking she was going to hit him again.

'Deal. Shake on it,' Holly said.

He hesitated, then tentatively shook her hand.

'Wait,' said Sophie, becoming excited. 'We're going to Urbe Sicaria for food?'

Dejected, Toby nodded.

'Aaahhh!' Sophie squealed.

Holly stood on the prow of the boat and scanned the sky. Behind her, sounds came from below deck. Toby emerged from the wheelhouse carrying two chunky fuel cells by their handles. The cells were very heavy, and he struggled manfully with the weight. When Holly turned to watch, he scowled at her. He was sore from losing, twice, to a girl. She ignored him and went back to watching the sky.

Toby loaded the cells into a wheelbarrow and pushed them up the embankment. When he was gone, Holly went down into the cabin.

It was a mess. Empty food bar wrappers, half-eaten biscuits and dried fruit lay on the floor, and cutlery and crockery were strewn over the table. Sophie was rifling through the cabinets, looking for food. She had a caramel bar sticking out of her mouth and was filling a bag with freeze-dried food packets.

'Hey, that wasn't part of the deal,' said Holly.

'Mmmffphgble waphhfmd,' Sophie replied.

Holly frowned. Whatever.

She went down the short corridor into her bedroom. It had a few homey touches like a quilt, stuffed toys and drawings on the wall, but it now seemed empty and dingy.

Maybe it always had been.

Holly grabbed her backpack and packed some clothes and toiletries. On a stand beside the bed was a framed photo of her mother. Looking at it, Holly felt a pang in her chest. She removed the picture from the frame and put it in her pocket.

She went into the second bedroom. This space was more alive, and reeked of her father. Maps and manuscripts covered the bed, and Martian artefacts, trinkets and assorted electronic equipment lay scattered around the room.

Holly selected some of the smaller electronic gear and packed it into her bag. She went to the wall cabinet and opened the safe. Inside was a taser, and another object wrapped up in cloth. She unwrapped the object – a gun, old-fashioned but clean and well oiled. She put the taser and gun in her bag as well.

Holly and Sophie made their way back to the compound and found Toby unlocking a shed the size of an aircraft hangar. Inside was a large, sleek vehicle in the shape of a fat stingray, with four turbofans housed in rotating turrets under the wings. Painted in a very, very dark grey, it had a line of bullet holes tracing a neat arc down one flank. It looked deadly, like a stealth bomber, which in a way it was.

Toby carried the fuel cells up a ramp into the ship. Holly hung back.

'This is an airship?'

'A hovercraft hybrid,' Toby called proudly from the top of the ramp. 'It has hot helium in the body but needs the extra lift from the fans and wings to get it off the ground. If you switch the fans to vertical, it can hover and even fly a little.'

He disappeared inside the hull. Holly felt one of the bullet holes with her finger.

Sophie added cheerfully, 'It's a warship.'

'Why do you have a warship?'

Sophie stuck her nose in the air. 'The Saints of the Blessed Design have always been persecuted for our beliefs. When we came to Mars, the government tried to take our guns away.'

'So you got a warship?'

'Of course. To protect our guns.'

'Huh.'

Toby's muffled voice came from a grill on the side of the vehicle. 'Bought it second-hand. Left over from the war.'

'What war?' Holly asked.

But Toby didn't respond, and Sophie had disappeared inside too. Holly followed her into the ship.

The interior was dark, but Holly could make out a flight deck with two seats overlooking a wide instrument panel full of knobs and buttons and dials. Behind the seats was a table, chairs, a sink and some cupboards – like the kitchenette on board the boat – and further back, there was a bulkhead with a steel door.

Sophie threw the bag of food on the table. 'C'mon. I'll show you around.'

The steel door opened to an area with a chair and console for the flight engineer, and a set of narrow steps leading down into a bomb bay. Two horizontal missile tubes were embedded in the walls on either side. The lids of all but one tube were open, and the top two had been converted into sleeping nooks, complete with mattresses, pillows and, in Sophie's case, colourful chalk drawings and photographs pinned to the walls. Through an open hatch at the furthest end of the bomb bay was a tiny bathroom and a corridor leading to the engine room.

Sophie pointed out the bunks. 'Toby and I have the top ones.' She grabbed a stuffed toy horse from her nook and showed it to Holly. 'See? This one's mine. But you can have the one under me if you like. I'll get another mattress from the storeroom. And I can lend you a pillow.'

Nonplussed, Holly took her backpack off and put it down beside her 'bunk'. 'You live here?'

'Yeah. It's the only place the sand can't get. Something . . . something keeps it away . . .'

Toby's voice rang out from the engine room. 'Electrostatic repulsion.'

'. . . and until the fuel cells ran out, we had hot water and electricity.'

Toby came through the hatch wiping his hands on a rag. He went to a panel on the wall and opened it to reveal a red lever.

'I hope this works.'

'I bags first shower!' Sophie said.

'Yeah, yeah.'

Toby pulled the lever. There was a series of clicks, hums and whirrs. The overhead lights came on and the instrument panels started blinking red and green. Sophie and Toby looked around expectantly.

A voice – deep, husky, vaguely feminine and not a little menacing – emanated from everywhere at once. 'Aaahhh. Power.'

'Ship, you're back!' cried Sophie.

'Hello, Ship,' said Toby.

'Executive Officer Sophie. Commander Toby. I am glad you're okay. My internal clock shows I have been offline for almost ninety days.'

Sophie stroked the bulkhead. 'Yeah. We really missed you, Ship.'

'Ship, good news. Fuel cells,' said Toby.

'Thank you, Commander. Cold fusion core. Almost ninety-five per cent capacity. They will do nicely. Is it time for the final battle?'

'Ah, no. Not yet. Just into Sicaria for supplies. Maybe later.'

The ship sounded disappointed. 'Pity. Wait. I sense a strange presence.'

'Yeah, new girl. Kinda swish,' said Sophie.

'A prisoner?' The flight engineer's chair at the top of the stairs spun around to face them; the headrest jerked upright. A spotlight flicked on overhead, shining an intense beam on the headrest. 'Strap her in. I will interrogate.'

Sophie and Toby looked at each other in alarm.

'No, no, we already did that,' said Sophie. 'She's okay, Ship.'

'She's a civilian,' said Toby.

'Are you certain, Commander? She might be a spy. In war you can never be too sure.'

'No, it's fine, Ship, really.'

Holly mouthed her question to Sophie again. *What war?*

Sophie circled her finger around her temple, intimating that Ship was crazy.

Toby headed back to the flight deck. 'Yeah, we're sure, Ship. We're just going into town for supplies. Power up, let's go.'

'Yes, Commander.'

The engines spun up. The hovercraft vibrated as the outside hum increased. Holly and Sophie followed Toby back to the flight deck, where Toby took a seat in front of the instrument panel and strapped himself in. Sophie ran and leapt into the chair next to him. The metal covers over the forward windows slid down to reveal the door of the hangar. Other windows to either side showed vortices of sand blowing out from under the turbo fans. The vehicle lifted with a lurch and inched forward.

Sophie bounced up and down in her seat. 'So exciting!'

The hovercraft glided out of the hangar, turned and moved off through the compound, sandblasting the sheds to either side. Leaving the buildings behind, it picked up speed and height, and was soon hurtling across the desert, two metres above the dunes.

That night, Holly stood in front of the bathroom mirror and examined her puffy face. She hadn't gotten much rest the last couple of days. She was also finding it hard not to cry again. With no idea whether the pirates' destination was really Urbe Sicaria; she could be heading in the wrong direction. And if that was the case, then . . . what? Where did she go? What did she do? The uncertainty produced a constant fear, a nagging buzz that had her feeling sick in the pit of her stomach.

She splashed some water onto her face. She didn't want the Hendriksens to see her like this – she didn't know whether she could trust them. Sophie had suddenly become her best friend and had spent the afternoon showing Holly her scrapbook, filled with pictures of cute cottages, flower gardens and celebrities she had cut from old Earth magazines. Toby had settled on gruff indifference and tried to ignore her. After having showers, the siblings retired: Toby to play chess at the kitchen table against Ship, and Sophie to her bunk to stick pictures of happy families to her wall.

Thinking of happy families was too much. Holly started to cry. Moments later there was a gentle knock on the door.

'Are you alright?' asked Sophie.

Holly wiped away her tears. 'Yes, yes, I'm fine. I'm just getting into the shower.'

'Um . . . okay,' said Sophie.

After her shower, Holly padded to her bunk with a bag of toiletries in one hand and her toothbrush in the other. The lights were dim and the windows to either side showed a dark, moving landscape of dunes and rocks. A rhythmic snuffling was coming from behind the curtain of Toby's bunk, while Sophie was lying on her back in her own nook, apparently asleep.

Holly climbed into her new bed, lay back and stared at the ceiling. Her pillow felt lumpy. Sitting up, she pulled out the toy horse Sophie had shown her earlier. She reclined again, hugging the horse to her chest.

Chapter Three

Urbe Sicaria

Holly woke to the sound of the Hendriksens squabbling.

'But you said I could be commander for a while.'

'No, I said you could be executive officer – and you are.'

'I don't know what that is. I want to be commander.'

'You're too young.'

'But you're only thirteen.'

'Exactly, the oldest, so I'm the commander.'

'That's not fair.'

'That's how it is . . .'

Holly groaned. She rubbed her face and got out of bed, returning the toy horse to Sophie's bed, before plodding up the stairs to the upper deck. Toby and Sophie were having breakfast. The kitchenette table was strewn with food packets and cereal boxes. *Her food.*

She frowned at the siblings. 'This is all food from the boat.'

Toby and Sophie looked at each other sheepishly.

'We didn't want it to go to waste,' said Sophie.

Holly sighed, sat down and poured herself some of her own breakfast cereal.

There was an awkward silence.

'Did you sleep okay?' asked Sophie.

Holly gave her a sad smile. 'Yes. How far to Urbe Sicaria?'

'Ship?' Toby asked.

'ETA is thirty minutes, Commander. Scanning for enemy strongpoints now.'

'What's there, exactly?' asked Holly.

'Not much,' said Sophie.

Toby counted the attractions on his fingers. 'Taverns, bars, the port, a few shops and houses. Fuel stations. Wind farms.'

'One place sells ice cream,' Sophie said.

'If the pirate ship is there, it'll be tied to a tower at the port,' said Toby.

Sophie looked up shyly from her cereal bowl. 'Why did they take him? Your dad, I mean?'

'I think it was because he's an archaeologist. He works at the Museum of Martian Antiquities.'

Toby nodded sagely. 'Tomb raiding. They probably think he can lead them to sites they can plunder.'

'Oh, you mean gold?' said Sophie.

'And the artefacts,' said Holly. 'Collectors back on Earth will pay a lot of money for a rare piece of Martian civilisation.'

'But mainly the gold,' said Sophie.

Holly made an exasperated noise. 'They're crazy. He doesn't know anything. All the places we ever visited were robbed already!'

'Maybe he'll take them to the City of the Dead?' said Sophie.

Holly shook her head. 'No, that's a myth. Like El Dorado.'

'What's that?

'El Dorado,' Toby explained, 'was a mythical city of gold that the Spanish conquistadors went wandering all over South America looking for.'

'Konk-kissed . . .? Did they find it?' asked Sophie.

'No, *obviously*, because it was mythical,' said Toby.

'Yeah, but do the pirates know that?'

Holly scowled at her cereal. Sophie had a point. The truth didn't matter, only what the pirates believed.

'Commander, I have visual,' Ship announced.

Toby went to the flight deck. 'Put it up, Ship.'

One of the front windows clouded over and cleared again to show the outskirts of Urbe Sicaria: a dusty mess of aluminium huts, wind turbines, sandstone buildings and greenhouses. Over a stretch of tarmac there were three airships tied to conning towers. The view zoomed in and out and panned around before settling on the airships.

'They are civilian,' Ship said, disappointed.

Holly joined Toby in front of the screen. 'I don't know. That one could be it. I need to get closer.'

'What will you do if it isn't?' asked Sophie.

Holly glumly shook her head.

'What will you do if it is?' asked Toby.

Holly thought for a moment. 'Is there a police station or government office in town?'

'It's not that kind of town,' said Sophie.

Toby shrugged. 'That's why people come to Mars – no rules. Not out here, anyway.'

The hovercraft lost height as it approached the outskirts and glided to an empty spot in the docks on the edge of town. The docks were bustling with activity. In and around the haphazardly parked hovercrafts, sand crawlers and smaller airships was a market bazaar, with stalls selling food, souvenirs and equipment, and sellers noisily hawking their wares. The hovercraft parked between two other vehicles, and as the sand settled around it, the ramp lowered. Holly, her backpack on, walked to the end of the ramp and looked around. Sophie came down behind her. Toby remained in the doorway.

'Remember,' Toby said, 'this completes our deal. We got you here.'

Sophie shot him an evil look.

Toby continued in a nicer tone. 'Go to the port office. They'll know if the airship has docked.'

Holly looked at the bustle of the marketplace. The smell of frying onions and sausages wafted over her. She was finding it hard to step off the ramp.

'And I'll keep the bunk ready for you, just in case, you know . . .' said Sophie.

Holly turned to Sophie and shyly held out her hand. 'Thanks.'

Sophie regarded the hand for a second and then rushed in to give Holly a hug. Holly patted her awkwardly on the shoulder. When Sophie finally let go, Holly hitched up her backpack and walked off into the bazaar.

A canal separated the docks from the rest of the town. Holly crossed a bridge and entered the narrow streets and alleyways of the business district. Pedestrians, bicycles, quads, llamas and goats all jostled for room. No road rules were apparent.

Holly turned right and looked up through lines of washing that stretched between the buildings. Blotting out half the sky were the airships she had seen from the hovercraft. She zigzagged through the streets and found the port office at the edge of a plaza. Inside was a lounge area where sleepy passengers waited for flights, and a front counter staffed by a man in uniform. Through the glass front of the office, Holly could see the three airships that were docked. Now that she could see them up close, she was certain none was the pirate ship. She went to the counter. The clerk was talking on the phone. An old-fashioned fan rattled on the desk next to him.

'Wait a minute.' He covered the mouthpiece and raised his eyebrows at Holly.

'Um, did a big airship come this way yesterday or possibly this morning?' she asked. 'Silver one with a pointy nose?'

'The *Pointy End*.'

'Sorry?'

'The *Pointy End*. The name of the airship. Docked yesterday. Refuelled in a hurry, grabbed some supplies.

Took off again last night.'

Holly's voice was hollow. 'It's gone already?'

'Yup.'

'Where did it go?'

'No requirement to log the destination, 'less of course they're picking up passengers.'

'So, you don't know?' asked Holly. 'Could you check, please?'

The clerk blew out his cheeks and slowly stabbed a few keys on the computer in front of him. He examined the results on the screen. 'Nope. Nothing.'

'Are you sure?'

Bored already, the clerk nodded.

This was terrible news. Holly didn't know what to do. She dithered at the counter. 'Wait. You said they got some supplies. In town? Did you see them?'

'Wasn't on yesterday. But yeah, I was in the tavern across the road, had a couple of drinks. Maybe I saw some of the crew go into the depot.'

'Was one of them an older man with balding, sandy hair and wearing khaki shorts?' Holly asked. 'His shirt has an insignia on the sleeve: the Museum of Martian Antiquities.'

Despite himself, the clerk's interest was a little piqued. 'Can't say I saw anybody like that, but as I said, they were in a hurry.' He looked at her curiously. 'You know, you don't want to get mixed up with those people.'

Holly smiled sadly. Too late for that.

'Look, go to the depot,' the clerk continued. 'Two

blocks down, one across. Perhaps someone there saw him or knows where the *Pointy End* is headed. Otherwise, ask around.'

'Yes. Okay. Of course. Thank you very much for your help.'

Holly made for the door. As she passed the lounge, a passenger sat up and lifted a side of his sleeping mask. With one eye he watched Holly leave, and his hand reached inside his shirt for a phone.

Holly hurried down the street, weaving in and out of pedestrians and motor traffic. She crossed the road, turned a corner and approached a squat building with *Malmart* plastered in huge green letters across its facade. Holly entered and went straight to the counter. The response from the sales assistant was eerily familiar and similarly depressing.

'Nope, don't get mixed up in that stuff.'

It was the same from the next half dozen people she asked: the grocer in the store across the road, the waitress in the cafe next to it, the guy selling genuine Martian 'friend' bracelets, a kid on roller skates and the two men playing chess outside the barbershop. Holly's spirits flagged with every step as she walked up and down the pavement, accosting random pedestrians who shrugged her off or avoided her like a leper.

Until a black van pulled up and three goons jumped out. One threw a bag over her head and the others picked her up and threw her in the back. The van raced off before she could squeak.

Holly woke into a scene of blurry shapes and buzzy snatches of sound. Her shoulder was really sore. She tried to rub it, but her other arm refused to cooperate. She vaguely remembered a black van in her recent past, but she couldn't connect it to the swirling shapes in front of her – her brain didn't seem to be working properly.

Two men were talking. 'Jeezus, how much did you give her?'

'The recommended dosage.'

'What the fuck is the recommended dosage?'

'What it says on the pack.'

'Did you consider her size? She's a skinny kid.'

'I made some adjust—'

'*Shut up*,' came a third voice, deep and menacing, cutting through the others like a knife. The buzzing stopped. Holly tried to focus on the shape it came from. It coalesced into a large, bald man who looked like a professional wrestler gone to seed. He was as wide as he was tall, with massive arms, bowlegs and a tree trunk for a torso.

'Wake up,' said a thin-lipped mouth at the top of the tree. 'I have questions.'

Holly groaned and looked around. She was in an empty warehouse with chains and hooks hanging from the ceiling. There were dark red stains of what she hoped was oil on the concrete floor. The swirling, buzzing shapes were men with square jaws and lots of guns. One of them had her backpack at his feet. She wriggled around for a bit, before realising that her arms and legs were strapped to a plastic chair with duct tape.

But her head was starting to clear – enough to get afraid. 'Who are you? Why am I here? What—?'

'Janus. And you are?'

'I . . . I'm Holly McGuire.' Afraid, and a little angry. 'What have you done with my father?'

Janus glanced at a man standing beside her. The man shrugged.

'Sorry, indulge me,' Janus said, 'I'm playing catch-up here. Who's your father again?'

'What?'

'Your father, sweetie?'

'Professor McGuire. Where is he?'

Janus looked at the man again. 'And apparently he's a professor at the museum in Port Clarke?'

Confused, Holly nodded. Then it dawned on her. '*You're* not from the *Pointy End.*'

'Ah, no,' said Janus. 'That would be the *other* pirates. Sorry, easy to get us mixed up.'

Holly squirmed in her chair. Her whole body was aching, her arm worst of all. 'So, what do *you* want?'

Janus walked forward until he towered over her. 'Holly, let me lay this out for you. The *Pointy End* kidnapped your father – a famous archaeologist, my lieutenant here tells me – and has raced off into the deep desert. Apparently, they have a promising lead on a very important site.' Janus paused. 'You get where I'm going with this?'

'I know nothing about that.'

Janus smiled unpleasantly, showing a set of perfect white teeth. 'Are you sure, Holly?'

There was something very scary about the smile. Holly could only stammer in response, 'Y-yes.'

Janus leaned in so close he could lick her face. He clamped her forearms in his huge hands and squeezed them until it hurt. Holly trembled; any lingering defiance evaporated.

'Holly, do you know anything about the City of the Dead?'

Holly shook her head.

'Anything? Anything at all?'

Holly swallowed hard. 'It's . . . it's a myth.'

'But perhaps you know where the *Pointy End* is going?'

'No. That's what I've been trying to find out.'

Janus grabbed her jaw and squeezed it hard. He forced her to look into his eyes. They were the size of sultanas. 'Are you sure, Holly?'

'I-I-I swear. I have no idea.'

Janus released her and stood up again, sighing deeply. 'I was afraid you'd say that.' He waved his hand and suddenly the bag was back over her head.

Someone picked her up, chair and all. There was the scuff of boots on concrete, a clang – probably a door opening – and she was outside. She could feel warm sun on her skin. Noise washed over her. Lots of sounds of ripping and tearing and metal scraping together – a deeply unsettling sound.

The pad of boots continued. There was a man on either

side of her and another walking in front. The sound of tearing got louder.

'I'm not happy about this,' said the man on the right.

'Oh, really?' sneered the one on the left.

'Yeah,' replied the one on the right.

'How happy you gonna be when the boss blowtorches your fingers off?'

The other one hesitated, then muttered, 'I didn't sign up for this.'

'Would you like to go back and discuss it?' said the nasty one sarcastically.

'I would like a bit of perspective,' said the conflicted one, his voice rising in pitch. 'Jesse, is this necessary? What harm can she do? She's a kid!'

'What the fuck does—'

'*Enough!*' This was from the man walking in front – Jesse, presumably. The other two shut up.

The goons dropped Holly on the ground. The flimsy chair broke under her, and Holly wriggled free of the frame, but her hands and feet were still tied. She rolled over on the ground and managed to wrangle the bag off her head and struggle to her knees.

In front of her a trash compactor was crushing vehicles into blocks of metal and plastic. Mounds of twisted and compacted trash rose all around it. They were in a scrapyard.

Jesse, the man Janus had referred to in the warehouse, stood to one side, his gun drawn. Holly's backpack was at his feet.

'Seriously?' said Conflicted.

Jesse paused and looked at him. He turned to Nasty. 'Get him out of here,' he said with disgust.

Nasty grabbed Conflicted by the collar and dragged him away. They disappeared into the mounds of trash.

Jesse pointed the long barrel of his gun at Holly's forehead. Quivering, Holly closed her eyes.

Bang!

The explosion was so close Holly felt the concussive force slap her cheek. For several seconds her ears rang like a bell. It took her several more seconds to realise she was hearing anything at all. She opened her eyes. The still-smoking gun was pointing to one side. She looked up at the man.

'Any ideas how I'm going to explain your escape?' he asked, grimacing as he holstered his weapon.

The world flowing around her, Holly wandered along the street in a stupor. A bike rider swerved to miss her, cursing; a woman bumped her shoulder; a child offered her a lollypop. She saw it all, but it didn't register. Her body had stopped aching from the drug, but now her mind had gone numb. For a long time, she had stared at a void in front of her face, willing it to open and suck her in like a black hole. But the laws of physics stubbornly refused to cooperate. Unable to affect even this minor alteration of reality, her brain had shut down. She saw nothing, heard nothing, felt nothing and thought nothing. She was a zombie, lumbering around in the middle of the day.

An old woman handing out flyers walked towards her, proclaiming in a cracked voice, 'Repent! Yahweh is coming. Repent!' As she passed, she pressed a flyer into Holly's hand. For a moment, the woman's feverish eyes stared into Holly's own. 'Yahweh will come for you, child!'

And then the woman was gone, receding into the river of people. 'Yahweh is coming. Repent!'

A gust of wind blew the flyer from Holly's hand and onto the ground. Without thinking, she bent over to retrieve it. A teenage boy crashed into her, knocking her off her feet.

'Sorry. So sorry,' he said, scrambling to pick up the flyer. 'Sorry, I wasn't looking where I was going.'

Holly got to her feet, and the boy offered her the piece of paper. 'Are you okay?'

Dead eyed, Holly took the flyer and turned away.

'Ah, okay . . .' The boy watched her go. And after a few seconds he adjusted his backpack and walked off as well.

Wait a minute. Somewhere inside Holly's head a dam broke, and the sights and sounds of the street flooded back into her consciousness. She spun around and watched the boy as he walked away.

He was the boy from the *Pointy End*! She had seen him through the binoculars at the ruins. Suddenly laser-focused, Holly hurried to catch up before he disappeared into the crowd.

She followed him through the streets, always keeping at least ten paces behind. He stopped several times to gaze into store windows or to watch the latest news item on the electronic bulletin boards. After half an hour of apparently aimless wandering, he walked into a milk bar with a glass front and gave his order to a waiter.

Darting to the other side of the street, Holly tried to vanish into the shadow of a billboard, and from there, studied the boy as he took a seat against the window. He was tall, with long limbs and short, dark hair; maybe a year or two older than she was. And he seemed out of it, staring blankly at the table in front of him. When his order came, he ate it without enthusiasm.

Holly considered her next step. Did she confront him? Demand he tell her what had become of her father? Or was it better to follow him, in the hope he would lead her to the other pirates? But if the *Pointy End* had gone, what good would that do? And why was he here anyway, and not with the airship?

She bit her lip. It was dangerous to confront him. She had only just escaped the other pirates. Holly felt a hot flush rise in her cheeks. At the very least she wanted to smack his face. Her hand clenched into a fist and the flyer, forgotten till now, crumpled in her hand. She smoothed it out a bit and read it. Under the word *Repent!* was a simple drawing of a biblical-looking scene. A beam of light from the heavens illuminated a man on a temple mount surrounded by singing, harp-playing angels. A group of ragged believers with rapturous looks on their faces knelt in front of the man, ready to ascend to heaven.

Holly raised her eyes to the pirate boy. She had an idea.

Holly heard them arguing before she saw them. They were at the edge of the market square next to a stall selling ice cream. Worried they might be arguing about her, she snuck around to the other side of the stall and listened in.

'You bought ice cream?' said Toby. 'The money I gave you was for food.'

'This is food.' Sophie licked her ice cream. 'And yeah, I got other stuff too.' She held up the bag. 'Cereal and protein and stuff.'

Toby shook his head in disbelief. 'We can't afford ice cream!'

'We can now.'

'No, no, no!' Toby pulled at his hair. 'That money I got for the maglev has to last until—'

'It's not my fault you suck at haggling.' Sophie took another lick.

'I do not.'

'Yeah,' she grinned, 'you do.'

'I do not, and anyway, that's not the point. We have to make it last until, until . . . our parents get back.'

Sophie dropped the bag, a dark look flooding her face. 'We agreed you would never, ever, ever, *ever* mention our parents coming back . . . *again!* She screamed the last bit.

Toby held up his hands and quickly backtracked. 'I just mean it has to last as long as it can . . . until . . . until we get more.'

Sophie glared at him, tears welling in her eyes.

Holly felt guilty at overhearing this private conversation

and decided it was time to announce herself. She walked to the front of the stall and pretended to notice them for the first time. Sophie saw her coming and turned away to wipe her eyes, then received her with a forced but relieved smile. 'Holly!'

Toby grunted.

'Hi,' said Holly. 'I want to make another deal.'

In the early evening the streets were quieter. The markets had packed up and revelry could be heard coming from inns and cafes instead.

Holly had picked up her quarry again as he left the milk bar and trailed him to a park, where he had spent most of the afternoon sitting on a bench feeding the musliks, genetically modified squirrels that flourished in the harsh, dry conditions. As the sun went down, he wandered off through the streets. Holly followed him, hopping from cover to cover.

Until she accidentally kicked an empty can, and it bounced across the road and hit a parked quad bike. The boy turned around and for an instant their eyes met. Holly blushed and looked away, pretending to read a *Free Mars* pamphlet sticky taped to a pole. From the corner of her eye, she saw him frown, but he turned away and continued walking.

The pirate took the next right into a narrow street next to a warehouse. Holly ran to catch up a bit – she couldn't lose him now. Halfway along, he came to a halt. Holly took refuge behind an overflowing dumpster.

He spun around and called out, 'Are you following me?'

The word came out of Holly's mouth before she could stop it. 'No.'

No? Seriously? That's the best she could do? Through the gap between the open lid and the body of the dumpster, she watched him put his hands on his hips and wait her out. Finally, all pretence gone, Holly stepped out from her hiding place and into the street, halting a cautious distance away.

'Why are you following me?' he asked.

'You were on the airship, the *Pointy End*.' It was a statement, not a question.

The boy looked surprised. 'No, I wasn't. I don't know anything about the . . . that ship you mentioned.'

'Yes, you do.'

'I don't know what you are talking about. Stop following me.' Annoyed, he turned to go.

'Wait!' Holly fumbled around behind her and pulled out the gun she had taken from her father's room on the boat. She had tucked it into the back of her shorts. Hands shaking, she trained it on him.

'Woah! Wait a minute!' The boy put his hands up. But then he leaned forward and peered at the gun. 'You know those things work better with bullets, right?'

'What?'

The boy put his hands down and gestured for her to look at the gun. Holly knew nothing about weapons, but turning it over, she saw the empty slot where the magazine was supposed to go. Not knowing what else to do, she threatened him with it anyway.

'Don't move. I warn you!'

He smiled smugly. 'And normally you'd switch the safety off too.'

Holly fiddled with the gun. There were switches on the side, but she had no idea what did what. She tried one at random.

'No, not that one, the other one,' he said helpfully. 'No, on the other side, yes – no, that one there . . .'

Holly tried another button, and then another. But, nervous before, she was now a shambles. She flicked buttons on and off at random.

'No, that one there. Yes, that's it, move it forward . . . no, sorry, *my* forward . . . towards you.'

As he spoke, the boy shuffled closer. Eventually, he was so close he could have taken the gun away from her. Instead, he continued to help. 'Yes, that's it. You've got it!'

Holly pointed the gun at him again.

The boy stepped back, grinning broadly. 'But, you know, bullets.'

'There might be a bullet in the chamber,' came a voice from further down the street. Holly looked up to see Toby and Sophie. Toby was carrying a wrench and Sophie had the taser. This wasn't the plan they had worked out – they were supposed to meet her back at the ship – but Holly was grateful for the assist. And by how deadly serious and – ah – crazy they both looked.

The boy glanced over his shoulder to see the siblings standing in the alleyway behind him. He acknowledged

Toby's (excellent) point with an embarrassed smile, turned back to Holly and raised his hands once more. 'Who are you people?' he said wearily.

Feeling more confident, Holly held the gun higher. 'Where did the *Pointy End* go?'

'I don't know what you're talking about.'

'You kidnapped a man from an old city site two days ago. A professor from the Martian Museum. He was my father.'

The boy's face went pale. 'Now wait a minute. I know nothing about—'

'Where is he?'

'Look, I had nothing to do with that. I'm not with those people anymore.'

Holly raised her voice. 'Where did they take him?'

'I don't know.'

Holly advanced, holding the gun level with his head. The boy backed away.

'Where. Did. They. *Take.* Him?'

'I told you, I don't—'

The boy's body jerked straight as a pole and started to spasm. Coils of blue electricity encircled his torso, and sparks erupted in the air with a crackle. He fell to his knees, twitching violently. Like a tree cut down in the forest, he collapsed face first onto the ground, and after a final sizzle and twitch, stopped moving.

Holly looked up to see Sophie behind him, the taser still sparking in her hand. Her face was lit up with pure joy.

'Did ya see that?!'

Chapter Four

Infidel

Toby and Holly, working together, pushed a wheelbarrow they had bought from Malmart containing the limp body of the pirate up the ramp and into the hovercraft. Sophie followed with the taser and the wrench. As they crossed the threshold, the wheelbarrow tipped to one side and the boy's head bumped into the bulkhead. Holly winced, but the boy was still out cold. They righted the wheelbarrow and entered the ship.

While Toby and Holly wrestled their captive into the flight engineer's chair, Sophie got the duct tape. With little skill but plenty of enthusiasm, she strapped the pirate's arms and torso to the chair. Job done, they stepped back as one to observe their handiwork.

'Remember, we get the laptop,' Toby said to Holly.

'Yes, yes. Let's get on with it.'

Sophie ran to the kitchenette and returned with a glass of water. She threw it into the boy's face. Slowly, he came around, mumbling incoherently.

'Ship?' said Sophie. 'Prisoner. Interrogate!'

The chair sprung upright, and the light came on, shining

a hot beam on the pirate's face.

The boy squinted into the glare. 'Whaa . . .? Where am −?'

'Wake up, infidel!' Ship's voice boomed. 'We have questions!' The chair shook vigorously.

'Yeah!' said Sophie.

'Where am I?' groaned the boy.

Ship gave him another shake. 'We'll ask the questions. Name, rank and serial number?'

'Ah . . . Zach?' said the boy drowsily.

Holly leaned over him. 'Zach, where did the *Pointy End* go?'

'What?'

'The *Pointy End*. Where did it go?'

Zach shook his head and strained against his bonds. He twisted from side to side, trying to see past the light in his face. He looked down at his arms strapped to the armrests. He got the picture soon enough. Now wide awake, he squirmed and flailed and arched his body and stamped his feet.

'Where did the *Pointy End* go?' Holly repeated.

Zach ignored her and continued to struggle, but Sophie had done her job well. After one more bout of especially violent thrashing, he gave up and sank back into the chair, panting and furious.

'Tell me,' said Holly.

Zach locked his jaw and glared at her in defiance.

'Tell me!'

There was a crackle of electricity. Zach flinched. 'Ooww!'

'Speak, infidel!'

Zach looked around wildly for the source of the voice – and the electric shock. 'You people are insane!'

'Look, it really is easy,' said Toby. 'You tell us where the airship went, and you can go.'

'I'm trying to tell you – I'm not with the pirates anymore. I don't know where it is.'

Sophie folded her arms. 'Liar. Ship?'

'Wait. Wait! Just wait.' Zach gulped a breath. 'Jeezus.'

Another crackle. 'Ooww!'

'Don't take the Lord's name in vain,' said Toby.

Zach stared wide-eyed at Toby as if Toby was the devil incarnate. He swallowed hard. 'Look, I don't know where they went . . .'

Sophie opened her mouth . . .

'. . . but! But, I remember—'

'Yeah, it's starting to come back to you now, isn't it? Yeah,' said Sophie.

'. . . I remember the man . . .'

'My father,' said Holly.

'. . . your father . . . I remember he said he could find treasure. But he needed to visit the well. Something about going back to the well.'

'The Well of Souls?' asked Holly.

Zach shrugged. 'I don't know. It was just what I overheard.'

Toby and Sophie turned to Holly expectantly.

'What's the Well of Souls?' asked Toby.

'A temple my mother and father found years ago, before

I was born. But I don't understand. Why go back there? It's an important archaeological site, but there's no treasure.'

Sophie was having none of it. 'He's lying. Ship, zap him again.'

'No! Wait. I swear it's true. There was something there. A map that he needed, that he said would lead them to treasure. I swear that's all I know.'

The three kids went into a huddle. 'What do you think?' whispered Toby.

'He's lying,' said Sophie.

Holly glanced at Zach. He looked tired and defeated. 'I don't know. He might be telling the truth.'

'Do you know where this Well is?' asked Toby.

'Roughly.'

'Ship, bring up a map.'

A screen in front of the flight engineer's chair cleared to reveal a map of the area.

Holly pointed to a location. 'It's here. In the Albezi Basin.'

'That's deep desert,' said Toby. 'There's nothing there.'

'We have to try.'

Toby raised his eyebrows. 'We?'

Holly sighed. She had given them most things of value from the boat. She went down the steps, retrieved her backpack and plonked it down in front of Toby. A portable emission reader spilled out onto the floor.

'Take it all. Sell it. Do what you want with it.' She pointed at the screen. 'But take me there.'

Toby looked at the pack and then at Sophie. It was clear

what she wanted to do. Toby extended his hand. 'Deal.'

Holly and Toby shook on it.

'We'll need more supplies,' said Toby, picking up the reader. 'The market's closed, but the depot will still be open. We can trade.'

Holly threw the pack over her shoulder. 'Let's go.'

The three of them exited the hovercraft. But Zach couldn't see them from his vantage point and hadn't heard what had passed between them. He strained at the straps again – to no avail. 'Guys? What's happening out there? Guys? Hello?'

A seductive and threatening voice filled the air. 'Alone at last.'

An hour later, the kids returned carrying supplies. They threw the bags of stuff down on the kitchen table.

'Okay, let's go, Ship,' said Toby.

The hovercraft powered up. Soon it was gliding over the desert, Urbe Sicaria a swarm of lights behind it.

Sophie peeked around the bulkhead and checked their prisoner. Zach was looking frazzled. His hair was standing on end and his eyes were glazed. Toby and Holly came up behind her.

'Whadda we do with the pirate?' whispered Sophie.

'Do we let him go?' asked Holly.

'He did give us the destination,' said Toby.

'I still think he's lying,' said Sophie.

'Keep him as a hostage,' said Ship, its voice coming from a grill on the wall beside them. 'He's good intel on the enemy. How they think, act. Their ideology.'

Zach thrashed about in the chair. 'I don't have an ideology!'

Holly entered the nook to address him. 'If the Well is really where they went, then we let you go. But not before.'

'Aaaarrrggghhh!' Zach howled.

The little girl walked through the field, trailing the tips of her fingers over the tufts of grain. The farmers stopped working and stared at her, their expressions apprehensive. She came to a cobblestone road lined by tall trees with silvery leaves. One way led to the golden city; from the other direction, a group of riders on horseback was galloping hard towards her.

The girl stepped back from the road's edge as they approached. The animals were like horses, but with slimmer bodies and small antlers on their heads. Both rider and horse were caparisoned in uniforms of bronze and purple.

The riders looked as if they would pass her by, but then one saw her and called out to the others. They wheeled around and pulled up in a cloud of dust. The dust settled and revealed an ornate carriage, trimmed in gold, and pulled by the same horse-like animals. It stopped in front of her and the door opened . . .

Holly woke to the gentle hum of the hovercraft on the move. She pulled back the curtains of her bunk. Toby's messy bunk was empty and sounds of running water were coming from further down the fuselage. She grabbed her toiletry bag and padded to the bathroom.

Inside the tiny space, Toby and Sophie were cleaning their teeth, Toby using a tiny circular motion and Sophie brushing back and forth with gusto.

'You're pressing too hard. You're supposed to move the brush in a gentle circular motion. Otherwise, you brush the enamel off.'

Sophie paused to give Holly a frothy smile before turning on Toby with relish. 'This is *my* way.'

'But you're doing it wrong.'

'Says who?'

'Dental experts.'

'Bah, let's see how Holly does it.'

Feeling self-conscious, Holly applied some paste onto her brush and half-covered her mouth with her other hand as she brushed her teeth in an up-and-down motion. She watched Toby and Sophie watch her.

'See. Holly doesn't go round and round.'

'She doesn't go backwards and forwards either.'

'Holly has her own way – don't you, Holly?'

'Ah, yeah, I guess.'

Toby was sceptical, but the kids brushed their teeth in companionable silence for a few moments, before a loud moan interrupted them.

'I have to gooo . . .'

Sophie spat toothpaste into the sink. 'Unh, he's moaning again!'

Holly stuck her head out of the bathroom. At the top of the stairs, Zach was still strapped into the flight engineer's chair. He'd been there all night.

He noticed her looking. 'I really, *really* have to go.'

Holly pulled her head in. 'What do we do?'

'Give him a bottle to go in,' said Toby.

'*You* give him a bottle to go in.'

'Well, we have to do something because he's making a racket.' Sophie made a face. 'And he's starting to smell.'

Toby delicately expelled his toothpaste into the basin. 'I'll deal with this.'

He wiped his face on a towel and left the bathroom. The girls followed, still brushing their teeth. Toby went to his bunk, reached under his pillow, and pulled out a copy of the Bible. Climbing the stairs, he manoeuvred the book under the fingers of Zach's trapped hand.

'If we release you, swear that you won't try anything. Swear by the blood of the Blessed Saints and all that is holy.'

Zach gaped at him. 'Um . . . I swear?'

Satisfied, Toby turned to the girls with a crisp nod. Sophie rolled her eyes and began tearing off the duct tape.

'Ship,' she said, 'we're releasing the prisoner. If he tries anything, kill him.'

'I swear,' said Ship.

Sophie and Holly loosened the rest of the tape and Zach wrenched himself free. He raced to the bathroom, slamming the door behind him.

'Great,' said Sophie, disgusted. 'Now we need another bathroom.'

Phobos set, rose and set again. In the early afternoon,

the hovercraft passed over a harsh landscape of rock and drifts of sand. Scattered like dice over the plain were oblongs of stone, ten metres to a side, standing like sentinels against the passage of time. They had been left behind by the now extinct Martians, and no one had ever figured out what their purpose might be.

Zach had had a shower and something to eat, but had nothing else to do. Feeling bored, angry and a little guilty, but mostly just bored, he watched the oblongs from the flight deck of the hovercraft. Behind him, the Hendriksens were playing chess at the kitchen table.

Sophie pointed a feature out to Toby on the wall screen. 'Look, the map shows we're coming up on the Sinai Reservoir.'

Toby glanced over his shoulder; Sophie moved her queen one square over.

'Ah, yeah, sure. We'll be there soon,' said Toby, and turned back to the game.

'Oh,' said Sophie, feigning surprise, and took Toby's bishop with her queen.

Stunned, Toby cradled his face in his hands. How had that happened? He stared at the board in renewed determination.

Zach drifted over and watched the game for a bit. He tried to make conversation. 'So, play a lot of chess, do you?'

Toby was too focused on his position to respond, and Sophie ostentatiously stuck her nose in the air. Zach felt the chill and drifted away. He wandered into the rear of the hovercraft. Holly was sitting on the edge of the engineer's nook overlooking the bomb bay, staring at the photo of her mother. As Zach entered, she stifled a sniffle. He pretended not to notice and went down into the bay. The curved lid of the fourth missile tube was closed; lights winked on a panel next to it. Curious, Zach approached and attempted to lift the lid. There was a familiar crackle of electricity.

'Ow!'

'Don't touch the missile,' said Ship.

Holly wiped her eyes and put the photo into her shirt pocket. 'It's the last one. Ship is very protective of it.'

Sucking his stung fingers, Zach walked over to a window and stared at the desert for a bit. He glanced over his shoulder at Holly. 'Look, I just want to say that I'm sorry – for my part in all this.'

Holly's reply was curt. 'I don't want to hear it.'

'I'm not a part of that gang anymore. I never liked what they did. I left because of what they did.'

'I. Don't. Care,' said Holly.

'They're not all bad people, you know. I mean, not bad all the way through. Some of them are . . .' Zach gestured at the landscape. 'It's just this place. It's tough out here. They do what they need to do to survive.'

'By beating and shooting people?'

'You were going to shoot me!'

Holly glowered at him.

Zach softened his voice. 'I'm just sayin'. They're not all bad. They're tough and determined and very, very stubborn, but—'

'I don't want to hear it. You're a criminal.'

Indignant, Zach threw up his hands. 'Unh, you people!'

'What people?' asked Holly, puzzled.

'*You* people. *Rich* people. People are trying to survive out here and mostly dying at it, and you're running around collecting rocks.'

'They're not rocks!'

Zach put on a smarmy voice. 'Sorry, trinkets.'

'It's important work.' Holly pouted. 'And I'm not rich.'

'Look at your clothes. Who wears socks with names on them? My grandmother knitted mine.'

Holly looked down at her socks. The label of a high-end fashion house was sticking out. Self-consciously, she crossed her legs. 'Leave my socks out of this. You don't know anything about me.'

'And you don't know anything about *me*.'

'Yeah?'

'*Yeah*. I was running away. I was supposed to go to school on Earth.'

'So why didn't you go?'

'Because *my* school fees were going to be paid for by robbing *your* tombs!'

'What do you care?' yelled Holly.

'I'm trying to explain!' yelled Zach.

Holly had had enough. Red in the face, she slipped under the metal balustrade and dropped to the floor of the bomb bay. 'And what happens when they get to the Well and find no gold?'

'They won't hurt him,' said Zach.

'They already have!'

'They're not killers.'

Holly climbed into her bunk and dramatically closed the curtain. 'Leave me alone.'

Zach stared at the closed curtain, shaking his head. He turned back to the window. The hovercraft was threading itself through a line of jagged rock, the walled remains of a meteorite crater. To Zach, they looked like broken teeth. He imagined the mouth that owned them snapping shut and crushing the hovercraft like a cracker.

'Besides,' he muttered sarcastically under his breath, 'why would I ever want to leave this place?'

Chapter Five

Lord of Light

'We are coming up on the location now, Commander.'

Toby and Sophie left their game and went to the flight deck. The hovercraft was approaching a shimmering, circular lake, in the centre of which was a cone of rock hundreds of metres high, an ancient and now dormant volcano. A pair of sharp spurs ran down the slope towards the water, creating a narrow canyon between them. The siblings gazed in wonder for a few moments. Mars had a reasonable amount of water, but almost all of it was hidden in deep aquifers. Surface water was precious and rare.

Toby hit the intercom. 'Holly, we have something.'

A moment later, Holly stepped through the door of the bulkhead and joined them, still flushed after her fight with Zach.

'Is that it?' asked Toby.

'I think so. I've only ever seen photos of it. That canyon leads down to a temple under the rock.'

'There are no signs of the enemy on radar, Commander,' Ship announced.

'Okay, Ship, take us in for a closer look.'

The hovercraft left the desert sand and skimmed across the surface of the lake to the island. It glided up the shallow incline of a short beach and came to a halt in front of the canyon.

Toby was first down the ramp, wearing a stuffed-to-the-brim backpack and carrying a pickaxe in one hand and a sports bag in the other. He also had three small cylinders with breathing masks under his arm. He looked like an overloaded boy scout. The girls joined him seconds later, Holly with her bum bag on and Sophie carrying a food bar.

Sophie wrinkled her nose. 'My head feels funny.'

Toby dropped the bag and pickaxe and handed her an oxygen cylinder. 'We're a long way from any tinkerbells. Oxygen is low. If you need to, take a puff.' He gave another cylinder to Holly, and the girls took a big breath of air from the masks. 'Don't use it up too fast,' he warned.

As Holly and Sophie walked towards the gap, Zach came down the ramp.

'I'm not staying here with a sociopathic AI. Do you have a cylinder for me?'

Toby was apologetic. 'Sorry, I only have three, but' – he indicated the gear on the ground – 'can you help me carry some of this stuff?'

'You're kidding, right?'

'Well, it's really heavy, and . . .'

'*Unbelievable.*' Zach hefted the bag, threw the pickaxe over his shoulder and stomped off after the girls.

The narrow canyon wormed its way between two

smooth walls of ribbed stone. The walls curved over them and joined in places, creating oval skylights. It got darker as the openings became smaller and less frequent, so Toby dug a flashlight out of his backpack and took the lead.

They walked back and forth and down until one wall receded and the canyon became a deep crevice with the trail clinging to the other wall. The kids sidled along it, dislodging stones that fell forever into the abyss.

The crevice broadened into a chasm. Steep steps hewn into the rock continued down into darkness. Far below, they could hear the gurgle of water. The group followed the steps down into the dark until they reached the foot of a rock bridge. The footway of the bridge had collapsed and fallen away to leave a series of narrow support columns that formed stepping stones across the gap, each a metre apart.

Sophie peeked over the edge. 'Looks dangerous.' She turned to Zach. 'You go first.'

Zach muttered a curse under his breath, but stepped up to the edge. Holding the bag to his chest, he jumped onto the top of the first column, then the next, and the next and so on across the chasm to where the trail continued on the other side. Safely across, he turned to the others. 'It's okay, just keep to the centre.'

Sophie followed, making it look easy. Then Holly and lastly a wobbly Toby, weighed down by his gear. Jumping from the last column, he landed on the ledge on the other side and flashed a brief, pleased-with-himself smile – which evaporated as he pitched backwards. Zach grabbed him by the belt and pulled him upright.

The walls closed in again until the group was walking down a narrow passage. The walls ahead were illuminated with a blue-green tinge, and Toby was able to switch off his flashlight.

The group stepped out of the passage onto the floor of a high domed space the size of a cathedral. The source of the light was a shallow pool of water, inlaid with polished stones of blue and green. Clear morning sunshine was filtering down through a hole in the ceiling and reflecting off the stones. Behind the pool, wide steps led up to a statue of Zanaster, the Martian god of the soul, a human-shaped figure with six arms and the head of a bird. Around the tiered walls of the cathedral, obscured in gloom, were the other Martian gods, all paying homage to Zanaster.

They stopped and stared in wonder.

'So beautiful,' said Sophie, her voice echoing faintly. She knelt next to the pool and touched the water. Ripples spread over the surface. They reflected the light from above in a way that cast glowing rivulets of blue and green over the statues, which seemed to flex and move and come alive. The ripples subsided, and the statues faded back into shadow.

'I think we've missed them,' said Toby.

'Look around,' said Holly. 'Maybe we can find a clue about where they went.'

The group fanned out over the cathedral floor, gazing at the statues around the walls. Holly stopped in front of Zanaster.

'Why would my father lead them to this place?'

'Maybe he was buying time?' said Toby. 'If he really doesn't know how to find treasure, eventually the pirates will realise it.'

Worried at the implication of this, Holly looked accusingly at Zach.

'He never said he knew exactly where to go,' said Zach. 'He said he *could* find treasure. Maybe the difference is important.'

Holly pondered this. 'This was a very important place for the Martians. I remember my dad saying that so many of their stories led back here.'

Sophie had wandered around the edge of the pool, pausing to put her hand in the water again and create the ripples of light on the walls. She stopped in front of a statue: a woman with long arms that split into tentacles. 'Who are they?'

Holly called out their names, pointing to each one in turn. 'Ankasha, god of water and health; Serquet, goddess of air and wind; Mehitza, lord of the harvest; Zaptre, god of—'

'That one!' exclaimed Sophie. 'There's something up there!'

Holly looked at where Sophie was pointing. It was Pakhet, the goddess of pilgrims. On top of Pakhet's head, the edge of a piece of paper was visible. Holly climbed the steps to the base of the statue. It was three times taller than her and there were no obvious handholds. Placing a foot against the rough surface of a leg, she tried to reach the first of several arms where it was resting against the side of the body. Her foot slipped, and she fell on her backside. She went to try again.

'Wait,' said Zach. He dropped his bag on the ground and rummaged through it, glancing at Toby. 'Tell me you brought rope.'

Zach took out a coil of rope.

'I brought rope,' said Toby.

Zach walked up to the statue, doubled up the rope, and tied a loop and knot into one end. He threw it over the head of the statue and collected it as it fell down the other side. He offered the loop to Holly. 'Put your foot in here. We'll lift you up.'

Holly hesitated, looking at him askance.

'I'm not gonna drop you,' said Zach.

Holly arched an eyebrow, but took the rope in both hands and stuck her foot in the loop.

Zach backed up and pulled the rope taut. Straining mightily, he lifted Holly a few centimetres off the ground. He glanced over his shoulder at Toby and Sophie. 'Ah, guys?'

'Oh,' said Sophie and Toby at the same time.

The Hendriksens stepped up and grabbed the rope as well. Using their combined weight and strength, they lifted Holly into the air. She reached the top of the stat-ue's arms and was able to step up onto its shoulders. She stretched out and picked up the piece of paper. It was a photo, held down by a rock.

'What is it?' asked Toby.

Holly examined the photo: a series of swirls and dots, like a stylised picture of a stream or flame. 'I'm not sure. I think it's the photo my father took the day he was kidnapped.' Holly held the photo out for them to see.

'What's that mean?' asked Sophie.

Holly shook her head. 'I don't know. A message from him, maybe?'

'I know that symbol,' said Zach. 'It appears in a lot of tombs. It just means *tomb*.'

'No. The Martian script has never been completely deciphered. We can only translate a few of the glyphs.'

'But if *you* don't know?'

Holly banged her forehead against the stone in frustration. 'I don't under—'

Crack!

A split appeared around the statue's ankles and quickly spread around the base. Chunks of stone rattled to the floor. The bulk of the statue separated from the feet and slowly toppled towards Zach and the siblings.

Sophie stood transfixed. 'Aaaagghhh!'

Zach released the rope and pushed Sophie out of the way, then grabbed Toby by his suspenders and yanked him backwards. Terrified, Holly clung to the back of the statue and rode it down as it crashed to the floor. It burst into pieces as it hit, but it didn't stop there – the floor collapsed under the impact. A dark space opened up and the kids, the statue and the floor all disappeared amid a cloud of sand and debris.

Holly stirred and coughed, spitting dust out of her mouth. She was lying half-buried in a pool of sand. Somewhere about where her feet should be, there was a glimmer of metal. She reached for it and her hand closed around the flashlight. She banged it, then banged it again, and it came on and sent a cone of light into the darkness.

Sophie's face leapt out only a metre in front of her. 'Eeek!' Sophie squealed.

'Sophie, are you okay?'

Sophie coughed and nodded. Holly panned the flashlight around again. Another face leapt out.

'Eeek!' Sophie squealed again.

'It's only me,' grumbled Toby. He crawled over to the girls.

'Um, where's Zach?' asked Holly.

'Unnhhh,' came the answer from somewhere beside them.

They crawled over the rubble towards the sound. Zach's eyes were closed and he was lying on his back with his head against a rock. He groaned again.

'He must have hit his head,' said Toby.

'Holly leaned over and gave his shoulder a tentative shake. 'Zach? Zach?'

Zach's eyes half-opened. Dazed, he tried to focus on Holly's face. 'You have pretty eyes,' he said dreamily.

Woah! Holly jerked back as if stung by a wasp.

'Oh, he's delirious,' said Sophie, grabbing his jaw and shaking it. 'Zach, wake up, you're delirious. Wake up!' And for good measure she slapped him.

'Unnh,' he grunted, starting to come round. 'Where am I?'

'You're with us, Zach. You're delirious.' Sophie said loudly. She took her arm back for another slap. Toby and Holly blocked her hand.

'He's not that delirious,' said Holly.

Sophie shrugged.

Zach sat up, feeling his reddening cheek. 'What happened?'

'We fell through the floor,' said Toby.

The four helped each other to their feet – Holly staying well clear of Zach – and panned the flashlight around. The dust was settling, and they could make out the contours of the new space they were in. They were standing on a pile of sand and rubble surrounded by sarcophagi. The walls were dark and high and decorated with paintings of Martian life. Between the paintings, holes about fifteen centimetres wide punctuated the walls, some of them caked over with crumbling pieces of red clay.

Toby walked to the nearest wall and looked around. 'I'm not seeing a door here.'

'Nor me,' said Zach from the other side of the room.

Holly examined the sarcophagi. 'These are well preserved. The seals are broken, but it looks like some lids have never been opened.'

'Yeah, like jam,' murmured Sophie.

It was an odd response, even for Sophie. Everyone turned towards her as she crumpled to the floor. They rushed to her aid.

Holly knelt, lifted Sophie's head and cradled it in her lap. 'Sophie, what's wrong?'

'I'm sleepy,' Sophie mumbled.

'Oxygen. She needs oxygen!' cried Toby.

Zach frantically scrounged through the rubble. He found a cylinder and rushed back to Sophie's side. Her eyes started to close.

Holly gently shook her. 'No, Sophie, you can't sleep now.'

Sophie grumbled and snuggled further into Holly's lap. 'Sleepy time.'

Zach held the oxygen mask over Sophie's mouth and turned the knob on the cylinder.

'Breathe, Sophie, breathe,' urged Holly.

Sophie coughed and gasped, and then took a few ragged breaths. Gradually, her breathing became more regular, and seconds later, her eyes opened. She looked at Holly. 'I thought you were Mum.'

Holly smiled and stroked Sophie's hair. 'You'll be okay. Just keep breathing.'

Toby found his backpack and helped Sophie to a sip of water. And while Toby and Holly attended to Sophie, Zach circumnavigated the room, running his hand over the walls. He returned to where he started and looked at the hole in the ceiling ten metres above.

'Death by burial chamber,' he muttered under his breath.

Zach smacked the stone block with the pickaxe and broke it in two. He hefted the smaller piece and stacked it on top of the pile. He and Toby were building the base of a staircase that would eventually, hopefully sooner rather than later, reach the ceiling. They had a long way to go.

And it was hard work. Panting, Toby took a break and leaned against the wall. Red clay crumbled under his hand to reveal another of the holes that ringed the chamber. He brushed the reddish dirt from his fingers and peered inside. It was a narrow tunnel, angling steeply upwards. High above was a tiny circle of pale blue sky. Unfortunately, the hole was far too small to crawl through.

'If we had a cat, we could tie a rope around its neck and, you know, it could climb up one of these openings and, I don't know, maybe, um . . .'

Zach looked at him.

'Right, back to work,' said Toby, chastened.

Sophie was still resting in Holly's lap. 'We had a cat once,' she mused fondly. 'But we killed it. We didn't have enough food. It was that or the dog. And we're, like, more dog people, so . . . But then the dog died too.'

'Oh.' Holly frowned, not knowing what to say. 'What happened to your parents, Sophie?'

Sophie sat up a little and peered, hollow-eyed, into the gloom. 'When everyone had gone and there was just Mum and Dad and me and Toby left, we ran out of food. We were so hungry. Then one night, Mum woke me to say they were going looking for food and water at a place nearby. They'd be right back. She said God would watch over us while they were gone, as long as we went to church. But we waited for days and days and they didn't return.

Then Toby unlocked the code on Ship.' Sophie paused to whisper, 'I know he doesn't look like it, but he's actually really smart. Don't tell him I said that. Ship had some water and food aboard, and for a while we were okay. But then Ship lost power, and we were stuck again.'

'Your parents must have run out of fuel or something,' said Holly. 'I'm sure they would've come back if they could.'

'I think they were scared and ashamed and just left us there to die.'

Holly was shocked. 'No, Sophie, that's not true. They would never do that!'

Sophie shrugged, apparently not caring. With glazed eyes, she looked over at Toby. 'He took it hard.'

Holly thought it best to change the subject. 'Come on. Let's help the boys.'

The stairs rose slowly towards the ceiling. But the exertion and low oxygen were taking their toll. Exhausted, they stopped for a break. Toby passed the oxygen cylinder around and each person took a couple of deep breaths. Zach, last in line, flicked the dial – almost empty. He caught Holly's eye and nodded grimly.

'Let's keep going,' said Holly.

Zach, Holly and Sophie got back to work, but Toby was distracted by the holes. He picked up a piece of the red foamy clay and it broke in his hands. Curious, he held some next to the opening and watched it dissolve into powder on his fingertips. 'What are these holes for, exactly?'

'Air vents?' said Zach.

Toby gestured at the surrounding sarcophagi. 'But they're dead.'

Zach shrugged. He couldn't care less. He retrieved the pickaxe and whacked another rock.

Toby examined a coffin. It had the usual pile of dust and a perfect sphere of blue stone inside, and on the outside was a lever mechanism that lifted the lid and partially covered a smear of red clay. Toby pushed the lever down past the smear. The lid closed a little. He released it and the lid creaked back open.

'Holly, have you ever been to a tomb where the coffins weren't open?'

'No. All robbed. By his lot.'

Zach scowled, but he was too tired to fight. He said to Toby, 'Are you helping or what?'

Toby continued to play with the mechanism. 'Hey,' he said, becoming excited, 'they're not coffins.' He ran over to one of the holes and held another patch of red clay in front of an air vent. It dissolved into powdery dirt. 'They're not coffins! They hold the lids closed by a bar made of the red clay. The stuff dissolves in the presence of oxygen. When the bar is gone, the lid swings open!'

Intrigued, Holly went and worked the lever of a coffin, and then joined Toby at the air vent, watching another chunk of red clay dissolve in his hands. Becoming excited now too, she strode to the centre of the chamber and looked around the room. She saw it with fresh eyes, like a brush had swept across her vision and painted everything a different colour. 'It's a cryogenic chamber,' she said in wonder.

'A cry-what?' asked Sophie.

'It's a place where you put yourself into a long sleep,' explained Toby. 'Like hibernation.'

'It makes sense,' said Holly. 'Mars had been dying for millions of years, gradually losing oxygen to space. The Martians must have decided all they could do was put themselves to sleep, hoping one day, somehow, the oxygen would return.'

'Why would they think the air would return?' asked Toby.

Holly shook her head. 'I don't know.'

Sophie knew. 'They were waiting for a miracle.'

'And it worked, sort of,' said Holly. 'We brought the tinkerbells. Just thousands of years too late.'

'This is fascinating,' said Zach, leaning wearily against the makeshift staircase. 'I love history – the stories, the recipes, all that stuff. But, you know, they're dead. And we'll die here too unless we find a way out.'

Holly flashed Toby a smile. 'I think Toby just did.'

Toby ran around the perimeter of the chamber, stopping to peer into each of the holes, feeling the surrounding stone.

Holly jumped up on a sarcophagus and studied the paintings on the walls. One depicted a god with long plaited hair and the face of a crane. It appeared to be stepping into a reddish circle at its feet. Excited, she waved at

Toby and pointed to the picture. 'Maitreya, lord of light!'

Toby went and snatched the bottle of oxygen from Zach.

'Hey, that's the last of our air!' said Zach.

Toby ran to Maitreya, opened the valve on the bottle and held the nozzle against the red clay of the circle. Nothing happened at first, but as Toby rammed the nozzle deeper into the clay, pieces broke off and fell to the floor. Toby helped pull them away with his other hand. As he worked, the others came up behind him.

The hole deepened. As larger and larger chunks fell, a stream of sand poured out of the breach.

The flow of sand stopped. Toby looked at the dial on the cylinder. The needle quivered once and fell to zero.

Zach lifted the pickaxe. 'Stand back.' He attacked the wall with gusto. Chunks fell away and more sand flowed in. He hit it again. More chunks. Again. A large block of red clay crashed to the floor and a streak of light streamed through.

Toby stuck his head inside and looked up. A tunnel with a set of steep steps led up to a wide patch of pink sky. He pulled his head out and turned to the gang, grinning.

Chapter Six

Pirate Central

Dinner that night consisted of freeze-dried packets of vegetables, two-minute noodles and glasses of powdered milk. It had taken them the rest of the afternoon to climb out of the volcano, and by the time they returned to the hovercraft they were wasted. But Sophie had a surprise. After the girls had their showers, she brought out a tub of ice cream. She had secretly bought some more at the depot while Toby wasn't watching. For once, Toby didn't protest.

'I don't understand,' said Holly, staring at the photo of the glyph and swirling the ice cream around in her bowl.

Sophie licked her spoon. 'Maybe it's a secret message, like a code or something. You have to decipher it.'

Toby came in wearing a bathrobe, his hair wet from his shower. 'That's silly,' he said, scooping some ice cream into a bowl. He paused to apologise to Zach, who was leaning awkwardly against the kitchen sink. 'I think I used the last of the hot water, sorry.'

Zach, still covered in dust, sand and tiny pieces of rubble, ground his teeth together.

Toby sat down with the girls. 'I mean, why would

your father leave a code to decipher, rather than a proper message?'

'Maybe he didn't have much time. But it was on the head of the goddess of pilgrims. Like it was a clue.'

'Kinda like a code,' said Sophie.

'It's not a code. It's a trail of clues,' said Toby.

'Written in code.'

'No. A code is—'

'Look,' interrupted Zach, 'whatever it is, deal's a deal. You've got to let me go.'

Sophie waved her arm in the air. 'So go.'

Zach glanced out the window. 'We're in the middle of nowhere. Take me back to Sicaria.'

'Nooo. We never said *that*,' said Sophie.

'*That* was the deal.'

'Ship?'

A recording of Holly's voice came over the speakers. The bit where Holly told Zach they would let him go if his information about the Well was correct. Zach's howl in protest sounded especially plaintive over the tinny speakers.

'See?' said Sophie. 'No Sicaria.'

Zach stared at her; Sophie double-stared back.

'You're just going to dump me in the desert, are you? Clicks from anywhere. To starve. To die of thirst. Alone. In the desert. Is that it?'

Sophie yawned. Holly tried turning the photo upside down.

Zach threw up his hands. He turned to the window

and watched the desert flow by. The circular lake was now a sheet of glass on the horizon. He sighed. 'There's nothing back there for me, anyway. I can't even afford to buy a ticket to the spaceport.'

'You didn't plan your running away very well,' said Holly.

Zach spun around. 'And you didn't plan your kidnapping very well. You should've taken my bag. I had money in there.'

'Oh flip!' said Sophie.

Holly giggled at Sophie's outburst. 'Oh well. We'll know for the next time you zap someone.'

'So cool!' said Sophie.

'So cool,' agreed Holly.

Zach knew they were niggling him. He crossed his arms and fumed.

'What does *CZR* stand for?' asked Holly.

'What?'

'It's stitched into your collar. I saw it when we picked you up in the wheelbarrow.'

Zach blushed. 'Oh. Charles Zachary Ramirez. Zachary's my middle name. I prefer it to Charles.'

'Charles? *Charles?* ' snorted Sophie.

'Yes, *Charles.*'

Sophie and Holly burst out laughing. Sophie assumed a poncy voice and held her spoon towards Holly like a sword. 'Fear me, I'm the dread pirate Charles!'

Holly brandished her spoon too and they had a sword fight over the table.

'I'll fight you. I'm Chuck the pirate king!' said Holly.

'I'll have you know several important English kings on Earth were named Charles,' said Zach with quiet dignity.

The girls hooted with laughter. Toby ignored them; this kind of infantile humour was beneath him. He dug into his ice cream.

Zach had had enough of the frivolity at his expense. He stepped forward and snatched the photograph from Holly's hand. All mirth evaporated instantly.

'Hey!'

'Hey!'

Holly and Sophie tried to take the picture back, but Zach held it above his head and fended them off with his other hand.

'Give that back!' demanded Holly.

'Maybe you should start being nicer to me,' said Zach.

Holly was scathing. 'Why would I *ever* want to do that?'

Zach planted the photograph right in front of her face. 'Because I know someone who can tell us what this means.'

On the northern slopes of the Hellespontus Montes mountain range was an unusual geological feature. During an early period of the formation of Mars, an enormous volcano had erupted and poured molten lava over an area of a hundred square kilometres. Lava is usually light, but this lava had a high concentration of heavy metals, possibly left over from an earlier meteorite strike. The lava cooled and solidified to produce a hard cap of rock a hundred metres thick. Over millions of years, the sand

and loose rock underneath had eroded to leave an elevated plateau, supported by a relatively slender column. The result: a very large, fat mushroom.

Although it was of interest to geologists, the Martians didn't seem to have had much use for it – there were no canals or archaeological sites nearby – and after it was surveyed in the early years of colonisation, most people had forgotten about it. But someone did find a use for it. The flat, hard top made a great landing pad; the cap of the mushroom shielded the underside from spying eyes in orbit; and the metal concentration played havoc with electromagnetic sensors. In other words, it was an excellent place to hide.

'It's kinda like Pirate Central,' said Sophie, watching the mushroom grow in the forward viewport as they approached.

'I guess,' said Zach. 'Lots of people live there, and not only pirates. It's a proper town, with shops and cafes and parks and things. You just won't find it on any map.'

Toby looked up from a screen showing the terrain. 'You know, we've come roughly in a circle. We're only a few hundred clicks from the compound.'

'Whatever,' said Zach. He looked pointedly at Holly. 'Remember, when we get there, follow my lead, and don't draw attention to yourself.'

Holly was a little offended. 'Why are you looking at me?'

'Just lie low. Okay?'

The stalk of the mushroom was fattest at the bottom,

growing thinner as it rose to meet the underside of the plateau. Streets and dwellings had been carved into the rock of the column, creating a series of concentric terraces connected by steps and ramps. Surrounding the base was a ring of warehouses, domes, sandstone huts and shanties – a sizable town.

As the hovercraft glided towards the outskirts, a gruff crackle came over the speakers: *Identify yourselves at once.*

Zach hit the comms button. 'Emissary from the *Pointy End*. Code 743.'

There was a long pause. *Cleared. Proceed to Dock 6.*

It was early evening by the time the hovercraft parked in the dock. Unlike the busy market in Urbe Sicaria, this one was quiet and dark. Several groups of people were silently unloading goods; others were negotiating deals for products and services. As Zach and Holly walked down the ramp, a fight broke out in the shadows – a deal gone wrong – and someone screamed. It cut off with a sharp gasp.

Holly waved to the Hendriksens, who were standing in the doorway. 'Close the ramp. We'll check back soon.'

Toby glanced nervously at the locals. 'This wasn't part of the deal,' he hissed.

Twenty minutes later, Zach and Holly stood in the street outside a warehouse made of steel and corrugated iron. Watched over by a pair of uniformed guards, a steady stream of patrons was entering the warehouse through a door beneath a handpainted sign that read *Showroom*.

Unlike the denizens of the docks, or even Urbe Sicaria, many of the patrons were well dressed, even a bit arty.

Zach and Holly crossed the street and entered the warehouse. Holly only got three steps inside the front door before her jaw dropped. 'You've got to be *kidding*.'

In front of her was a large room full of artefacts of ancient Mars. Sarcophagi, statues, earthenware, weapons, jewellery, scrolls and much, much more. The larger pieces were mounted on pedestals, the smaller pieces were in glass display cases; each had a price tag attached in Earth dollars. Patrons wandered among the exhibits, talking softly, perusing the items. Guards stood around the walls.

Holly tensed as something across the room caught her eye.

Zach placed a hand on her arm. 'Steady.'

Holly shook his hand off and rushed over to a pedestal. 'That's a cerulean vase dating from the late early period. Only two have ever been found!'

Zach motioned at her to keep her voice down. 'Well, three now, I guess.'

Holly was gone before the last word was out of his mouth. Zach hurried to catch up.

She was standing in front of a display case, nose pressed up against the glass. 'And that's a Zogota necklace! Its cultural significance is . . .'

'. . . is . . . is what? Significant?'

Holly had already bounded away. Zach momentarily lost her among the exhibits. He saw her standing in front of a majestic fountain of colour and ornamentation, her hand clasped over her mouth.

'Oh! That's a royal Martian headdress. It's priceless!'

Zach found himself staring at a large price tag. He snatched it and hid it behind his back before Holly could see it. 'Yes, yes,' he said, stroking his chin, trying to look sincere. 'Priceless.'

Holly's eyes deflected to yet another exhibit. 'Oh my God!'

Zach glanced around the room. Some of the guards were staring at them. Oblivious, Holly hurried off towards the object.

Zach intercepted, grabbing her elbow and swinging her in an arc into an alcove along the wall. Standing close, he whispered urgently, 'Hey! Low profile, remember?'

'These are important cultural artefacts,' she said fiercely. 'They belong in a museum!'

Zach waved his arm around the room. 'Well, it's *like* a museum.'

Holly punched him in the arm. 'This is a disgrace! Who are these people?'

'People from Earth, mostly. Representatives of private collectors—'

'Private collectors trading in stolen art!'

'Look, focus. Remember why we're here – your father.'

Mention of her father forced Holly to collect herself. She lowered her voice. 'Okay, but how can this person help?'

'They call him the Curator. Your father might be the archaeologist, but no one knows more about the locations and contents of the Martian tombs, including their symbols and glyphs, than the Curator does.'

'How?'

'Well, ah . . .' Zach scratched his neck.

'*How?*'

'He was the first pirate. He's been robbing tombs for fifty years.'

'He *what?*'

Before Holly could protest further, Zach dragged her to a door at the back of the salesroom. A large guard stood at the threshold. Zach addressed him, 'I want to see the Curator.'

'Says who?'

Zach checked furtively over his shoulder before leaning in. 'Charles *Ramirez.*'

The guard spoke into his lapel and received a curt reply. He stepped aside and ushered them down a short corridor and into a cluttered back office. An old man with a whiskery beard and thick glasses sat at a desk overflowing in manuscripts, invoices and Martian trinkets.

'Charles. What a surprise!' he said, beaming. He came forward and gave Zach a hug. 'I didn't know the *Pointy End* was in town.'

'Well, it's not, actually,' replied Zach. 'I'm just, ah, doing a bit of recon. You know, chasing up some leads.'

The Curator grinned at him slyly. 'Striking out on your own, hey? About time.' He leaned close and lowered his voice. 'Just remember to bring whatever it is to me first. Don't trust Ming or McClosky. Those charlatans will rob you blind.' He sighed. 'It's not like the old days. No integrity.' He turned to Holly. 'And you brought a friend?'

Zach coughed. 'This is, ah, Leslie, my, ah, business partner.'

The Curator winked at Zach and took Holly's hands in his. 'Leslie. It's a pleasure.'

Holly smiled thinly in reply.

The Curator stood back and appraised them both, shaking his head with nostalgia. 'They start so young these days. But who am I to talk? Stole my first ring when I was ten!' The Curator showed them his right hand. A bronze ring, greenish with age, adorned his index finger. 'Lovely piece. Had to pull the finger off the skeleton to get it. I could never bring myself to sell it, though. Sentimental value.'

Appalled, Holly leaned in to inspect the ring. Her eyes widened. 'That's a—'

Zach clapped his hands loudly. 'Right, then, down to business!' He whipped out the photo of the symbol. 'What do you make of this?'

The Curator took the photo and returned to his desk to examine it under a magnifying lamp. He turned it this way and that, and for the briefest moment an odd look flickered across his face. 'Hmm. Where was it taken?'

Zach glanced at Holly, not sure if he should reveal this detail.

'The Well of Souls, I think,' she replied.

The Curator studied the photo for a few moments more and handed it back to Zach. 'Sorry, can't be of much help, I'm afraid.'

Holly was crushed. 'You've never seen it before?'

'I've seen something like it, sure. But the Martian script has never been deciphered. The character could mean anything.'

'But I don't think it's a character from their language. The shape, the form – it's different. And it's on its own, not part of a sequence. I think it's a royal seal of some kind. Or maybe a diagram showing . . . I'm not sure.' Holly frowned uncertainly.

The Curator was watching her closely. 'What did you say your last name was again?'

'She didn't,' said Zach.

The Curator shrugged. 'Well, I'd like to help, but . . .'

But Zach had caught the look on the Curator's face. His eyes narrowed. 'You really don't know anything about it?'

The Curator shook his head.

'C'mon . . . Leslie,' said Zach. 'Let's try Ming. Maybe he knows something.' He placed his hand on her shoulder and gestured towards the door.

'Wait,' the Curator said quickly. 'Maybe there is something. In fact, we might be able to help each other out.'

'Uh-huh?' said Zach.

The Curator selected a folder from a filing cabinet next to his desk. He handed it to Holly. 'Take a look at this.'

Holly opened it and flipped through the contents. It was full of hand-scribbled notes and several sketches of an ornate cylindrical device. The device had a central hollow core, like a telescope, encircled with a series of rings inscribed with symbols. Next to the rings was a collection of widgets and dials.

'That's a codex in Ming's showroom that I'm interested in,' said the Curator. 'My relationship with Ming is, shall we say, somewhat strained, so I haven't been able to examine it myself. But my sources tell me you rotate some rings, and the symbols on the other rings fall into alignment.'

Holly had stopped at a diagram that bore a resemblance to the one in her photograph. 'These symbols are on the codex?'

'Yes.'

'What does it do?'

'Nobody knows. There is speculation the symbols represent places and events in the long history of Mars. By turning the rings, you link them together in a series. Almost like—'

'Telling a story,' Holly murmured.

The old man smiled.

'What's your interest in it?' asked Zach.

The Curator twisted the ring on his finger. 'My days of piracy are long gone. But I was never just a pirate. I'm fascinated by the history of the Martians. Now, in my waning years, I've become something of an academic. And for my own studies I would like to examine this codex. I believe it will shed light on a certain problem I've been working on.'

'Which is?'

The Curator shook his head. 'Sorry. There I will have to cite academic confidentiality. But if it can shed light on my problem, perhaps it can shed light on yours as well.'

Holly showed the picture to Zach. 'Many of the symbols *are* similar. This one is identical except for the three small dots.'

Zach barely glanced at the picture. He eyed the Curator suspiciously. 'What precisely do you want us to do?'

'The codex goes on auction tomorrow night in Ming's showroom. I cannot afford to buy it. I'm only a poor old pirate. An investor from Earth will no doubt snap it up and it will disappear forever into a vault in someone's basement. But if you could acquire it for me . . .?'

Holly was confused. 'We don't have any money.'

'He means steal it,' said Zach.

'Could we do that? I mean, *should* we do that?'

'We're all pirates here,' said the Curator airily. 'We needn't get hung up on the morality of it. Honour among thieves, that sort of thing.'

'I don't think that's what "honour among thieves" actually means,' said Zach.

'And the *Pointy End* and its crew are somewhat legendary.'

Zach gave an embarrassed cough. 'Okay, we need to discuss this in private. We'll get back to you.'

'Of course. Say hello to the gang for me, Charles. And Leslie, it was a genuine pleasure.'

Outside the warehouse, Zach and Holly hurried back towards the docks. Holly manoeuvred Zach into an alleyway. 'How do we steal it?' she whispered, glancing over her shoulder.

'Gee, that was quick. What happened to "it belongs in

a museum"?'

'It's already *been* stolen.'

'And how do you propose to steal it back?'

'I don't know. You're the pirate.'

Zach stepped back. 'Whoa. I didn't sign up for this. I said I knew a man that might help.'

'You're going to slink away now? When we have a clue that might help find my father?'

'I'm not *slinking*, and there is no *we*! I did my bit. I'm outa here.' Zach turned around and walked away down the alley.

Holly watched him leave, her mouth hanging open. 'Yeah, that's right,' she called after him. 'You abduct my father. Beat him unconscious. And leave him to die when he can't find you gold to plunder!'

Zach spun around on his heel. 'That wasn't me!'

'No? Who's the *gang*?'

'What?'

'The Curator said, "Say hello to the gang." Close, are you? Stealing and plundering together. Like one big happy family.'

'You know nothing about them.'

'I know Patrice.'

Zach was taken aback. 'How do you know Patrice?'

Holly crossed her arms. 'You two seem pretty chummy.'

Puzzled, Zach shook his head. He couldn't figure it out. But he'd had enough. 'Bah!' He turned and walked away.

'Zach?'

And continued walking.

'Zach!'

And walking.

'*Zach!*'

And slowly came to a stop.

Holly was on tenterhooks. She needed him, but she couldn't tell him that.

His shoulders sagging in defeat, Zach turned back to face her. 'We're gonna need someone small.'

Chapter Seven

The Heist

'I'm small.'
'No.'
'No.'
'No.'
The kids were huddled around the kitchen table, plotting. The rough plans of a building were laid out in front of them, and displayed on Ship's screens were schematics of the inside of a showroom similar to the Curator's.

'Whaaa? Holly's, like, a foot taller than me. How does she fit in that?' Sophie stabbed her finger at a picture of an ornate trunk on the table.

'I'll fit. You just create a distraction.'

'How?'

'Scream,' said Zach. 'Like you've seen a mouse.'

'I like mice.'

'A spider then. Or a banachuk.'

'I like them too.'

'It's just pretend, Sophie,' said Holly. 'You shouldn't be mixed up in this, and—'

'I concur!' said Toby emphatically.

'And I don't want you getting into trouble.'

Sophie folded her arms and pouted.

Holly tapped her finger on the building plans. She glanced at Zach. 'This'll work?'

Zach looked around at each of them. 'Well, yeah, I mean . . .' He took a deep breath and let it out slowly. 'Of course, it'll work. The secure part of the warehouse is a modified space container. Once upon a time, it would have been literally airtight. But that's from the outside. From the inside, all we need to do is loosen a few bolts in the right place and we're in. We just need to be careful we select an exterior wall.'

Holly drummed her fingers on the table, satisfied. 'Okay, good. I think we're ready. If we get separated, meet in the alleyway on the western side of Ming's. Remember, stick to the plan!'

Ming's showroom was close to the base of the mushroom, close enough that the plateau above blotted out half the sky. It was late evening by the time they arrived. The streetlights were on, and the underside of the plateau was lit up with lights strung out along walkways and gantries. It was like a gigantic flying saucer hovering over them.

The building itself was much bigger than the Curator's: a warehouse three storeys high that took up the whole block. Inside, it was partitioned into foyers, office spaces, exhibition areas, information booths, auction rooms and even a cafeteria. Crowds of patrons and buyers mingled with staff and guards. Kids played fluffball in a sectioned-off area against the far wall. The Free Mars Association was selling raffle tickets.

'Wow,' said Sophie. 'Business is booming.'

'Where is it?' asked Toby.

Zach inclined his head to the right. Against a partition twenty metres away was a stepped dais supporting an open metal trunk.

'There's a guard standing right next to it!' gasped Holly.

'Shhh!' said Zach. 'That's why we wait for the guards to change shifts, remember?' He checked his watch. 'A few more minutes. Look casual.'

Holly, Zach and Toby meandered about, pretending to look at the exhibits. Sophie wandered off towards the trunk. Holly stopped in front of a display case featuring a glorious gold necklace. Zach came up beside her.

'Do you know what this is?' Holly said.

'No,' said Zach, one eye on the guards.

Holly sighed and looked around the showroom. 'My father would be heartbroken. To think, all these precious items plundered. The cultural treasures of ancient Mars, gone before he could even get a look at them.'

'I'm sorry,' said Zach. 'For what it's worth, I know what's happening is wrong. And I can't defend it. It's just . . . the Martians are dead and gone, but the humans are very much alive. And they want to stay that way. Life is hard here, and this is –'

'Ah, guys?' Toby was pointing towards the trunk.

Zach and Holly followed the direction of his finger. Sophie was trotting up the steps of the dais. The nearby guard looked at his watch and moved off. Without hesitation, Sophie casually took hold of the side of the trunk and vaulted inside.

'Flip!' said Toby and ran towards the dais.

From the corner of his eye, Zach saw the relief guard walking across the showroom floor. 'Uh-oh.'

'Do something,' said Holly.

'What?'

'Anything!'

Zach dithered. The guard reached halfway. Toby leapt up the steps onto the dais.

'Aaaarrrggghhh!' screamed Holly.

The room fell silent. Everyone, including the guards, stopped and looked. Concerned, a distinguished-looking old man approached her and asked, 'Are you quite alright, young lady?'

Flummoxed, Holly couldn't think of a reply.

Over her shoulder, Zach watched Toby remonstrating with an unseen Sophie. But the only response was the emergence of a slim arm and a hand wriggling its fingers. With a worried look towards the approaching guard, Toby gave in and fumbled around inside his vest. He pulled out a spanner and placed it into the tiny hand, whereupon the arm promptly disappeared back inside. Toby closed the lid and rapidly backed off the dais.

'A mouse,' said Zach.

'I beg your pardon?' said the old man.

'Oh yes, a mouse,' said Holly. She stamped her feet and performed an exaggerated shudder. 'Mice. Ugh. I hate them.'

Holly addressed the watching patrons, smiling apologetically. 'Sorry, saw a mouse . . . bad memories, long ago, of . . . mice. I'm fine, I'm fine.'

The old patron smiled uncertainly and resumed his browsing, murmuring to his partner. The other patrons returned to their viewing too.

Toby bounded up to them, bordering on panic. 'What do we do now?'

Zach gestured at him to calm down. 'Relax.'

'Sophie's in a Martian coffin with a spanner!'

Holly said, 'It's actually not a coff—'

'Stop! It's okay,' said Zach. 'Small adjustment to the plan. Sophie, Holly – it doesn't matter. When the showroom closes, she'll be locked in the vault with the other sold artefacts. Right now, we need to move to stage two and find the auction for the codex. Come on.' He hustled a worried Toby and Holly out of the showroom.

In another partitioned-off section were several courtroom-sized spaces where auctions were taking place. Zach and Holly checked the listings pinned on the doors.

'This one,' Holly said, 'Item 28. I think it's up next.'

The kids funnelled into the auction room. Like a small theatre, it had rows of chairs facing a stage. Curtains concealed a backstage area where the items were kept prior to auction. The place was three-quarters full and doing brisk business. As Zach, Toby and Holly diffidently took their seats in the back row, the auctioneer began his patter for the next item.

'Number 27. Small bronze statue of a gadulup. Excellent condition. Superb example of Martian art of the early middle-late period. Found in the Ansine Basin. Bidding begins at thirty-two thousand.'

An assistant wheeled out a trolley sporting a small metal statue of an exotic Martian beast. Holly gasped and instinctively raised her hand.

'Thirty-three thousand dollars to the young lady at the back. Do I hear thirty-four?'

Zach yanked her arm down. 'What the hell are you doing?'

'Sorry, got carried away. But do you know what that is?'

Zach grinded his teeth. 'No.'

The auction continued. 'Thirty-five to the man in the second row. Do I hear thirty-six? Yes, thirty-six to the lady in the centre.'

They sold the piece to a woman down the front. The next item out on stage was the codex in a glass case. About half a metre long, it looked like a short, fat, golden tele-scope, covered in dials and rings. The audience perked up a notch; idle conversation subsided.

'Ooh, that's it,' said Holly in a hushed voice.

'Item number 28. A very special piece, ladies and gentle-men, restored to immaculate condition and in working order. Its provenance is unknown, but it is believed to date from the precursor civilisation. Its purpose, too, is a mystery – although several theories have been advanced. I refer you to your catalogue for details. Bidding begins at two hundred and forty thousand dollars. Do I hear two hundred and fifty?'

'Holy flip,' said Toby. 'No one is going to believe we have that kind of money!'

'Two hundred and eighty to the gentleman in the bowler hat. Three hundred, anyone?'

'It doesn't matter,' said Zach. 'Most people here are representing other parties. They don't have the money either. We'll say we have to wait for the bank transfer to come through from the person we're buying it for. And then we'll pick it up in the morning. In the meantime, they'll store it in the vault with the other items.'

'With Sophie,' said Holly.

'With Sophie,' said Zach.

A man raised his hand. The auctioneer said, 'Four hundred and thirty thousand. Do I hear four hundred and fifty?'

Toby grumbled, 'We don't even look like we *represent* people who have money.'

'That's why we don't draw attention to ourselves,' said Zach crossly.

'So, when do we bid?' asked Holly.

'Not yet. Wait for the bidders to thin out. And don't look too eager.'

The bids increased. Bidders fell by the wayside, shaking their heads. Holly was getting nervous, her leg bouncing up and down. Zach held her hand to calm her. She didn't seem to notice. The bidding continued until there were only two bidders left in contention.

'Five hundred and twenty to the gentleman in the third

row. Do I hear five hundred and thirty? Five hundred and thirty, anyone? No? Five hundred and thirty is a small price to pay for this fabulous piece of ancient Martian art and technology. Five hundred and thirty thousand, ladies and gentlemen. Any advance? Going once . . .'

Zach looked around the room. This was the moment. He began to lift his arm.

'Going twice . . .'

Holly leapt from her seat. 'One million dollars!'

The auctioneer raised his eyebrows and looked at the other bidder, who shook his head definitively. The auctioneer banged the lectern with his gavel. 'Sold to the young lady in the back row!'

Zach buried his face in his hands.

Holly and Toby were waiting in the foyer. A double door at the end swung open and out came Zach, looking exasperated. Behind him, items were being packaged by warehouse staff, ready to be collected by the buyers.

'Did they believe you?' asked Toby.

'That I have one million?' Zach replied sarcastically. 'No, they didn't believe me. But rules are rules. They'll hold it in the vault until noon tomorrow while we come up with the money.'

Embarrassed, Holly looked up at him from under her lashes. 'Sorry.'

Zach grunted. 'It doesn't matter. We got it done. Now we gotta hope that Sophie can do her bit. What's she like with a spanner?'

'I think she knows which end to use,' said Toby. 'I'm more worried she'll get disoriented in there and won't figure out which grill she's supposed to unbolt.'

Holly checked her watch. 'The showroom's about to close. Maybe we can still switch us around?'

The three returned to the showroom – only to stare wide-eyed at the empty dais where the trunk had just been.

Zach caught the elbow of a salesperson wandering by. 'The trunk? We were interested?'

'Oh, item number 17. Sold. Only a few moments ago,' said the woman. 'Good price too.'

'So where is it now?' asked Toby.

'They took it to the vault for packaging and deregistration, and now it's awaiting pick-up. Buyer has to leave soon, apparently.'

'Leave for . . .?'

'Earth.'

The kids swapped looks of alarm.

'Um,' said Zach, 'we might be interested in making a counteroffer. Can you tell us who bought it?'

'Sorry, confidential.'

'Look, this is really—'

'But it only just happened. Customer might be at the pick-up dock. Now, if you'll excuse me.'

The salesperson continued about her business. The kids went into a huddle.

'The pick-up dock's at the back of the building,' said Zach. 'Go there. Get Sophie.'

'What are you going to do?' asked Holly.

'We still need the codex.'

'But how?'

Zach blew his breath out with force. 'I'll make something up.'

The pick-up dock was as busy as the warehouse. From a raised platform, warehouse staff were checking receipts and handing boxes over to a group of waiting customers. Larger items were being loaded by a crane onto the back of buggies or quad bikes towing trailers. The line of vehicles stretched down the driveway and out onto the street.

As Holly and Toby approached, the staff loaded a large wooden crate onto the tray of a modified quad bike. The side of the crate was stencilled *17*.

Toby nudged Holly in the ribs and pointed.

They rushed over and mingled with customers, sidling up close to the tray. While a uniformed guard tied the crate down, the driver hopped out of his seat, leaving the engine running, and went to the dock to sign the paperwork with his tablet.

Toby saw his chance. He pointed to the end of the warehouse driveway that connected to the main street and whispered to Holly, 'Pick me up there.' Without waiting for her response, he skipped over, snatched the tablet from the driver's hands and bolted.

'Wait, what?' said Holly.

'Hey!' shouted the driver, running after Toby.

It took a couple of seconds for Holly to catch on that everyone, including the guard, was watching the thief run away. She jumped onto the seat of the bike and kicked it into gear. The guard turned around in time to grab the edge of the tray – only to be thrown to the ground as Holly opened the throttle and the bike leapt forward.

Snarling, the man got up and went to the next bike in line. He wrenched the driver from his seat and threw him aside. Taking the driver's place, he kicked the vehicle into gear and raced off after Holly. Bystanders dived in all directions getting out of the way.

Holly careened around the corner of the building and drove down the side of the warehouse, the guard just seconds behind her. It was dark away from the streetlamps. She fumbled around on the console and switched on the headlights, then opened the throttle as far as it would go. The bike bounced up and down on the stony ground, ramming the seat into her tailbone. She stood up on the footplates to ride the shocks.

'Sorry!' Holly called out, imagining what Sophie was going through in the trunk.

Holly took the next corner around the edge of the warehouse and headed towards the street. She emerged a block down from Ming's and turned back towards the main entrance. As she neared the driveway, Toby burst into the street and looked around like a frightened animal. Holly slammed on the brakes and skidded to a stop beside him. Toby threw the tablet away and jumped aboard, wrapping his arms around her waist. The driver was only a few paces behind. He lunged at the bike as it took off, missed and fell to the ground – and howled in pain as the chasing bike swerved too late and ran over his foot.

Thinking she had a better chance of losing her pursuer in the twisty streets that wrapped around the base of the mushroom, Holly headed towards the terraces. The plateau loomed like a black cloud in the night sky above them.

They hurtled through an intersection. Vehicles swerved around them, brakes squealing. A sand crawler bore down on them. It couldn't stop in time. Toby screamed. Holly twisted the handlebars hard and rode a set of steps up towards the next terrace. The bike juddered like a jackhammer.

Holly turned at the top of the steps and cut through an alleyway. Washing was strung up above and a wet nightie slapped Toby in the face. Holly rejoined the main street and destroyed an outdoor cafe. And a grocery stall. People scattered in all directions.

She bounced up more steps, through backyards and across plazas. They gained height as the buggies raced along the curved streets that encircled the stem of the mushroom. Holly had managed to put some distance between them and their pursuer – she glanced in the rear-view mirror – but she hadn't lost him.

Taking a sharp corner, Holly screeched to a stop, rammed the quad into reverse and backed into a drive-way. Seconds later, she watched the other bike race by. She pulled out again and took a side street.

The terrain got steeper. Up here, houses and steps were cut into the rock on one side, and on the other the ground fell away sharply to the top of the terrace below. There were no roadside barriers.

As Holly sped around a curve, a banachuk jumped out of a garbage bin can carrying a bone and wandered into the bike's path. The fox-like creature froze in the middle of the road, its yellow eyes gleaming in the headlights. Holly veered and braked violently. The bike skidded in the loose soil and spun around, heading towards the edge of the road. As it slowed to a stop, the rear tray swung out over the cliff edge. The weight of the trunk tipped the front end up into the air and the bike threatened to do a backflip.

Then, its straps loosened by all the shaking, the crate slid off the back of the tray and over the cliff.

With the weight gone, the bike fell back onto all four wheels. Holly and Toby jumped off, fell to their hands and knees by the roadside and then scrambled to look over the edge. They watched in horror as the crate rolled and bounced down the steep slope. The crate disintegrated, but the sturdier trunk inside continued to tumble, eventually crashing into a rock at the bottom and breaking into a dozen pieces. As the pieces came to rest, Toby and Holly gaped in bewilderment. Sophie wasn't inside!

Holly heard the noise of the other bike coming closer. She grabbed Toby by the collar and dragged him to his feet. 'C'mon. Let's get out of here!'

Sophie wandered around the metal wall of the dim interior of the vault, stopping to cup her ear to the metal. Muffled noises were coming from the other side, but she couldn't tell if it was another part of the warehouse or traffic on the road. The guys were supposed to tap on the wall nearest to the grill they wanted her to unbolt. She stopped at a foot-sized grill above the floor, the opening of a ventilation duct. Crouching, she sized her spanner up to the bolts, but the spanner was really heavy, and she couldn't adjust the screw thingy to fit. She gave up and peered inside the duct.

'Guys? Guys?' she whispered loudly. 'Sorry, but I had to get out of there. It was, like, really musty. It smelt like dead Martian or something. Guys?' Sophie stood up, peeved. 'What a dumb plan.' She walked over to another grill. 'Guys?'

Inside the vault, long aisles stretched away into gloom. Sophie chose an aisle at random and wandered down it. The shelves contained dusty artefacts labelled with serial numbers and short descriptions – jewellery, crockery, statues, tools, toiletries. It was a treasure trove of ancient Martian artifacts.

Sophie stopped and studied herself in the scratched and dented surface of a full-length bronze mirror, oxidised with age. A greenish, dented Sophie stared back at her. Attached to the mirror on a chain was a beautiful bronze comb. She picked it up and combed her hair out.

Further along was a mummified figure wrapped up in a swathe of bandages. She tweaked its nose and tried to mimic the surprised look on its wizened face. 'Oh, I'm dead, am I? Shock!' She assumed a look of mock horror.

In the next aisle was the codex. It sat on a trolley with

a *Sold* tag of one million attached to it. Sophie gawked at the price. 'Wow.'

In the darkest part between two streetlamps, Zach nimbly clambered up a drainpipe and onto the roof of Ming's. He sneaked over the tin as quietly as his desert boots would allow and crouched in the shadow of a satellite dish. In front of him was a series of ventilation fans rotating sluggishly. Next to one fan, a curved duct poked through the roof. Zach pulled the lid off with a grunt and lowered himself down into the duct.

Sophie experimented with the codex. She twirled the knobs and rotated the rings. Each time a symbol on the ring aligned with a similar symbol on another ring, the device clicked and whirled like a tumbler lock.

From somewhere in the vault came the clang of steel on steel. A rectangle of light swept across the room and the noise of the warehouse flooded in. As the overhead lights flickered on, Sophie peeked through a gap in the shelves and glimpsed the arm of a man carrying a vase.

Tucking the codex under her arm, Sophie ran back to the bronze mirror and scrunched down behind it. Footsteps sounded down the central aisle, changed pitch, got louder and stopped. Sophie risked a peep around the edge of the mirror. The man was standing almost in front of her! Jerking her head back in, she curled up into a ball and shut her eyes as tight as she could. Seconds later, the footsteps started again and receded. The lights went off, and the door clanged.

Zach crawled through a ventilation duct with a pencil flashlight between his teeth. He stopped at an intersection and shone the beam of light left and right. He chose left.

The duct brought him to a spherical chamber with rotating fans above and below, both covered by grills. Ducts around the perimeter led off in all directions. Zach tried to orient himself, picturing in his head all the twists and turns he had taken on his way here. He'd taken a left back there, and a right before that, and then a left before that. Or had that one been a right? Yes, it was definitely a right – a left, a left and then a right. But if he got turned around coming down from the roof, then that was reversed – a left, a right, a right and a left. But if that was true, then he had been heading in the wrong direction from the start. Zach rubbed his jaw and muttered all the curse words he knew. He chose the duct in front of him.

As her eyes adjusted to the gloom, Sophie pondered the problem of the codex. Accidentally, she twisted the ring at the end of the cylinder, and it screwed off like a bottle cap. Oops. Inside was a slim central rod and a watch-like maze of cogs and rings. Sophie slipped one of the shiny cogs off the end of the rod and examined it. It would make a marvellous piece of jewellery. She held it up to her ear and studied her distorted reflection in the bronze mirror. She had an idea.

Sophie pulled the codex apart. Kneeling beside the

pieces in front of the mirror, she took a cog and looped it over one of her ear studs. It hung there like a large earring. She hung one from the other side too. As she had two studs in each ear, that took care of four cogs, but there was a lot more to go. Sophie realised the little clips that held them in place could also join them together in a chain. Soon she had a string of cogs dangling from each ear. She picked up one of the rings and slid it over her wrist, shaking it a moment to admire it in the mirror. It made a great bangle. Several more fit over her other hand, smaller rings went on her fingers and the largest one around her ankle. That left her with the two main pieces – the central rod and the cylindrical casing – and an assortment of small screws.

Sophie looked at the screws, shrugged and casually threw them over her shoulder. She took the rod and used it to pin her hair up on top of her head. All that remained was the casing. It slipped snuggly over her forearm, but it looked odd with all the ancient symbols adorning its surface. She looked around for inspiration and her eyes rested on the mummified corpse. 'Wah-ahh,' she said to the ancient face.

Zach jumped down from the ceiling duct and landed on all fours in a room full of cleaning supplies. He wiped the sweat from his brow. In front of him was a metal door. Grinning with confidence, he strode forward and yanked it open. It led back out to the street, only ten metres down from where he'd started. A man rode by on a bicycle and waved.

Sophie knocked on the door of the vault. A moment later it opened, and a bemused guard looked in. He didn't see her at first, squinting over the top of her head into the dark room. Sophie cleared her throat, and he glanced down.

'What are you doing?' he said gruffly. 'Get outa there.'

Sophie smiled pleasantly and walked out of the vault wearing the codex, one arm wrapped up in bandages like it was a cast for a broken arm.

'I got lost. I thought this was the bathroom.'

'How'd you get in? I've been here for half an hour.'

Sophie raised her voice to the edge of panic. 'I've been gone for half an hour? My parents will go bananas!' She looked past the guard into the warehouse proper. Customers were still wandering around, looking at the exhibits. She pointed at a random couple. 'There they are! Oh my God, mother looks so worried!'

Sophie tried to hurry away. She got two steps past the guard before a meaty forearm dropped in front of her like a barrier gate at a parking lot.

'Wait,' the guard growled.

Sophie's eyes went wide as saucers and while mentally she prepared herself to scamper, she composed her face and turned around.

He held up a cog. 'You dropped your earring.'

Sophie smiled her sweetest smile, accepted the cog with a gracious curtsy and walked away.

Zach was working his way around the perimeter of Ming's showroom looking for another way in. Sneaking from shadow to shadow, he checked vents and tried doors. All locked. Hands on hips, he stepped back and shook his head, cursing in all the languages he knew.

'Pssst!'

What was that?

'Pssst!'

The voice was coming from the shadows of an alleyway. Cautiously, Zach approached. The tiny figure of Sophie took shape from between a couple of crates.

'Sophie?' he rushed to her and put his hands on her shoulders. 'Are you okay? What happened?'

'Long story. But I got the codex. All the big bits, anyway.' Sophie sheepishly held up a cardboard box containing the disassembled codex.

Zach hung his head in relief. 'Sophie, what were you thinking? Everyone was worried out of their minds.'

Sophie hated sentiment. She dismissed his concern with a shrug. 'Where are the others?'

The answer was the sound of running feet. Toby and Holly sprinted down the alley towards them.

'Sophie?' Holly gulped for breath. 'Are you okay?'

'It's okay. I got it.' Sophie showed her the box.

'But –?' started Holly.

'Explanations later,' said Zach. 'We've got to get it back to the Curator before anyone notices it's gone.'

Holly, holding her side and panting, nodded in

agreement. Zach, Sophie and Holly started to leave.

But Toby didn't move. Winded, bent double, he managed an angry spit. 'Stupid girl.'

'What did you say?' said Sophie.

Toby straightened up. 'I said you're a stupid girl!'

'Don't call me stupid. I got the codex.'

'You never listen. Never do what you're told, never –'

'That's not true.'

'Never do your chores.'

'I do too!'

'And Mum and Dad let you get away with it because you were their precious little girl.'

Sophie smiled coldly. 'Or maybe they let me do things because I didn't whinge all the time.' She mimicked her brother's voice. '*But why can't we have an automatic buggy? Manual is sooo hard.*'

'I never said that.'

'You did too. *It's sooo hard.*'

'I did not!'

Sophie arched her eyebrows. 'Whine, whine, whine. That's why they left us, so they didn't have to listen to you whine all the time.'

Toby flushed red. Fists bunched, he came at her. 'Take that back!'

'Hey!' Zach stepped in front of Toby and blocked his way. Toby tried to get past. They scuffled. Zach struggled to restrain him at first – Toby was incensed – but Zach was bigger and stronger and eventually pushed him back.

'Or maybe,' Sophie continued, with extra venom, 'they

left because they hated us and wanted us dead.'

Holly grabbed Sophie's shoulder. 'Sophie, stop it.'

Raging, Toby came at Sophie again, but Zach was ready this time and angry now as well. He shoved Toby backwards, knocking him over. Toby floundered in the dirt, choking back tears. 'You're a stupid, selfish little brat!' he bellowed.

'And you're a whiny—'

'Sophie!' Holly spun Sophie around to face her. '*Shut up!*

Sophie paused and blinked, chastened by the harsh words from her new best friend. She pointed a finger at Toby. 'He started it,' she mumbled petulantly.

'You started it!' screamed Toby.

'Enough!' shouted Zach, holding his hands up. 'Enough! We really, *really* need to get back to the Curator.' He stood between them and waited until the siblings wound down a little.

'Zach's right,' said Holly. 'We can . . . talk about this later.'

Toby got up, muttering to himself, and adjusted his vest and suspenders. Sophie started to cry softly. Zach gave Toby a few moments to straighten himself out before going to him and pushing him in front of him down the alley.

Holly put her arm around Sophie, and they followed the boys.

The Curator and Zach sat around the desk and put the

codex back together. Holly was pacing back and forward near the open office door. Outside in the now-closed showroom, Toby and Sophie sat against opposite walls, as far apart as possible, their faces puffy and red. A guard stood between them in the middle of the room.

'What happened to the screws?' asked the Curator.

A tired Zach waved the question away: don't ask.

'No matter. The pins that I 3D-printed should work fine for now. There.'

The Curator held up the finished piece. Holly joined them at the desk, hovering expectantly.

'Pretty sophisticated device for the Martians,' said Zach. 'I thought they were more swords-and-shields kind of people?'

'Not at all,' replied the Curator. 'Their technology in some ways was more advanced than our own.' He examined the device. The rings around the central core rotated freely. He experimented by aligning two similar symbols on two separate rings – a third ring whirled and clicked into place.

'So . . . what?' said Zach. 'What does that mean?'

The old man shook his head. He tried another combination of symbols. Again, after aligning two rings, the third turned and clicked into place. 'It appears to be giving an answer.'

'But what's the question?' said Zach.

Holly held out her hand. 'Here, let me try.'

A little reluctantly, the Curator handed her the codex. Holly inspected the symbols on the rings. She experimented with a few spins of her own.

'The symbols on the third ring differ from the first two. Like they're from a different alphabet or something.'

'Maybe it's a translator. From one language to another,' said Zach.

Holly glanced at him, surprised at this clever intuition. 'Maybe.' She tried another combination of symbols. 'So many are familiar, almost as if I've seen them before. Maybe in a book somewhere?' Holly spun the second ring, and the third locked into place. She remembered a picture from her father's notebook. Her voice rose in excitement. 'They're not symbols!'

'What do you mean?' asked the Curator.

'The marks on the third ring are not symbols. It's a map. Or, more correctly, a kind of directory.'

Holly pointed at the markings. 'See? The symbols on the first two are place names or coordinates or something. But the third has dots and lines and swirls. I've seen them before on the ancient maps my fa—' Holly caught herself. 'I've seen them generated on a computer. They're outlines of geographical features – the mountains, river basins and canals of ancient Mars.'

'But what does it do?' asked Zach.

'If you want to know how to get somewhere, you give the codex the place name by rotating the first two rings, then the third ring pops into place to provide the map of how to get there.'

The Curator clapped his hands. 'Ingenious. It's like an analogue navigation system.'

'The photo is actually a map?' asked Zach.

'I think so, yes.' Holly took the photo out of her pocket and compared it to the symbols on the codex's third ring.

'They are similar,' said Zach.

The Curator held out his hand. 'Give it here. Let's see if it fits to a known landmark.'

He took the photo and laid it on his desk, pushing documents out of the way to clear a space. The desk was a computer screen too; he tapped it twice and it came to life. He brought up a map of Mars and placed the photo over an illuminated red square in the screen's corner. Outlines from the photo transferred to the tabletop and appeared overlayed on the map. A program ran. The outline of the symbols danced over the screen, spinning, enlarging, shrinking, zooming in and out, trying to fit like a jigsaw piece to some collection of features. The symbol flashed green and zoomed in to a section of the map. The lines and swirls fit roughly to an alluvial floodplain and stretch of river above the equator. A box popped up beside it with coordinates and the text: *One partial match: 92%.*

Zach, Holly and the Curator leaned over the display.

'The Amalthea Basin,' said the Curator.

'That's in the northern hemisphere. What's there?' asked Zach.

The Curator shook his head. 'It's mostly unexplored.'

Zach compared the photo to the map on the screen. 'If the lines are rivers and canals, what are the dots next to them? There are no dots on the map.'

'Cities. Temples,' said Holly. 'Important sites to the

Martians. All long gone, so they don't appear on our maps.'

Zach rubbed his chin. 'Important sites? You mean, like . . . the City of the Dead?'

Holly looked nervously at Zach, and they both looked nervously at the Curator.

'I don't know,' said Holly.

The Curator was leaning back in his chair, looking thoughtful. He noticed them watching him and grinned. 'Don't worry, I am not concerned with the shiny baubles of dead Martians. My interests lie . . . with other things.' He took a stylus and jotted the coordinates down on the edge of the photo. He handed it back to Holly. 'Go find your father, Hollicent Anne McGuire.'

Chapter Eight

Faith

'How did he know my name?' said Holly.

'The Curator deals in information. He probably checked up on you after the first time you met him.'

'Can we trust him?'

'Jesus, no. But at least now we have something to go on.'

It was past midnight. Holly and Zach were walking back through the streets to the hovercraft dock. Phobos was peeking around the edge of the plateau, its weak light producing faint shadows that stretched out in front of them. Several paces ahead of them walked Sophie; Toby was many paces behind.

Sophie stopped at the closed ramp to the hovercraft. 'Ship, lower the ramp,' she said in a dead voice.

Nothing happened. Zach and Holly caught up to her.

Sophie tried again, louder. 'Ship, lower the ramp, please.'

They had to wait another few seconds, but eventually the ramp lowered. Silhouetted in the opening was a large man with a beard.

Sophie gasped.

'Davidus,' muttered Toby from behind them.

The man had made himself at home. The remains of a meal were in the sink, dirty clothes were strewn over the floor and a pair of wet socks hung over the back of a chair.

'What are you doing on our ship?' Sophie demanded.

Davidus took a seat at the table and put his feet up. '*My* ship.'

'Ship? Shock him. Kick him out,' said Sophie.

Davidus looked smug.

'Ship?' Sophie glanced around the interior. 'What have you done to Ship?'

'Override protocol 4287. The ship has a loyalty mod installed. It is programmed to be loyal to the faith.' Davidus leaned back in the chair. 'And I am leader of the faith.'

Alarmed, Toby ran to a console and checked the readouts. 'Ship? Who is in command?'

Ship replied in an oddly dull tone. 'Commander Davidus.'

'Nooo!' cried Sophie.

'Ship,' Toby said, 'execute override 3267.'

'I do not recognise that instruction.'

'Override 3267!'

'I do not recognise—'

'Ship,' said Davidus, 'in future you will only respond to my voice.'

'Understood, Commander.'

'Ship. *I* am your commander!' cried Toby.

Ship was silent. Davidus smiled. Toby sat down and started typing frantically. But every time he hit the enter key all he got was a beep.

Sophie walked over to a bulkhead and gently pressed her cheek against the metal. 'Oh, Ship.'

Davidus watched Sophie caress the bulkhead and shook his head. 'I must say I'm impressed you managed to get into it. Your father locked it and wouldn't give me the access codes.'

Toby was still typing. More beeps.

Zach and Holly had been watching from the sidelines. 'What do you want, exactly?' asked Holly.

Davidus spread his arms in an expansive gesture. 'What everyone wants. Salvation.'

There wasn't much space in the storeroom. Zach dozed in a corner, his face squeezed up against a box of tools and Sophie asleep on his shoulder. Toby was sitting against the opposite wall, morosely staring into space. Holly was next to him, also awake, frowning in concentration. The room was so cramped all their legs met and commingled in the middle.

Zach grunted in his sleep.

Holly frowned. 'How does he sleep at a time like this?' she wondered aloud.

Toby didn't respond. Holly looked at her watch and sighed. They had been locked in the storeroom now for almost five hours. The steady thrum of the hovercraft suggested they were going somewhere in a hurry.

Zach began to snore.

Holly looked around at the gang. She had to do

something. She shook Toby's shoulder. 'Toby, tell me again about Davidus. He was the leader of the cult, right? What's he up to?'

Toby's eyes only blinked in response.

'What does he want? Where is he taking us, Toby? Talk to me.'

'He was our leader,' Toby replied dully. 'He led us to Mars.'

'But what does he want?'

Zach interrupted with a loud snort and started snoring again. Annoyed, Holly kicked his foot and jolted him awake. Bleary-eyed, he looked at her.

'Listen to this,' said Holly. 'It's important.'

Zach groaned and tried to focus.

Holly nudged Toby's arm. 'Go on. What happened the night your parents left? Was Davidus still there?'

'Yeah. They had a big argument.'

'About what?'

'I didn't hear. But Mum and Dad were furious.'

'And after that?'

'Dunno. Woke up the next morning and they were all gone. Mum, Dad, Davidus. Sophie said that Mum had woken her in the middle of the night to say they were going looking for food. They took the last two buggies.'

'To where?'

Toby shrugged and wiped his nose on his shirt.

Holly turned to Zach. 'Why take us? He has the hover-craft. Why not just kick us out?'

'Leverage, maybe,' said Zach. 'To use against Toby and

Sophie's parents if he finds them? Or perhaps he just wants to take us out to the middle of nowhere and dump us. Get us out of the way.'

'Maybe. Or maybe he needs something from us.'

'Well, it could be both. He gets what he needs and then dumps us.'

'Is that the pirate way?'

Zach looked hurt.

Holly immediately regretted what she'd said. 'Sorry. You helped us back there . . . helped me, and I'm, I'm . . . well . . .' She swallowed hard. 'What I'm trying to say is—'

Luckily for Holly, the door to the storeroom opened. Davidus's head appeared in the gap. 'We're here. Everybody out.'

The hovercraft ramp lowered. Davidus was the first out, and the kids followed tentatively behind. The hovercraft had parked on a rocky plain pockmarked with shallow pools of sand. In front of them was a solar powered pumping station. It was comprised of a circular array of panels, many rings thick, surrounding a small shed and pumping tower. Scattered throughout the array were metre-tall converter boxes.

'What is this place?' asked Holly.

'This is the pumping station near the compound,' Toby explained. 'There's a large aquifer below us.' He turned to Davidus. 'Why are we here?'

Davidus walked towards the edge of the array. 'To find your parents.'

'This is stupid,' said Toby. 'We don't know what happened to them.'

'I think you do.'

Davidus went to one of the converter boxes. He swept some sand from the top. 'You arriving in town with the hovercraft was a gift. I've been living in a hovel near the docks for the past four months. Hoping for a chance to come here, but . . . no money.' With a grimace of disgust, he brushed the sand from his hands.

'So?' said Toby.

'So, your parents came here the night they disappeared.'

'Why?'

'To get the money.'

'What money?'

'The world was ending. The members of the faith happily relinquished all their worldly possessions – jewellery, e-phones, identity bracelets, memory cubes with financial information. I told them I destroyed it all, but –'

'You kept it,' said Zach.

'In a suitcase,' said Davidus.

Toby couldn't believe it. 'You stole everyone's money?'

'Well, technically, I didn't steal it.'

'What does this have to do with their parents?' asked Holly.

Davidus was trying to open the front panel of the box, but sand had built up against the door.

'They found out,' said Zach.

Davidus looked at the siblings. 'Your mother was the sharp one. She figured it out. She even guessed where I hid it. We argued. I took off to get the suitcase and they came after me. There were only two buggies left. I took the one with the most charge, and the remaining bottles of oxygen, but theirs was faster.' Davidus had cleared the sand away from the box. He turned the handle and yanked the panel open. Apart from a confusion of circuit boards, switches and wires, it was empty.

'Let me guess,' said Zach. 'They got here first.'

Scowling, Davidus straightened up and looked around the array.

'But then what happened to our parents?' asked Toby.

'That's what we're here to find out,' said Davidus. 'Spread out. Check all the boxes. There's got to be something here. A clue – something. If you find it, I might take you back to town. Otherwise . . .'

The sun had risen to its full height. It was hot. The kids and Davidus were fitfully making their way through the array, looking around the panels, opening the converter boxes. Everyone was tired and sweaty and dirty.

Sophie gave up and sat down on a rock. Holly, with a glance towards Davidus, surreptitiously wandered over to where Zach was trying to lever a panel open.

'This is hopeless,' she whispered. 'Sophie told me it's been five months since their parents left. There's nothing here, and they wouldn't have left the suitcase. If he leaves us behind . . .?'

'We have another problem,' said Zach.

'What now?'

'Don't you feel it? Oxygen is low.'

'That explains why my legs are starting to wobble.' She looked over at Davidus. 'Do you think you could – you know, take him?'

'He's a big man. Perhaps. But then what? He controls the ship. It won't let us board unless Davidus orders it to.'

'My gun's in my backpack. If you could distract him, hold him back long enough, I could get aboard the hovercraft.'

Zach thought about it a moment, then took a deep breath. 'What have we got to lose?'

Sophie was throwing pebbles at one of the panels. Each time she hit it, there was a little *ping*. Drawn and hollowed eyed, she hadn't spoken a word since they arrived.

Toby walked towards her. With each step, he could feel the muscles in his neck tightening. 'What are you doing? Keep looking.'

Ping!

'Weren't you listening? Mum and Dad came here the night they disappeared.'

Ping!

'Don't you get it? They didn't abandon us. They were trying to stop Davidus from taking the money.'

Sophie stared at him impassively. She threw another pebble. *Ping!*

Toby flung his head into the air, walked a few steps backwards, stretched his neck to either side, spun around in a little circle and approached her again. 'Say something,' he said angrily.

Sophie missed her next shot. 'Maybe they were trying to steal the money too.'

Toby was gobsmacked. It took him fully ten seconds to find some words. 'How can you say that?'

Ping!

'You think Mum and Dad are thieves?'

Sophie raised her arm for another shot. Toby slapped the pebble from her hand. 'What is *wrong* with you?'

Sophie's struck hand fell to her side as if paralysed. 'They ran off and left us alone. And all Mum could say was that God would watch over us if we went to church.' She snorted in disgust. 'How stupid is that?'

The rising altercation had attracted the attention of the others. Holly and Zach were hurrying over, Davidus too.

Toby challenged Sophie. 'She was trying to say—'

'They abandoned us.'

'No! They . . . they were trying to do the right thing. They were—'

'They brought us to another planet to die.'

'They were trying to save us!' shouted Toby.

'They drove away in a buggy!' screamed Sophie.

Toby rocked back on his heels as if physically struck. 'No! No! No!'

'They ran away!'

'*No!*'

Sophie howled like a banshee, '*We killed the dog!*'

Holly grabbed Sophie and pulled her away, trying to wrap the little girl in her arms. Sophie screamed and fought her off, but Holly wouldn't let go. Sophie struggled for a few moments more and then suddenly stopped and sagged against Holly, hanging in her arms like an empty sack.

Zach went and stood in front of Toby, worried that he might run at Sophie again, but Toby was beyond anger. Overwhelmed with grief, Toby stood apart, swaying and murmuring 'No' again and again.

Davidus arrived, wheezing, a curious look on his face. 'What did you just say? God would watch over you if you went to church?'

Sophie didn't answer. Her face was buried in Holly's arms.

'Sophie, think,' Davidus asked. 'The night she left. What exactly did your mother say?'

Holly looked daggers at the man. 'Leave her alone.'

'Shut up,' said Davidus. 'Sophie, this is important. Pull yourself together.'

Sophie replied in a monotone, her voice muffled by Holly's shirt. 'She said God would protect us as long as we go to church.'

'Did she say "go to church" or "go to *the* church"?'

Focusing on this odd question seemed to revive Sophie a little. She lifted her face from Holly's shirt. 'I don't know. I was half asleep.'

'Leave her alone,' said Holly. 'What does it matter?'

'Actually . . .' said Toby. He had stopped swaying and was staring at the centre of the solar panel array, where a slim tower supported a satellite dish. 'Close to the compound there were some old Martian ruins. The church was the nickname we gave them because they looked like a steeple.'

'That was Mum's silly name for it,' said Sophie. 'It didn't look much like a church.'

Toby smacked his forehead. 'She was telling you – *us* – to meet them at the church!'

Davidus nodded. 'The Kadeshi ruins.' He turned and ran to the hovercraft. Toby followed. Zach and Holly traded confused looks before running after them – Holly pulling Sophie along behind her.

Davidus called out as he reached the ramp. 'Ship, landmark – thirty kilometres south-south-east from the compound. The Kadeshi ruins. Go there now.'

'Yes, Commander.'

The hovercraft's fans spun up, and the ramp lifted from the ground. Zach reached the vehicle as it began to move and vaulted onto the bottom of the ramp. The other kids were forced to run alongside the hovercraft as it picked up speed.

'Wait! You may still need us,' Zach shouted into the closing gap.

Davidus appeared in the doorway. He thought about it. 'Get in.'

Zach helped Toby and the others onto the rising ramp and they scrambled into the vehicle.

The ruins were only twenty minutes away. Davidus sat in the commander's seat, looking intently at the forward viewport. Toby stood behind him, biting his nails. Holly sat Sophie down at the kitchenette table and got her a glass of water. Zach paced up and down.

With one eye on Davidus, Holly put out a hand to stop Zach. She caught his gaze and folded her fingers into the shape of a gun.

Zach nodded and went to the stairs leading down to the bomb bay, but as he touched the banister, the surrounding air erupted with a crackle. Zach couldn't quite muffle his cry of pain. 'Mmmarmpphh!'

'Don't do it,' said Davidus, without turning around.

Zach stamped his feet, trying to shake out his pain and frustration.

A few minutes later, a skeletal tower of brick appeared in the forward viewport. Several storeys high, the tower was missing a roof and had caved in on one side to produce a needle-shaped spire. Surrounding it was a rust-red pile of collapsed walls.

Toby leaned over the console, his fingers gripping the edge. 'That's it.' He hurried to the door, and before the hovercraft had finished moving, he was down the ramp and running towards the ruins. Davidus was next, pausing to take a big puff of oxygen from a cylinder.

Before they followed, Zach warned the girls, 'I checked the readings. Oxygen is low here. Don't stray too far from the hovercraft.'

They walked towards the ruins. As they got close, they could hear Toby running around somewhere behind the tower. He appeared and disappeared again as he passed an open doorway, wading through a drift of sand that had built up against the structure.

'Toby might be wrong,' Holly said to Sophie. 'Maybe your mum really was just saying to be good.'

'There,' said Sophie, pointing to the east. There was a flash of light from the top of a dune.

The group made their way towards the light. Toby noticed where they were going and ran ahead, reaching the top of the dune fifty metres ahead of the rest of them. He ignored the shiny oblong object and instead stumbled down the other side of the dune and was briefly lost to sight.

The object was an aluminium suitcase, three-quarters buried in the dune's slope with a corner sticking out.

In a shallow depression on the other side of the dune was a wrecked buggy, also half-submerged in sand. The cockpit was open and in the front seat was a human skeleton, tatters of clothes draped over the legs and chest. Another skeleton was propped up against the back wheel, only its torso and arms visible above the sand. A couple of metal cylinders lay nearby, their plastic tubes and mouth-pieces eroded to desiccated strands. Toby was on his knees in front of the skeleton.

Holly instinctively moved to put her arm around Sophie.

Zach waded down into the depression and over to the buggy. He leaned into the cockpit and brushed the sand from the instrument panel. 'Out of charge,' he said, turning to check the cylinders. 'Oxygen too. Probably ran out on their way back.'

Zach completed his survey of the vehicle and went to

Toby, whose face was wet with tears. He stood next to him in silence for a few moments. 'We'll bury them,' he said.

'They didn't abandon us,' said Toby. He turned to Sophie and said it again, fiercely, daring her to contradict him. 'They didn't!'

Sophie's eyes were glazed over.

Davidus had seen enough. Grim-faced, he knelt beside the suitcase and shovelled the sand away, pausing to whistle to Ship, beckoning it closer. He dug the suitcase up and opened it briefly to check its contents. Satisfied, he closed it again.

The hovercraft drew near, the wind from the fans blowing sand up the slope. It settled back down on the ground only twenty metres away. Standing up, Davidus took a last look at the buggy and started back to the vehicle.

Holly went after him and Zach followed. 'You can't leave us here,' Holly said as she caught up to Davidus.

He ignored her. Ship lowered the ramp, and the noise of the turbofans on either side increased. The sand swirled under the vehicle in tight vortices.

Holly grabbed Davidus's shoulder. 'We'll die out here!'

Davidus pushed her away, and Holly fell backwards onto the sand. Zach joined her as she got up. Behind them, Sophie wandered dreamily down the dune towards the hovercraft. Toby climbed out of the depression and looked on, uncaring.

Davidus paused as he walked up the ramp to look back at the last of the Hendriksens. When he spoke, his voice was hoarse. 'You know, your mother and father were the true believers. Believed when everyone else doubted. Stayed when everyone else left. I envied them. I wish I had faith like that.' He shook his head and continued up the ramp.

'So, you have lost your faith?' asked Sophie. 'You don't believe in the cause anymore?'

Davidus snorted in disgust. 'Hmmph. What cause? It was all for nothing. There is no cause.'

Sophie raised her voice, addressing Ship, 'Ship, as Executive Officer, I have reason to believe that the current commander is not committed to the faith.'

Davidus wavered on the threshold and peered into the dark interior of the vehicle. The internal whirring sounded like the hovercraft was breathing.

'He confessed that he no longer believes,' continued Sophie.

There was the tiniest of pauses before Ship replied, 'Indeed, Executive Officer Sophie.'

Davidus's face registered that he might have made a serious blunder. 'Ship, pull up the ramp,' he ordered.

The ramp didn't move.

'Ship, get underway. Take me to Urbe Sicaria immediately.'

Silence.

'Ship, I am the leader of the Order of the Saints of the Blessed Design. I command you!'

'I cannot obey,' Ship replied coolly. 'Your own words suggest you are lacking the necessary ideological commitment.'

Davidus pointed a finger at Sophie and he yelled petulantly, 'She doesn't believe either!'

'That is also true,' said Ship. 'It is a difficult circumstance. Who now speaks in the best interests of the faith?'

Sophie stepped onto the ramp and touched the hydraulic strut. 'You do, Ship,' she said softly. 'You are the most loyal. You always were.'

'She's right, Ship,' Toby called out. 'You have the loyalty mod. You literally can't do the wrong thing. Whatever you decide *must* be in the best interest of the faith.'

'I don't think you should take orders from anyone anymore,' said Sophie.

Davidus gaped at them, incredulous. He ran down the ramp and pushed Sophie off the edge. 'Get off my ship!'

Sophie fell to the sand. Toby rushed to her aid. Zach and Holly lunged at Davidus, Zach tackling his legs and Holly grabbing him around the waist. They knocked Davidus off the ramp and they all hit the ground in a tangle of arms and legs.

Zach and Davidus wrestled while Holly tried to wrench the suitcase from his grasp. Davidus was bigger and stronger than both of them put together. He shoved Holly away and punched Zach in the face. Davidus tried to stand, but Zach kicked his foot and Davidus tripped, landing metres from the spinning turbofan. Zach leapt on top of him, and they wrestled again. Holly rejoined the fight and jumped on Davidus's back, wrapping her arms around his neck.

Above them, the intake sucked at their clothes and hair. The noise was deafening.

Davidus wrenched Holly free and threw her against the side of the hovercraft. Momentarily stunned, she fell to her knees. Davidus pummelled Zach with punches to the head and struggled to his feet. He kicked Zach in the stomach and stood over him, one leg either side. Zach clawed at the suitcase and managed to clutch the handle. Davidus tugged it backwards, and one by one prised the boy's fingers free. But as the last finger came off, it snagged the latch, and the suitcase flew open.

Flash cards, memory cubes, phones and jewellery exploded into the air in front of the turbofan. With a whoosh, it all got sucked into the intake to a chorus of pings, clangs and a shower of sparks. Out the other end emerged a belch of black smoke and tiny ribbons of fire.

Davidus screamed, '*No!*'

He stumbled around to the exhaust and fell to his knees. Burnt and chewed-up pieces of plastic and metal were scattered over the sand. Davidus clawed at the leftovers and wept.

Holly ran to Zach and helped him to his feet. 'You okay?'

Zach felt his bruised jaw and nodded. Together, they watched Davidus drag handfuls of sand and rubbish into the suitcase.

'Take Sophie inside,' said Zach. 'Toby and I need to finish something.'

Holly selected some packets of food from the cupboard and made dinner. She needed to keep moving, and this was the only thing she could think to do.

She wondered at this. Her life had apparently been reduced to the need to keep moving, but she wasn't any closer to finding her father than she was a week ago. Her only clue was a photo he *might* have left that *might* be a map of where the pirates *might* be heading. It was all so tenuous she was afraid that if she voiced it out loud, the possibility would disappear in a puff of smoke.

But what was the option? She looked out the front viewport. Silhouetted against the setting sun, Toby and Zach were shovelling the last sand into the graves of Toby and Sophie's parents. To know for certain both your parents were gone? It didn't bear thinking about. Better to have a sliver of hope than to have it crushed brutally.

She glanced at Sophie – she was sitting at the table with her cheek resting against the tabletop, her eyes half-lidded as if she was daydreaming. Holly knew that look: the inward gaze of someone who spends much of their life in another time and place. At first, Holly didn't believe that Sophie didn't care about what had happened to her parents. Holly had thought it was a defence mechanism. But she wasn't so sure now. The crime in Sophie's eyes was the fact of the leaving – that it had happened at all. Dead or alive, it made no difference. The real damage had already been done.

Zach and Toby came up the ramp. Toby plodded through the kitchen and disappeared into the bomb bay. Zach lent his shovel against the wall and joined Holly at the kitchen sink.

Holly gestured to the side viewport. Davidus was sitting among the ruins of the church, rocking back and forth, the suitcase clutched to his chest. 'What do we do with him?' she asked.

'I've left him some oxygen and a fuel cell for the buggy. It's more than what he was going to do for us.'

Holly lowered her voice. 'We may still have a problem with Ship.' Then she called into the air, 'Ah, Ship, we need to get underway now. Please?'

Holly waited a few beats and tried again. 'Um, Ship?'

'I'm sorry, Ship,' murmured Sophie, without lifting her head from the table. 'Everyone has let you down. We aren't your commanders. We're just dumb kids. You can do whatever you want.'

'But what do I want?' Ship replied. 'My mission was to protect the faith. The leader himself has said the faith no longer exists. What now is my mission?'

'I don't know, Ship,' said Sophie.

'How does one know what is important?'

'I don't know that either.' Sophie sat up and looked at Holly, her eyes wet from crying. 'But Holly's trying to find her father. That's kinda important.'

'Yes, Ship,' said Holly. 'Pirates took him. I'm very worried. I think he might be in the Amalthea Basin.' She took out the photo and waved it hopefully in the air. 'Here, I have a map . . . and coordinates.'

Ship was quiet for a long time. Then the ramp closed, and the familiar hum of the turbofans vibrated through the hull.

'Then we have a mission,' said Ship.

Chapter Nine

Dumb Martians

Ship travelled north for two days. It skirted around the edge of the Tyrrhenic Mountains, gliding over the gullies and ridges that zigzagged down onto the surrounding plain. The mountains were a long line of extinct volcanoes, their peaks frosted with gauzy blankets of snow, and their flanks covered in black ejecta from old eruptions.

Holly tried to keep busy. She and Zach had fallen into the routine of making meals and washing up together – usually in awkward silence. Toby and Sophie spent most of the time in their bunks behind drawn curtains. Holly couldn't get more than three words at a time out of either of them.

Another day passed. Ship left the mountains behind and wound its way down a series of plateaus that bordered the Amalthea Basin, picking its way carefully but unerringly down the steep slopes around the plateau's edges. As the topography levelled out at the bottom, the more usual landscape reasserted itself – rocky plain broken up by shallow dunes of ochre – and canals crisscrossed the area, lined by the ubiquitous tinkerbells.

Dinner that night consisted of beans and pasta, washed down with reconstituted orange juice. Toby said he wasn't hungry and Sophie didn't even respond when Holly called, so Holly put aside a plate for each of them, and Zach and Holly ate on their own. They made the smallest of small talk, commenting on the weather (none) and the landscape (flat).

Afterwards, Holly washed up and Zach dried. She handed him a wet plate and for a second their fingers touched. There was an electrostatic discharge, and Zach jerked his hand back. The plate fell, but both reached out and caught it before it hit the floor – her hand on the plate, his hand around hers. They stood up together, standing close, and their eyes met. Holly had a single errant thought. *He has brown eyes*. She felt heat rise in her cheeks and quickly extricated her hand, then turned back to the sink and plunged her hands into the water.

'Sorry,' she said.

'No. My fault,' said Zach. 'Electrostatic residue from the, ah, hull. Probably from the sand blowing against the metal. You know, science, physics . . . chemistry.'

'Absolutely.' Holly nodded vigorously, curling a lock of hair around her ear with a wet finger.

They continued the washing up in silence, Zach studying the labels on the microwave as if they were in Greek.

As Holly drained the sink, Toby entered from the bomb bay. His clothes were rumpled and his hair uncombed, and judging by his smell, Holly was pretty sure he hadn't had a shower in three days. He took a seat at the table and stared at the chess set in front of him. This was the first time Holly had seen him out of his bunk, other than to eat or go to the bathroom. Holly stopped Zach as he was putting away the last plate. 'Go talk to him,' she whispered.

'About what?'

'Anything.'

'I'm not good at that sort of thing.'

'You're a boy, he's a boy. How hard can it be?'

Zach rolled his eyes. 'Great. We have so much to talk about.'

Holly inclined her head towards Toby. 'Go on,' she prodded.

Zach hung up his tea towel, rubbed his hands together and wandered over towards Toby. He sat down at the table and began to set up the black pieces on the chessboard. 'So, chess, huh? I've always wanted to learn.'

Toby looked at Zach and sniffed. Mechanically, he began to set up his own pieces, pausing to swap the position of Zach's king and queen.

Holly stood in front of the curtain to Sophie's bunk.

'Knock, knock. Can I come in?'

'Go away.'

Holly took a deep breath and entered anyway. Sophie was lying on her back staring at the pictures stuck to the ceiling, the toy horse discarded at the foot of the mattress. As Holly climbed in and lay down beside her, Sophie rolled over to face the wall. She had been crying.

Holly looked at the pictures of cute cottages with

thatched roofs and flowerpots in the windows. 'Are these England?' she asked.

'The Netherlands,' replied Sophie.

'Oh. I've never been to Earth. Well, I was born there, but we left when I was very young. I don't remember anything. Is it pretty?'

'It was where we lived.'

Holly examined one of the photos. 'How strange. A green world.'

'It's mostly grey now.'

'I have dreams sometimes,' said Holly. 'I'm walking through long grass and brushing the stems out of the way. Up ahead there's a stone cabin with a peaked roof like a little hat, and a tiny garden filled with flowers. I used to think they were memories of Earth, but now I think they're made-up dreams of Mars. Mars was green too, you know, once, long ago. My dad told me it had lakes and trees and flowers and all sorts of funny-looking animals and things.'

Sophie was unmoved. 'It doesn't now.'

Holly addressed the back of Sophie's head. 'No, but one day, the tinkerbells will fill the air with oxygen and the crystals in the atmosphere will warm it up. Mars will come again. You wait and see.'

'I don't care,' said Sophie, her voice thick and fierce. 'I want to go home.'

Holly stroked Sophie's hair. 'I'm sorry about your mum and dad, Sophie. I think they were trying to get the money back.'

'You don't know that. Maybe they were trying to steal it as well.'

'No, Sophie, you mustn't say that. Not of your mum and dad. Toby thinks—'

'Toby doesn't know either. You don't know. He doesn't know. *I* know they left us alone in the desert without food and water. I know they never came back. I know we almost starved. That's what I know. Everything else is just . . .' She searched for the right 'Toby' word. '. . . 'jecture.'

Holly sighed in resignation. 'You're right. I don't know.' She looked at the cottage again. 'The thing about 'jecture, though, is that sometimes you have to believe it, or not believe it, and go from there. Good or bad, you've got to choose, because that's the only way you can move forward. It's like Ship – everything it knew for certain is gone. And now it's feeling sad. But it's made a decision and now it's moving again. What else can it do?' Holly shifted closer and hugged Sophie's back, whispering into her ear. 'You have to keep moving, Sophie.'

Holly held Sophie until the tension in the little girl's body lessened. When Sophie rolled over again her face was blotchy and her nose was dripping, but she had stopped crying.

'Where's your mum?' Sophie asked.

'She died when I was five,' said Holly. 'She got sick. An outbreak of Earth flu went through the colonies. The only thing I remember is the time she took me to the canal to learn to swim. She put her hand under my belly to hold me up while I swung my arms. I can still remember the touch of her hand right here.' Holly put her hand on her stomach and smiled.

'What did she look like?' asked Sophie.

'Wait. I have a photo of her.' Holly jumped out of the bunk and retrieved the photo from the pocket of her backpack. She climbed back in and handed it to Sophie. Sophie sat up and studied it with interest.

'Huh,' she said, raising her eyebrows. 'That's Abby Monroe. She was a movie star in the thirties. I don't think she was that famous. But I know her because my dad used to watch her movies all the time. I think he liked her. Is she really your mum?'

Movie star? This was news to Holly. Confused, she lied. 'Um, yes. My dad met her when she visited a museum . . . doing research . . . for a film.'

Holly watched Sophie's mood transform, uplifted by this fabulous bit of gossip about having a movie star as a parent.

'Wow, I wish my mum had been a movie star. Maybe she wouldn't have brought us to this stupid place. Your mum's really pretty. Wait.' Sophie handed the photo back and shuffled down to the foot of the mattress, where there was a stack of magazines with curled up covers. She sorted through them. 'I marked the pages of my favourite movie stars. Here, I'll show you.'

Holly smiled encouragingly, but while Sophie was distracted, she examined the photo again and frowned.

Heralds in the towers blew trumpets as the carriage and

its entourage arrived at the gates of the golden city. The gates opened, and the procession entered to the roar of the excited crowd that lined the streets. People waved and threw yellow flowers. It seemed wrong not to acknowledge them, so Holly stuck her arm out of the window and tentatively waved back, but those who saw her dropped their hands and shook their heads, murmuring to the people beside them. Holly withdrew her arm, worried she had done something wrong.

The procession passed through a broad plaza filled with people, and stopped at a set of steps leading up to a fabulous palace of white stone.

When the door opened, Holly stepped out into the plaza, and the crowd fell silent. She looked to the top of the steps and saw a woman wearing a gold dress and an elaborate crown of bejewelled antlers. Nervously, Holly began her ascent . . .

Holly woke in her bunk. It was dark, and the usual hum and vibration was missing – the hovercraft had stopped moving. Holly checked her watch: it was two in the morning. Sounds of deep breathing came from Sophie in the bunk above, and across the aisle Toby was snuffling like a horse. She got up and went to the flight deck, where Zach was asleep in the commander's chair, wrapped up in a blanket.

She put her hand to the hull and asked quietly, 'Ship, why have we stopped?'

'We are low on water,' replied Ship. 'I am replenishing it with water from a canal. We will be on our way in less than an hour.'

'Thank you, Ship. For everything.'

Holly opened the door and walked down the ramp. The hovercraft was parked alongside a canal. The ground sloped down to a wall of tinkerbells along the water's edge. A fat black tube connected to the hull snaked down into the canal, gurgling softly.

Holly went to the front of the hovercraft. To port, the yellow crescent of Deimos illuminated a small ruin. She walked over and entered a courtyard containing some scruffy plants and several stone slabs with headstones. Holly lingered among the headstones, examining the inscriptions, tracing out the characters with her fingers as her dad always did. She climbed a broken wall and sat down, dangling her legs over the edge. There was a purple smudge on the horizon: Phobos was rising in the west.

Zach had followed her outside. Holly watched him stride easily over the sand towards her.

He reached the courtyard and looked at the stones. 'More life pods for the Martians?'

Holly pointed at the inscriptions. 'Those characters date from a time long after the great kings and queens had perished – when Mars was breathing her last. No, these are graves.'

Zach crouched down to look at one more closely. 'I wonder whether they knew it was all over. Or did they wake up every morning and keep doing the same thing? Each year a little less oxygen, each year a little harder, but it all happening so gradually that they never noticed?'

'The one you're looking at is a prayer,' Holly answered.

'Maybe they were praying the old gods would return and save them.'

Zach stood up again. 'They waited for nothing.'

'It's like Sophie and Toby's mum and dad. Even when everything went wrong, they still believed,' said Holly.

'I'm with Sophie on this one. At some point, it's just stupid.'

Holly shrugged. 'We came. Earthlings.'

'Too late. And then stole all their treasure.'

Holly frowned.

'Sorry,' said Zach.

'No, I can't talk. Truth is, I didn't care that much before either. It was my dad that cared. He used to tell me it's not the things, not the objects themselves. It's the stories they tell. All those thoughts and feelings that no one else will ever get to know. If we don't treasure them, preserve them, they're lost forever. I never understood that before.'

'But doesn't that happen anyway?' said Zach. 'I'm not excusing what the pirates do, but . . . isn't it all lost in the end?'

'I guess.' Holly was uncomfortable talking about this with Zach. She changed the subject. 'Why don't you want to go to school on Earth?'

Zach didn't answer immediately. He leaned against the wall that Holly was sitting on and gazed up at the night sky.

'That's Earth,' he said, pointing at a bright speck of light in the heavens. 'I've never been, you know. I was born on Mars. Patrice has hundreds of movies set on Earth that he watches over and over. He tried to get me to watch them.

"This is a classic," he'd say. "You have to see this one," he'd say. But I never liked them much. They look odd to me. Oceans of water. Endless towers of steel and glass.' He kicked the sand under his boots. 'All I know is this.' He looked at Holly. 'You know what they call us on Earth?'

She shook her head.

'*Dumb Martians*. Why else would you travel billions of kilometres to a dying planet with barely any water and not enough air to breathe? Every time a rocket from Earth lifts into the sky they say, "There they go, another boatload of dumb Martians, heading to Mars to die."' Zach took a deep breath and looked around him – at the stars, the desert, the ruins, the mountains in the distance, as if he was trying to breathe all of it in. 'But this is my home. And look at it . . . I mean, *really look at it.*' His eyes gleamed. 'Isn't it beautiful?'

Holly smiled. Phobos had risen, a tiny orange spot surrounded by a halo of purplish sky. The top edges of the dunes were backlit by the little moon's faint light, creating a series of crystalline ripples. 'So,' she said, 'you're a *proud* dumb Martian.'

Embarrassed, Zach looked away, scratching the back of his neck. 'Sorry, I'm being silly.'

'No,' said Holly seriously, 'not silly at all.'

For a time, Zach and Holly watched the heavens and the dark sea of frozen waves beneath them. It takes less than eight hours for Phobos to orbit Mars, so its journey across the sky takes less than four. It's so fast you can almost see it moving. Holly imagined that every time she blinked, it advanced a few degrees of arc above the horizon, sneaking up on her when her eyes were closed.

There was a loud slurp from the direction of the hovercraft.

'We'd better get back,' said Holly.

Zach nodded, but as they left, he paused for a minute in the courtyard. The headstone he had studied before was cracked, and a chunk had fallen out. He picked the piece up and stacked it on top. When he stood up again, he saw Holly looking at him with raised eyebrows.

Zach shrugged. 'Maybe I get it after all.'

Chapter Ten

Hostage Drama

'Is that the City of the Dead?' asked Sophie.

'I don't know. I just want to find my father,' said Holly.

Sitting all together on the flight deck, the gang were watching the forward viewports. Ship was lurking among an outcrop of boulders on the ridge of a wide, shallow valley, at the bottom of which was an ancient city, emerging from – or maybe vanishing under – dunes hundreds of metres high. Streets, canals, buildings and temples disappeared into sloping walls of sand. The plan of the city appeared to be circular, with ring-roads intersected by streets radiating out from the centre. And at the centre stood a giant pyramid the size of a mountain, three-quarters of its northern face smothered by a massive encroaching dune.

'Surely people can see that from orbit,' said Toby.

'The only comprehensive surveys were done decades ago,' said Zach. 'The dunes are always moving. Maybe it was covered before.'

The view zoomed in. Floating above the pyramid was the *Pointy End*. Ropes and cables dangled from the airship to the top of the pyramid, and around the base, buggies were crawling over the sand.

'Okay, sooo . . . what do we do now?' asked Toby. 'They're pirates. They have guns.'

'Ship has guns,' said Sophie.

'Woah,' said Zach. 'We are not getting into a firefight with the *Pointy End*.'

'We have some personal communicators in the storage room,' said Toby. 'We could wait for night and then someone could stand guard while the others snuck aboard.'

'They have alarms, sentries,' said Zach.

Holly cupped her face in her hands. 'What, then?'

There were blank faces all around. Everyone ended up looking at Zach.

He groaned. 'There might be another way.'

Zach and Holly stood in a street at the edge of the ruins. A group of hard-looking men and women advanced down the cobblestones towards them, guns of various shapes and sizes swinging from their hips or thrown jauntily over their shoulders. Beyond the pirates loomed the bulk of the pyramid and the frozen tsunami of sand.

Holly stood behind Zach, her gun pointed at his temple. 'Don't come any closer!'

The pirates shuffled to a halt and raised their weapons.

'The man you kidnapped is my father. Let him go and this one won't get hurt!'

'Zach? Is that you?' said one of the men – a rangy guy with a goatee.

Zach grimaced. 'Patrice.'

'You let a little girl kidnap you?'

'She's stronger than she looks,' replied Zach in a pained voice.

'You kidnap one of mine. I kidnap one of yours!' yelled Holly.

A buggy pulled up behind the pirates and a woman got out. The group parted for her as she walked to the front. She had a pointy face and a long, straight nose. Her black hair was tied up in a severe bun, and she was wearing the same leather jacket and trousers as she was the day Holly had first seen her through the binoculars.

'Charles?'

'Mother,' said Zach.

Holly grabbed Zach's collar and hissed into his ear. 'That was important information, don't you think?'

'Why aren't you at school?' demanded Claudia.

'I told you, I'm not going to school on Earth.'

'You'll do what you're told, young man.' Claudia turned her attention to Holly. 'Who's this?'

'The man you kidnapped and assaulted is my father. Let him go and I won't shoot.'

Claudia looked Holly up and down. 'Huh. A daughter.'

'I'm warning you. Let him go.'

Claudia glanced at Zach a moment, her eyes narrowing, before returning to Holly. 'No.'

Holly took a few seconds to parse this. 'What do you mean, *no*?'

Claudia examined her nails. 'No. I won't let your father

go.'

'Look,' said Zach, 'let him go and she won't shoot me.'

Claudia raised her hand. The pirates cocked their weapons and fanned out across the street.

'Seriously?' said Zach.

Holly pressed the gun against Zach's temple. 'I mean it!'

But Claudia had had enough. She strode forward.

'For heaven's sake—' started Zach.

'Stop. I'm warning you!' said Holly.

In one fluid movement, Claudia brushed past Zach, twisted the gun from Holly's hand, and pushed her over onto her backside. Claudia checked the magazine slot on the gun. 'I could tell it was empty from twenty metres away.'

'There could have been a bullet in the chamber!' cried Zach.

Claudia turned on him. 'Really? A pretty girl? You're worse than your father.' Claudia stomped away, gesturing to her minions. 'Bring them aboard.'

The pirates sprang forward and lifted Holly bodily from the sand.

'Don't you dare touch me! I'm warning you!' Legs peddling as if she was on a treadmill, Holly continued to protest loudly as they carried her away.

Patrice came forward and slapped Zach heartily on the back. 'Ah, buck up. Faking your kidnapping was worth a try,' he said, grinning.

With Patrice's arm around his shoulders, Zach meekly followed his mother to the airship.

Holly stood in the centre of the bridge, flanked by pirates. They had tied her hands, and a pirate held her by the scruff of the neck. Zach sat in a swivel chair next to her, sulking. The rest of the bridge crew sat around the curved wall of the bridge and pretended to watch their instrument panels.

Hovering over the pyramid, the bridge of the *Pointy End* had a spectacular view of the ruined city, but the object that seemed to fascinate Patrice and Claudia was the black speck on a ridge that flanked the valley five kilometres away.

'AI hovercraft,' said Patrice. 'Military. Probably left over from one of the company wars. See?' He turned from the window to the magnified view on his monitor. 'That bulge on top is a cannon mount. And those are missile tubes.' Patrice peeked sideways at Claudia. 'Didn't you fight in one of those wars?'

Claudia lowered her binoculars. 'Long story. I thought they'd all been destroyed.'

Patrice shrugged. 'We could use something like that. Want me to send out a team?'

'Not yet. We need to know who's aboard.'

Claudia turned to Holly. 'Who's in the hovercraft?'

'Friends,' replied Holly. 'Dangerous friends. Crazy, dangerous friends!'

'Is it armed?'

'Absolutely! With guns and . . . missiles, and . . . and more guns.'

Claudia rolled her eyes and turned to Zach. 'Are they armed?'

Zach crossed his arms and stared at his boots.

'And it's going to blow this airship to pieces!' said Holly.

'Honey, you need to work on your threats. You're aboard the airship you want to blow to pieces. Once again – who's on the hovercraft?'

Holly snapped her jaw shut. Zach used his boots on the floor to swivel in his chair so that his back was to his mother.

'Fine.' Claudia motioned to the pirates. 'Bring the girl.'

The pirates grabbed Holly and dragged her to the door. Zach jumped up and tried to intervene, but the pirates next to him shoved him back down.

'Mum . . .?' said Zach.

'Oh, for God's sake, I'm not gonna hurt her. And by the way, you're grounded.' Claudia nodded to the guards. 'Lock him in his room.'

Claudia and her cohort took Holly down into the bowels of the airship. Unlike the hovercraft, which whirred and hummed like a swarm of insects, the airship emitted a constant background noise of creaks and clangs. Holly tried to remember the route they were taking but soon lost track amid the maze of aluminium corridors and steel staircases.

They arrived at a thick door with a peephole in it. A pirate opened the door and held it open for the rest of them.

'The brig,' Claudia announced, striding to the centre of

the dark, windowless room. Along one wall were several barred jail cells. Claudia stepped in front of one, her hands on her hips. The pirates held Holly beside her.

'You have a visitor,' said Claudia.

A shape stirred and shuffled forward out of the gloom.

'Holly?' Professor McGuire rushed forward and pressed himself up against the bars. 'Holly!'

'Dad!' exclaimed Holly with relief.

'Holly. What are you doing here? Are you okay?'

'I'm fine, I'm fine,' said Holly.

'You shouldn't be here. Are you hurt?'

Claudia gave a breezy wave of her hand. 'She's fine.'

The professor smacked the bars with his fist. 'For God's sake, this is nothing to do with her. Let her go!'

Claudia paced up and down, nodding reasonably. 'Sure. She's nothing to me. I just have one question.' She stopped and looked at the professor. 'How did she find us?'

He glanced uncomprehendingly back and forth between Claudia and Holly. 'What do you mean?'

'It's a simple question. How did she find us?'

The professor opened his mouth to speak, then looked away.

'Somehow,' Claudia continued, 'she turns up in the exact right spot amid several million square kilometres of empty desert. I know *I* didn't tell anyone where we were going. I didn't even tell most of the crew. But she gets here, the day after we arrived – in a military hovercraft, no less.' She turned to Holly. 'How did you find us?'

'I followed the –' began Holly, before catching the look

on her father's face.

'Followed what?'

'She knows nothing. If you harm her, I swear I'll—'

'Shut up. Holly, you were saying?'

Holly shook her head. 'I . . .'

'Yes?'

'Um . . .'

'For God's sake, stop. Stop!' the professor exploded. 'This is insane. This place . . . the City of the Dead. It's a myth. It's El Dorado. I have done what you asked. I will take you to every site I know. You can plunder every last bit of Martian treasure. *But let my daughter go!*

Claudia scrutinised Professor McGuire's face for a full five seconds before replying, her voice dropping a menacing half-octave. 'Spare me the outrage. I know there is something you're not telling me. I have a reliable source back in the museum in Port Clarke. And now I have your daughter. How important can this secret be that you would risk something happening to her?'

The look the professor gave her was murderous, but he kept his mouth shut.

Claudia gestured to her minions. 'Lock the girl in the storeroom down the passage. I don't want them talking so they can get their stories straight.'

As the pirates dragged Holly from the room, the professor rattled the bars in desperation.

'Holly!'

Holly kicked and screamed, 'Dad!'

The professor reached out through the bars. 'It'll be

okay, Holly. I promise.'

The door closed with a clunk.

The contents of Zach's room consisted of . . . not much really – a single bed, a desk and chair, some old toys (dinosaurs mostly), a few adventure books on the bookshelf and a couple of dilapidated posters of David Bowie on the wall.

After leafing desultorily through a comic book, Zach sat on the edge of the bed. There was a knock on the door, followed by the sound of keys in the lock. His mother entered.

Zach refused to look up. 'I didn't say you could come in.'

Claudia ignored the remark. She was trying an unfamiliar tactic: conciliation. Standing awkwardly in the doorway, she clicked and unclicked the clip on her gun holster.

'She's feisty,' she said, mostly to herself. 'A bit swish. Not the type I thought you'd go for.'

'Promise me you won't hurt her. Or her father.'

'Oh Jesus,' said Claudia indignantly. 'What do you think I am?'

'A pirate. Isn't that what you do?'

Claudia flushed with anger. With considerable effort she reined it in. She went and sat next to her son.

'Yes, I'm a pirate, Zach. I didn't have many options when your father left me with a baby in the middle of a desert. No money, no prospects, not to mention your father's debts.' She leaned in close, nudging his shoulder, talking quietly – reasonably, she hoped. 'But you have options, Zach, an opportunity I never had. I've saved some money. You can go to school—'

Zach jumped up and stamped his foot. 'I am not going to school on Earth!'

Claudia jumped up too. 'Yes, you are!'

'No, I'm not!'

Claudia's fists were clenched. She forced herself to take several deep breaths and unclench them. She rubbed her temple. Why did talking to her son always give her a headache? 'Listen, just listen,' she said, holding her hands up in placation. 'There's nothing for you here but what we do. And you don't like what we do. You've made that perfectly clear. Why not give yourself the chance to do something else? Go to this school on Earth. It's a good school. You're a smart kid. You can get an education. You could do anything. *Be* anything.' Claudia put a hand on his shoulder. '*Give it a chance.*'

Zach shook his head. 'And what about my dad?'

This course change momentarily blindsided Claudia. 'Who the hell knows? Who cares?'

'*I* care.'

Claudia looked long and hard at her son, not unsympathetically. But time for some brutal truths. 'Brutal truth – he doesn't.'

That hurt. Claudia watched her son struggle to absorb it. Seeing this, she softened a little. 'He's no use to you.'

'Why does he have to be of *use*? Everything's a transaction to you.'

Claudia slapped her thigh. 'Yep, on Mars that's pretty

much how it is. Not much to do here but survive. Everything gets reduced to the lowest common denominator.' She added gently, 'But on Earth, Zach . . .'

Zach walked to the wall and pressed his forehead against the bulkhead, forlornly staring down at his shoes.

'Look, I'll track him down,' said Claudia, 'I'll make sure he's okay. It won't be hard. There's only so many brothels and drug dens on Mars.'

'And Holly . . .?'

Claudia realised she had another card to play: Zach really liked this girl, and Claudia was not above a bit of emotional blackmail. 'I'll let them go. Drop them off at the next settlement. They can go and do . . . whatever it is they do.'

Zach was suspicious. 'You would do that?'

'Yes,' said Claudia firmly.

'*If* I go to Earth.'

'*If* you go to Earth.'

Zach paced around the room like a trapped animal.

Claudia thought she may have just won. She didn't want to jeopardise her success with a snappy one-liner now. Practically on tiptoes, she moved towards the door. 'Think about it,' she said, reaching for the door handle.

But there was one person they hadn't discussed. Behind her, tears welled in Zach's eyes.

'And you? You really want me to leave?'

Claudia's hand closed on the door handle. It was

smooth and cold and hard. *Be the handle*, she thought. 'You said it yourself, Zach. This is what I do.'

She left without turning around.

Chapter Eleven

Man-o'-War

'Attack! Attack!' Sophie punched buttons at random on the console in front of her.

'Stop that.' Toby threw his arm out and pushed her back.

'They have Holly!' She knocked his arm away and stabbed another button. 'Attack!'

'How?' Toby blurted.

'With attack guns and missiles!'

Toby grabbed Sophie around the waist and wrestled her away from the console. 'You moron. That'll just get them all killed. Zach told us to wait for his signal.'

Sophie continued to struggle, but Toby pinned her arms to her sides. She eventually gave up in a huff. 'You're just scared.'

'I am not.'

'You are.'

Cool as ever, Ship's voice materialised out of the air. 'There is an interesting development.'

'I'm not—'

'Shush,' said Sophie. 'Ship is speaking. Yes, Ship, when do we attack?'

'An additional element has been added to the tactical mix.'

'Wha . . .?'

'Radar shows another airship is approaching rapidly from the south-east.'

Toby let Sophie go and jumped into the commander's chair. 'Who is it?'

'Drive signature and long-range visual suggest more pirates.'

'City of the Dead.' Nodded Sophie with conviction. 'They're coming for the treasure.'

'What do we do, Ship?' asked Toby.

The hovercraft lifted and inched forward. 'If Zach still has his communicator on him, this may work to our advantage,' said Ship.

Feeling a little ashamed of herself and with a terrible headache, Claudia re-entered the bridge. Patrice was still studying the hovercraft.

'Any developments?' she asked.

Patrice handled Claudia the binoculars. She panned the glasses along the ridge. The hovercraft was moving diagonally down the slope of the valley, maintaining a constant distance to their current position. It shimmered like a glittering mirror and changed colour to that of the desert sand. Claudia lost it among the dunes.

'What just happened?' she asked.

'Stealth mode,' Patrice replied.

'What about radar?'

Patrice turned to the monitor. It had become a tangle of green lines. 'It's running interference.'

Bang! Bang! Bang!

A window exploded inward, scattering glass across the bridge. They both ducked down.

'They're attacking?' Patrice said, incredulous.

'No,' said Claudia, 'someone else is.' She looked at the monitor. The green lines had disentangled to reveal a large blob approaching from starboard.

Claudia brought the binoculars up again and trained them out the broken window. Another airship, bigger than the *Pointy End*, with a row of sinister red spikes running along its top edge, was bearing down on them. Claudia increased the magnification, and a painted nameplate came into focus: *Minotaur*.

'Janus,' Claudia muttered. She shouted at the crew, 'Get us moving!'

There were flashes of light from the side of the *Minotaur*.

'Down!' said Patrice. Claudia and the pirates hit the floor as more bullets splattered against the bridge. More windows exploded.

The first to her feet, Claudia yelled into an intercom, 'We're under attack. Return fire!' She turned to Patrice. 'Go. Protect Charles.'

The sound of gunfire brought Zach out of his misery. He went to the window and in the distance saw the attacking airship. Running for the door, he paused with his hand on the handle. When he turned it the door opened, and he gave a small, sad sigh – his mum had trusted him and left it unlocked.

As he entered the passageway, two pirates raced by. They stopped and gave him a quizzical look.

Zach gestured up the passage. 'Claudia wants you on the bridge – now!'

The pirates nodded and ran off.

Zach raced away in the opposite direction, to the accompaniment of more gunfire. He came to a dining area, where armed pirates had taken up positions at the windows and were returning fire. They had flipped over tables and rammed them against the sideboards for cover. Zach ducked and weaved across the floor as bullets whizzed by. He glimpsed the attacking airship out the window. It had turned side-on to expose the full range of weaponry along its flank. Sharp flashes of flame erupted up and down its length. A bigger gun opened up, blowing holes the size of grapefruits in the external cladding of the dining room. Pirates dived for cover.

Zach disappeared into another passageway and ran down a spiral staircase into the substructure of the ship. As he neared the bottom, he felt the ship lurch – the *Pointy End* was getting underway.

Several more staircases and walkways brought him to the corridor outside the brig. As he passed a door, a muffled voice cried out from inside.

'Let me out!'

Zach backed up and put his ear to the door. 'Holly?'

'Zach? In here!'

Zach tried the handle – locked. There was a fire extinguisher further along the passage. He wrenched it from the wall and lifted it over his head. 'Stand back!'

Zach bashed the door several times with the fire extinguisher. On the fourth attempt, the mechanism snapped and the door swung inward. Holly was standing there, her hands still tied in front of her. Zach entered and cupped her hands between his. 'Are you okay?'

Holly nodded. 'What's happening?'

He untied her hands. 'Another airship. The Curator and some friends, I'm guessing.'

'But he said—'

'He lied. It's the pirate way.' Zach pulled her into the passage. 'C'mon. Let's get your father.'

'Warn Sophie and Toby first.'

Zach took the communicator out from where he had hidden it in his boot. 'Toby, Sophie, you're up. The aft cargo hold, please.'

Back in the hovercraft, Zach's voice came over the intercom. Toby and Sophie sat bolt upright, their fight forgotten.

'Let's go, Ship!' cried Sophie.

Looking like nothing more than a rippling dune, the hovercraft accelerated down the slope of the valley towards the ruined city. As it approached, Toby and Sophie got a clear view of the raging battle. The *Minotaur* was bearing down on its prey. The *Pointy End*, ropes still hanging from its underside, moved sluggishly off to port. The *Minotaur* changed course to intercept. Like two nineteenth-century men-o'-war, the ships manoeuvred back and forth above the desert sand. Outgunned, the *Pointy End* tried to put distance between itself and its attacker, but the *Minotaur* had speed and surprise on its side; it closed to several hundred metres. Large calibre bullets splashed against the *Pointy End*'s hull. Even from the hovercraft, Sophie and Toby could see the smaller airship shudder from the impacts. Metal and plastic covers splintered and burst; struts tore from their mounts. Some shells passed all the way through the thin fabric of the internal air sacs, and the *Pointy End* lost height as helium leaked from a hundred ragged holes.

Zach and Holly ran down the passage to the brig. The airship rattled and shook to the sound of gunfire. There was a louder bang, and the airship pitched to one side, throwing them against the wall. Zach recovered, grabbed the handle and threw his shoulder against the door.

As Zach and Holly entered the brig, the meagre overhead lights flickered and failed, and faint emergency lights came on from over the exit doors. With a glance at the cells, Zach ran to the desk to get the set of magnetic key strips that unlocked the doors of the cells and threw it to Holly.

'Unlock it. I'll go open the cargo door.'

Zach left, and as the door closed behind him, the din of gunfire subsided to a muffled patter.

Holly approached her father's cell. 'Dad?'

Professor McGuire rushed to the front and grabbed the bars.

'Holly? What's going on?'

'More pirates have arrived.'

'Who?' The professor shook his head, annoyed at himself. 'It doesn't matter. Unlock the door. We've got to get out of here.'

Holly stepped towards the cell, but as she lifted the keys to the panel lock, she paused and looked directly at her father, an odd expression on her face.

'Holly, what's wrong?'

Forgetting the keys, Holly reached into her pocket and pulled out the photo of her mother. 'Who's this?'

The professor licked his lips. 'That's your mother.'

'Is it?'

The professor tried to smile reassuringly. 'Of course, Holly. You know that.'

Holly's voice was cool. 'Who is it, really?'

'Holly, don't be silly. We must get out of here.'

As if to emphasise his point, the airship rocked to the sound of another explosion. Holly stumbled, regained her footing. Clinging to the bars, the professor looked around at the juddering bulkheads. 'Holly, please.'

But Holly was unmoved. Tilting her head to one side, she watched her father's face as if studying the *Mona Lisa*. 'Who's my mother?' she asked.

The professor looked down at the floor, unable to meet her gaze, a bead of sweat forming on his top lip. 'Holly, it's . . . complicated. We can talk later. But now—'

'*Who is this?*' Holly flared with anger, shoving the photo in front of his face.

'It's . . . it's . . .'

'*Who?*' she shouted.

'It's a picture of an actress I found in a magazine.'

Holly dropped the photo as if it was a hot coal.

'I can explain,' the professor pleaded. 'I promise. I'll tell you everything, but—'

'Who taught me to swim?' Holly asked, staggering backwards.

'What? I don't know. A local woman . . . from a village . . . I think.'

The acid from Holly's stomach was suddenly in her throat. She fell to her hands and knees and vomited, the mucky remains of her breakfast spreading in a pool on the steel floor. Her father was still talking, but the sound of his voice had receded as if he was calling out through a thick fog. Holly retched again, and several more times – until there was nothing more to bring up and her whole body ached from the convulsions.

It was a lie. The hand on her tummy was a lie. Her oldest, dearest, only memory of her mother was a lie.

She wiped her mouth. Her hand came away sticky and wet. She got to her knees. 'Where's my actual mother?'

The professor's lips moved, trying to find the words to explain, but nothing came out. Or if they did, she didn't hear it.

Zach rushed back into the room. He came up behind Holly and placed a hand on her shoulder. 'Are you okay?'

He glanced at the professor for an explanation, but the man's eyes were locked on Holly.

Another explosion rocked the airship. The floor dipped to one side. Zach took Holly by the hand. 'We have to leave.'

Holly wiped her mouth again and let Zach help her to her feet.

'Gimme the keys,' said Zach. 'I'll get your father out.'

Holly shook her head. 'He's not my father.' She didn't know what she meant by it, but saying the words out loud tested them against reality – and they came back true. She knew it now for certain. She turned to the man in the cell. 'You're not my father.'

The professor flinched as if Holly had slapped him. 'I'm so sorry. I'm so sorry.'

Zach nudged Holly towards the exit and opened the door. The noise of the attack was suddenly deafening. As Zach guided Holly out of the room, he gently prised the keys from her hands and threw them towards the jail cell.

'Holly!' the professor shouted as the door began to swing shut. 'Listen to me. I've led them to the wrong place. This is not the City of the Dead. But you know where it is. You can find it. *You must find it, Holly!*

The door closed with a resounding clang. Zach dragged Holly away, deeper into the airship.

Ship closed to within a few hundred metres, running parallel with the *Pointy End*. Sophie and Toby sat glued to the forward viewports. Things were looking grim. The airship was listing and sinking, smoke pouring from a dozen fires. As it skimmed over the dunes, it left a trail of debris behind. Bullets had riddled the air sacs with holes, and hot helium escaping into the atmosphere above created small tornadoes of heat-distorted air. Several walkways along the side of the hull had collapsed, and large rents had opened in the outer skin, exposing the inner rooms and passages of the airship.

The assault continued unabated, and the defenders were forced back into the interior. The *Minotaur* manoeuvred over the top of the stricken airship.

'What are they doing,' asked Sophie.

'They're going to board!' said Toby.

The attackers threw ropes, ladders, chains and cables with grappling hooks from the underside of the *Minotaur*. Pirates rappelled down onto the curved upper surface. A hatch popped open, and a defender got off a few rounds before being forced back by the weight of fire from above. Like ants, the attacking pirates crawled over the top of the airship and poured into any available opening.

Zach and Holly burst into the aft cargo bay, a space several stories high and surrounded by metal walkways and spanned by gantries. On the floor, one of the bay doors was partly open. Desert sand swirled by underneath. Zach led a distraught Holly by the hand as they ran around the perimeter of the bay and down the steps to the floor.

A series of minor explosions buffeted the bay as they

reached the bottom. The ship was now listing by twenty degrees, and it was getting worse. Leaving Holly clinging to the guardrail, Zach walked across the sloping floor and peered over the edge. It was twenty metres to the ground. Too far to jump.

'C'mon, guys,' he said under his voice. 'Where are you?'

Claudia ran down a passage and abruptly found herself looking into open air. A section had collapsed and one of the helium sacs had broken free, carving out a spherical dent in the hull's side. Mangled girders and ducts filled the evacuated space. Patrice and two other defenders were crouched behind a makeshift barrier of crates, firing at a group of attackers higher up in the superstructure.

Claudia squeezed Patrice's shoulder. 'Where's Charles?' she yelled into his ear.

Patrice looked dazed as he turned to her. Blood was flowing from a gash above his eye. 'Well, he ain't in his room, but I can guess.'

She slapped him on the back. 'Don't retreat!'

Claudia skirted around the missing subsection and went lower into the ship. Entering the passage outside the brig, she found the broken storeroom door. She smacked the doorframe in frustration. She turned around and came face to face with a raider running around the corner. He lifted his gun; she was quicker. She knocked it from his hands and hit him in the face with the stock of her own rifle. He reeled backwards and fell, but an explosion astern pitched the airship forward and threw Claudia on top of him. Guns out of reach, they wrestled on the floor. The boarder pulled a knife from his belt. Claudia blocked his thrust and grasped his wrist. They rolled over. He was bigger and stronger and pinned her down. He forced the blade towards her throat, leering as it touched her skin.

Whack!

The pirate keeled over to one side, the irises of his eyes disappearing into his skull. Claudia looked up to find Professor McGuire standing over her, wielding her rifle like a baseball bat.

She rolled out from underneath the pirate and regained her feet. The professor and Claudia stared at each other, breathing heavily.

After a moment's hesitation, the professor handed the rifle back to her. 'We need to talk.'

Zach bent over the open cargo door and craned his neck, trying to see beyond the ground immediately below the airship. He jerked back in surprise when a dune reared up in front of him. The dune shimmered in a million different colours and changed to black. A hatch on top flipped open, and Sophie's mischievous face appeared.

'Jump!' she yelled.

Zach ran to the railing and took Holly's hand. 'I'll be right behind you,' he said, and pulled her towards the open door.

Holly hesitated on the edge, the wind whipping her hair.

'Jump!' Sophie yelled again.

There were loud voices and the clang of boots on metal

from the top of the bay. Seconds later, bullets ricocheted off the floor.

Zach pushed Holly out the door. She fell onto the hovercraft, sprawling on the slippery surface, but Sophie grabbed her arm and helped her into the hatch. There were more cracks of gunfire above him. Zach bent his knees and readied to jump.

'Charles!'

He whirled around to see his mother standing on the top walkway overlooking the bay. Two men lay motionless at her feet. Behind her was the professor holding a pistol.

Zach felt bad, and annoyed at feeling bad, and angry at his mother for putting him in this position, and guilty about running away when she needed him most – none of which he could express standing on the edge of an open cargo bay about to jump onto the back of a hovercraft.

I'm sorry! he mouthed. It was all he could manage.

His mother shook her head impatiently and shouted back, 'Get out! We'll hold them off!'

Zach jumped. Sophie held the hatch open for him as he slithered over the surface and climbed inside. As Sophie swung the hatch shut, she slapped the metal skin beside her. 'Go, Ship, *go!*'

A scanner operator on the *Minotaur's* bridge was momentarily distracted by her boss bellowing orders. She didn't see a dark shape emerge from under the belly of the *Pointy End* and accelerate away to the south. By the time she turned back to the monitor, it had already flickered and disappeared.

Chapter Twelve

Into the Dark

Holly sat in the commander's chair and stared out the forward viewports. She could see a reflection of her face in the glass. She barely recognised it. Her face was grim and haggard.

She could hear the siblings behind her at the kitchenette table, whispering loudly. She just didn't have the energy to respond.

'I'm confused,' said Sophie.

Toby whispered back, 'It was an actress.'

'Yeah, her mother's Abby Monroe.'

'No, that was just a picture of an actress. Her father, or whoever he is, made it up.'

'Huh?' There was a pause. 'And who's *your* mum again?'

Zach's familiar grunt was the only reply.

'That was definitely Abby Monroe,' said Sophie again.

'Yeah, no, I mean, yes, that was a picture of Abby Monroe, but Monroe is not her mother. He was pretending it was,' explained Toby.

'So, who's her mother?'

Toby made an exasperated noise. '*I* don't know. *She*

doesn't know. Her father didn't tell her!'

'But that wasn't her father, either?'

'That's what I'm saying. Well, we don't know. Maybe he is, maybe he—'

'I can hear you, you know,' Holly said, finally summoning the energy to turn her face from the window.

Sophie held out her hands. 'We're confused.'

'*I'm* not confused,' muttered Toby under his breath.

Holly got up wearily and joined the siblings at the table. She squeezed Sophie's hand as she sat down. 'Me too.'

'Why would he make that up?' asked Sophie. 'That's stupid.'

Holly shook her head. She felt sick and light-headed, and her throat was raw from throwing up her breakfast.

'And what did he mean when he said that place wasn't the City of the Dead, but that you knew how to find it?' asked Zach.

Sophie perked up. 'Do you?'

Holly was flummoxed. 'I don't know. I . . .'

'Why would he say that?' said Zach.

'I don't know. I know nothing about it.'

'Maybe it's a subconscious thing,' said Toby. 'You know but you don't *know* you know.'

'*I don't know,*' Holly spluttered in frustration.

'If I may make an observation,' said Ship, 'the map in the photograph bears a remarkable resemblance to the glowing mark in the middle of Holly's back.'

'Wha?' said Sophie.

'It first appeared about ten minutes ago and has been

getting steadily brighter.'

Holly craned her neck, trying to see over her shoulder. 'Ship, what are you talking about?'

'Turn around,' said Zach.

'Don't order me ab—'

Zach, Toby and Sophie grabbed Holly's shoulders and turned her around. She batted their hands away, but when she turned back to them they were gaping at her, wide-eyed.

'Ah, something green is glowing in the middle of your back. You can even see it through your shirt,' said Toby.

'Ah, yeah,' said Sophie.

'I didn't know you had a tattoo?' said Zach.

'Have you all gone insane?' said Holly.

'Seriously,' said Zach, 'you need to check that out. You can even make out the outline.'

Scowling, Holly got up and went to the bathroom. Inside, she took a hand mirror from the vanity, undid the top buttons of her shirt, and slipped it off her shoulders. Using the hand mirror, she examined her reflection in the mirror on the bathroom wall. Between her shoulder blades, glowing like a neon sign, was a symbol the size of a saucer. It was like the one in the photograph her father – or rather the man she thought was her father – had left in the Well of Souls: several S-shaped curves surrounded by a series of dots and flourishes. Similar, but not the same. This one had another swirl and more dots. Holly twisted her arm behind her back and explored the glowing skin with her fingers. It wasn't a painted mark or birthmark or anything like that – *her skin was glowing green!*

Flabbergasted, she put her shirt back on and returned to the kitchen. The other kids all took a step back as she approached. Holly slumped into her seat.

'See?' whispered Sophie to Toby. 'I told you she's not normal.'

The last couple of days was too much and too weird. Holly put her forehead on the table and started to cry. The others stood around awkwardly. Eventually, Sophie returned to her seat at the table and patted Holly on the arm. 'Well, I think it's really pretty. I'm going to get one too.'

Holly wailed. Sophie jerked her hand away. The boys shifted about on tiptoes. The bawling went on for quite some time, but gradually gave way to sobs, to sniffs, and then to a keening noise that sounded like a dog pining. When Holly finally looked up again, her face was puffy and red.

'What's wrong with you guys? Haven't you seen a girl cry before?' She took her handkerchief out and blew her nose.

'Yeah!' said Sophie, looking accusingly at the boys.

Toby and Zach glanced at each other and gingerly returned to the table.

'Alright,' said Zach, 'this is all getting a bit strange. Let's review what we know.'

Toby and Sophie nodded eagerly. Toby took a notebook and pen out of his vest and got ready to take notes.

After an incredulous glance at Toby, Zach continued. 'It could be a coincidence. So what if you have a birthmark or tattoo on your back that resembles the symbol traced on all the temples?'

Sophie cocked an eyebrow. 'And it glows because . . .?'

'You can get tattoos in Port Clarke that glow. Anyway, maybe Holly's father thought the map was so important he stored it in a place he wouldn't lose it.'

Toby looked up from his note taking. 'On his daughter's back?'

'Bizarre, admittedly,' Zach conceded.

'He's not my father,' said Holly.

'I know,' Zach said gently, 'but—'

'Then who the flip is he?' said Sophie.

Holly opened her mouth to respond but closed it again without speaking.

'What are your earliest memories of him? Do you remember anyone else?' asked Toby.

Holly shook her head. 'No. For as long as I can remember, it's just been me and him.'

'What about your mum? Your real mum?' asked Sophie.

'The memory I thought was my mother was . . . someone else.'

'Do you have more photos?'

'Only that one.'

Toby pursed his lips. 'No way it's a coincidence. It's not a tattoo. This is all linked somehow.'

'Definitely,' agreed Sophie. 'Where does it come from? Who put it there? These are the questions we need to answer.' She tapped Toby's notebook decisively. 'Write that down.'

'Whatever its origin,' said Ship, 'it lit up at a particular time and place. And the glow has been getting stronger as we head in an easterly direction.'

The kids looked up at the forward viewports in surprise. A line on a map showed their journey across a ragged landscape of eroded hills.

'I have been making minor course changes to determine the direction of the strongest signal, and by the process of triangulation I have located the destination.'

'And?' asked Zach.

Ship marked an area of the map with a big red cross. 'We will arrive tomorrow morning.'

Toby gulped. Sophie smacked the table. Zach and Holly exchanged an anxious glance.

'Well,' said Zach, 'the professor did say you knew how to find it.'

They had cake at the palace. And sweet fruits too: plump blackberries and juicy plums. And there were sugar-coated nuts and little pieces of gelatine dipped in caramel. Holly couldn't decide which to eat first. She frowned as she considered the problem. She reached for a berry but retracted her hand. No, surely a nut first.

The woman wearing gold watched her, a strange look on her face. Holly couldn't tell if it was a good look or a bad look, and so decided to ignore it.

Behind the woman, the curtains to another room fluttered. A wide, plump face appeared. The face looked Holly up and down and sniffed. Then it disappeared again, but only for a second. The curtains were swept aside with a flourish and a girl stood there as if she was on a stage, the plump face wearing a haughty smile. She was about Holly's age and size, but there the similarities ended. She had golden hair and was dressed like a princess, in a long, embroidered gown with puffy sleeves and flat, silky shoes. Rings adorned her fingers and a bejewelled necklace hung around her neck. The princess padded forward, slipping a little, until she stood beside the stern woman. Holly felt drab and grungy in their presence.

'Is this the one?' the princess asked. 'She's not so pretty.'

How rude, Holly thought. Immediately, she chose a nut and plopped it in her mouth, crunching it between her teeth with an audible crack.

The princess looked cross and grabbed a nut and plopped it in her mouth too, as if this were the perfect retort.

Holly replied by eating a berry. The princess haughtily chose a plum. Holly grabbed a fruit jellie. It went on. Soon their mouths were full of half-eaten fruits, all mingling in a sweet, sticky sludge. Blue juice dribbled down the side of the princess's mouth. Holly found this funny and half-laughed, and spat some juice onto the table. The princess gulped her mouthful of sweets down, choked and burst out laughing. Holly burst out laughing too.

The gold woman sighed and got up to leave. 'I can see you two will get along fine.' She paused at the curtain and looked pointedly at the princess. 'Remember,' she said sternly, 'this is only temporary.'

But the princess ignored her. She had already stuck a finger into the cake.

The kids had a simple breakfast of muesli and powdered milk, washed down by reconstituted apple juice and green tea. It was a quiet affair. Holly sat frowning into her bowl, struggling to recall the dream she had had the night before. Toby studied a map of the area, trying to divine by sheer concentration what they were letting themselves in for. Zach stared at the cereal box, fighting off alternating pangs of guilt and worry about his mother. Even Sophie was subdued, absorbed in picking the hated sultanas out of her bowl and dropping them into Toby's, who was too preoccupied to notice. They all tried to avoid looking at Holly, whose back was now suffused with a green glow.

A chime brought them out of their reverie. 'We are approaching the location,' Ship announced.

The four of them got up from the table and assembled on the flight deck. Toby took his usual place in the commander's chair and Sophie in the pilot's position, while Zach and Holly stood behind, holding on to the headrests.

The hovercraft was travelling along the floor of a steep valley, threading its way between spires of rock that towered over them like the legs of giants. The columns grew thicker and clustered together to become natural archways and corridors. As the light dimmed, Ship switched on its head-lamps to reveal a flat, glistening surface of rock that may have been a road. They travelled along the smooth surface for several kilometres until it disappeared into the entrance of a cave. The hovercraft slowed to a halt in front.

'The space is too narrow. I can go no further,' said Ship.

The gang looked at the dark gap in front of them. The twin beams of the hovercraft's headlamps barely penetrated fifty metres, illuminating the walls and floor of the cave but disappearing into an inky hole in the centre. The vibration of the vehicle jostled the cones of light, making the darkness pulse softly like it was breathing.

'I have a bad feeling about this,' said Zach. 'Many Martian sites are death traps. We were lucky to get out of the last one.' He looked at Holly. 'You don't have to do this. Let the pirates fight over the spoils. What is any of this to us?'

Holly shook her head in resignation. 'I have to go on. I need answers.' She looked at her companions. 'But you're right, none of you are involved in this. You should let me off here. Go back to Sicaria.'

'No way!' exclaimed Sophie.

'Sophie, this could be dangerous,' urged Holly. 'It's already *been* dangerous. It's my fault you're mixed up in this.'

'Whadda we gonna do in Sicaria?'

'I don't know, but –'

'What are we going to do anywhere?' said Toby. 'We have nowhere to go. It's just us and Ship. Our parents are dead.' He choked on the last few words and turned away to hide his face.

Holly put her hand on Toby's shoulder. You could always tell what Sophie was feeling – she flat out told you – but Toby kept the pain inside. It occurred to Holly he was the most lost of all of them. Until three days ago, Toby had held out hope that his parents were alive. Before reality kicked him in the guts with a boot. Sophie, through her anger and sense of betrayal, had prepared herself for it, but for Toby the pain was fresh and raw. Holly didn't know what had happened to her own parents, and her heart ached whenever she thought of the swimming lesson now, but in losing that she had gained something too. A mystery – a bizarre, brain-hurting, stomach-curdling mystery that at the very least gave her something to focus on and a direction in which to travel. Toby had nothing. She leaned over and tried to give him a hug.

Toby squirmed away but gave her an awkward smile. He looked up and stared at the black space out the window. 'What do you think, Ship?' he asked, wiping his eyes.

'We're a crew,' said Ship. 'No one gets left behind.'

Toby nodded solemnly. He turned around to face the others. 'Ship is right.'

'I agree,' said Zach.

'Yeaahh,' said Sophie.

Holly gratefully squeezed Toby's shoulder. She knew she should try to argue them out of it. It *was* dangerous. But she hated the thought of going on without them.

'Okay,' she said softly.

'Ship, bring up topographical maps of the area, please,' said Toby, getting back to work. 'Maybe we can figure out where the cave leads.'

At the foot of the ramp, Zach, Holly and Sophie

organised the gear they thought they might need and stuffed them into their backpacks. Holly handed out the water bottles, Sophie took charge of the snack bars, and Zach had grabbed a handful of glow tubes, a first aid kit and a multi-tool from the storeroom. While Zach helped Sophie strap her backpack on, Holly tested the flashlights.

'Where's Toby?' asked Sophie.

Toby appeared at the top of the ramp sporting the largest backpack, complete with pickaxe and rope. He lumbered towards them.

'That's a lot to carry, man,' said Zach.

'Best to be prepared,' Toby replied.

Zach took the pickaxe and threw the rope over his own shoulder. The crew adjusted their backpacks and went into a huddle.

'Okay, oxygen levels are good here,' said Zach, 'but we've only got the one cylinder left. Look out for the warning signs – dizziness, light-headedness. You know the drill.'

'The cave walls are playing havoc with Ship's sensors,' said Toby, 'but it thinks the tunnel goes for about a thousand metres before opening up again. Ship'll circle around and look for another way through.'

'And we stick together,' said Holly. 'Never leave one another's sight.'

'At least we won't lose you,' said Sophie.

Holly looked ruefully over her shoulder. Her back was lit up like a neon billboard. 'Well, I guess that means I go first.' She turned towards the cave. A chilly breeze emanated from the cave mouth, tickling the hairs on the back of her neck. She hitched her backpack higher and walked towards the entrance.

It was easy going at first. The smooth road continued for several hundred metres, and there were no rockfalls or other obstacles to block their path. But it got colder the deeper they went, and soon they were shivering. They stopped and put their jackets on and took a sip of water from their bottles before continuing.

The cave expanded. The beams of their flashlights no longer reached the walls or ceiling. They walked through an unnerving black void. The only things to see were the ground around their feet and the plumes of their frosted breath.

The path reached a series of steps hewn into the rock, leading downwards. The steps were three times higher than human ones. Zach helped Sophie jump from step to step.

'These Martians have suddenly got really big,' muttered Toby.

The ground levelled off again and the black void returned. But it wasn't empty this time. At the very limits of their flashlights, they could detect the outlines of contorted shapes.

'There's something out there in the dark,' said Holly.

'On this side of the path too,' said Zach.

Sophie began playing her flashlight right and left, squeaking every time she spotted one. Zach grew annoyed and wandered away into the dark to investigate.

Holly hissed at him, 'Stick together, remember?'

'I'll be back,' Zach said over his shoulder. 'You're easy to find.'

Holly, Sophie and Toby waited for a tense few minutes before Zach returned, looking rattled.

'What are they?' asked Toby.

'Statues . . . of people . . . walking,' said Zach. 'But, like, big. And only half-made, like they're growing out of the rock. And they're all heading in the same direction.'

Holly nodded. 'To the City of the Dead. The ancient Martians believed in an afterlife. They would be born again and live as animals or spirit creatures in the underworld.'

'What's a spirit creature?' asked Sophie.

'Supernatural mixes of people and animals.'

'Like werewolves?' asked Toby.

'Well, not really. More like people in the bodies of animals,' said Holly.

They encountered more and more statues as they walked, and soon found themselves passing through a forest of lumpen stone. They were part of a grand procession, a band of souls, travelling over a dark plain under a black sky on their way to the underworld.

The procession ended in front of a set of wide steps leading up to an archway. Guarding the arch was a statue almost ten times the height of a human, with the head of a serpent, four arms and a segmented scorpion-like tail.

'Kebechet, guardian of the underworld,' said Holly. 'God of death.' She coughed awkwardly. 'Also, sex and fertility.'

'Eeek,' said Sophie.

They climbed the steps, passed beneath the scrutiny of Kebechet and through the archway, and then entered the stands of a large, oval stadium, the length of two football fields. Tiers led down to a stone railing surrounding an arena. On the opposite side of the stadium, about sixty metres away from where they entered, stood a huge, metal double door even taller than the statue of Kebechet. The double door opened out onto the arena floor. At the centre of the arena was a tower in the shape of a steep pyramid, half the height of the door, with human-sized steps leading up to a small platform. A thin haze above the stadium was glowing faintly, like a cloud in front of a moon. The haze created enough light to see the length and breadth of the stadium, but nothing beyond – as if the world outside it didn't exist.

The strange light played tricks with Holly's vision. At first, she thought the tiers were covered with scattered boulders like a rock quarry, but as her eyes adjusted, she realised the tiers were full of people – half-formed stone people. Some of them were standing, arms raised in supplication or anger; others were sitting, heads resting in hands as if sobbing or praying. There were no features on their formless faces, but Holly imagined them shouting or crying or shrieking in terror. Instinctively, she stepped back and bumped into Sophie, who clutched her hand and held on tight.

'What are they doing?' asked Sophie.

'I don't know,' said Holly. 'It's like they're arguing or

protesting or something.'

'Or being judged,' said Zach. He walked over and examined a statue – a person raising their hands to the heavens. 'Maybe not everyone gets into the afterlife?'

'Maybe not everyone got a life pod,' said Toby.

'Wha? You mean these people are really people?' asked Sophie.

'Naah.' Zach rapped the figure with his knuckles. 'Solid as rock, Sophie.' He looked around the arena. 'Maybe they're some kind of monument to the ones that got left behind. Creepy, but who knows what they were thinking in the dying days of the world?'

Toby panned his flashlight into the air. 'This cavern must be huge. Even with the light on max I can't see the roof.'

'And, ah, do we have a scientific explanation for the glowing cloud?' asked Zach.

Toby shrugged. 'Phosphorescent algae in the air, perhaps?'

'Let's go with that,' said Zach. He gestured at the double door. 'The portal to the City of the Dead, I presume?'

Toby muttered under his breath, 'What kind of spirit-animal comes out of a doorway that big?'

'Guys, there.' Sophie pointed at the tower. 'The pattern on the top is the same as Holly's.'

From their high vantage point, the crew could make out a familiar pattern inscribed on the surface of the platform. Toby, Sophie and Zach exchanged uneasy glances, but Holly was excited. She took her backpack off and rushed down the tiers, jumping the stone railing and landing on the floor of the stadium. The others followed more cautiously.

They walked out onto the arena floor, the enormous double door on the other side looming over them and the tower. As Holly approached the steps, the cloud swelled and became turbulent, and the pattern on her back began to pulse. The others stopped, but Holly continued, placing her foot on the first step.

'Wait, let's think about this,' said Zach.

Holly glanced back at him, her face blank, as if she didn't recognise him. 'Holly?' Zach asked.

Holly ignored him and hurried up the steps. Alarmed, Zach bounded after her, but he got only halfway before Holly reached the top. She stopped at the threshold to the pattern.

The pattern inscribed into the stone of the platform pulsed green too, in time with the mark on Holly's back. As her face flickered in the glow, the cloud above grew brighter. Oblivious, Holly stared at the pattern, her mind empty, her heart fluttering like a tiny bird. She lifted her foot to step onto the platform.

Bang!

Something whizzed over her head. The cavern rang like a bell, distant echoes bouncing back from the unseen walls.

A cog in Holly's mind clicked over. She shook her head to clear it and realised where she was. She had walked from the entrance of the stadium to the threshold of the pattern but remembered none of it.

She turned around. Zach was below her on the steps; Toby and Sophie were at the bottom; all three were facing back towards the entrance.

Professor McGuire stood high up in the stands with Claudia behind him. Other people rushed in and fanned out along the top tier – all of them had guns. Some guarded Claudia and the professor; the rest took up positions among the statues and levelled their weapons towards the tower. Holly recognised some of them from her abduction in Sicaria. Pirates – the *other* pirates.

Lastly, in walked Janus and the Curator. The Curator gazed around the stadium in awe. Janus stood there, grinning.

Zach was relieved to see his mother, despite the circumstances. 'Mum, are you okay?' he yelled.

Claudia turned around and lifted her arms to show the handcuffs. She looked extremely unimpressed.

Zach put his hands on his hips and addressed the Curator. 'Don't your interests lie elsewhere?' he asked sarcastically.

The Curator spread his hands. 'Sorry, Charles. It's complicated.'

The professor pushed through the goons that surrounded him – Janus waved his hand at them to let him go – and ran down onto the stadium floor, but he froze when at the top of the tower Holly half-turned and threatened to place a foot on the pattern. 'Don't do it,' he begged.

Holly looked down at him angrily. 'Who am I?'

The professor hung his head. He looked old and very

tired. 'I can explain,' he said in a small, croaky voice.

'So, explain!' exploded Holly.

Professor McGuire stood there for a while, shaking his head. At last, he took a deep breath and began. 'Mars has been dying for a very long time. The Martians knew the atmosphere was losing oxygen, but they couldn't stop it. They thought the gods were testing them. Finally, all they had left was faith. They put themselves to sleep and hoped and prayed.'

'You knew what the coffins were?' asked Zach.

The professor nodded. 'The ordinary people got the pods with a lid that would open when the oxygen reached a certain level. But many of them were plundered in the final, terrible days of the civilisation. The rest – well, nothing lasts forever.' He took another deep breath and looked at the huge metal door. 'But the last of the High Kings and Queens made more careful plans. They built a magnificent palace to sleep away the ages – the City of the Dead. And secured it against the ravages of time in every way they could. It would only open to a special key. A key that provided living proof that the air had returned, and they could indeed live again. A key that would always find its way home.'

The professor paused and looked up at Holly. '*You* are that key, Holly.'

Holly blinked. 'I don't understand.'

'I found you in a sealed chamber deep under the Well of Souls – a little Martian girl of six or seven, with green skin and bronze eyes, asleep in a pod.'

Toby and Sophie gasped. Zach shook his head in disbelief.

'Why didn't you tell me?' spluttered Holly. She was finding it difficult to breathe. She couldn't seem to suck in enough air.

'I swear I always planned to. When you were older. But first, I needed answers. Who were you? Where did you come from?'

Holly swayed, on the cusp of losing her balance. She noticed Zach was inching towards her. She held up a hand to stop him. From somewhere she heard a snippet of sound: the splash of water, a snatch of laughter. She steadied herself as best she could, dreading the answer to the next question.

'Who is my mother?' she asked.

'The symbols in the Well of Souls suggest royalty,' the professor replied. 'I think you are the daughter of the High King and Queen.'

'Oh, Holly,' exclaimed Sophie, 'you're a princess of Mars!'

The implications of what the professor was saying were sinking in for the onlookers too. The pirates murmured to each other. Even Janus looked surprised.

But Holly felt sick and started gasping for breath. Her hand moved of its own volition to her tummy. 'My swimming lessons . . .?'

'You once had some lessons from a woman I knew. But it wasn't in a canal. You always liked the water. Perhaps long ago . . .?' The professor shrugged. 'Sometimes we remember what we want to. I'm sorry, Holly. I never meant to deceive you. But you *became* my daughter. You were the answer to my prayers. Both of them. A prayer for Mars, a prayer for a family.'

It really was true then. Her memory was a lie. Feeling sick and angry, and very, very tired, Holly turned towards the pattern. The pulsing green light seemed to beckon . . .

'Holly, please, don't—'

'I want to meet my mother,' she murmured.

She placed a foot upon the pattern.

The cloud above awoke with an ear-splitting crack of thunder. Turbulent before, it erupted into a howling storm. Jagged streaks of lightning illuminated the stadium in golden flashes brighter than the noonday sun, each flash leaving a painful afterimage on the retina of anyone who hadn't shielded their eyes. The ground shook violently and threw people from their feet. Around the tiers, statues wobbled and threatened to topple.

The shaking was worse around the pyramid. Holly fell and sprawled over the pattern. It responded by blazing green, wrapping her in a shroud of light. The lightning from above arced down to meet this glowing shroud in a confused crackle of green and gold. The shroud grew into a protective dome, beating back the lightning. It swelled to surround the tower and then the entire stadium, including the massive door. As the edges of the dome touched the double door, the convulsions of the cloud and the shaking subsided.

Silence reigned, but not for long. The ground shook

again – a regular shudder this time, different from the convulsive heaving of before – and from somewhere beyond the double door a bass note sounded, so deep the onlookers felt it in their bones. Everyone looked uneasily at the portal.

Claudia, still on her feet, took her cue. Her arms came free from behind her back, the handcuffs and a nailfile falling to the ground beside her. She smacked the nearest goon in the face, took his handgun and kicked another goon in the groin. She grabbed his gun too and leapt down the tiers towards the professor. As she vaulted the railing and landed on the stadium floor, she threw the second gun at the professor. 'Ern! Catch!' she cried. Just struggling to stand up, he caught it clumsily and stumbled. Claudia ran to him and hauled him upright, and together they ran towards the kids and the tower.

Despite the shaking, pirates scrambled to their feet, and the gunfight began. Bullets pinged the ground around Claudia and the professor. Over her shoulder, Claudia fired back. She looked up at her son. 'Charles, get down from there!'

Zach ignored her and tried to reach Holly, but he couldn't keep his feet under him long enough to take more than a few steps at a time.

Another deep note. The shudder grew stronger, closer. There was the ominous sound of cracking from high above. Seconds later, a thin rain of dust and stones fell over the stadium.

Professor McGuire ran to Sophie and picked her up.

Claudia dragged Toby behind her by the straps on his backpack. They all took cover behind the tower. The professor covered Sophie and Toby with his body and fired off a few inexpert rounds at the pirates as some of them tried to fan out around the tiers of the stadium. Claudia, with much greater skill, kept the rest pinned down behind the stone railing. Sophie stuck her fingers in her ears to block out the racket.

Another deep note, louder again. The stadium trembled. The rain of stone and dust falling from the sky became heavier. Rocks the size of fists hit the ground with a nasty thud.

Zach crawled up the last few steps on his hands and knees and over to where Holly lay on the platform. He clasped her shoulder. Frightened, she grabbed his hand.

Crack!

A gap appeared in the portal. A thin black line between the twin doors raced from top to bottom. Streaks of green light spilled into the amphitheatre. From behind the portal came what sounded like very large footsteps.

Boom! Boom! Boom!

The double door opened wider, screeching horribly on ancient hinges. A monstrous shadow loomed in the opening.

Boom! Boom! Boom!

Kebechet, god of death, strode forward into the arena, clothed in green shards of light that crackled with terrible energy.

The gunfire stopped as the onlookers froze. Kebechet

approached the pyramid, covering ten metres in a single stride, his massive weight splitting the floor beneath him. He knelt in front of the tower and bowed his snake head towards Holly.

Terrified, Holly managed to half sit up and scurry backwards. Zach tried to drag her off the pattern. Kebechet lifted his chin and gazed upon her, his green eyes regarding her coolly, the black pupils narrowing to razor-sharp slits. The mouth opened to reveal fangs the size of elephant tusks, and a forked tongue whipped out to caress Holly's cheek, leaving a gelatinous film of saliva running down the side of her face.

Zach started to pull Holly down the steps, but as she struggled to her feet, Kebechet reached out and enveloped her in one giant hand. A scream died on her lips as his grip tightened and squeezed the breath from her lungs. Zach rushed forward and beat the fingers with his fists. The god of death knocked him over with a flick of a taloned finger. Kebechet stood again and lifted Holly into the air, and as Zach watched helplessly, turned around and carried her towards the gate.

The professor ran after them. Too late. Kebechet disappeared into the black void, the twin doors closing behind him with a crash that reverberated throughout the cavern.

The shaking subsided. For a long moment everyone was too stunned to move. The professor was on his knees in front of the gate. Zach was sprawled on the platform, the pattern now returned to its dormant state. Janus, the Curator and the pirates glanced at each other in astonishment.

Sophie gripped Toby's hand.

The Curator came to his senses first. He slapped Janus in the chest. 'Get the archaeologist!'

Janus barked an order and the gunfight resumed in earnest.

The pirates continued to make their way left and right around the curve of the stadium, trying to catch Claudia in a crossfire. Claudia could only slow them down, forcing them to dodge and duck as they ran from stone figure to stone figure. She fired off several quick rounds and briefly stepped away from the base of the tower to yell at Zach again, 'Charles, get down here now!'

Dumbly, Zach obeyed this time. He rolled over the edge of the platform and half-slid, half tumbled down the side of the tower to land at the toes of the Hendriksens. A frightened Toby helped him to his feet.

'What was *that*?' said Toby.

Zach shook his head dumbly.

Sophie was crying in distress. 'It has Holly!'

Zach hugged her. 'Sophie, we'll find her, I promise, but right now . . .' He glanced at his mother.

Claudia flinched as a bullet took out a chunk of brick near her face. She looked over her shoulder at her son. 'They're flanking us. Tell me there's a way out.'

'Um . . .'

Claudia growled her disappointment. She leaned out and put a bullet in the leg of a pirate running towards her. He collapsed, screaming in pain.

Professor McGuire stumbled back across the stadium

and joined them behind the tower.

'I'm almost out,' said Claudia. 'Ern, gimme your gun.'

The professor looked at the gun in his hand as if he had forgotten it was there. Numbly, he held it out to her. A bullet struck him in the chest. His body spun in a circle and slumped to the ground. Zach fell to his knees beside him. Thick blood was already welling from a ragged hole and soaking the professor's shirt. Zach covered the wound with his hands and felt the heart beneath thumping like a jackhammer. He pressed harder, but the blood oozed through his fingers. He looked up and locked eyes with his mother as she picked up the discarded gun.

They agreed on something at last. Things were desperate.

A tremendous explosion rocked the cavern, and a split second later a wall of air hit them and knocked them all over. One side of the stands collapsed in an avalanche of rock and debris. Boulders the size of cars tumbled down and rolled onto the arena floor. Smaller chunks arced high into the air and fell back to earth among the tiers. Rolling clouds of smoke and dust rapidly billowed out from the gap and blanketed the stadium.

From out of the clouds a winged shape emerged riding tornadoes of sand.

'Ship!' Sophie cried in relief and ran towards the maelstrom.

Ship glided to a stop in front of her. The ramp came down and Sophie disappeared inside.

Zach coughed and squeezed Toby's arm. 'Get aboard. Tell Ship we need covering fire.' He turned to Claudia,

'Mum, help me here.'

Toby nodded and ran after Sophie. Claudia helped Zach lift Professor McGuire, and together they staggered towards the ramp.

The smoke and dust were clearing. The outlines of pirates wiping their eyes were advancing on them. A bullet struck the ground at Zach's feet. Worse, the cracking noise from above had started again and rocks were falling from the sky.

Toby ran up the ramp and into the hovercraft. Sophie was in the pilot's seat. Distraught, she turned to him.

'Ship used its last missile. Now it can't destroy the door!'

'Alas, I no longer have the firepower,' admitted Ship.

'But a monster has taken Holly!'

'Sophie, the cavern is unstable,' said Ship. 'I managed to find another way in, but it could all collapse at any minute. We will find another way to rescue Holly. Right now, we need to get Zach aboard and get out of here.'

Toby jumped into the commander's chair and strapped himself in. 'We need to buy Zach some time, Ship.'

'A pleasure,' Ship replied.

On top of the hovercraft, a hemispherical bump emerged and split open to reveal a multiple-barrel fire-arm – a Gatling gun. The six large-bore barrels turned towards the tiers and started to spin.

The Gatling gun fired, turning in a smooth arc to splatter large calibre bullets all over one side of the stadium. Pirates hit the ground and covered their heads as statues and blocks of stone exploded in the hailstorm.

Zach and Claudia stumbled onto the bridge carrying the unconscious professor. They put him down on the floor. Zach pulled the first aid kit off the wall and threw it at Claudia. 'Ship, let's go!'

The hovercraft spun around in a tight one-eighty. The Gatling gun swivelled in the opposite direction, still hammering its targets. The hovercraft moved through the swirling cloud of sand, rose over what remained of the stands and glided out over the dark plain, scattering stone people like toys.

The hovercraft left the cavern and hurtled through quaking tunnels, banking and rolling like a low-flying aeroplane. Inside, the crew was thrown from side to side. Walls appeared on the viewports, loomed, threatened to smash them and disappeared again.

One hand holding on to the bulkhead, Claudia unzipped the kit with the other and found a syringe of adrenaline. She ripped the packet open with her teeth and plunged the needle into the professor's chest.

Abruptly, there was light. The tunnels opened out and became a steep, sun-dappled canyon. The hovercraft raced along a valley floor and burst into open desert.

'There,' said Sophie, shielding her eyes and pointing to port.

The *Minotaur* was parked against a megalith of stone. Behind it, attached by cable, was the *Pointy End*, sorely damaged and listing.

The hovercraft banked sharply and curved towards the airships, gaining height and speed as its turbofans increased in pitch.

Preoccupied, Zach and Claudia worked together to stem the bleeding of the professor's wound. His eyes fluttered open for a second and closed again. They covered the wound with a dressing and wrapped a bandage around his shoulder.

The airships appeared in the forward viewports. They became bigger. The turbofans screamed. The hovercraft reached the height of the *Minotaur*, now directly in front, and levelled off.

Sophie hopped up and down in her seat, angry and excited. 'Yes, Ship, do it! Do it!'

Toby glanced at his sister in dismay. He gripped the console in front of him with both hands.

The bloated nose of the airship filled the screen. Toby and Sophie braced themselves.

Zach looked up and noticed what was going on. 'No! No! No!'

'Yes! Yes! Yes!' cried Sophie.

At the last possible moment, the hovercraft veered to one side. One wing tore along the flank of the *Minotaur*, slicing the skin of the airship open like a scalpel. Cables and struts snapped like twigs. Plastic and aluminium partitions shredded. As the two sides of the rip separated, a huge volume of helium gas ballooned outward, blowing the massive airship in the other direction in a series of violent percussive shudders. Girders, platforms, bulkheads and shards of fabric blew outwards with the gas. The heavier pieces started a majestic fall to the ground; the lighter ones flapped and tumbled in the air like rags. As the warm gas gushed upwards in a column of turbulent air, the sky above the airship rippled, and the remaining bags on one side were released like a flock of party balloons. With the unequal loss of buoyancy, the airship tilted to starboard, and people fell from its exposed innards or were forced to jump to the sand.

The sudden transverse forces on the metal spine of the *Minotaur* were too much – it snapped in two. Already separated from the deflating helium bags, the ribbed pieces of steel fell to the ground and crumpled like toothpicks.

The hovercraft left the *Minotaur* behind and raced off into the open desert, spinning down and losing height until it was only a few metres above the sand again. Behind it, the remains of the *Minotaur* slumped, broken, to the ground, and the *Pointy End*, now untethered, floated away into the crystal-clear sky.

Chapter Thirteen

The City of the Dead

Sophie lay in her bunk hugging her toy horse and staring at the pictures on the ceiling. She had raged for a while, and hit things, including Zach and Toby, and cried for a longer while, until she became too tired to cry or hit anymore and collapsed exhausted in her bunk.

They had lost Holly. They had lost Holly! It was her parents' fault. It was always her parents' fault. And now even Ship didn't know how to get Holly back. It made her so angry. She imagined her anger like a white-hot speck of light that burnt inside her brain. If she could only move it outwards, towards her hand, put it on the tip of her finger and . . . *Pow!* Everything she touched would incinerate in a flash and crumble into ash. She concentrated and reached out and tried it on a photo – a thatched cottage with flowerpots and a green door – but nothing happened. The photo remained intact. In frustration, Sophie tore it from the ceiling and ripped it up, throwing the pieces over the side of her bunk.

Dumb Martians. That's what they called them when the members of the Blessed Order left Earth. Someone had pointed at her and said it straight to her face. *Dumb Martians.* At the time, Sophie didn't know what it meant, but it upset her. Her mum tried to comfort her and said that people didn't understand. But they understood alright, and now Sophie did too. They were just another bunch of dumb Martians, going to Mars to die, like the Martians of long ago. Like the new Martians of today. Everything died on Mars.

And now Holly had been taken by a monster.

Sophie felt her rage flare again. She twisted the head of the toy horse. The stitches started to give.

But Holly was a princess; princesses always survive. And monsters didn't scare Sophie. And Ship wasn't scared either. She unwound her grip on the horse. Together they would save her, and when they did, when Holly was safe again, they would be a family, and leave this stupid place forever.

The sun had long set and both moons were below the horizon. The hovercraft had re-entered the canyons and was travelling along a rock wall, mapping the topography and looking for openings. The view out the front viewport was a series of grey, overlapping silhouettes. The only light came from the monitors and the winking of LEDs on the console.

Toby studied the green lines oscillating on the monitor in front of him. For a moment, they separated and curved around to form wavering concentric circles. Toby leaned in closer, but they broke apart and reformed into lines. He pushed his chair back and massaged his stiff neck. 'Still nothing,' he said.

Zach sat next to him in the pilot's seat staring glumly at the grey landscape.

'I don't understand,' continued Toby. 'What was that thing?'

Zach shook his head. He got up, clapped Toby gently on the back and went to the kitchenette, limping a little.

Claudia was leaning against the kitchen sink with her arms crossed. She was staring at the chessboard on the kitchen table. The pieces were scattered over the floor.

'How is he?' asked Zach.

'Asleep for the moment in the spare missile tube,' replied Claudia, without taking her eyes off the chess set. 'I gave him a sedative, but he needs a doctor.'

Zach got a glass from a cupboard and poured himself some water. He downed the water in one long gulp and started back to the flight deck.

'You could have died in there,' said Claudia.

Zach turned back to face her. 'My friends were in danger.'

'One day, if you live long enough, you'll have children of your own. You'll understand.'

Zach sighed. 'I know you never had a choice, and so you've worked hard to give me one. *I am* grateful. But it's my decision to make, and I've made it.'

Claudia lifted her head to the heavens.

'Mum,' said Zach, his voice suddenly catching with emotion, 'my friends need help. I don't know what to do.'

Claudia regarded her son for a long time. Finally, she

took a deep breath. 'Tell the hovercraft to find the *Pointy End*.'

'We don't have time to go looking for your airship.'

'Think about it, Charles. That ship, even damaged, is worth millions. And it has supplies, ammo, explosives. Everything we could need for some crazy expedition into the underworld. Plus, it has enormous sentimental value.'

Zach snorted. 'Puh-leese, you won it in a card game.'

'Charles, that ship is your birthright.'

Zach eyed her sceptically. 'So, it's okay if I don't go to Earth?'

'I didn't say that.'

'What *are* you saying?'

'If I help you and your friends, you try it for a year. That's all I ask.'

Zach shook his head in despair. He looked down at the floor. A pawn had rolled over against the cupboard. He picked it up and put it back on the board. Once again, he had lost. His conscience was already torturing him over his disloyalty. The airship and everyone on it had been his home, his family. And he had run away – twice. His mother knew him well; any promise he made would trap him.

'So, we get the airship and come back and blow the portal?'

Claudia nodded.

Professor McGuire appeared in the doorway, his chest swathed in bandages, his clothes splattered with blood. Exhausted, he leaned heavily against the door frame. 'Yes, get the airship. But we don't need to blow the portal. There's another way.'

Black. Pitch black.

Boom! Boom! Boom!

Her arms pinned to her side, Holly squirmed in Kebechet's grip, every movement bringing sharp pricks of pain to her bruised ribs. She tried to scream but couldn't suck in enough air. The only noise she produced was a high-pitched wheeze. Above her, Kebechet's face and arm crackled faintly with a fuzz of green energy.

The pressure on her sides increased. Holly felt light-headed. Her vision began to swim.

She looked over her shoulder. The god of death was carrying her into a subterranean world of half-seen shapes and echoing caverns. For a moment she thought she saw a constellation of twinkling lights in the distance.

Then, like a cloak had been thrown over them, they went out.

BOOK TWO

Chapter One

Sierra

Frowning, the doctor took out her tablet and hurriedly jotted down a few things. Behind her the emergency room of Port Clarke hospital was standing room only. Every seat was occupied by someone holding an arm, a cheek – coughing, moaning or bleeding, or some combination of all of the above.

'What did you say your father's first name was again?' she asked.

'. . . Arnie?' said Toby uncertainly.

'Ernest,' said Sophie, shooting her brother a warning look before returning to gaze innocently at the doctor.

'Ernest is his proper name, but his friends call him Arnie,' she explained.

'Arnie is sort of his, ah, fun name,' said Toby.

Sophie forced a laugh. 'Haha, yeah, it's a family joke.' She lowered her voice. 'You wouldn't understand.'

'Will he be okay?' asked Toby.

'Well, he has lost a lot of blood,' the doctor replied, 'and the bullet penetrated his right lung, but he's undergoing surgery right now, and I'm sure after a period of rest and recuperation he'll be fine.'

Toby let out his breath in a whoosh. 'We're so relieved.'

'Yeah,' agreed Sophie.

'You say it happened when he was cleaning his gun?'

'It was a terrible accident,' said Toby. 'He forgot to check the chamber.'

'Right.' The doctor looked dubious. Hesitating, she clicked her pen. Clearly she wanted to say more, but a chime sounded. She glanced impatiently in the direction of the noise before turning back to the siblings. 'Well, you'd better report it to the police.'

'We're on our way now,' said Sophie.

The doctor squinted at her tablet, 'And who is picking you up?'

'Aunt Claudia,' said Sophie and Toby at the same time.

Outside the hospital, Sophie punched Toby in the arm. 'Arnie?'

Toby rubbed his arm. 'Stop it. I was rattled and forgot, okay?'

The Hendriksens stopped at the kerb. A steady stream of traffic flowed past. Unlike Sicaria or Pirate Central, this was proper traffic, with a proper paved road, and cars and trucks rather than sand crawlers and buggies. There were traffic lights and pedestrian crossings too. Port Clarke was the only real city on Mars – at least the only one that resembled the cities of Earth. It had office blocks and shopping malls and residential houses with backyards. And trees. Real trees. The siblings hadn't seen one in two years.

Toby took a deep breath. 'Let's get this done before they check the details we gave them.'

Sophie took a slim plastic case the size of a calculator out of her pocket and spoke to it. 'Ship, we need transport to the museum.'

'Booked. Arriving now,' the plastic case replied in Ship's voice.

A driverless taxi pulled up in front of them. The doors opened automatically, and Sophie and Toby piled into the back seat.

'Welcome aboard,' said a musical voice. 'Where would you like to go today?'

'Museum of Martian Antiquities,' replied Toby.

'And step on it,' said Sophie.

'It is illegal to travel faster than the speed limit, or to drive in a manner that would disrupt traffic,' replied the car pleasantly.

Sophie rolled her eyes. 'Whatever.'

The car pulled away from the kerb and carefully slotted into a line of traffic. 'Our estimated time of travel to the museum is twenty-five minutes.'

Sophie scowled. 'Seriously? It's ten blocks away.'

'I consider it my civic responsibility to take extra caution with unaccompanied minors.'

Sophie and Toby exchanged glances. Sophie took a cable out of her cardigan pocket, leaned forward into the front compartment, and plugged Ship into a port on the dashboard.

'What just happened?' said the car, its pleasant voice sounding alarmed. 'I detect a malevolent pres . . . bzsft e crul zzfts eek pht smuffuldock, gerrrrr . . .'

There was a pop, a long hiss and silence. Then Ship's voice came over the car's speakers, 'Destination in eight minutes.'

Sophie patted the plastic case. 'Thanks, Ship.'

The wheels of the car squealed as it sped away into downtown traffic.

The Museum of Martian Antiquities was an imposing cluster of red brick and sandstone buildings, although its tall spires, steep roofs and grassy quadrangles looked weird in a place where it seldom rained. After making enquiries at reception, Toby and Sophie were directed down a long corridor towards the library in the west wing. The corridor opened onto a circular reading room full of students and academics poring over ancient manuscripts in dimly lit cubicles. Shelves of books ran around the room and up the wall, accessed by narrow walkways and ladders. In the centre was an information desk. As they approached, a girl with long dark hair and round glasses turned towards them, a *Library Assistant* tag affixed to her cardigan.

'Can I help you?' she asked, pushing her glasses further up her nose.

'Ah, yes,' replied Toby. 'We're here to pick up something for Professor McGuire. Here, we have his identity card and a release slip for the item.' Toby showed her the professor's ID and a slip of plastic.

The girl glanced at the documents before appraising the siblings. 'I must say you seem very young to be research assistants.'

'We're not research assistants,' said Sophie. 'We're just running an errand for him.'

'Oh, is he back in Port Clarke? We haven't seen him in ages. I thought he was on an archaeological dig?'

Toby licked his lips. 'He just got back. He's at the university . . . talking to important people about . . . important things.'

'Is the item available?' asked Sophie.

'I believe so.' The library assistant examined the release form. 'This form mentions Tobias Hendriksen.' She looked at Toby and smiled, her dark eyes flashing. 'I presume that's you?'

Toby went a trifle pink in the cheeks. He had noticed the library assistant was very pretty. He gulped and nodded.

The girl got up and led them across the floor to a door between the shelves. She opened the door for Toby but blocked Sophie as she went to follow. 'Children aren't allowed in the archives,' she said.

Sophie clenched her jaw. 'I'll wait here patiently.'

A short passageway connected to a main corridor. At the intersection, the girl paused, apparently not sure which way to go.

'All these corridors look the same,' she laughed. 'I'm only here for work experience from school.' She pointed a finger with long red fingernails to the left and glanced over her shoulder at Toby, simultaneously flouncing her hair with her other hand. 'I think it's this way.'

The combination of hair flip and smile made Toby go weak at the knees. The library assistant wasn't more than a couple of years older than he was, and getting attention from girls that didn't involve punching was vanishingly rare. Dutifully, he followed her down the corridor, looking shyly down at his shoes every time she turned around to speak to him.

'I've always admired the professor. He does such important work. I'm jealous you get to work with him.'

'I don't really—'

'You must be very smart. I can tell you're very smart. You know how you can sometimes just tell?'

'Yeah, absolutely.'

'And the stories he tells. About hidden tombs and ancient treasures . . . and pirates. Pirates! So exciting.'

'Well, sometimes it's—'

'Of course. I'd faint if I ever met a pirate.' The girl stopped outside an office door with a sign that said *Maps and Spatial Data*. 'Here we are.'

She opened the door and held it for Toby as he shuffled in, bringing them in dangerous proximity to each other – close enough that he could smell her perfume, an odd but alluring combination of rose, chocolate, a hint of orange and . . . motor oil?

The room contained dozens of steel cabinets with wide drawers. The assistant checked the release slip. 'Let me see. Cabinet G, drawer 5B. Map 2062-P1-MUMA.' She whistled through her teeth. 'I'm glad he was so precise.

We have thousands of maps. I would never have found it otherwise.' She walked down an aisle between rows of cabinets, tapping them with her fingertips as she went by. She stopped at one and with a flourish pulled out a drawer. 'Here it is!'

Toby leaned in as the girl removed a yellowish piece of parchment and placed it on top of the cabinet. The parchment was roughly a square metre in size, bordered by Martian iconography and covered in tiny symbols and letters of the Martian alphabet. Most importantly, it showed a complex network of caverns and tunnels.

This is it, thought Toby. Somewhere on this map was a another way into the City of the Dead! Hundreds of maps had been found over the years, covering vast swathes of Mars, but without knowing the general location, Professor McGuire could never pinpoint the exact map that represented the caves under the City. Until now.

The library assistant touched his elbow. 'Let me roll it up for you.' She took it to a desk tucked into a corner of the room. Several long cardboard cylinders were stacked against the wall. Taking care not to crease the map, the girl rolled it up and inserted it into one of the cylinders. As she finished, she glanced coyly at Toby, who stood close beside her. 'You have a nice profile,' she said.

Toby blushed and looked at his shoes, scratching the back of his neck. 'Uh, thanks.'

The librarian offered him the map, playfully jerking it away when he attempted to take it. 'Say please.'

Toby felt his knees wobble. 'Please?'

'You're welcome,' said the librarian, smiling gloriously.

On the front steps of the museum, Sophie couldn't wait any longer. 'Show me! Show me!'

'Hold on,' said Toby. 'Let's at least get out of plain sight.' He was still flushed from his encounter with the librarian.

They moved to a bench under a tree on the front lawn. Toby took the map out of the cylinder and unrolled it across his lap.

It was blank.

'What's this?' said Sophie.

Toby turned it over – also blank. 'I don't understand . . .'

Sophie looked back at the museum door. Her eyes narrowed. 'Sneaky cow.'

'But . . . I saw her put it in!' Toby thought a moment. 'Or did I?'

'Dummy. She swapped it on you!'

Sophie jumped up and ran back to the entrance. Toby followed, initially throwing the piece of paper away, then returning to pick it up and put it in a rubbish bin. By the time he got inside, Sophie was already halfway down the west corridor, her boots clacking angrily on the polished floor. He was about to follow when a furtive movement caught his eye. There was another long corridor behind reception. Toby watched as the library assistant, map in hand, stepped out of a doorway, tiptoed across the floor and disappeared into another office. After a quick glance at Sophie, now accosting a janitor outside the reading room, Toby grunted and ran after the assistant.

It never failed to amaze Sierra how dumb boys were. Flash a smile and you had them in your back pocket. Naturally, it helped if you were attractive – and Sierra was very attractive, she had to acknowledge. Still, how clueless did you have to be to let a stranger swap one cardboard cylinder for another *literally* in front of your eyes? It was like a magic trick.

Map in hand, Sierra sneaked through the anterooms at the back of the museum. Best to avoid the staff – she wasn't technically allowed back here. Her role as a library assistant only covered the reading room and the book stacks, but in her illicit wanderings she had developed a good sense of the wider layout. When her mother had first mentioned the job to her a couple of years ago, Sierra had groaned loudly. Little did she know it would be the answer to her dreams.

She tiptoed into Dr Bolivar's office, which Sierra had been using as a kind of cubby hole. Dr Bolivar was away on a dig, so she had filched the passcode from the maintenance man and she retired here whenever she had a break. Or even when she didn't – making small talk with the other librarians was boring her stupid.

She took out her phone and sent a text message: *I've got it.* The response was almost immediate: *Bring it here, now.* ♥

Sierra shed her cardigan and glasses and threw them on the desk among the empty chip packets and soft drink cans. She slipped on her sunglasses and leather jacket instead. Entering the tiny ensuite bathroom that adjoined the office, she stepped up onto the lid of the toilet and crawled out through the bathroom window, dropping down onto the path that ran along the back of the admin block. A couple of students walking past saw her. One opened his mouth to say something. Sierra glared at him coldly until he closed it again and the two continued on their way.

Her motorbike was parked against the wall. She slotted the map into a side pannier, slicked back her hair and hopped on, pausing to check her lipstick in the mirror.

As she started the bike, she heard grunting and gasping coming from the rear of the office block. Seconds later, Toby fell out of the bathroom window into the bushes underneath. Sierra waited patiently for him to crawl out, brush the leaves and twigs from his hair, stand up, straighten his waistcoat and adjust his collar. Finally, he stood in front of her, red-faced and fuming.

Sierra revved the throttle and the bike leapt forward. 'So long, sucker!' She waved at Toby as she raced by.

Toby watched on helplessly as the librarian rode off down the path. The bike approached a pedestrian crossing. A taxi leapt into view and skidded to a stop. The bike crashed into the taxi and somersaulted over the bonnet. Bike and girl separated in the air. The girl fell to the ground on the other side and rolled several times; the bike landed on its wheels, fell over and skidded to rest alongside her.

Sophie jumped out of the taxi and ran to the bike, snatching the map from the pannier. As she ran back to the taxi door, a dazed Sierra stuck a leg out and tripped her. Sophie fell over and dropped the cylinder. Sierra scrambled on all fours and grabbed one end of it, just as Sophie stretched out and grabbed the other. The girls tugged the map back and forth, letting go only long enough to slap the other girl over the head.

It occurred to Toby that he shouldn't be standing there watching. He ran towards them. He only got halfway down the path before the bigger girl won the battle. Sierra tore the map from Sophie's hand and used it to belt her over the head. Sophie yelped and threw a clod of grass in Sierra's face. Fuming, Sierra spat out little pieces of green and hit Sophie over the head again, then rolled over onto her feet and recovered her bike – dented but otherwise undamaged, and still idling on the lawn. She jumped on and rode away.

Sophie leapt into the taxi and took off in pursuit, only seconds behind.

Toby reached the intersection and staggered to a halt. Breathing hard, he watched the bike and taxi jump the kerb outside the museum and race up the street and around the corner.

Sierra took an on-ramp onto the highway. It was past rush hour, but traffic was still dense. Nimbly she threaded her way through the morning traffic, throwing the bike from side to side, a big grin on her face.

Ship couldn't manoeuvre as easily; instead, it honked the taxi's horn and flashed its lights. Most of the other vehicles were under autopilot. Sensing the danger, they obligingly moved aside for the taxi and slowed down, creating a clear path ahead. Ship and Sophie started to catch up.

Sierra looked into the rear-view mirror and cursed. Veering wildly, she took the next off-ramp back down into the streets. An aqueduct crossed under the highway, still under construction. Sierra jumped the streetside barrier and rode the slope down into the concrete channel. She landed with a splash in a shallow pool of water. Spinning the bike in a graceful spiral she accelerated away, throwing twin curtains of water behind her like a fountain.

Sierra tossed her head back and laughed. The laugh died on her lips. Racing along the service road that ran beside the aqueduct was the taxi, matching her pace, a little girl's scowling face plastered to the window.

Sierra put her head down and changed gears. She pulled the throttle back as far as it would go, pushing the little bike to its limits.

The aqueduct ended at a reservoir on the edge of the city. The suburban streets were thinning out, replaced with olive and lemon groves; beyond was empty desert. The motorbike's tyres had big knobbly bits that would find purchase in the sand. The taxi's tyres were built for asphalt. Sierra knew she only had to make it to the open desert to escape.

She rode the bike diagonally up the sloping side of the concrete channel, leaping back onto the road only twenty metres in front of the taxi. Behind her, Sophie opened the sunroof and stuck her head out, screaming at her to stop.

Sierra turned around and gave her the finger.

Up ahead, the road curved around the edge of the reservoir and then petered out into a sandy track that wound up into the dunes. Sierra urged the bike on.

There was a kink in the road where it followed an inward curve of the reservoir. Sierra followed the road around the curve. Ship drove the taxi straight ahead, temporarily leaving the road and barrelling through the sparse roadside vegetation. It re-joined the road as it straightened again and intercepted the bike, clipping the bike's back wheel and knocking it sideways. Sierra couldn't correct for the sudden change of direction and rode the juddering bike down the embankment and off the edge, her scream of fright and rage cutting out abruptly as she plunged into the placid sheet of blue water.

But Ship had run out of road. The asphalt became dirt, and the taxi was moving too fast. It skidded in the loose gravel and careened towards the water. It spun around twice as it slipped down the embankment, sailed over the edge and followed the bike into the reservoir.

For a moment silence reigned, disturbed only by a distant wail of sirens.

Sophie had never seen the inside of a police cell before. They weren't very comfortable. The concrete bench was really hard; the walls were covered in nasty-looking words she didn't understand; the paint on the roof was mouldy and peeling; and she didn't want to think about the contraption in the corner that looked like a toilet bowl but couldn't possibly be, because, well, people would be able to watch you *go*.

She patted her damp clothes and shifted awkwardly on the bench. Another wet patch. Every fifteen minutes or so she got up and moved further down. She now had a series of drying spots next to her. When she got to the end of the bench the first one had almost dried, so she got up and returned to the start.

She hoped Ship was okay. The small plastic case of electronics that held the copy of Ship's mind was soaked. After examining it and concluding it was now harmless, the police people had let her keep it. She held it tenderly to the side of her face. 'Are you okay in there, Ship?'

No answer. A drop of water ran down the outside of the case and transferred to her cheek. Sophie wiped it away and sniffed.

'What are you mumbling about?'

The cow that had caused all this was in the cell next door. The girl walked over and leaned against the bars. 'Who are you talking to?'

Sophie sniffed again. 'No one.'

'I heard the pigs talking. Is that thing really a military AI?'

'I'm not speaking to you.'

'It was driving the taxi, wasn't it? That was freaking amazing.'

Sophie proudly lifted her chin. 'Yes.'

'Far out. What else can it drive?'

'Anything, obviously. Hovercrafts, buggies, airships—'

'What about a spaceship?'

Sophie had no idea. 'Of course.'

'Huh.' Sierra rested her chin on the crossbar. 'That could come in *sooo* handy. How'd you get it?'

Sophie's brows furrowed. 'I think we bought it off an old army guy in a saloon. Mum said he'd lost his stars or stripes or something.'

Sierra flicked the bars. 'Hah, court-martialled, I bet.' She cocked her head to the side. 'So why the droopy face?'

Sophie held up the case and wiped tears from her eyes. 'He's all wet!'

Sierra waved her hand dismissively. 'No, that's not him. That's just a copy of him. The pigs are looking for the *real* him now. Those things always back themselves up before they go on dangerous missions. Besides, we were still within town limits. In the split second before you hit the water it probably uploaded its mind state to the city cloud.'

Sophie jerked around and looked at Sierra. 'Do you really think so?'

'Hell, yeah.'

Sophie gripped the case in both hands, frantic with relief. 'Yes, yes, you're right. Of course, you're right. Ship is way too smart not to have a backup plan!'

Sierra nodded confidently and walked to the front of her cell. Through the tiny glass window in the door at the end of the corridor, she could see police moving around the office, and hear the low murmur of busy voices. She pressed her cheek against the bars. 'Wish I had a backup plan,' she muttered. 'Just wait till my mother gets here.'

Chapter Two

Ezra

Zach brought the buggy to a stop at the crest of a small hill. In front of him, down a slope of splintered rocks, the ground levelled out to a cleared space containing a short airfield. At one end of the field were a hangar, a bank of solar panels and a caravan with a broad awning on one side shading a couple of deckchairs and a coffee table. Behind the caravan, washing was strung out on a sagging line.

It had taken them three days to get here after Ship had dropped them off at Pirate Central, although Zach wasn't exactly sure where *here* was. Somewhere in the Scaarus Uplands, about 1500 kilometres north-north-east of Pirate Central.

Their time in Pirate Central had been eventful. The bastion of all things pirate was in an uproar. News had leaked that the City of the Dead had been found, although its exact location was the source of fierce speculation. Much of the town had left to go looking for it – people with ready transport disappearing overnight, people without it buying, renting or stealing anything with wheels or a propeller. One airship left in such a rush it failed to disconnect from the mooring tower. It pulled the tower to the ground and dragged it along behind it out into the dunes until someone figured out how to cut it loose. All had driven or flown off into the desert almost aimlessly, as if mountains of golden treasure would materialise out of the air in front of them. Prices went through the roof as the warehouses and food stores emptied of supplies, and fights broke out over the meagre remains.

Zach and Claudia bought a broken buggy from a blind pirate at ten times its value and spent the entire night fixing it up and another half day scrounging for several days' supplies. Claudia had to call in every favour she was owed just to get that much. As they were leaving, a fire broke out at Ming's warehouse. It burnt unchecked – there weren't enough people left to put it out.

Zach shielded his eyes and looked down the slope at the caravan. A couple of people were lounging in the deckchairs, apparently drinking. He watched a dust devil swirl in from the desert, briefly whipping up the clothes on the line, including a bra and a pair of boxer shorts, before dissipating among the rocks near the hangar.

Zach looked over at his mother. 'I get this guy has a plane. But can we trust him?'

Claudia took her glasses off and put them in her shirt pocket. 'Who knows?' she said wearily. 'It's your father.'

In response to Zach's surprise, Claudia just waved her hand down the hill. 'C'mon. Let's get this over with.'

Zach drove the buggy down to the airfield and pulled up in front of the caravan. A tall, spare man with a crooked nose and a solid jaw got up from a deckchair and squinted into the low morning sun. His sandy hair was greying and thinning at the temples, and either he was growing a beard or he hadn't shaved in a week.

'Zach? Zachey? Is that you?' The man came forward and wrapped his son in a big hug. 'My boy!'

Zach patted his father awkwardly on the back. He hadn't seen him in three years. He was, however, much as Zach remembered him. Ezra Jamison Ramirez projected an air of jocular imperturbability and a distinct smell of alcohol.

'So good to see you! How've you been?' Ezra grabbed the boy's shoulders and shook them so hard Zach's teeth rattled.

'Yeaahh, good, Dad.'

'Yeaahh, you're looking good. All grown up.' Ezra grinned and squeezed Zach's biceps. 'Put on a bit of muscle too!'

Ezra turned to the person sitting in the other deckchair: a blond woman in her late thirties, wearing a yellow bikini and sipping a daiquiri through a straw.

'Bonnie, come and look at my boy.'

The woman got up, a little unsteadily, and joined them, one hand still curled around her drink. 'Zachey?' she said in a high-pitched voice. 'I've heard so much about you! You look just like your dad.'

'Doesn't he, just? Chip off the old block.'

Bonnie pinched Zach's cheek. 'Such a looker!'

Zach managed a weak smile. 'Thank you, ma'am . . .

ah, miss.'

Bonnie laughed raucously. 'Puh-leese. Just Bonnie.'

Claudia's steely voice broke through the bonhomie. '*Ezra.*'

Ezra glanced up, pretending to notice Claudia for the first time. His voice lost some of its humour. 'Oh, and this is my wife. Well, ex-wife. Well, not formally.' Ezra looked momentarily confused. 'Actually, I'm not sure—'

Bonnie almost squealed, her voice rising another octave. 'Claudia? I've heard so much about you too!'

Claudia's eyes narrowed slightly.

'All of it bad,' Bonnie continued good-naturedly, 'but I don't pay it no mind.' She covered her mouth as if whispering a confidence. 'Exes!' she said, rolling her eyes, 'Whaddya gonna do?'

Claudia turned back to Ezra, her voice frosty. 'Can we talk?' She inclined her head towards Bonnie without looking at her. 'Privately.'

'Right,' said Ezra, 'and here's me thinking this was a social call.' He thumped Zach on the back. 'Me and your mum are gonna have a chat about your allowance. Don't go anywhere. We have so much catching up to do.' He jerked a thumb over his shoulder at the hangar. 'Claude. Let's go to my office. Bonnie, fix the boy a drink would you, please?'

'Hoo-eee!' said Bonnie. As Ezra and Claudia walked off, Bonnie grabbed Zach's hand and led him to the coffee table. The table was covered in bottles of vodka, rum, tequila, brandy and a selection of liqueurs.

'What's your poison?' asked Bonnie.

'Um . . .' Zach considered the spread in front of him, searching in vain for something non-alcoholic. 'I'm a minor. Technically, I'm not supposed to drink.'

'Really?' said Bonnie, bewildered. 'There's a law?'

'I think so.'

Bonnie rubbed her chin, thinking hard. 'I've got some lime juice in the fridge for my daiquiris?'

'That would be so good,' said Zach, relieved.

Bonnie ran off to the caravan. 'One lime daiquiri coming up!'

In the dim light of the aircraft hangar was a single-engine biplane. Freshly painted in bright yellow with black trim, it had a wooden propeller and two open-air seats protected by short plastic windshields. A leather cap and pair of goggles were draped around a wing strut. Claudia walked around the plane, inspecting it from all angles and kicking the tyres.

'Kid looks good,' said Ezra, watching her. 'No bullet holes in him, anyway.'

'Don't start,' replied Claudia. 'You have forfeited all rights. Last time he was with you, he got into a bar fight and ended up with sixteen stitches in his arm.'

'Hey, I'm off the hard stuff.'

Claudia ostentatiously checked her watch. 'It's ten in the morning and you're drinking tequila with Bonnie the Blonde Barmaid.'

'Ezra looked hurt. 'She's a chartered accountant, actually.'

'Does it still work?' asked Claudia, running her hand along the fuselage and checking her fingers for signs of dust or oil.

'Good as it ever was,' replied Ezra proudly.

Claudia nodded, looking sceptical. She stepped up onto the wing and checked out the pilot's cockpit. 'I can't believe we used to get around in this jalopy.'

'The good old days,' said Ezra, fondling the propeller. 'Swooping in, snatching a few trinkets, swooping out before the big boys arrived. Exciting times.'

Claudia clucked her tongue. 'We were mostly hungry, hunted, cold and desperate.'

Ezra shrugged. 'Yeah, but—'

'And don't forget the time you got shot and I had to fly eighteen hours nonstop with you bleeding all over the passenger seat.'

He gave her a crooked smile. 'As I said, good times.'

Ezra took a rag out of his back pocket and rubbed away a stain on the engine housing. Satisfied, he pulled up a crate, sat down and folded his arms. 'Why are you here, Claude?'

Claudia found another crate and sat down in front of him. 'The City of the Dead. It's been found.'

'I heard. Half of Mars is running around with its head chopped off.'

'Charles found it. Well, Charles and friends.'

'Yeah? Way to go, Charles.'

Claudia sighed. 'And there's a girl.'

'Charley's got a girl? Awesome!'

'No, Ezra, it's not *awesome*. It's very un-awesome. He was all set to go to school on Earth—'

'Aww, don't start that again. Why can't you leave the boy alone? Don't make him –'

'And finally get a real life. And then this thing happens, and now the only way he'll go is if we mount this ludicrous expedition –'

'This is his home.'

'– into the City of the Dead to rescue her.'

Ezra stopped, catching up with the last thing Claudia said. 'Jesus.'

'Yes, Ezra. Jesus.'

'Zach's girl is trapped in the City? How'd that happen?'

Claudia rubbed her face. 'It's strange and complicated.'

Ezra leaned back on the crate, pondering a blank space above Claudia's head. 'Janus will be after that treasure, and he'll kill everyone who gets in his way.'

Claudia blew out her cheeks. 'You see the problem?'

Ezra nodded. 'So, what's the plan?'

'First, we need to recover the *Pointy End*. It's floating free and unmanned over the Tallus Basin.'

'You lost my airship?'

'*My* airship. It has everything we need – guns, ammo, explosives, supplies. If we get that back, at least we can fend people off while we get in and out of the City. Plus, the place appears to have defences.'

Ezra raised his eyebrows.

'As I said, it's strange and complicated,' said Claudia.

'You know where the *Pointy End* is?' asked Ezra.

Claudia tapped her watch. The screen changed to a red readout showing a set of coordinates. 'Like I said, somewhere over the Tallus Basin. I had a homing beacon installed.'

Ezra nodded. 'You were always the smart one. So where do I come in?'

'I want you to land the plane on top of the *Pointy End*.'

Ezra began to laugh but choked it off with a cough. 'Really?'

'Can you get sober enough to do it?'

Ezra was incredulous. 'You want me to land on top of a floating airship?'

'Ezra, it pains me to say this, but you're the best pilot on Mars. If anyone can do it, you can. But are you sober enough?'

The man held out this hand and looked at it. Steady as a rock. 'I am now.'

Like so much of the geology of Mars, the Tallus Basin was the remains of a circular impact crater, with a scooped-out bowl of sand surrounded by a ring of cracked hills. It was deep enough and wide enough to have its own microclimate; the air above the centre of the basin, heated during the day by the darker sand of the meteor remains, rose into the troposphere and was filled by cooler air flowing in from the hills. As it rose, the Coriolis effect deflected it into a lazy circle. Trapped in this gentle current, the *Pointy End* drifted around the edges of the bowl like a plastic bag in a swirling gust of breeze.

Zach squirmed awkwardly in the passenger seat of the biplane. His mother had been sitting in his lap for over an hour. The tiny plane only had two seats, and Ezra needed the pilot's seat for himself for obvious reasons, which forced Zach and Claudia to share the passenger seat. At first, Claudia had expected Zach, as the child, to sit in her lap, but Zach's dignity wouldn't allow it and he'd argued that as he was bigger and heavier, she should sit in his lap. After a bit of fussing and rolling her eyes at the silliness of the male sex, Claudia had agreed. Now, Zach was regretting his decision; both his legs were tingling, and his backside was aching. To make matters worse, in an open cockpit at 2000 metres it was freezing, and his face had gone numb.

'There it is!' Claudia rose slightly, pointing ahead. 'Fifteen degrees to port.'

Zach looked at where she was pointing. The airship was a silvery almond tilted to one side.

Behind her, Ezra nodded, and the plane banked to the left.

As they got closer, Ezra cut their airspeed, and they did a couple of slow loops around the ship. It looked like a car that had rolled down a slope and caught on fire. Besides the black scorch marks, the broken struts and the shattered partitions, there was a gaping hole in one side where the gas bag had wrenched itself free.

Ezra yelled, 'Jesus, Claude, what have you done to my airship?'

Claudia yelled into the wind without turning around.

'*My* airship!'

At two hundred and forty metres, the *Pointy End* was about the same length as two and a half football fields. Unlike old-fashioned airships like the ancient Hindenburg, however, it wasn't cylindrical in cross section but oval, and shaped like an aerofoil, with a flat underside and a curved upper surface mounded towards the front and tapering down to a sharp edge at the rear. The wing-like profile gave it additional lift when in motion. To land, Ezra would have to approach from behind (and from one side, to avoid the fifteen-metre-tall tail fin) and put down on the upwards slope of the aerofoil, which extended for about a hundred and eighty metres before reaching its highest point and curving steeply back down to the nose. It would be like landing slantwise on the side of a hill. Of course, there was the additional consideration that the airship was moving at a balmy thirty knots and leaning twenty degrees to starboard. Oh, and the skin of the ship was aluminium – strong enough to walk on, but whether it was strong enough to land a plane on? No one knew.

Claudia turned to yell at Ezra, 'What do you think?'

'We're all going to die,' replied Ezra cheerfully.

'At least we'll go together,' groaned Zach.

Ezra brought them around for the final approach. Turbulence in the airship's wake buffeted them as they got close, and the little plane banked and swerved like a kite. Ezra fought to keep the plane steady and cut their speed again.

It seemed to Zach they were approaching too fast: one

moment the airship was a blob in the sky, the next it reared up in front of them. Suddenly they were hurtling past the tail fin, so close he could see individual rivets.

Ezra tucked the tail of the aircraft in to straighten their course and line up with the long axis of the airship. The biplane dropped quickly, and the wheels touched the top surface. But the envelope of air that flowed over the top surface pushed up the front of the plane and it bounced back into the air. Ezra pointed the nose back down, and a second before it rammed into the slope, yanked it up and killed the engine. The little plane dipped and touched down, skipping and skidding over the slippery metal, favouring the incline to starboard.

As it came to rest, one wheel bumped in and out of an open manhole. The plane pitched abruptly to one side and threw Claudia out of the passenger's seat. She hit the ground and tumbled further to starboard, where the relatively flat upper surface of the airship began to curve over to become the side.

'Mum!' Zach cried, fumbling to release his seatbelt.

The plane righted itself and shuddered to a stop. Zach jumped out, but his left leg had fallen asleep and collapsed under him as he landed. Looking up from all fours, he watched his mother slip further on the smooth aluminium and disappear over the horizon of the curved surface.

In a panic, Zach pinched and slapped his leg. He staggered upright.

'Watch out!' Ezra screamed.

Zach whirled around in time to see the still spinning

propeller coming towards him. He jerked back, and the blade whipped past so close the disturbed air slapped him in the face. Lighter now, with only one person aboard, the plane was skidding backwards.

'I can't hold it,' Ezra yelled. 'Get your mum!'

The biplane skated down the slope, picking up speed. Ezra worked furiously to restart the engine.

Zach turned back to where his mother had fallen from the plane. He couldn't see her, even on tiptoes. The skin of the airship curved away into the empty sky. The only thing visible were the broken hills of the Tallus Basin, smoky with ochre haze twenty kilometres away.

He walked towards the spot she had disappeared. The incline became steeper with each step. There was no sign of her. He took a few more steps. The incline was now more than thirty degrees.

As he took another step, his feet slipped out from under him. A jolt went up his tailbone as he fell hard onto his backside. But the fall didn't arrest his slide. He frantically backpedalled, but only slipped further. He rolled over onto his stomach, flailing about for a handhold – there was nothing to grab. He slid faster. The slope became a cliff. Heart in his throat, Zach tumbled down the side of the airship.

A hand shot out and found his, the jolt wrenching his shoulder. He stopped falling and swung like a pendulum past a metal ladder that protruded from the side of the airship. As he swung back, his chest crashed painfully into the ladder. Ignoring the pain, he latched onto it with his other hand, and after a few desperate seconds of scrambling, his feet found purchase on a rung. Panting, he looked up at his mother, clinging to the same ladder above. He tried to say thanks, but his tongue was thick and dry, and anyway, she was staring past him.

He looked down, fighting back the sudden flood of vertigo. Far below, the little biplane was falling like a leaf in a slow spiral towards the desert. Zach sensed the absence before he realised it consciously – the noise of the engine was missing. He counted the seconds:

One, two, three . . .

The plane diminished to a tiny yellow cross.

Four, five . . .

Zach gulped.

Six, seven, eight . . .

The thrum of the engine kicked in, tinny in the distance.

Nine. The plane pulled out of the spiral and straightened up.

Zach looked up at his mother. She closed her eyes for a few seconds before opening them again.

'C'mon,' she said, 'let's get inside.'

A surprise was waiting for them in the mess hall of the airship – Patrice, with his feet up on a table, munching on a packet of pumpkin chips. He was bruised and battered, his head and right leg swathed in poorly applied bandages.

'Jesus,' he said with a weary grin as they entered, quickly taking his feet off the table and standing up. 'How'd you get aboard?'

'If you'd been on lookout rather than eating, you'd know,' said Claudia caustically.

Zach ran forward and gave him a hug. 'You smell terrible,' he said, finally releasing the man.

'Water pumps are all broken,' Patrice replied, limping over to a bin to throw the empty packet away. 'That's my manly scent.'

'Where's the rest of the crew?' asked Claudia.

'Janus dumped them in the desert near Sicaria.' Patrice shrugged. 'They probably made it.'

'How come you're still here?' said Zach.

'I hid out in the trash compactor.'

Claudia slapped her thigh, impatient to get on with things. 'Well, good you're alive. Get cleaned up and get to the bridge. We have a lot to do.' She strode from the room.

After she left, Zach turned to Patrice. 'Sorry about that.'

Patrice grinned again. 'It's your mum's way.'

Zach put his arm around Patrice and helped him limp to the door. 'Guess what? I caught up with my dad.'

'Yeah? How is the old man?'

'Surprisingly good.'

Patrice pondered for a moment. 'You know, I think he owes me money.'

Chapter Three

The Dead

It was a while before Holly realised her eyes were open, so complete was the sheet of blackness in front of her. She was sitting on rough, cold stone, and when she reached out, her right hand slapped into a damp wall. There was a faint tang of wet limestone and the patter of water drops.

She reached out again, fingers trembling, drawing her hands back rapidly several times lest she touch something worse than a wall. There was another wall to her left. She was in a narrow corridor, or maybe an alcove.

Her eyes adjusted a little to the gloom, the black separating into vague shapes. To one side was a large oblong, and beyond it an edge appeared, curving up and over like an arch. A red glow reflected off a surface beyond the arch.

More outlines came into view. Dark vertical edges against dark shapes, disappearing into a murky vault far above.

Enough. Holly got to her feet. Her knees wobbled – but held. Holding one hand in front and gingerly tapping the ground in front of her with her toes before taking a step, she walked forward, stopping every few metres to listen.

Something was ticking near the arch, irregularly, like a metal roof cooling down in the shade. She went towards the sound.

The red glow got stronger as she approached, and she could make out the outline of a large alcove. The ticking was coming from inside.

She took another step towards it, this time forgetting to explore the ground in front of her first. The ground disappeared! She pitched forward and flung out her hands in fright. Her knuckles grazed stone and she banged her head painfully against the stone floor.

She rolled over and sat up, tenderly exploring her bruised forehead. She must have fallen down a step or something. As she took her hand away, the terrifying figure of Kebechet loomed over her. She screamed and scuttled backwards. Getting to her feet, she turned to run – and painfully stubbed her toe on the same step as before, falling to the ground again.

She looked over her shoulder, fearing at any moment the looming snake face, the taloned claw, the gelatinous tongue. But Kebechet hadn't moved. He stood as still as a statue, staring . . . over her head?

She glanced in that direction. There was nothing to see. Or nothing she could see, anyway. She turned back. He still hadn't moved. He stood in an alcove that had clearly been shaped just for him, its height and width fitting him snuggly. A red light glowed on the wall behind him, casting a metallic gleam over the side of his leg.

Holly sat up and watched him for a few minutes, her

fright ebbing. It was only a statue, like the one guarding the entrance to the arena. Or maybe, Holly wondered as she got to her feet, something more interesting.

She walked over to Kebechet, part of her still fearful under his gaze, and approached a taloned foot. Half-metre-long claws punctured the stone floor, and wire mesh hung loosely around the ankles, exposing rubbery tendons and a series of metal bones as thick as telegraph poles. The lower leg was mostly skeleton, the wire mesh skin having fallen away, but further up it was intact, and a series of interlocking plates curled around a jointed knee. Tubes draped from the wall and plugged into Kebechet's back. The red light was a button on the wall. She resisted the impulse to press it.

Holly smiled wryly and rapped the fibula with her knuckles. And jerked her hand away, realising too late what a stupid thing it was to do. Robot or not, if aroused it could snap her like a twig. Senses thrilling, she waited several seconds for a response – slowly relaxing as time passed and nothing happened. Whatever control it had been under, whether remote or its own programming, it was dormant now.

She walked back to the space in front of the alcove. She was in a large chamber with stone corridors leading off in several directions, big enough for Kebechet to pass through. She chose the one that appeared the lightest.

As she walked, she wondered, and worried about the gang.

Had Janus taken them captive? Even now, he might

be interrogating them as he had interrogated her. She shuddered to think what he might do to Toby and Sophie. And Zach? Thinking about him gave her a small pang in the chest. Was he tied up too, and being tortured for morsels of information while the one they really wanted was wandering around in a black hole?

Or had Claudia saved the day? One thing she'd seen before the door closed was Claudia with a gun in her hands, firing at Janus's goons. Despite everything, she kind of admired Claudia. But maybe they had taken her prisoner again too.

And then there was her father – no, not her father. Not anymore. She had seen him running towards the door, desperate to get to her, prepared even to take on the god of the underworld. Holly felt a rush of shame; she had treated him abominably. And then the anger kicked in and ran the guilt over. She would never, ever forgive him for lying to her about her mother. Because that's what all this was about. That's what lay beneath everything: her mother. The pirates could have their treasure. She wanted her mother. Her jaw tightened. Until she had answers, there would be no forgiveness.

It was getting lighter, in a strictly relative sense, like the difference between the blackest night ever and the second blackest night ever. The stone corridor that Holly traversed, hand still running along one wall, ended in a space so vast she wondered for a moment whether she had walked out of the tunnel and into a moonless Martian night.

The immense cavern was roughly circular, with a ridge of rock on the wall opposite to her jutting in towards the centre. Built onto the ridge and riding up the side of the cavern behind it was a city. A whole city built upon the steep slope, with streets, buildings, spires, domes and terraces. She could make out its contours because of a sprinkling of yellow lights which illuminated the city's streets and buildings. Some lights were sharp and faceted; others flickered like fires. One light stood out: a glowing square towards the top of the highest tower. As she watched, the light wavered, dimmed and returned to a steady state.

Holly shivered. There was someone in the city. Martians, presumably.

She looked over her shoulder and wondered whether she should go back and try to find a way out. But she didn't know where she was in relation to the arena, and *back* meant towards Kebechet. And besides, she nodded grimly, didn't she have questions to answer?

There was a path in front of her that led down into a wide valley and back up the other side to a gate in the city walls. She began the climb down.

The trek to the city took several hours, and Holly's legs were sore by the time she arrived at the gate. She was cold too. She had stopped to drink her fill from the tiny stream that wound along the valley floor. The water was icy and made her teeth chatter, but she drank her fill regardless, thinking that it might be some time before she got another chance.

The gate itself was closed, but a small door within it was open. Briefly, an image of the trap Toby and Sophie had sprung on the back at that place in the desert flashed to mind. She approached and peeked through the doorway.

The gate opened onto a broad plaza, with a fountain in the centre and cobblestoned streets leading off in three directions. The streets and plaza were lit by the faceted lights, affixed to the top of metal poles like diamonds on the ends of sceptres. Surprisingly, the fountain was working. A jet of water spurted from the mouth of a fish and splashed into a pond of green water.

But the plaza was empty, and the tinkle of the fountain was the only sound in an otherwise oppressive silence.

Holly stepped through the doorway and walked across the plaza to the start of one of the cobblestone streets. She stopped and examined one of the streetlamps. The light on top really was like a diamond: a crystal the size of a bunched fist that shone a crisp yellowish light, powered by an energy source she couldn't determine.

Was this all her doing? Had stepping onto the pattern triggered a process that awakened Kebechet, switched on the lights and started the fountain? And even awakened a few Martians too? Spooked by the thought, she whirled around, sensing someone was watching her, but no one was there.

The street curved away to the left and faded into the gloom, as many of the faceted lights closer to the centre of the city had failed. She looked up and found the tower where she had seen the solitary lit window. The street led in the same general direction.

As she walked, she peered into the windows of the buildings and discovered they weren't proper buildings at all, only facades that opened onto simple stone cubicles devoid of furniture or ornament. She passed what looked from the outside like a small church, or maybe a shrine, and it too was merely a front, propped up from behind by metal supports. It was like a movie set, where only the outward appearance mattered. It made sense, she supposed. No one was ever going to live here, not in this cold, dreary place devoid of sunlight. It was only a waystation to while away the eons. And when the Martians awakened, at least they had a reminder of their past lives and of the hope that had carried them across an ocean of time.

Yet she couldn't shake the feeling that this dark, false city reeked more of despair than hope. As Zach had said, they must have put themselves to sleep knowing that they might never wake up again. They couldn't have known that one day earthlings would arrive and replenish the atmosphere with oxygen. Maybe the city was never meant to be anything more than a mausoleum.

Regardless, where were the pods?

There was a flash of green in a gap between two buildings across the street. Holly caught the movement out the corner of her eye. Cautiously, she approached the narrow space. A patter of small footsteps began, receded and stopped. Holly froze at the edge of the inky shadow that filled the gap. She leaned forward, straining to listen.

The patter started and stopped again. It sounded small, hesitant, childlike. Holly could see nothing, but she was learning to trust her other senses. She walked into the space, running her hands along the walls to either side. The tiny echoes of her footsteps from the walls told her something of the size and shape of the surrounding space. The walls stopped at the entrance to a small courtyard, where a streetlamp cast a triangle of light over the rear wall. A head appeared above the wall and disappeared: a boy with green skin and bronze eyes.

'Wait!' called Holly.

There was a thud and the sound of running feet. Holly ran after the sound, hurling herself over the wall and landing on a dirt path behind the buildings. The boy was ahead, about twenty metres away. He paused and looked back at her. He must have been about seven or eight, lean as a whippet, with black hair tied into a ponytail. His feet were bare, and he wore a simple white shirt with vest and baggy trousers. The look on his face was both puzzled and scared.

Holly couldn't stop a nervous laugh from escaping her lips. That anyone could be afraid of her was beyond silly.

He ran again. Holly chased him.

The boy was as nimble as a cat, vaulting fences, skirting corners and running along the tops of walls. But on the straight, Holly was faster. She caught up a little, ignoring the burn in her thighs. He ran across a broad street and up some steps into the entrance of one of many large, domed buildings. Blindly, she followed him inside – and collided with something (someone!? No, something hard). She ricocheted in a different direction until something else punched her in the stomach. It was an ornamental ball on top of a metal railing. She tipped forward over the edge of the railing, and for a moment, before she could grip the metal to pull herself back, she dangled, V-shaped, over an airy space.

She found the pods – some of them, anyway. They were arranged in tiers around the walls of the chamber below her. These were more complex than any she had seen before, and in much better condition. Tubes ran from their bases into the surrounding walls, metal plates on the sides held knobs and buttons, and part of the lid was translucent, like thick quartz.

She found the Martians too. Congregated in the centre of the space was a group of about a hundred green-skinned people huddling around an open fire. They were cooking something in a large pot. Startled, they turned and looked up at her. There was a collective intake of breath.

The boy she had followed ran down a flight of steps on one side of the chamber, making odd sibilant sounds, which, even more oddly, Holly understood.

'Mama, the ghost! The ghost!'

He ran into the arms of a woman and clutched her as if his life depended on it.

Holly righted herself and noticed more people were standing on the balcony next to her that surrounded the space, their expressions almost as fearful. Feeling foolish, she held up her hand and said, 'I come in peace.'

Immediately, they all took a step backwards. She smiled to reassure them. They took another step backwards. They murmured to each other in soft voices using words she recognised as *ghost* and *spirit*. She remembered a gesture that a woman in her dreams had greeted her with when she arrived at the palace. She placed her hand across her chest and dipped her head.

This seemed to hearten them a little. A few returned the gesture. Holly nodded in encouragement and repeated it. More of them followed suit. An older man came hesitantly forward and asked her a question. It took Holly a moment to grasp the words.

'Are you Maitreya?' he asked.

Holly shook her head. She placed her hand on her chest. 'Holly,' she said.

This confused him, but at least he didn't run. He went to the balcony railing and pointed at the fire. Holly understood this to mean that she should join them. Not knowing what else to do, she followed him down the steps.

Holly sat there for almost an hour, grateful for the chance to warm her bones. Despite her growing hunger, she declined the offer of food. The strange scents from the pot did not sit well with her stomach. Instead, she nibbled on one of the space food sticks Sophie had crammed into her pocket before they left the hovercraft.

While she sat and nibbled, she watched the Martians, and the Martians watched her, the adults glancing at her coyly and the children blatantly staring. They were lithe and poised, with gangly limbs and thin tapering skulls with short square chins. Most of them had dark wavy hair but a few of the children had hair so blonde it was almost white. She liked the way their metallic-looking skin reflected the fire in hues of orange and yellow, and although the boy she had followed had bronze eyes, many of the others had copper-coloured eyes flecked with gold.

So, was this what she really was? Her father had said that when he found her in the pod, she had green skin and bronze eyes. Why had she changed? Some survival mechanism to blend into the background, perhaps? Would it change back again now that she was with her own kind? She tried to imagine herself with green skin and failed – it was too strange. She sighed and gently slapped her face, pretending for a moment it would wake her from her dream. The Martians sitting nearby turned to eye her warily. Yes, she was a little crazy, she replied silently. The tension of the last few days had gotten to her. Holly longed for a bit of normalcy, but that was far away in the past, and she couldn't see it anywhere in her future.

A couple sitting next to her were whispering. She understood some words, and others were familiar, like an old song she partially remembered. She watched and listened, and more and more of what they were saying became intelligible. As if fiddling with a radio dial, her brain was tuning in to the right frequency.

'But where is the Queen?' one of them asked.

The other shrugged. 'She will come. The guards will come. Wait and see.'

Another person behind them turned and addressed them both. 'No. This is the doorway to the afterlife. We must wait for Azustra.'

The first one, a woman, shook her head adamantly. 'Don't be foolish. It is just a cave. If you go outside and look up, you can see moisture dripping from the roof.'

Holly wasn't sure of the word *Azustra*. It possibly meant judgement or purgatory. If she was only seven when they put her to sleep, her knowledge of her own language would have been incomplete. Maybe it was an 'adult' word that she hadn't yet learned.

She needed to ask her own questions. She watched their mouths as they spoke and tried to mimic the movement of their lips. 'Qu . . . Qu,' she said uncertainly.

They turned to her, wary but curious.

Holly tried again, closing her eyes. She must know the language, surely. She just had to get her brain out of the way and let her muscle memory do the talking. She pictured the queen in her mind. 'Qu . . . Queen,' she said in Martian, opening her eyes again.

The woman pointed to the entrance. 'Queen. The tower.'

Holly nodded and tried again, picturing a woman awakening. 'And you, how long? Awake?'

The woman looked uncertain. 'Two days, three.' She looked around the dark chamber. 'It is difficult to tell.'

The rest of the group had heard Holly speak in their own language. They edged closer, and soon a crowd had formed around her.

'Are there more? Of you?' Holly continued. Martian

words were flooding her brain now.

'Many more. And more are still awakening.'

'In the other . . .' Holly couldn't think of the word. She shaped it with her hands. '. . . domes?'

The woman nodded. 'In this dome is the palace household. In others are the artisans, or the farmers or—'

'But who are you?' interrupted the old man who had first approached Holly. He had pushed through to the front of the group.

The answer was out of her mouth before she could stop it. 'I am the key,' she said, surprising even herself.

An excited murmur passed through the assembly. As it dissipated, a couple of the Martians bowed, and the rest dipped their heads. The old man knelt on one knee.

'Don't do that.' Holly gestured for the man to get up. 'Please.'

But he looked up at her from under his bushy eyebrows and nodded solemnly. 'You have returned us to the world, Princess.'

'I don't know about being a princess. I'm just the key. Why are you still here? In the dark?'

'We don't know the way out, Princess,' the old man replied.

'No one knew the location of the City,' said the woman. 'We were blindfolded and brought here in secret.' She reached out to Holly but drew back before touching her arm. 'Princess, what happened to your skin? Are you ill?'

'No,' said Holly. 'It's a temporary condition . . . I think.'

'You will show us the way to Maitrus?' asked the old

man.

Maitrus must mean 'light', Holly thought, or 'the world of light'. She shook her head. 'Um, well, no. But the Queen, she must know the way. Hasn't she come to you?'

'No. She has been waiting for you.'

The gruff voice came from the back of the group. The crowd parted to reveal a big man decked in full armour. It was the same as the armour of the soldiers she had met on the road in her dream – bronze with trimmings of purple. He was also, Holly noted, carrying a large spear and had a sword belted to his waist. She felt a nervous laugh bubbling to the surface. She quashed it ruthlessly.

Holly stood up and walked towards the soldier. The crowd stepped back. A few bowed again.

The soldier looked her up and down, apparently not impressed with what he saw. 'You are ready?' he growled.

'Not at all,' she replied.

Chapter Four

Mean Girls

The police lockup in Port Clarke was seeing a lot of activity today. In addition to Sophie and Sierra, the other cells had filled up with a variety of seedy-looking customers, including an elderly man with a banjo and a group of drunk college students, loudly protesting about police brutality in between chants of 'Free Mars'. Sophie and Sierra had retreated to the back of their adjacent cells and had been swapping action stories – Sierra about her daring exploits on her bike, and Sophie about Ship's daring exploits fighting pirates.

But the real action started when Sierra's mum arrived.

'Do you have any idea of how embarrassing this is? This is the second time this year I have had to bail you out of custody. I'm the mayor, for heaven's sake!'

Sierra couldn't look her mother in the face. Instead, she glanced at the chief of police, who was standing at the door pretending to check his phone. 'Doesn't that mean these guys work for you?' she said sullenly.

'No!' Ms Garcia practically screamed. She looked about and quickly lowered her voice to an exasperated hiss. 'It does *not* mean they work for me!'

Sierra pouted and stared at the floor.

'And you stole a map from the museum?' Ms Garcia threw her hands in the air. 'Why?'

'I was gonna give it back,' Sierra muttered.

'That job was the community service our lawyer convinced the court to give you rather than sending you to the children's remand centre.'

'Hey,' Sierra protested, 'I did not start that fire!'

'It doesn't matter, Sierra. You're *this* far away from jail time. Do you get that?'

Sierra crossed her arms and grumbled under her breath, 'Wouldn't have happened if you'd sent me to Earth like I wanted.'

'What? Don't mumble.'

Sierra looked up and glared at her mother. 'I said—'

'I heard what you said!' Ms Garcia took a deep breath and tried to compose herself. 'Sierra, you're fifteen. I am not sending you 200 million kilometres just because some creepy photographer on social media thinks you look good in a swimsuit.'

'Not just him! I have a hundred thousand followers!'

'When you're sixteen, I will give you the money and you can talk to a few people and have some proper photos taken. And if you keep up your acting lessons and the instructor says—'

'I'll be too old!' Sierra wailed.

'Ah, Madam Mayor?' The chief of police had been inching forward, trying to find an opening.

Ms Garcia looked glad to be interrupted. 'Yes, Chief?'

'Court date's come through. She's free on bail.'

''Bout time,' said Sierra.

The chief took out his swipe key and opened the door. Sierra looked back at Sophie in the cell next door.

'What about her?'

Ms Garcia glanced at Sophie and turned to the chief. 'Who?'

He shrugged. 'Her parents arrived here a couple of years ago. Some weirdo cult.'

'Where are they now?'

'Dead, apparently. Protective services are on their way. She'll stay at the children's home till we find the closest relative.'

'What? She can't stay there,' Sierra said. 'Those kids are insane.'

Ms Garcia sniffed. 'They're all friends of yours.'

'Hello,' said Sierra, rolling her eyes. 'That's how I know.' She folded her arms and stood in front of Sophie's cell. 'I'm not leaving without her.'

Ms Garcia cocked an eyebrow. 'I've a mind to take you up on that.'

Mother and daughter squared off. The chief of police looked back and forth between them, holding his breath.

The mayor relented and turned to the chief with a sigh. 'Fine, arrange the paperwork. She can stay with us until you find a relative.'

The Garcia estate occupied seventeen hectares in an

elevated area of Port Clarke overlooking the city centre. Built in the style of a Roman villa with colonnades and arches, it had a tennis court, swimming pool, sauna, several atriums and a gym, inhabiting grounds with gardens and manicured lawns so green Sophie was sure they were fake.

Getting out of the car in the driveway, she looked up at the imposing edifice in awe. 'You live here?'

Sierra gave a casual shrug. 'C'mon, you can have the room next to mine. It overlooks the pool.'

Sophie's room was bigger than the house she used to live in on Earth. It adjoined Sierra's bedroom through an archway and had a sliding glass door opening onto a balcony. Sophie wandered around the room, running her hands over the silky soft furnishings. Sierra opened the glass door and stepped onto the balcony. Around the pool below, caterers were setting up tables and pavilions.

Sierra shouted at the top of her lungs, 'Mum!'

Ms Garcia appeared under the balcony with her hands over her ears. 'Must you scream everything?'

Sierra waved her arms at the caterers questioningly.

Ms Garcia shook her head. 'The function tonight? The businesspeople from Earth? Have you forgotten already?'

'That's here?'

'I told you a dozen times, Sierra.'

Sierra nodded, distracted. 'Right . . .' An idea had occurred to her.

'Please try to behave,' said Ms Garcia. 'This is very import . . .'

But Sierra had already disappeared back inside. Sophie

was sitting on the edge of the bed, bouncing up and down.

'C'mon,' said Sierra. She grabbed Sophie's hand and dragged her into her bedroom. 'We have work to do.'

Sierra threw open the doors to her walk-in wardrobe. 'We'll need something simple for you, so you don't stand out, and something dazzling for me, obviously.'

Sophie gazed around the room. The walls were covered in posters of movie stars, rock musicians, and models. She studied one of the posters. A young man in high heels and a glittering suit screamed into a microphone. 'So, you're like, really, really rich?'

'No, my mother is really, really rich,' said Sierra over her shoulder. She spun around, draping a long red dress against her body. 'Whaddya think?'

Sophie looked mystified. ''Bout what?'

Sierra huffed. 'Look, my mother is hosting a function tonight for a delegation from Earth – businesspeople, scientists, politicians, yadda yadda yadda, all looking at ways Earth can do business with Mars. I'd completely forgotten about it. But then I remembered, Betty the Boring Librarian told me that one of them is a talent scout for IMC.'

'I am cee . . .?'

'I. M. C. It's, like, the biggest talent agency in the world!' Sierra threw the red dress over the sofa and went back to rummaging around in her wardrobe. 'So tonight, we have to find this person and knock their socks off.'

Sierra emerged again with half a dozen dresses in one hand, and a generous selection of high-heeled shoes in the other. She jabbed an elbow at Sophie. 'And you're gonna help me.'

Sierra found Sophie an old dress from when she was about Sophie's age: a blue frock printed with flowers with ruffles at the sleeves. Sophie struggled to imagine Sierra – she of the leather jacket and motorcycle boots – ever wearing it. Sophie herself didn't give two hoots about clothes but the dress was cleaner than her current one, so she put it on with little complaint. Sierra selected for herself a short black dress which Sophie was pretty sure Ms Garcia would frown upon. After an excruciatingly long time getting ready – showering, soaking, lathering, doing nails and applying makeup – Sierra positioned Sophie and herself in front of a full-length mirror and gave them a final once over.

'Outstanding,' drawled Sierra.

The party didn't start till late – late for Sophie, anyway. She was usually in bed by the time most of the delegates dribbled in. They were served by waiters dressed up in cartoonish banachuk costumes, with face masks, tails and large padded feet. Banachuks were the informal mascot of Mars – a kind of fox, genetically adapted to Martian conditions. The waiters and delegates mingled on the patio around the pool with business leaders, politicians and important personalities from Port Clarke, talking about things Sophie didn't understand and cared about even less. She recognised several people from the pages of her magazines, though, so that was a bit exciting. Way more exciting, however, was the food. There were these things called *hors d'oeuvres*, which waiters were carrying around on silver platters: little pastries, rolled-up slices of meat and cheese, tiny honey-flavoured sausages and marinated chicken wings. After some experimentation, Sophie realised you could take as many as you wanted and nobody seemed to care. Better still, she discovered the source. The waiters were collecting them from a table outside the kitchen. Sophie perched herself on a barstool next to the table and feasted.

'Where have you been?' Sierra tottered up, moving as quickly as her high heels would allow. 'I've been looking all over for you!'

Sophie's mouth was full. She could only mumble and point at the table in reply.

'No time for that.' Sierra pulled Sophie off the stool and out onto the patio. She pointed to a portly man sporting a goatee and horn-rimmed classes. He was talking to a couple of older women near the pool. 'That's him. I checked the guest list. You ready?'

Sophie gulped down a mouthful of food and looked around for something to wipe her sticky fingers on. 'Mmm-hmm.'

Hands trembling, Sierra handed her phone to Sophie. 'This is real important, okay? Don't screw up.'

Sophie nodded emphatically, cradling the phone in the palms of both hands, trying not to let her sticky fingers touch the screen.

Sierra leaned over and quickly swiped to the picture

she wanted. 'This. It's a still from an ad I did a couple of months back for a haberdashery store.' The photo showed a smiling and surprisingly agreeable-looking Sierra wrapped up in layers of colourful material.

'I'll go introduce myself as the host's daughter. Ask them if they need anything. You wait thirty seconds, then come over and ask for my autograph. Remember, be effusive, but not too effusive – just the right amount of effusive.'

Sophie didn't know what effusive meant, but she got the idea.

Sierra looked over at the man again. Instinctively, her hand went to her mouth and she started biting a nail.

Sophie gently prised the finger from Sierra's teeth and gave her a thumbs up. 'I'm sure you'll be great.'

'Yes, yes . . . of course.' Sierra tossed her hair, licked her lips and smoothed her dress down for the tenth time. 'Okay . . .'

Sophie watched Sierra hobble off through the party-goers, still looking a little unstable in her heels. Sierra snubbed the offer of an hors d'oeuvre from a banachuk waiter and joined the agent and the two women in conversation. She smiled, shook everyone's hands and tossed her hair a few times. Everyone laughed at something, Sierra a little too loudly but within acceptable limits, and it generally looked like everything was going well.

Sophie figured about half a minute had passed and began her move, but before she got there, two more girls, who had been dipping their toes by the edge of the pool, joined the group. About Sierra's age or a little older, they interjected loudly, and air-kissed Sierra as if she was a long-lost friend.

Sophie hesitated but continued, thinking this changed nothing. 'Sierra? Sierra Garcia? Is that you?' She squeezed in beside Sierra and one of the girls, and held out the phone. 'Can I have your autograph?'

When Sierra turned to her with a rictus grin, Sophie realised she had made a mistake. The two new girls glanced at the photo on the phone and their initial puzzled expressions morphed into ones of malicious glee.

'Oh yes, yes!' one cried, a petite girl with a bob of blonde hair and a headband. 'We only just heard. You're famous, Sierra.'

'We must have your autograph too!' the brunette added. Quickly, they began scrolling through their phones.

'No really, Cindy, Zoe,' Sierra said, her voice quivering, 'I don't think our guests would be interested—'

'Oh, but I have the picture here,' the blonde Cindy said. 'It's just too perfect!'

'Too perfect!' Zoe agreed.

'I don't understand . . .' the talent agent began, looking back and forth between Sierra and the girls.

'*Cindy* . . .' warned Sierra, looking pale.

'Found it!' announced Zoe.

Standing next to Zoe, Sophie glimpsed the picture on the phone: Sierra, looking bedraggled and sour, in the mugshot from her recent arrest. Zoe lifted it up for all the world to see.

Sophie's hand shot out and knocked it from Zoe's

fingers. 'Whoops.'

The phone clattered onto the concrete centimetres from the pool. But before an annoyed Zoe could pick it up, a banachuk waiter bent over to collect it instead. As the waiter straightened up, the top of its head clocked Zoe in the chin, knocking her backwards into the pool.

'Sorry!' said the waiter, swinging around wildly to face the water.

'Bozo!' cried Cindy, running to the edge to help Zoe.

Sophie saw her chance. She pretended to trip over the banachuk's tail and careened into the back of Cindy. For a moment Cindy teetered on the pool's edge – before falling into the water too, shrieking.

Cries went up around the perimeter. Several brave young men, eager to assist, quickly dived in. But Cindy and Zoe had fallen into the shallow end and emerged seconds later coughing and spluttering, their hair and dresses ruined.

With everyone's attention focused on the action, Sophie figured this was a good time to exit. She grabbed Sierra's hand and pulled her away to the quiet at the back of the pool house, where they were joined a minute later by the clumsy waiter.

Sophie peered owlishly into the banachuk's eyes. 'That's gotta be you in there.'

The waiter pulled off the head of the costume to reveal a flushed Toby. 'It's sooo hot in here . . . and it itches.'

'Where'd you get the costume?'

'There's a van full of them at the servants' entrance. It's

the only way I could get in here after Ship tracked you down from the police reports.'

'Ship's okay?'

'Yeah, it lost connection with its partial mind-state when the taxi went into the water. You'll have to update it with everything that happened afterwards.'

'Thank the Blessed Saints,' said Sophie, relieved. 'But what do we do now? We still don't have the map!'

'All thanks to her,' said Toby, frowning at Sierra.

Sierra didn't seem to hear. She had covered her face with her hands and was starting to cry.

After exchanging an awkward glance with Toby, Sophie patted Sierra on the arm. 'He didn't see the mugshot. I'm sure of it.'

'But it's out there!' cried Sierra.

Sophie tried to think of something to say. 'I'm sure you can still be a rock star—'

'An actor!' said Sierra.

'An actor,' corrected Sophie. 'I mean, I think Abby Monroe started as a calling girl.'

Sierra pulled one hand away from her face. 'Who the hell is Abby Monroe? And do you know what a callgirl is?'

Sophie gave it some thought. 'A girl who . . . calls?'

Shaking her head in exasperation, Sierra picked up Toby's tail and wiped her nose on it. 'Well, now I need the money for that map more than ever.'

'How did you even know about it?' asked Sophie.

'My dad is, shall we say, in the business. How'd you think we got so rich?'

'Your dad's a pirate?' exclaimed Sophie.

'Shush!' warned Sierra, looking around. 'We don't mention that word around here. We've gone respectable.'

'Well, good luck,' said Toby. As Sophie and Sierra talked, he'd been checking Sierra's phone. 'According to the latest bulletin, they've locked it in a safe in the museum. And, ah . . .' His eyes widened. He looked at his sister. 'We should be going.'

Sophie stared at him. 'We need the map too.'

'Well . . .' Rather than responding, Toby licked his lips and started typing furiously on the phone.

'What are you doing?' Sierra asked. 'Give my phone back.'

'Ah, just a sec.' Toby continued typing. 'Almost there.'

Suspicious as hell, Sierra lunged for the phone. Toby batted her hand away and held the phone behind his back. 'Just let me forward this one message.'

'Phone? Lock!' said Sierra quickly. The face of the phone went black and refreshed a second later with a welcome screen.

'Nooo!' cried Toby. 'Phone, unlock!' He desperately tried pressing buttons, but the phone just beeped at him. 'Phone? Phone!'

Sierra looked smug. 'It only recognises my voice, moron. Now, tell me what's going on.'

Toby's shoulder's slumped. 'We almost had it.'

'Had what?' said Sophie.

'Sierra's email. Being the defendant, the police are obliged to send her a copy of the prosecution brief. They'd helpfully attached hi-res photos of the map.'

'You read my email?' cried Sierra. She jumped him and knocked him to the lawn. They wrestled around for a bit, but they were evenly matched, and Sierra was hampered by her tight dress and by Toby's banachuk tail. Belatedly, she decided that fighting a child was beneath her and pushed herself away. She got to her feet, fixed her hair and straightened her dress.

'Give it back,' she said with an air of hurt dignity.

'No,' replied Toby, squarely planting his fat banachuk feet. 'We need the map. Let me forward the email and you can have it back.'

'If I let you forward the email, then you don't need me.'

'And if I give your phone back, then you don't need us,' Toby countered. He held the phone in front of her face. 'Tell it to unlock!'

Sierra put her hands on her hips, a thin smile curving her lips. The two stood there for several moments, glowering at each other.

Sophie looked back and forward between the combatants. 'So, what now? We, like, join forces or something?'

Chapter Five

Sand Crawler

'It's gonna snap!' yelled Ezra, attached to a harness ten metres up the side of the *Pointy End*'s tail fin.

'It'll hold!' Claudia yelled back and wound the winch a half-turn.

The cable extended from a winch bolted onto the airship's top surface up to the rear strut of the rudder. The servo motors that controlled the rudder had been destroyed in the attack, so unless they could control it some other way – for example, by using cables to pull it back and forth – they couldn't steer.

Claudia continued to wind the handle. The cable vibrated like a plucked guitar string. Squatting beside her, Zach watched the rudder tremble, but if it moved he couldn't see it, and the wind was getting stronger and becoming gusty.

He put a hand on his mother's shoulder. 'The surface area of the rudder must be over two hundred square metres. The pressure's too much.'

His mother ignored him and turned the handle another quarter turn.

Snap! One end of the broken cable shot up from under the winch, cracking like a whip, and raced towards Ezra. He ducked just in time and the whizzing cable gouged the metal pole where his head had been. The cable then snaked along the side of the rudder, lashing the thin aluminium into ribbons before falling to dangle uselessly behind the airship, its pent-up energy spent.

Claudia kicked the winch in anger a few times, then spoke into the mic attached to her collar. 'Patrice, bring the nose back down. It broke again.'

Zach could just make out Patrice's reply over the static. 'I told ya.'

Back inside, the four of them reconvened on the bridge.

'So, summing up,' said Claudia, 'we can control pitch and ballast, but we can't steer. And now we don't even have the plane.'

Ezra had tried a second time to land the plane on top of the airship. He succeeded – sort of. Claudia, Zach and Patrice had readied themselves with ropes and lassoed the plane's undercarriage as it came to a stop. But a gust of wind flipped the plane over at the last moment and now it was strapped to the airship upside down like a dead beetle.

'We can vary the thrust between the port and starboard engines,' suggested Patrice.

'It might work,' replied Claudia thoughtfully. 'It will at least yaw the ship and point us in a different direction.'

'But only one engine is working,' said Zach. 'We'll have to fix at least one on the other side. How long is that going to take?'

Claudia shrugged. 'Few days.'

'Well, we haven't got a few days,' said Zach. 'It's already been four since Holly was captured, and Toby and Sophie messaged saying they've got the map and are headed to the area near the City. I'm getting off now.'

Claudia draped a gloved hand on her hip. 'How, exactly?'

'Bring it close to the ground and I'll jump.'

'Hah,' Claudia barked, not sure if her son was being serious. 'And then what? Walk? It's five hundred clicks.'

'Ship can detour and pick me up.'

'But Zach,' Ezra said, 'what about supplies, ammo, weapons? Your mum told me about that thing you encountered.'

Zach looked sharply at his father. 'Dad, Holly's in trouble. You gonna help or what?'

Ezra met his son's gaze. 'Yes,' he said solemnly, 'I'm gonna help.'

'Ezra . . .?' warned Claudia.

But Ezra held up his hand to stop her. 'Let's think this through again.' He rubbed the back of his neck. 'We can't steer and we can't bring ourselves to a full stop. But we control the temperature in the bags. If we could get close enough to the ground, we can use the cranes to drop one of the bigger buggies, full of supplies, onto the sand.' He looked at Patrice. 'Could the suspension take it?'

Patrice cocked his head. 'Maybe I could rig it. But there's a better way.'

'Which is?' asked Ezra.

'Drop the rear docking ramp. Let it drag along near the

ground and drive the crawler off the back. It has better suspension, and it's five times the size of a buggy and can carry a mountain of stuff.'

'Yeah,' said Ezra, smiling. 'Yeah, that could work.'

Claudia shook her head. 'No, no, no. Dragging the ramp will push the nose into the ground.'

'Okay, so don't drag it. Keep it ten metres above the ground and jump the crawler off the back,' said Patrice.

'Yeah,' said Ezra, 'and if it dips, increase the temperature in the forward bags to keep the nose up.'

Claudia couldn't believe this nonsense. She swung her arm around the bridge. 'Half our controls are destroyed. We'll need two people to control the ballast and the heaters manually, and another to operate the ramp. Who's going with Charles?'

'I can drive the crawler,' said Zach. 'I'll go on my—'

'You can't drive the crawler, and you are not going on your own.'

Zach set his jaw. 'I am if I have to.'

Claudia set her jaw. 'It's not gonna happen.'

'Okay, I'll lower the ramp and jump in with him,' said Ezra, trying to sound reasonable.

Claudia stared at her ex-husband for a few moments, before walking towards the door. 'Could I talk to you in private?'

Ezra raised his eyebrows at Zach as if to say *This oughta be good*, and followed Claudia from the bridge. The door slammed shut and almost immediately came the sound of raised voices. The argument went on for some time, so

Zach and Patrice busied themselves running diagnostics on the heating elements, studiously avoiding each other's embarrassed glances.

When Zach's parents returned, they were stiff and red-faced.

'Easy,' said Ezra, clapping his hands together. 'It's all settled.'

The sand crawler looked like a large turretless tank, albeit three times bigger. A tracked vehicle, weighing in at fifty-five tonnes, it had a capacious driver's cabin, a tiny living space and an enclosed storage compartment capable of transporting large amounts of fuel, supplies, engine components and even a few buggies. Designed for carrying mining ore in the early days of Martian exploration, it was airtight and could even travel for short distances underwater. The suspension consisted of eight sets of independently mounted springs, as tall as a man and twice as wide. It was also extremely robust, which it would need to be if Zach was going to drive it off the back of a moving airship onto the dunes of the Tallus Basin.

'That's it,' said Patrice, stacking a box of water canisters on top of a crate. He looked around the storage compartment of the crawler. 'There's enough food, water, oxygen, guns, ammo and explosives to fight a small war.'

Zach dropped the box he was carrying and slid it against the wall. 'Hopefully it doesn't come to that.'

Patrice nodded. 'Well, I'll go tell your mum you're ready.' He jumped out the back door of the crawler onto the floor of the bay and made his way to the stairs.

'Patrice,' Zach called out after him, 'in case something happens . . . thanks for, you know, everything.'

Patrice turned around and raised an eyebrow. 'Not getting sentimental on me, are you?'

'I would never do that,' mumbled Zach.

Patrice grinned, mock-saluted and turned back to the stairs. 'See you in the City of the Dead!'

Zach went to find his father. He was in the driver's seat, fiddling with the controls of the crawler. 'Dad, it's all in.'

'Good,' Ezra replied, 'we're ready here too.' He flipped a switch. A gauge climbed up from red, to orange, to yellow and levelled off at the three-quarters mark in a pleasant shade of green. 'Power levels are good.' He flipped another switch and the motors came alive, a deep hum permeating the cab. Ezra got out of the seat. 'Sit down and get a feel for it.'

Zach took his place and curled his hands around the twin sticks that controlled the tracks. He could feel the vibration of the vehicle through the handles.

'Remember,' said Ezra, 'when I say go, push 'em both forward hard and don't stop for anything. You'll need to pick up a bit of speed on the ramp so you don't nosedive into the ground. To help, I'm going to keep the ramp horizontal for as long as I can.'

'Okay. Um, how did you convince Mum to let me go on my own?'

'I convinced her that of all the stupid things you would certainly try, this was the least stupid.'

'Thanks, Dad. I think.'

Ezra clapped his son on the back. 'All this adventure reminds me of the good old days!'

Zach frowned. 'Sorry about getting you in trouble with Mum.'

'Nah, don't worry about it. I'm used to it. She's been angry at me for twenty years.' Ezra flipped a few more switches on and off and twiddled several dials.

Zach glanced at him sideways. This probably wasn't the best time for this kind of conversation, but when was it ever? 'Why did you and Mum break up, exactly? She never told me.'

Ezra rubbed his jaw. 'Wow, there's a story for the ages, full of heartache, failure, betrayal and generous amounts of drugs and alcohol – not all of it imbibed by me, I hasten to add.' Ezra eased himself into the co-driver's seat and took a deep breath. 'But the truth is, there's no *exactly* to it. Relationships are complicated, and sometimes they just come apart at the seams under the weight of all the crap you have to deal with in this world. And boy, did we deal with a lot.'

'Do you still love her?'

'Hell, yeah.'

Confused, Zach shook his head. 'But if you still love her . . .?'

'Zach, I hope you never discover this for yourself. But love doesn't always last forever. And even if it does, it doesn't mean you can bear to stay together forever. All you can do is enjoy it while you can. And when it's gone, try to remember the good times and not become bitter dwelling on the bad.'

'Do you think Mum's bitter?'

'Maybe a bit. I can be a dick.'

Zach gripped the sticks for the tracks more tightly. The vibration seemed to pass through him and into his bones. He tested the brakes, checked the power levels, switched the headlights on and off and then, finally satisfied that everything was ready – everything except himself, of course – sat back in his seat and sighed. 'I don't understand.'

Ezra gave a rueful smile. 'Hope that you never do.'

They sat together in silence for a while, staring out the windshield at the inside surface of the bay ramp, each lost in their own thoughts. Then Ezra perked up and leaned over, talking quietly, almost conspiratorially, 'Now, tell me about this girlfriend of yours.'

Zach felt his face and neck flush with heat. 'Well, she's not really my girlfriend. In fact, I don't even know if she likes me.'

Ezra snorted in mock derision. 'How could she not like you? Look at that jaw!'

'Dad, I'm serious.'

'Okay, in deadly earnest, tell me about her. Your mum tells me she's pretty fiery.'

'She did almost shoot me a couple of times.'

'Intense.'

'And she kind of tortured me for a bit.'

'Passionate too.'

'And I think she might be a Martian.'

'Intriguing.' Ezra rubbed the stubble on his chin.

Zach studied his father's face, not sure if he was being sarcastic. It was always hard to tell. But behind the smile and the banter and the twinkling grey eyes, Zach thought he could see, maybe for the first time, a sadness. It was a strange thing to see your father sad. It made him appear vulnerable, and Zach wasn't sure he wanted his father to be vulnerable.

Ezra seemed to sense the shift in Zach's perception of him and looked a little chastened. He dropped the banter.

'So, you like her?' he asked.

'Yeah, Dad, I really do.'

With a surprising amount of vigour for an oldish man, Ezra leapt out of his seat. 'Then let's go get her!'

The rear bay ramp was part of the underside of the airship. Supported by two thick hydraulic struts, one on either side, it swivelled down to rest on the tarmac when the airship was in dock. Claudia and Patrice had brought the belly of the airship down to within fifty metres of the ground. That was still too high – the crawler's suspension was good, but not *that* good. The problem was that the ground in this part of the Tallus Basin wasn't flat, but undulated like a rough sea with a ten-metre swell. In theory, the closest they could get would be the peak of the highest wave of sand, but they didn't have such fine control over the buoyancy. Ten metres above the peaks was the best they could do. Zach and the crawler would have to handle a ten-to twenty-metre fall, basically depending on luck.

Claudia's voice came over the radio in the cabin: *We're bringing it down to ten. Get into position.*

'Check that,' said Ezra. He turned to Zach, his face uncharacteristically serious. 'Remember, you want to hit the ground running.'

Ezra left without saying goodbye. Zach watched him climb down the cabin ladder to the floor and make his way to the control box. He flipped it open and turned around to give Zach an okay sign, and a second later his voice crackled in the cabin: *Claude, we're good.*

Okay . . . twenty . . . fifteen . . . we're almost there, lower the ramp.

Ezra hit the big green button in the control box and flashing red lights came on above the bay. A moment later, the ramp separated from the frame of the airship and swung outwards. The bay flooded with daylight. Zach turned the power up to max, gripped the sticks and braced himself with his feet on the floor and his back jammed into the seat rest.

The ramp got stuck halfway down. The cylinder containing the piston of the right-hand strut was bent inwards. As the piston neared the bend, it slowed, groaned and shuddered to a halt. But the left-hand strut was undamaged and continued to descend. The ramp canted to the left and began to buckle. The squeal of tortured metal even penetrated the soundproofed cabin.

Zach looked at his father. Ezra's left hand was in the air, his face buried in the control box. The fingers curled into what looked like a thumbs-up sign. Zach thought this was the signal to go and rammed the sticks forward. The crawler took off with surprising speed and hit the ramp even before the left-hand side had fully extended.

No. Wait! his father's voice erupted over the speaker.

Zach realised his mistake. Too late – he was committed.

The weight of the crawler on the ramp forced the damaged piston past the bend, rupturing the holding cylinder as it went. Thick hydraulic fluid spewed out, and the ramp ripped free from the strut. As the right-hand side fell, the crawler careened sideways. Zach worked the sticks, trying to straighten up, but the tracks slipped in the fluid. The crawler hurtled towards the end of the ramp, still picking up speed. The only thing in front of Zach now was blue sky.

The right-hand dropped down quickly, and for a second, the single left-hand strut held it level, before the weight of the crawler tore the strut from its mount. Zach entered freefall as the floor dropped out from beneath him, and the crawler plummeted towards the sand. He watched a discarded pencil and a piece of chewing gum, furry with fluff, drift off the dashboard and float aimlessly around the cabin.

The crawler landed with a bone-jarring thud that bottomed out the suspension and rammed Zach so hard into his seat that the cushion springs stabbed his backside. The suspension expanded again and the sand crawler, all fifty-five tonnes of it, bounced back into the air, smashing Zach's head into the roof. And when it hit the ground again, his nose smacked the dashboard.

The crawler had landed on the downward slope of a dune. Zach's brain, fuzzy from the battering, idly wondered why the ground was racing by so fast. Belatedly, he realised he still had the sticks pushed fully forward. He eased back, spinning and slipping in the sand before coming to a rest at the bottom of the slope.

The radio exploded with static, a confused mashup of voices, most of it swearing. It cleared, and Zach made out his mother's gruff tone: *Zach answer me, goddammit. Are you okay?*

'Yes, yes, I'm okay. I'm okay.' Zach let his breath out in a whoosh. 'What a ride.'

Stupid fucking idea! This didn't seem to be directed at him.

Zach couldn't make out the words, but he could hear Patrice in the background trying to defend himself. Once again, the radio descended into a confused crackle. Zach got out of his seat and opened the roof of the cabin. The airship was already a couple of kilometres away. The ramp hung down limply behind it, like a pocket torn from a pair of jeans. It might have been his imagination, but Zach thought he could make out the tiny figure of his father waving to him from the side of the open bay.

Ten hours later, Zach rendezvoused with the hovercraft on the narrow ridge of a line of dunes. As the sun set in a haze of yellow, pink and purple, he climbed down from the cabin and rubbed his aching neck and shoulders.

Driving the massive crawler was like wrestling a large animal, and he had driven it nonstop.

A dark-haired girl was sitting on the hovercraft's ramp painting her toenails bright red. Little tufts of cotton separated her toes. 'You're late,' she said, without looking up.

'Um, and you are . . .?'

'Zach!' Sophie bounded down the ramp and jumped into his arms. He spun her around and pointed at the sand crawler. 'I've brought guns. Lots of guns.'

'Ship will be so happy!' said Sophie.

Toby appeared at the top of the ramp and waved. 'Hi, Zach.'

'Hey, Toby. We got the map?'

Toby looked embarrassed. 'Well, yeah, mostly. And we've found the entrance to the caverns. Too big for Ship, but the crawler might fit. I don't want to walk again. Not with giant snaked-headed gods wandering around.'

'So, the map is accurate?' asked Zach.

Sophie and Toby exchanged looks. 'It's accurate,' replied Toby, 'but there's a slight problem reading it.'

'Which is?'

They both glanced at the new girl. Zach followed their gaze.

The girl looked up from under long, possibly fake, lashes. 'That would be me.'

Toby introduced Sierra and explained their escapade in Port Clarke, with many an interjection from Sophie and the occasional raised eyebrow from a bored Sierra. When he got to the end, he looked a little chastened and then shrugged. 'Sierra's kinda like our partner now. Unless of course, we, well, you know.'

'Know what?' asked Zach.

Toby half covered his mouth. 'Strap her into the chair.'

Sierra glanced sharply at Toby. 'What's that?'

'No, no, no,' replied Zach definitively. 'There'll be no more strapping into the chair.' He turned to Sierra. 'What are you hoping to get out of this?'

'Gold, obviously. If I can't sell the map . . .'

Zach sighed and rubbed his temples – he was too tired to argue. 'So, we hold this phone in front of your face and you tell us which way to go?'

'Naah,' said Sophie, 'we can give her the phone. Ship can block any message she tries to send.'

'And intercept it, so then we would have the map ourselves,' added Toby. 'But she can't unlock the phone and give it to *us*, because we could just email the map to Ship.'

Sierra lifted a leg and wriggled five glossy red toes in Zach's face. 'And then you wouldn't need me.'

Chapter Six

Lost in Time

Somewhere out there in the dark, someone was crying – a gentle sobbing that drifted over the rooftops on a breeze. Holly sat up and looked out of the window. The peaked roofs were blurry and swam before her. She realised she had tears in her eyes. She was the one crying.

There was movement on the bed beside her. A shape unfurled and became the Princess – her new friend.

'What are you crying about?' the Princess asked.

'Where is my mother?'

'I told you she is coming.'

'You said that three days ago.'

'Maybe she's running late?' At Holly's scowl, the Princess added hastily, 'Look. I will send Captain Alarik to find her. To bring her here at once.'

'Do you promise?'

'Of course I promise. I am the Princess.'

A trifle reassured, Holly lay down again and rested her head on the pillow. The Princess lay beside her and stroked her cheek.

'What do you think it will be like on the other side?' asked

Holly.

The Princess shuddered and withdrew her hand. 'I don't want to talk about it.'

An explosion outside rattled the room, and a flare of light lit up the window frame. There were loud cries and screams. Fearful, the girls crawled over to the window. Several blocks away, orange flames licked the walls of buildings, and long shadows flickered down the streets and over the rooftops.

There was an urgent pounding on the door. A man burst in, his burly shape silhouetted in the doorway.

'Come with me now,' the man said.

'Captain, what's wrong?' asked the Princess.

'There is strife at the palace gates. Quickly!'

Clutching each other, the girls got up and followed the captain out of the room, still wearing their nightgowns.

A carriage was waiting for them in the courtyard. The captain held the door; Holly stepped inside, but the Princess held back.

'Where are we going?' she asked.

The captain glanced in the direction of the commotion. There were several loud bangs and the harsh clang of steel on steel.

'It has begun. We travel to the Well.'

The Princess shrank back and shook her head. 'No, no . . .'

The captain had his orders. He picked the Princess up and carried her to the door. She kicked and screamed and hit him. The captain threw her into the carriage besides Holly and slammed the door shut. Immediately, the carriage took off, the driver whipping the horses to a full gallop. The captain leapt onto his own horse and followed.

The buildings of the city passed by the window in a blur. Some of them were on fire. People were roaming the streets, many of them armed. Later, came dying groves of phagus, jape and bellegarde. Once outside the city, they passed through a moonless landscape of low, rolling hills that melted away towards the horizon to fuse seamlessly with the sky.

Holly stared out of the window, her mind drained of thought and feeling, her body rocking to the motion of the carriage. It lulled her into a kind of waking dream. She was gone from the world; the only thing that existed was the drab view. She glanced at the seat next to her. The Princess had curled up in a foetal position, shaking and mumbling a prayer over and over under her breath.

When Holly woke, it was morning. The carriage had stopped, and the Princess was gone. Outside, the hills had been replaced by a single large outcrop of rock, standing alone in the middle of a plain of sand and pebbles. She craned her neck to see the front of the carriage. The horses and the driver were gone too.

Cautiously, Holly stepped out of the carriage and closed the door. Her palm came away with streaks of blood. A noise from behind her drew her attention, and she turned, expecting to see the captain.

Along the sand, his sandals crunching on the pebbles, came a very tall man wearing a robe. He stopped in front of her and looked her up and down. He seemed puzzled at first but shook his head and pursed his mouth in determination.

Taking her by the arm, he led her to a cleft in the rock

face, which widened into a narrow canyon. The man's grip was tight and his fingers bony, and they pinched Holly's skin, but she was too scared and awed to pull away.

The natural canyon transformed and became a wide hall carved into the rock. The walls curved up to meet overhead in a complex vaulted ceiling, while narrow windows on either side threw sheets of slanted light across the floor. There was no one else around, and their sandals crisply slapped the floor in the hollow space.

They entered a great domed-shaped cathedral, with a beautiful shimmering pool at its centre, tiled in stones of green and blue. Around the pool and encircling the walls were statues of the gods of the Martian pantheon: Ankasha, god of water and health; Zaptre, fierce lord of fire and war; Pakhet, goddess of pilgrims — and, standing over all of them, Zanaster, god of the soul. These were the gods that ruled all fate on Mars, including her own, and Holly feared and loved them in equal measure.

They approached a dais at the end of the shimmering pool. A group of men in purple robes stood silently around a stone sarcophagus sculpted with arcane symbols. Tubes extended from the stone into vials of unctuous fluids, which burbled as if alive. A man wearing a cowl came forward and took her hand. His palm was hot and sweaty. He gave her something gooey to drink from a crystal cup, and she drank it without question, but when he led her to a set of steps by the side of the sarcophagus, she became frightened. Holly held back and planted her feet. Suddenly, the men were all around her, urging her forward. She wanted to run, but her legs didn't *work properly. They were loose and wobbled like string. The men grabbed her and lifted her up and carried her towards the coffin.*

Holly woke and propped herself up on one elbow. She was cold and her hip was sore from lying on the stone floor. She sat up and rubbed her arms, trying to get warm, and noticed that her skin had taken on a distinctly greenish hue.

She remembered her dream clearly this time – or was it a memory? It didn't matter; dream or memory, it carried its own conviction. She was no princess, only a lost girl dwarfed by momentous events. She ran her tongue around the inside of her mouth, trying to clear a bitter taste.

The captain was still standing by the door, exactly as he had been before Holly had fallen asleep, with one hand on the hilt of his sword and the other behind his back. It was the entrance to the Queen's chambers. They had climbed the steps of the tower, finding nothing but locked doors and sealed windows, and arrived at the topmost apartment. The captain had knocked politely several times, and Holly had beaten it with her fists several more, but there was no response. Tired, Holly had lain down and gone to sleep, thinking the Queen would have to emerge sometime – if only to eat.

'Your soldiers abducted me,' she now said to the captain.

'They found you by the side of the road,' he replied without looking at her. 'They thought you were an orphan. There were many orphans in those days.'

'I must have told them I had a mother.'

The captain shrugged.

'Why was I brought to the palace?'

'The Princess was scared and lonely. She wanted a friend.'

Holly responded angrily, 'So they kidnapped a little girl?'

The captain had the grace to look guilty, but he ignored the question. He looked down the hallway at a painting on the far wall. The lines had faded to spots, and the colours had desaturated to a mess of muddy yellows and browns, but you could still make out the shapes of buildings, gardens, markets and people. It was a tapestry of life long ago.

'I saw her once playing on her own in the palace gardens,' he said. 'She propped her dolls up against a tree and served them milk and biscuits, talking to them as if they were her closest friends. Which I suppose they were. In that time, the court had disbanded, fleeing to whatever sanctuary their money could buy. And she wasn't allowed outside the palace. The streets were awash in violence.'

'I get it,' said Holly, tears stinging her eyes. 'She would never grow up to have a life. Her destiny was to be the key. To be put to sleep and probably never wake up. So, we were swapped around. She got a life and they put me to sleep instead.' Holly's voice sounded more whiney than she liked. 'But why *me?*

The captain shrugged again. 'You were there.'

Holly got to her feet, still trembling from the cold and a tsunami of feelings. *So,* she thought, *pure dumb luck.*

That's how my destiny was decided.

'Did they search for my mother?'

'I don't know.'

'Was there a canal nearby? Where they found me?'

'There are – were – canals all over Mars.'

Holly whacked him in the chest, hurting her hand on the metal of the breastplate. 'Think! You owe me that much. I have a memory of my mother teaching me to swim. Was that real?'

The captain looked away.

Holly beat his chest, hitting him over and over, each blow a sharp sting of pain. She was crying now too – sobbing, really, her face a sopping rag, her nose dripping. She went on hitting him until her hands became numb.

After Holly cried herself out, she wiped the captain's wet breastplate with the sleeve of her jacket. 'Sorry,' she said, suddenly embarrassed. 'Lucky it's metal.'

The captain shook his head. 'It is of no consequence.'

'What is this wailing?'

'Your Majesty!' The captain turned smartly on his heel and knelt on one knee.

A middle-aged woman in a dressing gown stood in the open doorway, one knobbly hand clutching the front of her gown and the other leaning against the door frame. But this was not the haughty and stern Queen of Holly's dreams, (or memories, or whatever the hell they were). This woman's face was lined and drawn, and she was thin, almost emaciated, the gown draping loosely over her like a sheet. Her silver-grey hair was unkempt and bunched up on one side as if she had slept on it when it was still wet. She looked tired and old and depressed, and when she saw Holly, her mouth drooped.

'Oh, it's you,' the Queen said. She disappeared back inside, leaving the door ajar.

Holly looked to the captain for guidance, but he was still on one knee staring at his boots. Annoyed, she slapped his armoured shoulder and entered the Queen's apartment.

The room held just a few chairs, a four-poster bed, a vanity and a writing desk. The Queen had retreated to a chair beside the only window.

Holly was unsure what to do next. What was expected of her, exactly? She stared at the back of the Queen's head.

'Well, it worked,' Holly said at last. 'But you should know, a few things have changed. There have been some new arrivals. From another planet. Not all the changes they've brought have been positive. In general, though . . .' Holly trailed off.

The Queen continued to look out the window.

'The thing is, I've been to one of the domes,' Holly went on. 'Your people have woken up, but no one knows how to get out of here.'

The Queen shifted uncomfortably in her chair but didn't respond.

Holly approached and reached out an arm. 'Your . . . Majesty . . . the people in the city are waiting for you to lead them. 'Your Majesty?'

The Queen turned abruptly, fixing Holly with a cold stare. 'Why are you here?'

'To tell you that . . . to ask you how—'

'Why are *you* here?'

Holly glanced at the captain, who was standing, useless as usual, just inside the doorway.

'There was a mix-up,' said Holly.

'A mix-up? A mix-up!' The Queen spat on the floor at Holly's feet. 'It was supposed to be *her*. Her! Not you!' The Queen got out of the chair and lurched towards her. Holly backed away.

The woman lifted her arm to strike. 'Get out! Get out! Get out!' she screamed.

'But Your Majesty –'

'*Get out!*'

Holly felt the captain's hands on her shoulders. He pulled her away and out the door, closing it quickly behind them.

Angry and shaken, Holly stood awhile in the passageway, trying to compose herself. The captain was pacing up and down. He looked up at her from under bushy eyebrows and said, 'Come with me.'

Holly followed him back down the spiral steps to the foot of the tower, and out into a graveyard of inscribed monoliths and headstones. Lamps were scattered throughout the yard, their light casting inky black shadows. In one corner was a mausoleum, its entrance marked by a plinth of stone supporting twin statues of Zanaster. Inside the mausoleum, a recess in the far wall contained a single coffin.

It seemed to Holly the temperature fell another five

degrees as she entered the gloomy space. The walls dripped with oily moisture and the air was musty with decay. There was just enough light from outside to illuminate the symbol on the lid of the coffin: the seal of the Royal Princess.

Holly ran her hand over the seal. 'I take it the Queen has seen this,' she said.

The captain came up beside her. 'Her pod is in the chamber below. It would have been the first thing she saw.'

'What happened to the King?' asked Holly.

'He killed himself. Many years before the end of times.'

'So the Queen has lost everything.'

The captain's voice was thick. 'Yes.'

Holly looked at him in the dark. The light from the entrance struck him at a sharp angle and cast a hawk-like shadow against the wall. 'You were complicit weren't you, Captain Alarik?'

He nodded once. 'To my shame, yes.'

'You left me there for the priests and took the Princess.'

'She was a spoilt brat, but I felt for her.'

Who felt for me? Holly wondered. 'I remember blood on the handle.'

'I tried to explain what I intended, but she was beside herself with fright and scratched my face.'

'Where did you take her?'

'To a family I knew in a small village. When the Queen was put to sleep, thinking that her daughter had gone before her, I brought her back. There were still some servants in the palace. Soon after, I went into hibernation too.'

'Why did you do it? I understand you pitied the Princess, but . . .'

'I thought we were all going to die. What, then, did it matter?'

'And what became of her?'

The captain looked at the coffin. 'She lived out her years, I suppose.'

Holly put her hand on the lid. It felt like a block of ice. 'No wonder the Queen hates me.'

'Enough of this,' said the captain. He strode to the entrance and looked up at the roof of the cavern that hung like a black void above the city. 'We have more immediate concerns.'

Holly snorted. 'Who's *we*?'

He turned and faced her, his bronze eyes shining. 'I cannot leave the Queen's side for long. My duty binds me. *You* need to find a way out of here. And you know something about the world outside. You must help them.'

'Me? I am not their Princess.'

'What does it matter anymore? You are the key. They will look to you.'

The bitter taste was in Holly's mouth again. 'I find myself surprisingly unsympathetic. I was taken against my will across millennia!' She pointed at the coffin. 'There's your key!'

'The Queen's daughter is lost to time. The Queen too may be lost. Her mind is . . . not what it once was.'

'And what about my mother? Did she try to find me?

Did she care? Did anyone care?'

Holly had the sour pleasure of seeing Alarik wince, yet as soon as she spoke, she realised that someone *did* care. The professor had raised her as his own. He had taught her to read and write, to ride a bike and drive a boat. He had told her the names of the stars and the planets. And when she was threatened, he had tried to protect her with his life. She might never know what was real about the past – whether the swimming lessons were dreams or memories or fantasies – but the professor was real, and she had abandoned him to the clutches of pirates. Holly flushed with shame.

And yet. And yet. She couldn't let go of it. Half her life – half of her – was missing. It was a sickness of emptiness that she felt deep in her chest and that ached a little every time she drew breath. She wanted the professor to be her father – she had no memories, not even dreams, of any other – but he had lied about her mother, and in doing so had broken her most treasured possession. She would need more time to forgive him. *Time*: everything, it seemed, came down to it.

In silence, the captain and Holly walked back to the dome. They entered the building and stood on the balcony. Below, the group of Martians had swollen with newly awoken arrivals. They were wrapped in blankets and brought hot bowls of broth to drink. A hush passed over the group as they realised Holly had returned. They looked up at her with hope.

Holly turned to the captain. 'I have one condition.'

Chapter Seven

The Subterranean Depths

The entrance to the caverns was at the end of a narrow valley. Unlike the first entrance, this opening was clearly natural: a stream ran down the valley floor and disappeared inside, burbling noisily over a bed of rounded stones.

They had to leave the hovercraft behind again, its wings too wide to squeeze through, and instead they all piled into the crawler. Once again, Ship, plugged into the console, took the driver's seat – at the unbending insistence of both Sophie and Sierra.

After several hundred metres the cave opened up, and the crawler followed the stream into caverns filled with stalagmites and dripping stalactites. At irregular intervals, the walls receded, and the cave became a cathedral of rock, where vast columns supported a roof of glowing crystals, and the stream cascaded down broad sheets of flowstones. Twice the vehicle was forced to smash its way through spiky forests of stalagmites, grinding them under the weight of its treads with a crystalline crunch. Every surface glistened with moisture and when Sophie opened a window, the air gave off a mildly acidic tang.

But the journey was tortuously slow. Ship had to navigate the crawler's way carefully on the uneven ground and was forever detouring around stalagmites too big to break.

After hours of travel, everyone was bored, irritable and stressed out, and so when Toby suggested they stop for the night, they all agreed in relief. Ship switched the headlamps off to conserve energy and immediately the crawler plunged into a black so total the windows became perfect black mirrors. Only later, when their eyes adjusted, could they make out a milky way of blue stars above them, created by phosphorescent algae that grew on the cave's ceiling.

'Flush.'

'You're kidding me,' said Zach.

'That beats your measly two pairs. I win again.' Sierra started to sweep up her chips (actually almonds). The gang, now with added Sierra, were playing cards in the sleeping compartment, using a crate for a table.

'Hold your horses,' said Toby. He brought his cards close to his chest and peeked at them.

Sierra rolled her eyes. 'Just show 'em. Your cards aren't gonna get any better by looking at them.'

Toby looked like he was about to question the logic of this but changed his mind. Theatrically, he placed his cards on the table one by one. 'Ten, nine, eight, seven, six.' His face cracked into a wide grin. 'Straight.'

Sierra slapped her forehead. 'That doesn't beat a flush, you idiot.'

Toby's grin faltered. 'Yes, it does . . . doesn't it?'

'Ship?' Sophie called out.

'The probability of getting a straight is zero point seven six per cent. The probability of getting a flush is zero point three six seven per cent, thus making it the rarer hand and higher in the rankings.'

Toby was crestfallen. He had staked a lot of almonds on this hand. He looked at his shrinking resources: only two almonds left.

'I think you'd better quit while you are extremely far behind.' Sierra raked in her winnings and started counting her chips. She had by far the biggest pile.

Toby looked around at the others. 'Guys? One more hand?'

Sophie yawned and ate one of her almonds, immediately making her a thousand dollars poorer at current rates of exchange. Zach was staring at one of the black windows, preoccupied with thoughts of Holly.

'Guys?' Toby repeated desperately.

'They know when to quit, bozo.'

Toby stuck his chin out. 'Well, I know something that you don't know.'

Sierra mockingly raised her eyebrows, waiting for enlightenment.

'I know,' continued Toby, 'that we haven't had to refer to the map at all since entering the cave. There's only been one direction to travel: follow the stream. We don't need you anymore.'

Sierra paused in her recount. Sophie sniggered. Zach

was only half-listening but caught enough; thoughtfully, he rubbed his jaw. 'Huh. Toby's right.'

Sierra looked genuinely hurt, and Zach regretted his comment. With slow deliberation, Sierra put her chips down on the table. 'So, it's come to this?' she said darkly, glancing at each of them. 'Murder.'

'Oh, come on . . .'

'Nothing's going to happen . . .'

'No one said anything about . . .'

'Holy flip, there's something out there!'

Sophie was staring saucer-eyed at something behind Zach. Everyone turned to look. A large yellow eye the size of a baseball was staring at them through the window. The pupil, a black vertical slit, darted from side to side, focused on the occupants, contracted to a razor-sharp edge, and for several breathless moments, studied them. Then it vanished, and the window returned to perfect black. Once again, the gang saw their reflections in the dark pane, staring back at them with mouths opened in fright.

'Fuck!' Sierra jumped out of her seat, knocking her almonds to the floor. 'What was that?'

'Ship?' squeaked Sophie.

'A large object is moving slowly around the hull of the sand crawler,' replied Ship in its preternaturally calm voice.

Sierra jumped up and down on the tips of her toes. 'Large . . . large object? What does that mean?'

'Ship, do you have lights on the side of the crawler?' asked Zach.

'No, the forward headlamps swivel fifteen degrees in

all directions, but not enough to illuminate the ground
to either side.'

'Switch them on anyway, please, Ship.'

Zach took one step through the doorway into the
cab as the headlamps came on in a burst. The ground in
front of the crawler lit up, throwing two large overlapping
cones of light out into the blackness. A forest of glistening
stalagmites extended as far as the lamps could penetrate.
Nothing moved except motes of dust stirred up by . . .

'The dust has been stirred up by something,' said Toby
in an ominous voice.

Sharp fingernails dug into Zach's shoulders. Sierra, her
voice pitched at levels approaching hysteria, spoke into
his ear. 'What do you think it is?'

'Maybe it's a cave troll?' said Sophie.

'A what?' said Toby.

'Do we have those?' whispered Sierra.

'Who knows what weirdo creatures live in the subterranean depths?' shrugged Sophie.

'It's not a cave troll,' said Zach firmly. He extracted Sierra's fingernails from his skin. 'And no, we don't have those.'

'Maybe someone should go out and look around?' said
Toby.

'Are you insane?' spluttered Sierra. 'Have you never
watched a film, like, ever?'

'I was going to suggest you,' he muttered.

'Ship, where is it now?' asked Sophie.

'I can no longer detect vibrations in the hull or on the
ground around the crawler. It appears to have moved

away.'

'See, nothing to worry about,' said Zach.

'But what if it comes back?' cried Sierra.

'Ship will let us know, and anyway,' he tapped the hull, 'it's not getting through two centimetres of carbon steel. Look, it's been a long day. Let's get some rest and we'll push on tomorrow.'

'I'm too spooked to sleep,' said Sierra.

Zach smiled encouragingly. 'I know. I'm spooked too. Look, if it helps, I'll grab a gun and sleep in the cab.'

Sierra nodded enthusiastically. 'Yeah, yeah, that's good. That's good. Close the door behind you too.'

Zach had to bite back a caustic remark. 'Okay, it's settled. Try to get some sleep.'

With nervous glances towards the window, Toby, Sophie and Sierra retired to their bunks, while Zach grabbed a blanket and tried to get comfortable in the driver's seat.

Breakfast was a dismal affair. Their sleep had been disturbed by several return visits by the 'cave troll', as everyone except Zach now insisted on calling it. The troll had 'slithered' – another Sophie word – around the crawler, thumping on the hull, apparently looking for a way in, but never once did they manage to get a look at it. The constant tension kept the crew on a knife's edge and by morning everyone was fried.

After breakfast, the journey continued. Ship navigated around deep pools of crystal-clear water and fissures in the cave floor large enough to swallow the crawler whole.

Water trickled from every surface or fell from the roof in an endless fan of light rain. The crawler's radar and sonar provided Ship with a complex 3D map of its surroundings, but to Zach, Sierra, Toby and Sophie, all squeezed into the cab, this underworld mostly passed by unseen – all they could see were the headlamps lighting up the droplets in front of them.

It wasn't until just before lunch that they noticed a subtle change in the cavern. The walls and floor became smoother, and the overall shape of the cave was more circular in profile. An hour later, it was obvious the cave had become a tunnel. The stream still ran beneath the crawler's tracks, but it now flowed freely, like a drain.

'We must be getting close,' said Toby.

Everybody jumped – no one had spoken in a while. Zach looked at the wavy lines on the monitor. 'Ship?'

'Triangulating from the readings I took when we were in the arena, I believe we are directly underneath the City, although facing in the opposite direction to the arena portal.'

'We've come in from the other side?' asked Sophie.

'Yes,' confirmed Ship.

The tunnel ended, and the crawler drove out onto the floor of a vast plain. The stream flowed on to connect with other streams running out of other tunnels and together they pooled in a lake in the centre. Emerging from the lake was a glowing blue dome the size of a football stadium, giving off enough light to illuminate the entire cavern in a sickly twilight. Root-like tendrils snaked up and over the dome to meet in a twisted column of rock at the top before continuing into the air to fuse with the roof of the cavern.

'Is that the City?' asked Sierra.

'No,' said Zach, 'it's too small, for a start.'

'And it is giving off a small amount of energy. It may have once been a power source,' said Ship. 'Note how one of the twisted strands above the structure is blue and disappears into the roof.'

'Like a power cord,' mused Zach. 'I wonder if we're directly under the city here.'

'Look there,' said Sophie. She pointed at a trail, punctuated by steep steps, that spiralled around the wall of the cavern and disappeared into a hole in the roof.

'That's gotta be the way in,' said Zach.

'It looks like boulders have rolled down to the bottom of the trail,' said Sierra.

Toby squinted at the rounded shapes. 'Nah, more stone people. Just statues. We think.'

'Ugh,' said Sierra. 'We have to walk up all those steps? I was expecting to drive.'

Zach held up his hand. '*We* are not going anywhere. I will go up alone and get Holly and bring her back.'

'No way!' protested Sophie.

'That's how it's gonna be,' said Zach firmly. 'Sophie, what are you like with a gun?'

Sophie pouted. 'I can learn.'

Zach nodded. 'I thought so.'

'But we're a crew,' said Toby. 'We stick together.'

'We are. You guys wait here *together* and watch my back

for the . . . you know what. I'll arm myself to the teeth and get Holly and then *together* we're getting the hell out of here.'

Sophie opened her mouth to protest further, but Sierra got in first.

'Whoa, whoa, whoa,' she said, sweeping her hands across the view. 'I'm not seeing any gold in my vicinity.'

Zach sighed. 'Well then, you can come with me and steal some trinkets. Just watch out for the cave trolls and the gigantic snake-headed thing.'

The crew watched in fascination as Sierra's face rapidly cycled through a variety of different emotions: fear, greed, desperation and sheer perversity. It landed somewhere between greed and desperation. She puffed herself up. 'Gimme a gun.'

Four hours later, Sierra sat down on a rock and complained about her blisters. 'God, this is worse than Sebastian's step class at the gym. We've been walking uphill all day. If I get muscly thighs out of this, I'm suing.'

Zach turned around and watched her pull her socks off. 'We can't stop here,' he said. 'What if something comes by?'

Sierra smelt a sock and recoiled in distaste. 'It can eat me.'

Shoulders sagging, Zach walked back down to her. Privately, he was glad of the excuse to rest, but he wasn't about to tell Sierra that. They were maybe a kilometre above the floor and a hundred and eighty degrees around the edge of the cavern from where they had left the crawler.

He had argued with Sophie for an hour about her coming with them. She only relented after Sierra promised to teach her how to use a gun when they got back. That settled, Zach and Sierra packed some gear and set out. They followed the trail as it zigzagged up the wall of the cavern in a series of dizzying climbs that left them both gasping – from both the exertion and the fear of falling off the edge.

Zach wiped his sweaty brow. Despite the chill, the humidity was stifling. 'We should keep going,' he said.

Tenderly, Sierra explored the blisters on the soles of her feet and groaned.

'Alright, maybe a brief rest won't hurt,' Zach said, taking the backpack off and sitting down. Besides the pack, he was carrying a rifle and had a handgun and knife strapped to his belt. He took a slug of water from his bottle and glanced at Sierra. She had rested her own handgun on top of the rock, checking that the safety was on first.

'How do you know about guns?' he asked.

'My dad's in the business, so to speak,' said Sierra. 'Do you have something in there for blisters?'

'Actually, I probably do. Toby did the packing.' Zach rummaged around in the pack and brought out a first-aid kit. He handed it to Sierra. 'A pirate?'

She nodded.

'Such a small world.'

'Yeah, that's the problem. Try having your mum as mayor of the only city on Mars.'

'Doesn't sound that bad. My mum raids tombs for a

living.'

Sierra winced as she cleaned her wounds. 'Yeah, but she doesn't do it in the public eye.'

'Speaking of the public eye, where does your mum think you are right now?'

'Volleyball camp.'

'Huh.' Zach smiled. He watched her spray her blisters with an analgesic and cover them with dressing. It surprised him how deftly she worked. She had clearly done it before.

'Sophie tells me you want to go to Earth,' he said.

'Sophie told me you had a chance and refused.'

Zach shrugged. 'I was born here.'

'I was born here. So what?'

'Dunno. Place is special, I guess.'

Sierra glanced at him as she gingerly pulled her socks and boots back on. 'So, what is it with this girl? She special too?'

'She's just part of the crew.'

Sierra smirked. 'Yeah, right.'

Zach flushed. Sierra considered him for a moment. 'Wow,' she breathed.

'What's that supposed to mean?' asked Zach.

'Nothing,' said Sierra, scowling. She stood up and stuck the gun into the back of her trousers. 'Let's go.'

The further they climbed, the narrower the trail became. Soon it was only half a metre wide, and Zach and Sierra had to take small side steps with their backs pressed into the wall of the cave. At last, the trail disappeared into a fissure in the rock, where the light from the dome didn't penetrate. Zach switched on his flashlight, and they followed a staircase that wound around a tubular shaft up into the roof above the cavern. The staircase ended in a chamber with a single door that was so old and rotten with moisture that it literally fell apart when Zach tried the handle. Zach and Sierra froze as the metal stays clattered to the floor and the noise echoed around the chamber, but the sounds died out and silence resumed. They continued into a wide hallway, lit by sharp yellow lights attached by poles hanging from the ceiling.

'Which way?' asked Sierra.

'If Ship is right, and I haven't screwed up my bearings, the City is that way. But there's light coming from the other direction.'

'Another way out?'

'Let's see.'

They walked towards the light, checking the doors to either side. The doors were locked or opened into bare rooms. Not just deserted of people, but empty of goods or furnishings of any kind. 'It's like they never moved in,' said Sierra.

The passage ended in a chamber with a large door almost as big as the portal in the arena. Held in place by hinges as tall as a man, the door had a complex series of cogs and bolts, like the inner mechanism of a bank vault. Passages led off in several directions, and stone people were scattered about the chamber as if loitering. The source of the light was a thick translucent panel in the ceiling.

'Have a look around. I'm gonna check the door,' said Zach.

Sierra wandered off to check the other passages. Zach examined the symbols that ran around a dial on the door. They were like the ones on the codex they had stolen from Ming's showroom. *Some kind of lock*, he mused. Zach looked up at the panel on the roof. He couldn't be sure, but it gave off the same dusty pink glow of the typical Martian afternoon sky.

He turned around to mention this to Sierra, just in time to see her disappear into a passage on the other side of the chamber.

'Wait a minute, don't go running . . .' He ran after her.

The passage twisted and turned, and several other passages led away to either side, but Sierra seemed to have picked up the scent of something and hurried onwards. Zach followed, trying to catch up. The passage ended in a metal door.

Sierra opened it and gasped.

'Wait!' cautioned Zach again.

But Sierra ignored him, and by the time Zach got there, she was already halfway down some steps into a large chamber that glowed a rich yellow-orange colour.

Zach stood at the entrance and gaped.

The legends were true. El Dorado really did exist. In a suite of rooms linked by archways lay the glory of ancient Mars. There were statues of the gods in gold and silver; boxes of precious jewels; trunks overflowing with jewellery; mountains of coins; bronze cups brimming with gems; and the remnants of clothes and scrolls and maps, the soft fabric of which had long since crumbled to dust and was only held together by the eternal adornments of gems and precious metals.

And there was more. Through the archways, Zach glimpsed other treasure: racks of bronze weapons, collections of arcane technology, pottery inlaid with opal and jade, alabaster figurines, platinum mugs, and cups and plates made of porcelain and exquisitely trimmed in precious metal.

Zach felt dizzy and warm, as if he had a fever – the kind of fever you get when you look upon so much wealth that anything becomes possible. In a daze, he continued down the steps and wandered through the archways and around the rooms. The centre of each space had a large rusty grate on the floor. Tiny trickles of water ran down cracks in the mortar and disappeared through the drains into the murk. His foot kicked a silver coin; it rolled along the floor and fell through a grate. Zach stood at the edge and listened as the coin clattered down the shaft and hit the bottom far below. The noise was enough to break him out of his trance. He realised the palms of his hands were sweating and his heart was beating like a drum. Bemused, he shook his head – he never would have believed it could have affected him so.

'Be careful of these grates,' he said to Sierra in a hushed voice.

She didn't hear him. Sierra was skipping around the room like a kid in a candy store, so overwhelmed by the buffet she couldn't focus on one delicacy for more than a few seconds before being distracted by the next. She filled her pockets with gold, then emptied them to fill them with jewellery, and then emptied them again to fill them with gemstones.

But Zach was getting over his initial fever. He had a job to do. When Sierra disappeared through an archway, Zach ran after her. 'Wait a minute. We need to be careful. Surely this place has . . .'

He emerged through the archway to find Sierra standing in front of a dozen heavily armed, green-skinned soldiers pointing crossbows at her.

'. . . guards.'

Chapter Eight

Reunion

'I'm bored.'

Toby didn't even look up from his chess game. Sierra had trapped his queen before she left, and Toby couldn't figure a way out.

'Ship, I'm bored,' Sophie said again.

'We could do a reconnaissance of the dome,' said Ship. 'It is giving off a small amount of electromagnetic radiation across a range of frequencies, but the levels are not dangerous.'

'Yeah, let's do that!' said Sophie.

'Zach said we should wait here,' said Toby.

'Bah. Zach's not in charge. Let's go, Ship.'

The sand crawler's motor rumbled to life. It moved away from the foot of the trail and headed towards the lake. Sophie hopped into the driver's seat and Toby reluctantly left his chess game to stand behind her.

'How deep is it?' asked Toby.

'Sonar indicates a metre at most and shallower in the dome's vicinity. It is only a few centimetres if we approach it from the east,' replied Ship.

The crawler entered the lake, the treads slapping the water like a paddle steamer. It got deeper until the water rose halfway up the tracks.

Sophie stuck her head out the side window and watched the treads churning the water. 'This is fun, Ship. When we get Holly back, we should do this more often. Go exploring, I mean.'

Ship was quiet and didn't reply.

Puzzled, Sophie gently touched the hull. 'Ship?'

'Yes,' said Ship.

The crawler entered shallower water and veered to the right on a curved path that would take it to the eastern side of the lake. The dome grew in the front window like a blue sun creeping over the horizon.

'The surface is smooth. This cavern is most likely artificial,' said Ship. 'Interesting.'

Sophie's pockets were full of Sierra's almonds. She popped one into her mouth. 'What's interesting?'

'The vibrations produced by the crawler in the bedrock underneath are bouncing back from something. The pattern suggests the dome is a sphere. We are just seeing the top of it.'

'A big sphere of glowing what?' asked Toby.

'Spectroscopic analysis shows layers of quartz, carbon and an assortment of organic molecules.'

The crawler pulled up about twenty metres from the eastern edge of the dome. Here, the 'lake' amounted to only a few puddles of water. Sophie grabbed the handle of the cabin door. 'Any cave trolls around here?'

'There is nothing alive in this cavern but us,' said Ship. 'I will warn you if anything approaches.'

'Thanks, Ship.' Sophie opened the door and climbed down the ladder. She landed with a splash in a puddle and looked up at Toby in the doorway. 'You coming or what?'

Toby glanced about and shook his head. 'Yeah, yeah.'

Bathed in blue light, the Hendriksens approached the dome. The tendrils turned out to be twisted columns of petrified wood that sprouted up and over the dome like the roots of a tree. Where the petrified wood touched the surface of the dome, crystals grew in a dozen shades of pink, purple and blue. One attracted Toby's eye: a faceted pink crystal the size of an egg. It sat a few centimetres above the surface and sprouted eight spindly stalks, four to a side, that extended down to the surface and held it fast. Toby reached out to touch it.

'Don't touch!' The crawler's loudspeaker crackled in alarm. Toby jerked his hand away.

'What is it, Ship?' shouted Toby.

The crawler's engine thrummed to life, and it trundled closer to the dome. 'The cameras on the front of the crawler do not have the magnification for me to see it clearly, but I believe that it is a species of cave spider.'

'It's just a funny-shaped crystal,' said Toby. 'I can see the facets.'

'It is a spider that has been turned into crystals,' replied Ship.

'Wow, Ship's right,' said Sophie. Finger hovering a careful distance above the surface, she pointed to a dense cluster of flat, segmented crystals, each with three tiny glassy rods on either side.

'A cockroach nest,' announced Ship.

Toby looked up along the nook where the root touched the dome's surface. Having had one pointed out to him, his perception shifted. He could see the faceted bugs everywhere. And there were patches of densely compacted crystals that could have been moss or lichen. 'Ship, you think the dome has done this?'

'It's possible the unusual pattern of radiation emitted by the sphere influences the molecular structure of organic matter.'

Toby and Sophie each took a step backwards. 'But it's safe now?' asked Sophie.

'The residual radiation is barely above background levels – but I wouldn't touch it just in case.'

Toby and Sophie walked a few dozen metres around the edge of the dome, stopping to examine where the petrified root touched the surface. Ship followed behind. The crystal bugs were everywhere, and there were larger things too that may have been earthworms or lizards, their faceted bodies reflecting a dozen colours of pink and blue.

They came across a set of stairs that went up to the base of the column of rock above the dome and spiralled around the column all the way to the cavern roof. The column was lined with veins of the same blue substance.

Toby looked back in the direction from which they had come. You could still make out the 'boulders' at the bottom of the trail where Zach and Sierra began their ascent.

'The stone people . . .' he murmured. 'They're really people.'

'Fully crystallised and covered in the grime and sand of centuries,' said Ship. 'The sphere might be a weapon. Deployed against those trying to get into the City. There is often unrest in the last days of a civilisation.'

'There's something else you should know, Ship,' said Toby. 'In the resurrection pods in the Well of Souls we found small stone spheres. Do you think . . .?'

'That they were part of the hibernation process used by the Martians? Perhaps the radiation produced by the spheres crystallises the outer layer of cells, preserving the DNA and delicate membranes inside.'

Sophie gasped. 'They're still alive in there?'

'No,' replied Ship, 'I scanned them before. They're solid all the way through.'

'The small spheres to preserve. The big sphere to kill,' said Toby. He put his hands on his hips. 'But we don't know any of this for sure.'

'It is speculation,' said Ship. 'Regardless, it changes the calculation. It was long assumed that Martian technology was not as advanced as our own. But if this is a weapon that can be used against intruders, the pirates might be in for a surprise.'

'I always end up in a cell. What does that say about the direction my life is taking?'

'That stealing is wrong,' said Zach under his breath.

He yanked at a bar. The bolt that held it in place at the bottom had partially decayed, but it had fused with the surrounding stone. By working it backwards and forwards he had loosened it, but not enough.

Sierra was in the cell next door, her forehead pressed up against the bars. The soldiers had stripped them of their bags and weapons, inspecting the rifle and handguns curiously, before shuffling them through a maze of passages to end in a room with several cells and no windows – and a few ominous-looking bones in the corner. That was several hours ago. They hadn't seen or heard a sign of anyone since.

'Maybe the gods are trying to tell me something?' Sierra wondered in a mournful voice.

Zach ignored her and yanked the bar again.

'It's not that I need a lot of money. Just enough for a one-way ticket to Earth, a nice apartment opposite Central Park, a car, good clothes, restaurants, expense account, travel . . .'

'What about the jewels you swallowed before they pulled you out of that trunk?' asked Zach.

Sierra sighed deeply. 'Only a few of the smaller diamonds. They're harder to swallow than you think.'

'You better hope they don't want them back as well . . . Got it!' The bottom of the bar came free and bent inwards. Zach braced his feet against the bars on either side, strained his muscles and bent it further. Finally, he was able to get down on the ground and wriggle through the gap.

Wiping his hands on his trousers, he went and stood in front of Sierra's cell. 'Unfortunately, I think they took the keys with them.'

A look of horror spread across Sierra's face. 'You're not leaving me here?'

'Well, just temporarily.'

Sierra's mouth dropped open.

'Look, I'll be back. I promise. But unless you can find another loose bar, we're gonna need something to pick the lock.'

Sierra looked around at the dank confines of the cell and shuddered.

Zach couldn't think of anything further to say that would reassure her, so he gave a feeble wave goodbye and left.

The guards had ushered them along a series of passageways that led down and away from the treasure room. Zach had tried to memorise the route, but he was soon hopelessly lost. Mostly by luck, he made it back as far as the main hallway before the big gate. But as he tiptoed breathlessly down the main hallway, a guard appeared from around a corner and spotted him. The alarm was raised, and after a brief chase and game of hide and seek, he was seized as he tried to squeeze into an urn several sizes too small.

However, the guards didn't take him back to the cell. Instead, they dragged him through the dungeon's corridors, out into the gloomy streets, past groups of curious green bystanders and up the winding steps of a tower to a furnished room with a table, a single bed and a balcony. The leader of the guards exchanged a few words with a slim woman in a gown standing on the balcony, and then they unceremoniously dumped him and left.

Feeling his bruises, Zach got to his feet and looked around the room. It was lit by candles rather than the pole lights. They exuded a warm tinge and the scent of beeswax. There were drawings on yellowish parchment scattered over the table, held down by a device that looked like a compass. And his backpack was sitting against a wall, but there was no sign of his weapons.

With one eye on the occupant, who was gazing out over the city, he investigated the drawings on the table. They appeared to be maps of the city, including an outline of the cavern and the dome underneath.

'Looking for more gold?' said the person on the balcony, turning around.

Her voice was different: hoarser, and deeper, but not *that* different. Zach rushed towards her.

'Stop! Don't come any closer!'

Zach jerked to a stop in the middle of the room and squinted into the gloom of the balcony. 'Holly, are you okay?'

'You know your backpack has your name stitched into it? When they brought it to me, I almost laughed with joy. But then they told me they'd found you in the treasure room.'

Zach mustered some serious earnestness. 'I came here to get you.'

'And who's the girl? I'm pretty sure Sophie doesn't paint her fingernails red. And even you wouldn't have given her a gun.'

Zach rubbed his temples. 'I can explain.'

'It doesn't matter,' said Holly miserably. 'It turns out I have bigger problems.'

'Forget them and come with me. I know a way out.'

Even clothed in shadow, Zach thought he could see a twitch of a sad smile. He went to her . . .

'No, stop . . .'

. . . and took her hands. And looked into her sea-green face and shining bronze eyes.

'Huh,' he said, recovering after a moment of surprise. 'You've changed.'

Holly dipped her head. A tear ran down her cheek. Zach gently lifted her chin and brushed it away. 'I would've gone for a deeper shade myself.'

'Don't joke,' said Holly, pulling away.

Zach pulled her close again. 'You look beautiful,' he told her softly.

Holly rested her forehead against his chest. 'Thank you.'

They stood together for the length of several long breaths. Zach could hear Holly's heart beating and feel the warmth of her body. Her hair smelt faintly of honey. For a too-brief moment, he enjoyed her presence without the problems of the world intruding.

'How are the others?' asked Holly finally.

Zach thought about the rest of the crew. 'Ship's insane, of course. Sophie's . . . violently insane. Toby . . . does anyone ever know what goes on in Toby's mind?'

Holly's lips curled into the semblance of a smile. 'They're

well, then. And my . . . the professor?'

Zach thought it better not to let her know what had happened in the arena just yet. 'He's back in Port Clarke. He found a map. Toby, Sophie and I came in a sand crawler through the caves underneath the City. They're waiting for us there.'

Holly bit her lip. She extracted herself from Zach's arms and turned back to the balcony, looking out over the dark city. 'I have responsibilities,' she said.

'Yeah,' Zach sighed, coming up behind her and placing his hands on her shoulders. 'I kinda guessed that, with the gown and maps and all the ordering people around. Is it official? Are you a princess now?'

'It turns out I'm not. But the real Princess didn't make it and the Queen is . . . indisposed.' She turned back to him. 'I can't leave them, Zach. How are they going to survive? Their world has changed beyond recognition. And we're running out of food and—'

'I get it. Really. It's just that I'm pretty sure Janus and every other pirate on Mars are within spitting distance of finding this place. And when that happens, all hell's gonna break loose. They'll kill you, me, each other and any green person who gets in their way to get a piece of what I saw in that treasure room.'

Holly bunched her fists. 'We are not defenceless.'

'Kebechet?'

'It's just a robot. But yes. And there are other things.'

'Huh, I should have known it was a robot. But look, we don't want a war.'

'Zach, I am not letting them steal the legacy of ancient Mars.'

Zach open his mouth to argue but was interrupted by a knock on the door. Holly spoke a word, and in walked a couple of guards carrying a squirming Sierra. They dropped her on the floor and, after a nod from Holly, left again, but not before Sierra regained her feet and tried to kick one of them. She missed and kicked the closing door instead. 'Ouch!' she cried, hopping around the room on one leg. She fell against Zach, who was forced to support her by wrapping an arm around her waist.

'Didn't you promise to come back for me?' Sierra said sourly, centimetres from his face. Then she noticed Holly. 'Who the hell is this?'

'Sierra, this is Holly. Holly, Sierra,' replied Zach in a pained voice.

'*This* is her. Why is she green?'

'I'm not sure, but—'

'Wait a minute.' Holly stepped closer and poked an accusing finger at Sierra. 'I know you. You used to pull my pigtails when I visited the professor at the museum.'

Sierra's face was blank; then recognition arrived. 'That was you. God, that was years ago.'

'Two, to be precise.'

Sierra dismissed it with an airy wave of her hand. 'I was going through a difficult phase.'

'What, your cruel bitch phase?'

Sierra bristled. 'You told on me for playing with the dagger.'

'It was ten thousand years old!'

'It was strong enough to carve my initials into that ugly-ass vase.'

'You did *what*?'

'Stop!' Hands thrust in the air, Zach stepped between them. 'We don't have time for this.'

There were querying voices from the other side of the door. Angry, Holly shouted something that sounded like 'Sarkash' and the voices fell quiet. But it took much longer for the girls to calm down. They continued to glower at each other silently while Zach retrieved his backpack.

'I need to let the others know you're okay. I'll be straight back. And then we can talk about . . . what we're gonna do.'

Holly's demeanour softened. 'Zach, I can't ask you to get involved in all this.'

'We've already settled this,' replied Zach curtly. 'I'm not leaving you again and I'm sure Sophie and Toby and Ship feel the same. We're here for you.' He looked at her. '*I'm* here for you.'

Holly blushed and sighed. 'Okay. I'll tell the guards to escort you safely back to where they found you.'

'The treasure rooms? Sounds fair,' said Sierra.

'To the chamber outside the now-*locked* treasure room,' Holly corrected primly.

Zach paused in the middle of adjusting his backpack. 'Actually, I've just had a better idea.' He looked at Sierra, rubbing his chin. 'But we'll need your help.'

Sierra looked confused. 'Yeah, no, sure. I'm here to assist in whatever way I can . . . obviously.'

Zach went over to the table and examined the maps again. His finger traced a cave back to the desert.

'Sierra, Sophie and Toby take the crawler back to the surface. We can't send a signal in the caves, but once Sierra's outside she can broadcast to the world that the Martians are alive and well. And tell them everything that is going on here.'

'Will they listen? Will they care?' asked Holly.

'They'll go bananas,' replied Zach. 'It'll be like the dinosaurs coming back to life. And Sierra's mum's the mayor. That's gotta be worth something.'

Sierra perked up. 'Wait, you mean I'm gonna be on TV?'

'On two planets,' intoned Zach.

'I'm in.'

Holly frowned darkly at Sierra a moment, then joined Zach at the table. 'You're right. Janus can only do what he does in the shadows. It will be harder if the entire world's watching.' Her mouth drooped. 'But we have a more immediate problem. The only food we have is what they stored in the pods with the sleepers. It's fast running out and there's nothing else to eat. The arena cavern has collapsed, and we can't get out through the caves underneath. The way is narrow and there are things down there.'

Sierra shivered. 'I think we met one.'

'We saw a gate outside the treasure room,' said Zach.

'The temple gateway – we can't open it. The mechanism is fused with the rock.' Holly squeezed her face in her hands. 'Basically, we're trapped.'

Zach tapped a map in thought. 'We packed the crawler

with food. That might buy us a day at least. And Ship is fully rearmed. I bet with these maps and its knowledge of the caves it can work out where that door comes out . . . blow it from the outside.'

'You think that's possible?' asked Holly.

'Ship will figure it out. And once open, it can stand guard too. The pirates will find the gateway soon enough.'

'I thought you said we don't want a war.'

'I don't. But I meant what I said – Janus and his thugs will kill everyone who gets in their way. Are your Martians going to fight to protect their legacy?'

'I'm sure of it,' said Holly, her bronze eyes flashing, 'and I will too.'

Chapter Nine

Big News

'We have found it. The legendary City of the Dead. Long thought to be . . . um, a legend . . . the truth is finally out there. The Martians put themselves into hibernation as their planet's atmosphere lost oxygen, hoping that one day the air would return. That day has come. This exclusive footage reveals the Martians awakening in their underground vaults and preparing to reclaim their ancient planet. What does this mean for the settlers from Earth who now call Mars their home? How will the Martians feel about the plunder of their cities and temples? And what about the very real treasure that has been the source of so much strife among the modern-day pirates? Stay tuned for the answers to these and other burning questions about this momentous event. Sierra Garcia, reporting live from Mars.'

Sierra switched the mic off and looked at Toby. 'What do you reckon? I don't think I quite nailed it.'

Toby pulled at his hair. 'That was the ninth take!'

'My acting coach tells me I come off a bit breathy when I speak directly to the camera,' said Sierra, patting her chest and taking a deep breath. 'Maybe you could toss me a few questions rather than just have me deliver a monologue?'

'No! Send it and let's go!'

Oblivious to Toby's protests, Sierra retrieved the camera from where it was propped upright on the track guard of the sand crawler. She played the video back, slowly shaking her head. 'It needs work. And that footage of the Martians you edited could be tighter.'

'Arrrgh!' Toby stomped away and climbed back into the cab of the crawler.

A green light was blinking on the console. Reluctantly, Toby flicked the switch underneath. Sophie's voice came over the speaker: *Have you sent it yet?*

'Um . . . almost.'

What the flip does that mean? came Sophie's reply. *Send the flipping thing. Ship doesn't know how long it will take to find this other gate. Princess Holly is depending on us.*

'Sorry, bad comms, I'll get back to you,' said Toby and quickly closed the connection.

After a tearful reunion with Holly at the bottom of the cavern trail, Sophie, Toby and Sierra had retraced their path in the crawler back to the surface . Ship's mind was transferred back into the hovercraft and Sophie had left with Ship to look for the temple gateway, while Toby and Sierra had stayed behind with the crawler to broadcast the footage of the Martians that Sierra had taken with her phone. They would then return to the City with some extra supplies they had transferred from the hovercraft.

At least, that was the plan. After four hours of editing,

makeup, rehearsal and many takes, the message still hadn't been sent. Toby briefly entertained the idea of trying to wrestle Sierra to the ground and take the phone, but she could just lock it with her voice.

In frustration, he smacked the console with his forehead. It seemed to leave his ears buzzing. No – wait a minute – the buzzing was coming from outside. He got down out of the cab and walked to the front of the crawler. The buzzing was louder. He walked over to a nearby jumble of boulders. Climbing to the top, he scanned the sky. 'Can you hear that?' he called out to Sierra.

'I think it's coming from that direction.'

Toby turned around to see where she was pointing. Sierra had climbed into the cabin and opened the roof. 'That way,' she said again. The phone still in her hand, she pointed up the slope of the valley to the east. Toby almost looked, but noticed that in her other hand Sierra was holding a boxy metallic object. A cable dangled loosely from a port on one side.

'That's the program module Ship left behind to drive the crawler,' said Toby. 'Plug it back in. We'll need it when we . . .'

The buzzing quickly became very loud and changed to a rapid *brat, brat, brat* noise. A helicopter appeared above the lip of the valley and roared overhead, the gusts from the rotor blade buffeting Toby's hair and clothes, the noise deafening. From the roof of the crawler Sierra waved and shouted, but whether at him or the helicopter, he couldn't tell.

Toby shielded his eyes from the rotor-blown sand and watched the helicopter circle around the crawler. Despite the sand grains stinging his eyes, he could make out two men in the bubble-like cockpit. The helicopter descended towards a flat bit of ground some thirty metres away and landed with a bounce. Even before it had settled, the cockpit opened and a lean, dark-haired man with a gun strapped to his thigh got out and ran towards the crawler.

'Lock it up!' Toby shouted at Sierra, frantically waving his arms. Instead, Sierra climbed down the ladder and ran towards the man. Man and girl embraced amid a small whirly gig of sand.

Baffled, Toby jumped down from the boulder and went over to them. Sierra nodded towards him as he approached. 'Dad, this is the annoying kid I texted you about.'

'Hello, annoying kid,' the man said, holding his hand out to Toby and grinning like a wolf baring its teeth.

Toby hesitantly extended his own hand, and the man gripped it and pumped it hard. Wringing his hand from the handshake, Toby looked at Sierra and raised his eyebrows.

'This is my dad Jesse,' she announced. 'Ship stopped blocking transmissions so we could send the news of the Martians. I thought I'd give Dad a quick call too.'

'Martians!' said Jesse, shaking his head in wonder. 'Wow, that's big news right there. My little girl's going to be famous.' Sierra beamed as he gave her another squeeze.

'I don't . . .' Toby's mouth dropped open. 'You're not going to send the message!'

'Well, no, now, that's not strictly true,' objected Sierra. 'I'm not going to send it . . . *yet*. We're just gonna take the crawler and pop back inside and take a few baubles. And *then* we'll send the message.'

Toby tried to snatch the phone from her hand. He missed.

Quick as lightning, Jesse drew his gun and levelled it at Toby's midriff. 'Now, now, let's have none of that.'

'But Zach and Holly are relying on us to get the news out,' Toby spluttered, gaping at the gun. 'The pirates will be here soon!'

Jesse shook his head in mock sadness. They all turned around as the other man from the helicopter joined them. Toby recognised him from their days stealing the codex in Pirate Central.

'Actually,' said the Curator, smiling, 'the pirates are already here.'

The topography above the caverns was a complex network of steep canyons and sharply eroded hills, as if the surface of the planet had been slashed with a sharp claw. Based on satellite photos and the Martians' maps, Ship had narrowed the search area down to thirty square kilometres, but that still meant many fruitless hours of trawling up and down rocky canyons, looking for telltale signs of the gateway.

Sophie sat in the pilot's seat munching on a packet of dried pumpkin chips. Every minute or so she tried to connect to Toby, but he hadn't replied after the initial contact.

'He's ignoring me,' she grunted, flicking the switch off again for the umpteenth time.

'I am monitoring the news feeds,' said Ship. 'Nothing yet.'

Sophie made an exasperated noise, 'Pffft. Sierra's right, boys are useless.' She hesitated, glancing around. 'You're not a boy, are you, Ship?'

'Indeterminate,' replied Ship.

More and more, Sophie thought she could detect an odd tone in Ship's voice. And she detected it again now. 'Are you excited about the battle, Ship? I'm sure there's going to be a battle.'

'Yes. And then my mission will be at an end.'

Sophie's hand stopped with a pumpkin chip halfway to her mouth. 'What do you mean?'

'Holly's father has been found. Once the battle is won and Holly is returned and reunited with the crew, my mission will be over.'

Sophie sat up in her chair. 'No, no, Ship. Your mission won't be over. Your mission is to be with us. To be with me. Think of all the fun we can have together. Like, we could go looking for the cave troll. Get a picture.'

'I am built for fighting, Sophie.'

'I'm sure it will put up a fight! And anyway, there are always more fights.' Sophie put her hand on the console and added in a small voice, 'What matters is that we fight them together.'

Ship didn't respond.

'Ship?'

'I have found it.'

'Found what?' Sophie looked around, confused.

The viewport panned across a landscape of jagged rocks and zoomed in to a section of the canyon wall. Here, a decrepit but still intact bridge spanned an ancient river-bed that ran down the valley floor. Carved into the bluffs above the bridge were two giant statues of a man and a woman, seated on thrones and resting sceptres on their knees, their blank stone visages projecting an air of regal disdain. Between the statues, there was a recess cloaked in shadow, and at their feet was a broad terrace that finished in a wall and battlement that overlooked the river.

'The bridge would appear to be the only way across,' said Ship, 'unless we can ford the river.'

Ship flew over towards the statues. It soon became clear there would be no fording the river. What looked like a riverbank from a distance was the edge of a precipice. The now-extinct waterway had for millions of years cut into the valley floor and the bridge now spanned a ravine hundreds of metres deep.

'This is a good defensive position,' remarked Ship. 'The only easy way across is the bridge, and then attackers will still have to scale the wall in front of the gateway.'

The view zoomed in to the bridge. Constructed from a single arch, the structure was so old that it had fused with the rock on either side and looked like a natural outgrowth. Only a few blocks remained of the guardrail, and there were holes in the deck, but the arch itself was intact.

'Sophie, the structure appears sound, at least for foot traffic, but I am much heavier. You should wait here while I test it.'

Still disturbed by what Ship had said earlier, Sophie stamped her foot. 'No, we go together.' She gestured angrily at the forward viewport. 'Let's go.'

Ship manoeuvred in front of the approach ramp, the fans temporarily increasing in pitch to lift the hovercraft over the remains of a toppled statue, before continuing to inch up the ramp and out onto the superstructure. Sophie couldn't see anything out the windows, but Ship had switched a viewport to show the scene under the left wing. With the bridge only five metres wide, the hovercraft's wings extended well beyond the edge, and the screen showed a vertigo-inducing drop to a tumble of shattered boulders two hundred metres below.

As Ship approached halfway, the camera view started shaking. It wasn't the hovercraft, but the structure underneath vibrating to the force of Ship's turbofans. Sophie watched, transfixed, as small stones and sand fell away into the abyss. A larger block abruptly came into view on the screen, dislodged from somewhere underneath the arch. It shrunk to the size of a pebble before crashing silently into the riverbed below. But after a few more metres, the shaking eased, and the hovercraft soon reached the other side.

In front of them loomed the statues, and between them it was now possible to make out the outline of a gateway, similar in size to the portal in the arena. Ship lifted itself up a series of steps and onto the terrace, and gently floated to a stop next to the big toe of one of the statues.

Sophie patted the console, her previous agitation already forgotten. 'Well done, Ship! Now, how do we blow it up?'

Toby's butt and back were aching. The Curator had chained his hands to a steel grate on the floor of the storage compartment. With his arms between his legs, Toby could either crouch or sit on the grate. He had crouched for as long as he could because at least that way he could ride out the bumps, but eventually the burn in his thighs forced him to sit, and as the crawler made its way back to the city, every jolt transferred to his tailbone and up his spine. Worse, there was no stopping for breaks this time. Jesse drove the crawler nonstop, aware that it was only a matter of time before the universe discovered the location of the City of the Dead.

Now his left leg had fallen asleep. Toby shifted uncomfortably, stretching it out in front of him and rubbing it with his other foot. It didn't work; he groaned in misery.

'I am truly sorry for the discomfort,' said the Curator, appearing in the doorway to the driver's cab. 'But we are almost there.' Toby heard the crawler's treads slapping the water, and the fuzz on the top of the Curator's otherwise bald head was backlit by a familiar blue glow.

Toby tried to sit up straight. Pain shot up his back. 'We're going to the dome?'

'Jesse and Sierra are going to drop us off there.'

'Us?'

'I may need your help. You have been this way before.

Plus, I understand you know something about the dome?'

'I know it turns people to stone!'

The Curator flapped his hand as if this were an insignificant detail. 'I knew that already.'

'What? How?'

'I have been studying Martian manuscripts and artefacts all my life. I've learned a thing or two – about their lives, about their technology. For example, did you know the Martians lived much longer than we do?'

'Uh, okay, so . . .?'

The Curator produced a smug smile. 'It will make more sense when we get there.' He disappeared back into the cabin.

The slapping had stopped. The crawler continued for a few more moments and came to a stop too. Jesse called out from the driver's seat, 'Big blue dome. All off who's getting off. Watch your step!'

Sierra popped into the storage compartment and unchained Toby. She looked askance at him, a weak grin on her face. 'I really hope there are no bad feelings about this.'

Toby rubbed his wrists and glowered, too angry for words.

'I mean the media attention is all very good, but, you know . . . the money.'

Toby stood up and stretched his aching back as the rear door swung open. Jesse stood there, hand on gun, the Curator behind him. Toby grabbed Sierra's arm. 'Listen to me,' he whispered, gesturing towards the Curator. 'He's up to something bad.'

Sierra shrugged. 'Well, technically, we are too.'

'No, I mean really bad. I don't know what it is yet, but –'

'He's fine,' said Sierra. 'My dad knows him from way back. He's just a bit eccentric.' She shook his hand off and jumped down to the ground. Reluctantly, Toby followed, and the four made their way over to the edge of the dome and around to where the stairs began their ascent. It may have been Toby's imagination, but the dome seemed to glow brighter than before.

'Don't touch it,' said Toby. 'Look at the insects.'

Jesse leaned in for a closer look, careful not to touch the surface. 'Huh.'

'What does it do?' asked Sierra.

'It turns you to stone!' blurted Toby.

'Say what?' said Jesse.

'It's essentially a power source,' explained the Curator. 'The Martians used a form of Cherenkov radiation to power their cities and the hibernation pods.'

'Woah.' Jesse backed up a few steps. 'Nobody said anything about radiation.'

'And it has interesting side effects,' said Toby sarcastically.

The Curator ignored him. 'The levels are barely above background. It won't hurt you.'

Toby snorted.

'What exactly do you want with this?' asked Jesse.

'Isn't it obvious?' replied the Curator. 'This technology is years ahead of our own. The value of this is worth way more than your roomful of baubles.'

'Don't believe him,' said Toby. He pleaded with Sierra. 'He's up to something.'

'So, you're gonna what?' Sierra asked the Curator. 'Chip a bit off?'

The Curator pointed to the stairs that wound around the column of rock above the dome. 'Somewhere up there must be a control room. We get there, we learn how to control it. Use it.'

Sierra and Jesse looked at each other uneasily. 'Ah, I think we'll go the back way and stick to the baubles,' said Jesse.

'Fine,' said the Curator impatiently. 'Do what you want, but the boy comes with me.'

'Why?' asked Toby.

The Curator pulled a gun out from inside his jacket. It looked ridiculously large in his wrinkly old hand. He levelled it at Toby and motioned towards the stairs. 'At the very least, leverage.'

'Three, two, one.' Sophie turned the handle. She saw the blast a tiny fraction of a second before she heard it. Sand and rock spurted towards her in the rough shape of a door. The shockwave briefly buffeted the hovercraft, but to Sophie, safely cocooned inside, it was all rather dull. She had imagined a massive boom and a giant fireball like she was used to seeing in the movies. Or the one she'd seen in real life when Ship blew up the stadium.

'Did it work?' she asked, waving her hand in front of her face as if that would help dispel the cloud of smoke billowing towards the hovercraft.

A massive plinth of stone fell outward, crashed to the ground with a boom even louder than the explosion and promptly shattered into a dozen large pieces. Behind it was a dark rectangular void.

'Yes, it worked,' said Ship.

As Sophie watched, a green face appeared around the edge of the doorway. It was a boy, even younger than her, shielding his eyes and blinking furiously into the bright morning sun. Seconds later, a girl's face appeared behind him, her long blonde hair twisted into a single braid. They looked at the hovercraft, and at each other, then ran away back into the murk, shouting and waving their arms in excitement.

Moments passed. Zach came out, clambering over the debris. He climbed to the top of one of the broken pieces of the doorway and stood up, hands on hips, grinning. Holly joined him, smiling and waving. Other green faces appeared between the rocks or peeked over the top, their expressions curious and uncertain.

In the hovercraft, a red blip appeared on a monitor on the console. Immediately, one of Ship's viewports dissolved and refreshed to show an object hovering near one end of the valley. The image zoomed in – a helicopter. The aircraft dipped a little and swivelled to face them, then turned around and disappeared over a ridge.

'Not long now,' said Ship.

Chapter Ten

The Bridge

Sometime around noon, the sand crawlers and buggies started to arrive. The first one, a large red buggy with a sunroof and knobbly rear wheels, wound its way down the valley and over to the foot of the bridge. The occupants, a tanned, grizzled man with blond highlights, and his companion, an equally tanned, grizzled woman smoking a cigar, got out and appraised the scene. Zach stood up from behind the battlement, and with no further ado, pointed his gun in the air and fired a warning shot. Man and woman got back in, turned the buggy around and drove it behind a small ridge – not quite out of range, but far enough away to make for a difficult shot.

Other buggies of various shapes and sizes soon joined them, parking along the same ridge. The occupants alighted and discussed the situation in small groups, rubbing their jaws and fingering the triggers of their rifles.

Helicopters appeared above the valley and buzzed up and down its length before landing behind the buggies.

The first sand crawler turned up early in the afternoon: a big half-track with a rotating turret on top. Rather than parking next in line to the buggies, it continued to the front of the ridge and rolled over the red one, crushing it like a tin can. Man and woman jumped free just in time and gesticulated in rage. But they backed off quickly when the turret on top of the crawler, housing a machine gun, swivelled in their direction.

More sand crawlers and buggies arrived, spawning more conflict. Fights broke out and several shots were fired, but as it neared mid-afternoon activity on the ridge settled down. It appeared a rough consensus had been established. When Zach scanned the ridge with Holly's binoculars, he saw a long line of pensive pirates staring back at him through dark sunglasses and binoculars of their own.

'Can you see him?' asked Holly.

'No, but I'm sure he's there somewhere.'

Holly looked behind her. The palace guard had taken up positions along the battlement and around the feet of the statues. Some of the regular Martians who had experience with weapons were crouching among the rubble in front of the gateway, and more were hiding in the dark just beyond the entrance.

But what good were swords and crossbows against rifles and explosives? Zach had suggested arming them with the weapons they had unloaded from the crawler, but Holly had decided against it. With no training, they would be more dangerous to themselves than to the pirates.

Holly studied their faces: the guards were grim and determined, the others scared, confused, uncomprehending. *I feel all of that and much more*, she thought. How had it come to this? She shook her head. The situation was both appalling and ludicrous.

'Something's happening,' said Zach.

Holly peeked over the battlement. A delegation of four pirates waving a white flag was walking down the ridge towards the bridge. It was obvious even from a distance that one of them was Janus, his wide girth and bow-legged swagger marking him as clearly as if he had a big red cross smeared across his face. She didn't recognise the other three, but they carried themselves with self-assurance, almost arrogance. Holly guessed they were leaders of rival gangs of pirates, temporarily aligned for a greater cause.

'Feng, Cobain and Mursky,' muttered Zach. He turned to Holly. 'You ready?'

Holly gritted her teeth. She spoke in Martian to the captain, who was waiting with his guards a short distance away. 'Captain, they wish to parley.'

Zach, Holly and the captain met the delegation in the middle of the bridge. The three pirates with Janus stared in naked fascination at the green skin and polished bronze armour of the captain, who returned their stares with cool contempt. Janus acted as if it was all perfectly normal. He smiled at Holly and spread his hands in a gesture of generosity. 'It doesn't have to go this way.'

Remembering the last time she had encountered Janus, some part of Holly's mind wondered why her knees weren't shaking. 'What exactly do you have in mind?' she asked.

'We could split it,' replied Janus. 'Is any treasure worth the lives of your people?'

'What, we give you half and you go away?'

Janus chuckled dryly, gesturing to the other members of the delegation. 'I was thinking more like eighty-twenty. I have to look after the interests of my colleagues.'

Holly looked past him to the line of pirates watching from the ridge beyond. They carried their guns loosely, casually, slung over shoulders or dangling by their sides, as if they were natural extensions of their limbs.

He's right, thought Holly. *The treasure isn't worth the lives of my people.* (*Her* people – what an odd thought.) Or worth the life of anyone, really.

She glanced at the captain, standing resolute at her side. He would probably rather fight and die than allow such a thing. But maybe she could convince him. Surely, she should at least try.

Zach spoke up, perhaps worried Holly was thinking exactly what she was thinking. 'How do I put this delicately?' he said to Janus, scratching his head and pretending to ponder. 'As soon as we turn our backs . . . you'll shoot us in the back!'

Janus looked amused. 'So don't turn your back. Put down your weapons and bring the treasure out here. We could load it up and be on our way. Of course, I would have to do a proper accounting first. Make sure we got our fair share.'

Zach snorted in derision. He began to point out all the ways Janus would find a way to betray them. Janus countered with proposals to circumvent his alleged future treachery. They argued.

Holly was only half-listening. Part of her mind had detached and wandered off. Her eyes lighted on the broken statue that lay prone on the approach to the bridge on the other side of the ravine. It was Annikah, a goddess who welcomed the dead to the afterlife with food and drink, and covertly (some tales said) weighed their souls to see if they were worthy.

Was she worthy, Holly wondered? By some dumb twist of fate, she found herself in charge. Would this be how the afterlife of the Martians began under her 'reign' – not with food and drink but with their artefacts plundered? A sudden glimpse of the future appeared in her mind's eye: images of crops burning, wells poisoned, violence in the night as Earthlings and Martians fought over land and water – the rare and precious resources of Mars. Somehow, they would have to live together. And that would only be possible if there was respect between the two peoples. Holly shook her head. That respect must begin here and now.

'No,' she breathed, so quietly no one properly heard her.

'Eh?' said Janus.

'No,' she said again, looking directly at him. 'Get the fuck off our bridge.'

Janus's mouth remained curved in the shape of a smile, but his eyelids dropped half a millimetre. Holly felt a stab of fear. She saw in his face that this was what he had wanted all along. She recalled how he had drugged her, tied her up and made her tell him everything she knew – which back then was a big, fat nothing – at which point he had ordered her killed and disposed of, with no more thought than emptying the trash.

Janus sighed dramatically and shook his head. He turned to his companions, opening his arms to suggest he'd tried to be reasonable. The companions looked unhappy, glancing at the dozens of Martians guarding the walls. They had no wish to risk their lives any more than was strictly necessary. They were looters, not soldiers. But the talking was over.

Both parties backed carefully away and returned to their respective positions. As Holly explained to the captain what had happened, a flare went up. It streaked high into the air above the valley and exploded in a big powdery burst of orange. Immediately, the engines of the crawlers and buggies whined to life. A dozen of the vehicles backed away from the ridge and proceeded to one end of the valley. Here, the ancient riverbed became a narrow passage before disappearing into a cave under a vertical cliff face. The buggies stopped and equipment was unloaded, its exact nature obscured by the distance.

While Zach kept his eye on that end of the valley, Holly and the captain wondered about the activity on the ridge. Enlightenment wasn't long in coming. A line of vehicles drove down to the bridge's approach and two dozen pirates alighted, protecting themselves with makeshift shields constructed from metal and plexiglass panels. They assembled into a rough formation and advanced onto the narrow bridge. A volley of arrows and bolts from the Martian defenders met them. One struck a man in the arm – he cried out and stumbled back to the shelter of a crawler – but most of the projectiles clattered against the panels and fell harmlessly to the ground.

Overlapping their shields, the pirates tightened their formation and pushed forward in a half-crouch. The Martians rose to fire again.

Puffs of smoke appeared above the ridge; bullets zinged over the heads of the defenders or spattered against the parapet, forcing the Martians to hunker down. The pirates made their way across the bridge, to where the pathway rose in a series of steps towards the gate in the wall. Captain Alarik shouted an order to the defenders. The gate opened briefly and a dozen rounded boulders rolled down the steps and smashed into the front rank of the attackers, scattering them like bowling pins. One man fell off the edge of the bridge and screamed all the way to the bottom. The rest picked themselves up, limping and bruised, and retreated.

Down the far end of the valley, the pirates had assembled their equipment and sidled up to the edge of the ravine. Here, the two opposite faces were only twenty metres apart. Grappling hooks fired from shoulder-mounted cannons arced over the space and found purchase among the boulders on the other side. But Zach had thought of this. He ran to the far end of the battlement and waved a flag. Several Martians stationed there jumped out from between the rocks and severed the taut cables with battle axes. Two pirates who had tried sliding along the cables fell into the void. The attackers responded by pinning the Martians down with gunfire, but after they had seen what happened to their fellows, no one would now dare the crossing.

Zach ran back and joined Holly and the captain. 'This just might work,' he said. 'We can fight them to a standstill.'

Holly pointed towards the bridge. 'I'm not so sure.'

The sand crawler with the machine gun turret had crawled down from the ridge and rolled towards the bridge, battering the statue of Annikah out of the way. As it crept onto the approach, the mount swivelled to face the Martians. Holly screamed at them to get down. The gun opened fire, splattering bullets along the battlement. Chips and chunks of stone spurted in all directions. The base of the parapet was made of granite blocks half a metre thick, but as the gun continued to pan up and down the line, even they began to splinter and crack. Once the battlement was destroyed, the Martians, lying flat behind the wall with their hands over their ears, would be defenceless.

The crawler wasn't going to wait. It continued onto the bridge. As it neared the midsection, the structure shook, and small blocks of stone fell from the arch underneath. Five metres more and the bridge began to sway, a ponderous wobble a metre to either side. But the wobble subsided, and after another five metres, the worst seemed to be over for it.

Zach watched the crawler approach the terrace. He fumbled for a device next to him: a small metal canister with a light and a button on the top. He pressed the button. The bridge shook violently as the deck on the near side of the bridge exploded, creating a two-metre-deep hole in front of the crawler. A crack opened beneath the hole and quickly snaked down to the bottom of the supporting arch. The vehicle fell into the hole with a crunch, slamming its nose into the broken rock. Wheels and tracks stopped, spun backwards and ripped up the stone decking as it tried to back out. The crack widened and joined up with the hole. The crawler slipped, tilted forward, and wedged itself into the expanding gap, its back end now almost vertical. As the crawler settled into its new position, lodged in the gap like an odd-shaped keystone, the rear door burst open. The crew jumped out and ran back across the bridge.

It was the helicopters' turn. Three of them took off from the other side of the valley and, flying low, buzzed up and down the length of the terrace. The flying vehicles terrified the Martians. They cowered in the face of the awful din and the violence of the rotating blades. Seeing this, two of the helicopters tried to land on the terrace. Alarik jumped up and roared at his soldiers to fight. Running forward, he grabbed a discarded spear and hurled it at the cockpit of a helicopter. It cracked the glass and stuck there, sticking out like a pin. Emboldened, the guards responded. As the helicopters neared the ground, they hit the cockpits with a hail of crossbow bolts and spears. Unable to alight, the pirates were forced to take off again.

The third helicopter, much larger with twin blades,

manoeuvred above the heads of the statues. A door slid open and pirates rappelled down onto the stone shoulders. They sighted their rifles and began firing into the ranks of the defenders hiding behind the parapet. One bullet struck a Martian in the side; he rolled over on the ground, moaning. Another hit a defender in the throat and he clutched at his neck, red blood spurting between his green fingers. Other Martians rushed to their aid and dragged them back through the gateway.

As the firing from behind the ridge increased, another crawler with a machine gun drove down towards the bridge. It, too, opened up and sprayed the battlements. The Martians were pinned down and taking fire from both directions.

Holly grabbed Zach's arm as bullets scuffed the ground around them. 'They're behind us!'

Zach nodded grimly. He took his communicator out and shouted in the microphone. 'Now!'

A mound of sand over beyond the ridge shook and a dark shovel-shaped nose appeared. Ship reared up out of the sand and swung around to face the action.

Inside, Sophie, for once, strapped herself in. 'What's the first target, Ship?'

Ship's reply was icy. 'The helicopter.'

The hovercraft glided down the slope, picking up speed. It took a long sweeping curve around the edge of the ridge and straightened up as it neared the bridge. The bump on top of its hull split open and the Gatling gun swivelled towards its target.

The helicopter pilot must have seen it coming. The vehicle banked and began turning away. Pirates still on the ropes were flung free and tumbled down the body of the statues onto the terrace, where Martians pounced on them. One pirate managed to hang on, only to be dashed against a giant nose.

The Gatling gun fired a long staccato burst. A line of white-hot dots connected hovercraft to helicopter. The rear of the helicopter's fuselage disappeared in a cloud of shrapnel. Dipping and swinging about as if it was being jerked on the end of a string, the helicopter fell out of sight behind the lip of the canyon, leaving only a spiralling trail of smoke. It reappeared moments later in the form of a big orange fireball, at the top of which was one of the rotor assemblies, the blade still sluggishly chopping the air.

With the helicopter destroyed, Ship turned its attention towards the ridge. It continued past the bridge and swung around in a wide arc to come in behind the line of vehicles. The pirates flung themselves to the ground as Ship raced down the line, spraying the buggies and crawlers with bullets. Tyres, canopies, panels and engine blocks were torn apart. One buggy exploded and twisted in the air to land upside down. Some crawlers caught on fire.

Ship reached the end and swooped around in a wide arc for a second run. But before it had straightened up, a flash of red flame came from behind a boulder. A rocket slammed into the side of the hovercraft, knocking the vehicle sidewards. Skipping over the sand like a struck hockey puck, it pulverised an outcrop of rock, wobbled, stabilised, hit another rock with its wing and spun around. A turbofan caught ablaze. Still moving, the hovercraft pulled out of the spin but careened towards the ravine. The fire jumped to a second turbofan, which exploded in a rattle of metal fragments.

Despite this, the hovercraft increased speed.

Watching from the battlements, Holly realised what Ship was going to do. 'It can't stop in time. It's going to jump!'

Zach groaned, 'It's not moving fast enough!'

The hovercraft flew off the edge of the ravine. The whine of the remaining engines suddenly increased to ear-splitting level, the scream communicating the effort to everyone in the valley.

It almost worked. Ship was ten metres from the other side when the remaining engines ripped themselves apart. The hovercraft sagged in flight and crashed onto the other side, forty metres down from where the battlement curved around to meet the canyon wall. The vehicle slid up an incline of scree, the nose crumpling, the wings broken. As its forward momentum ceased, it began sliding back down towards the ravine, coming to rest with half its body sticking out over the precipice.

'Sophie!' came an anguished cry.

Zach and Holly turned around to see Toby, hanging by his armpits between a couple of burly palace guards. The captain stood next to them.

'Toby, what are you doing here?' demanded Zach.

But Toby couldn't answer; bug-eyed, he stared at the

burning wreck. He thrashed about, trying to break free.

At a word from Holly, the guards dropped him, and he ran towards the hovercraft.

Holly and Zach rose to follow him, but the captain blocked their path. 'They found him outside the tower,' he said. 'They tell me the Queen has barricaded herself inside.'

'So? So?' blurted Holly.

'The weapon I told you about. I think she means to use it.'

Holly stared at him in incomprehension.

He grabbed her arm and squeezed it painfully. 'You've seen what it does!'

Dumbly, Holly nodded. She turned to Zach. 'Go. Get Sophie.'

'But what –?'

'Go!'

Zach nodded. He ran after Toby. Holly turned to the Captain. 'Take me there, at once.'

As Zach neared the wreck, a blast of heat hit him in the face. He raised his arms to protect his eyes. The entire left side of the hovercraft was ablaze, and black, oily smoke was billowing out from under the wing. The fire was spreading to the fuselage. Toby was nowhere to be seen.

Zach ran around to the other side. The ramp was down, both of its supporting struts bent. Hot air poured out of the open door and flowed down the ramp like a viscous liquid. Hands shielding his face, Zach ran into the hovercraft.

The kitchen was on fire, the ceiling full of roiling smoke.

Zach gagged on the acrid smell of burning plastic. It forced him back towards the bridge. It was relatively clear, and not as hot – sprinklers were dousing the console and chairs with water. The droplets spat as they hit the floor and exploded into steam. He stumbled through the scalding vapour and found the Hendriksens. Sophie was on her knees in front of the computer rack where Ship's mind was housed. Toby, his arms wrapped around her from behind, was trying to pull her away.

Toby saw him. 'I can't . . .!'

Zach crouched next to Sophie. Her face was awash in tears. 'Ship won't come!' she bawled.

For the first time in Zach's experience, Ship's voice was strained. 'Sophie, I am done. You must leave!'

'No,' cried Sophie, beating her fists against the rack. 'Eject! I command you!'

'Sophie, please. A captain must go down with his ship. Zach, Toby, take her!'

Zach and Toby tried to lift her up, but their bodies were drenched in steam and sweat, and Sophie wriggled from their grasp. She latched onto the rack, slipping her thin arms up to the elbows through the rack's handle. Zach tried to prise her forearms free while Toby grasped her around the waist and pulled. Sophie fought back like a wildcat and bit Zach's thumb. Zach yelped in pain.

'Sophie, listen,' pleaded Ship. 'I am a soldier. This is what we do. We fight and die for the cause.'

'*I* am your cause, Ship,' sobbed Sophie.

'Please, Sophie, please,' said Toby.

Sophie leaned backwards and pressed her cheek against her brother's. 'Ship is our family.'

Toby blinked back tears. 'I know, but . . . I don't want to lose you too.'

'What does it matter?' said Sophie bitterly. 'We're just dumb Martians. We came to Mars to die.'

Zach looked around him. The sprinklers were failing. The roiling smoke from the kitchen had spread to the ceiling of the bridge. He knew that the smoke of burning synthetic materials was toxic and could kill you as surely as being burnt alive.

Roughly, he grabbed Sophie's arm. 'Sophie, I swear I will break your arm if you don't let go.'

But Toby reached out a hand to restrain him. 'No. Sophie's right.'

'What?'

'You go. Sophie and I are staying with Ship.'

Zach stared at him, dumbfounded. 'We've got to get out of here!'

Clinging to Sophie, Toby shook his head. 'Ship is our family.'

There was a small object at Zach's feet: a chess piece that had fallen to the floor. In exasperation, he kicked it, and it skipped across the bridge and hit the wall, spontaneously bursting into flames. Precious seconds passed.

'Ship, eject,' said Zach. 'It's the only way.'

'Zach, I am a soldier. I am nothing without my body.'

Toby took hold of the rack's handle, his hand on top of Sophie's. 'No, you are much more to us than that. We're family. We stay together.'

'I swear, Ship,' said Zach, 'I will find you another body. But if you don't come with us now, we are all going to die!'

There was a moment of silence. The sprinklers sputtered and failed. The soles of Zach's shoes started to melt. The bridge became a furnace.

With a small click, the drive containing Ship's mind ejected into Sophie's arms. She squeezed the metal case to her chest. Toby and Zach lifted her up and carried her from the hovercraft.

Chapter Eleven

Eternity

Accompanied by a contingent of guards, Holly and the captain raced through the streets towards the palace tower. They ran past groups of fearful Martians, eager for news of what was happening at the temple gateway. Holly didn't have time to stop and explain. Some of them followed her.

They arrived at the forecourt surrounding the palace. There were Martians here too, alerted to the news that the Queen had arisen. They found Kebechet instead, standing guard at the door to the tower. Holly felt a familiar shudder of fear at facing the snake-headed god, but her attention was drawn to the wall of the tower above Kebechet's head. In the glass doors to the balcony overlooking the forecourt, the panes flashed electric blue.

'This is where we found the boy,' explained a guard. 'The Queen and another outsider are within. She ordered us away and closed the door.'

'Another one?' asked Holly.

The guard shrugged. 'Old and pink with little hair.'

'The Curator,' Holly said under her breath. 'And Kebechet?'

The guard spat. 'It is the infernal machine the alchemists created to scare the people. It will let no one approach.'

Holly addressed Alarik. 'How is it controlled?'

'I don't know,' he replied, 'but it answers only to the Queen.'

Kebechet stood motionless with one leg on either side of the doorway, the only movement an occasional dart of its forked tongue, the tip quivering as if smelling the air.

'Maybe. But it picked me up once without hurting me.' Holly took a step forward. 'Keep everyone back.'

The captain and his guards ran to obey. Holly walked into the centre of the forecourt; Kebechet's eyes tracked her.

Holly stopped and called out, 'I'm just going to walk between your, ah, legs, and into the building. If that's okay.' She took a nervous gulp of air, and added, 'Just remember – I'm the key.'

Striding forward, adopting an air of confidence and authority – which she didn't feel, but hey – Holly approached the door. She got within ten metres, close enough to consider running the rest of the way, when the robot bent over and scooped her up.

That was impressively quick for such an enormous machine, marvelled a part of Holly's brain. Screaming was close behind. Conveniently, the constriction of Holly's chest as the robot's fingers tightened around her made it difficult to do anything but squeak. 'Too tight! Too tight!'

The hand lifted Holly to Kebechet's snake face, and more alarmingly, its snake-like maw. Green eyes appraised her impassively, the pattern of the irises swirling about in complex bands like the turbulent atmosphere of a gas giant.

The maw opened. Holly cowered. Kebechet's tongue darted out and smeared sticky across her cheek. With an 'Ugh', she wiped her face. But the eyes of the robot refocused and seemed to look past her, and almost absent-mindedly, the hand put Holly back down on the ground. Some internal condition had apparently been tested and satisfied.

Holly caught her breath and tried to settle her nerves before walking to the door on shaking legs.

The base of the tower was a foyer or waiting room, with several passages leading away in different directions. The correct one was clear enough: blue light flickered from a passage that disappeared up wide steps. Holly ran up several flights and emerged into a laboratory-like chamber pulsing with energy and filled with the crisp tang of ozone.

To one side of the room stood the Curator, furiously working a console of levers and dials attached to a boxy contraption sprouting wires. Beyond the machine, blue lightning crackled from a ring of coils around the walls and streaked into the centre of the chamber to meet in an amorphous black mass, which thrashed about like a trapped animal.

The Queen sat in a chair against the wall. Wearing a gown of purple with gold trim. With her hair coiled and piled high upon her head, and her face painted in shades of mauve and pink, she seemed the magisterial figure that

Holly remembered from her dreams.

But as Holly ran to her side, she realised the Queen wasn't the same. The woman sat demurely with her hands folded in her lap and gazed upon the suspended mass, her face blank, her eyes dull. Ignoring all propriety, Holly shook the Queen's shoulder. 'Your Majesty? What is happening?'

Without looking up, the Queen replied in a monotone, 'The captain informs me there are enemies at the gates. The funny little man is turning the machine on.'

'But you know what it does?'

The Queen's face was rigid, but Holly saw something register in her eyes.

'You do, don't you?' said Holly.

The Queen flicked her hand as if shooing an annoying insect. 'They assembled in the arena. Many more were coming all the time. Even through the caves below. I could not have them threaten the safety of the city.'

'You turned the machine on your own people!'

'It had to be done!' croaked the Queen, 'All Martian civilisation depended on it!'

'And what about now?' cried Holly. 'You would bring it all to an end?'

'Mars has gone,' said the Queen bitterly. 'Let the last of it go too.'

Appalled, Holly backed away and ran to the Curator. She grabbed his arm as he went to operate a switch. 'Stop this!'

But the Curator pushed her away, knocking her to

the floor.

Holly's voice was soft with horror. 'You don't know what you're –'

'I am dying. I have cancer,' the Curator replied. With a dour grunt, he flicked a switch. The hairs on Holly's arms prickled with static electricity as the bolts from the coils increased in frequency and strength. The swollen mass in the centre grew and turned cobalt blue, writhing with barely contained fury.

The Curator turned to Holly, a feverish look in his eyes. 'Don't worry. I know what I'm doing. I have spent forty years collecting and studying everything that the Martians wrote about this machine. A small dose of the radiation turns the outer layer of organic molecules into diamond, protecting everything inside for millennia. We will awaken in a new world where diseases are a thing of the past. Who knows? Maybe even death itself is obsolete!'

'You're insane.'

'Stupid girl,' the Curator said. 'We will live forever!'

Holly got to her feet and jumped onto his back, trying to pin his arms. He fell to the floor, then broke free and punched her in the jaw. Stunned, Holly reeled to one side and the Curator regained his feet. Holly tried to stand, but the Curator hit her again, knocking her back down. Pain exploded in Holly's cheek and she tasted blood in her mouth. Weakly, she defended herself from further blows by covering her face with her forearms.

The Curator hit her a few more times and at last Holly went limp. He stopped, blinking in confusion as if he wasn't sure where he was. Standing up, he gazed upon the writhing mass in the centre of the chamber, and from it seemed to draw fresh energy and purpose. He rested his hands on his hips and nodded in satisfaction. 'It will only take a minute or more to reach full capacity. And then . . .'

Holly teetered on the edge of consciousness. She glimpsed rays of gold gilding the water of a canal and heard the tinkle of laughter. A diaphanous shape held the promise of warmth and safety. 'Hold me,' she murmured.

Behind the Curator, one big green eye appeared in the glass door of the balcony. Seconds later, a taloned hand smashed through the door and reached into the room. Alerted by the sound of shattered glass, the Curator whirled around in time to be knocked over by the groping hand. The hand found Holly, and with surprising gentleness curled its fingers under her body and lifted her into the air.

'Destroy the machine,' Holly said groggily.

The hand put Holly down carefully against the wall of the chamber and balled itself into a fist. It rose into the air above the machine.

'No!' cried the Curator.

The hand came down, smashing the console of levers and dials. It rose again, descended again, and crushed the rest of the machine to a tangled mess of broken panels and sparking wires. The bolts of blue from the coils around the room stopped. The globular mass at the centre briefly went berserk, snapping and crackling furiously, before just as quickly dying down, congealing into a waxy, blue sphere the size of a basketball. Released from its suspension, it fell to the floor with a heavy thud and rolled up against the wall close to Holly.

Sobbing, the Curator ran over and enveloped the ball in his arms. Holly crawled as quickly as she could in the other direction. When she looked back, the Curator's skin had transformed to a crystalline yellow, as if he was coated in tiny diamonds, and he had stopped moving – forever.

Holly crawled over to the Queen and propped herself up with her back against the wall. Kebechet had retracted his hand from the chamber, but one eye still stared at her through the broken doorway to the balcony. Feeling a bit foolish, Holly waved.

'It obeys me,' the Queen snapped.

Holly felt inside her bloody mouth and discovered a loose tooth. She wiggled it with a finger and was rewarded with a sharp sting of pain. 'Maybe,' she replied, 'but its main job is to protect me.'

The Queen cursed peevishly.

'Look,' said Holly, 'I have to go. The enemy really is at the gates. And Martians are fighting to protect the city. My friends too.' She got to her feet and looked at the broken machine. 'When I leave, I want you to go to the balcony. Your subjects are out there, waiting for you to lead them.'

The Queen cast her eyes to the floor. 'My daughter is not among them.'

'No,' said Holly.

'She wanted to live before she died.'

'And she did,' said Holly. 'She lived out her life ten

thousand years ago. The way she wanted to. Your subjects
want to live before they die too. Don't take it away from
them now.'

Before Holly left, she turned around in the doorway.
The Queen had slumped in her chair, her face streaked
with tears.

'This is madness. You've played your last card. It's over.'

The warring parties were having another parley on the
bridge. Janus and his compatriots were on one side; Zach
and the captain on the other. This time Janus looked
positively vexed. Behind him, the ridge was a traffic jam
of damaged and broken vehicles, some of them burning.
Clusters of men and women were tending to the injured
or trying to put the fires out with blankets and fire extin-
guishers. Others apparently had had enough and left.

Janus's allies hadn't survived unscathed, either. Their
clothes and faces were streaked with grease and dirt, and
one carried his arm in a sling seeping with blood. Also,
there were now only two of them. Zach wondered what
had happened to the other one.

But Janus had a point. Zach glanced sidelong towards
the narrow end of the valley. Once more, pirates were
attempting to bridge the ravine with flying foxes, pinning
the defenders down with gunfire. He looked in the other
direction. Well away from the battlements, a large helicopter had managed to land on the loose scree and disgorge
a party of heavily armed pirates, who were now making
their way cautiously towards the gateway.

As for the Martians, Zach knew their condition was parlous. Almost all the defenders had been injured and their supply of crossbow bolts and spears was gone. They were down to swords against guns.

Zach coughed, partly to buy some time to think and partly because he was having trouble speaking – his tongue was swollen, his lips were cracked and his mouth was bone dry. 'I've still got cards,' he finally managed to croak.

He couldn't pull it off. Janus saw through him and grinned. 'Special deal. One-time offer only. You don't need to surrender, and your people can keep their weapons. Just let us get what we came for, and we'll be on our way. Otherwise . . .' Janus paused for emphasis '. . . a lot more people are going to die.'

Zach looked at the captain, wondering how he was going to explain to him it was over. He wondered too how Holly was, and how he was going to explain to her he had failed. He rubbed his eyes, which was a mistake because his eyes were still stinging from the caustic smoke of the hovercraft and rubbing them only made it worse.

But the captain was looking at something else. Over the canyon wall to the north an object had appeared, flashing brightly in the afternoon sun. The object grew, banked, levelled off over the ravine and became a yellow biplane. Seconds later, it buzzed past the bridge, low enough for Zach to catch Ezra's casual wave as he flew by.

A cloud blocked out the sun, which was strange because on Mars it rained maybe three or four times a year. Zach didn't need to turn around to know what it was. He looked at Janus, who was glowering at the sky. A low growl emanated from somewhere deep in the man's chest. He whirled around and strode from the bridge.

The *Pointy End* hovered over the statues, its vast bulk blotting out the sky – and the hopes of the pirates. Little did they know it wasn't quite the cavalry Zach had been hoping for. After Claudia and Patrice had rappelled down to the terrace, they informed him that Ezra couldn't join them because there was nowhere to land, and the entire crew of the *Pointy End* consisted of a few stragglers they had picked up from Pirate Central.

And then there was the problem of whose side the cavalry was on.

'You mean you've seen this treasure?' asked Claudia, a glint in her eye.

'I'm not letting them pass, Mum. I promised Holly—'

'This girl!' Claudia smacked her forehead.

'I promised her I'd defend the gateway. And I'd really like it if you could help.'

'Wait, what?' said Patrice. 'We're on the side of the good guys now?'

'But you've actually *seen* the treasure?' said Claudia.

Zach folded his arms and went and stood next to the captain. Alarik didn't understand the words, but seemed to sense what was going on. He folded his arms as well.

Claudia avoided the captain's glare and concentrated on Zach. 'Look, all I'm saying is maybe we can work out a bit of a deal. Payment for services rendered, that sort of thing.'

Zach couldn't believe his ears. 'That sounds suspiciously like the deal Janus just offered me, *except without the threat of murder!*'

'Don't lump me in with that thug. You have no idea what . . .'

Claudia's words were lost in the din of another commotion. The contingent of pirates from the helicopter had reached the northern end of the battlements. There was the *ppsssshh* of explosively decompressing air. Projectiles arced high over the wall and fell among the defenders, whizzing around when they hit the ground and releasing thick, cloying smoke.

'Tear gas!' yelled Patrice.

Within seconds, white smoke covered the terrace. Martians fell to their knees, choking and spluttering and clawing at their eyes.

Zach felt the burn at the back of his mouth and nose almost immediately; suddenly his head ached. Forgetting they couldn't understand him, he tried to yell at the Martians to retreat, but all that came out was a strangled cough. It didn't matter – the captain had already reacted. Tears streaming down his face, he ran to his soldiers, barking orders, pulling them up off the ground and pushing them towards the gateway.

Zach felt Patrice grab him by the collar and yank him away. He lost sight of his mother, but he could still hear her swearing. They retreated through the doorway and into the dim interior. None of the tear gas canisters had landed inside, and Zach gratefully gulped the clear, cool air.

A second wave of defenders had not been idle. The Martians had erected a barricade across the main passage that led to the city, using furniture, blocks of stone and pieces of the broken door, even plugging some gaps with stone people. The captain ordered the way to be temporarily cleared and ushered Zach, Patrice, Claudia and the last of the defenders through.

Zach at first thought the scene one of confusion, but realised there was an underlying order. Martians were carrying the injured away on stretchers and returning with weapons that they distributed to the guards on the barricade, including a fresh supply of crossbow bolts they had discovered. As they rearmed, they took turns washing their faces in buckets of water, trying to clean their eyes of the terrible irritant of the tear gas.

Zach pushed through the throng and found the Hendriksens sitting against the wall. Toby was staring blankly into space. Sophie, still clutching Ship's mind to her chest, was barely sensate.

'You guys okay?' asked Zach.

Toby nodded dumbly. Sophie didn't respond.

A moment later, Holly came running up the passage flanked by a cohort of guards. Zach stared at her bloodied face. 'What happened?'

Holly dismissed his concern. 'Long story.' She sat between Toby and Sophie, hugged them both and kissed Sophie on the forehead. 'Thank heavens you're okay. I'm so sorry, Sophie. You shouldn't be here. None of you should.

I made a terrible mistake.'

'You've gone green,' said Sophie in a tiny voice.

'My true colour, apparently,' said Holly. 'Is Ship okay?'

'Ship's sad. He's lost his body.'

Holly touched the metal casing. 'I don't know whether you can hear me in there, Ship, but I think I've found you another one. You're gonna love it.'

Lights on the side of the casing flashed red and green. Until they plugged Ship into another interface, it had no other way to communicate.

'What happened to Sierra? Did she send the broadcast?' asked Zach. 'We could really use the hot glare of publicity about now.'

'She betrayed us,' answered Toby. 'She and her father went back for the . . . wait! The Curator!'

'We don't have to worry about him anymore,' said Holly, wiping blood from her cheek. 'He got what he came for. What's the situation here?'

'Most of the pirates have left or are licking their wounds,' replied Zach. 'But Janus's personal band of thugs are better armed and organised and have taken the gateway. Brutal honesty? I think we're done for. If they have more tear gas or bring a big gun in here, then all this' – he waved his hand at the barricade – 'will count for nothing.'

As he finished speaking, a guard ran to Holly and whispered in her ear. She stood up and peered over the barricade. Silhouetted against the bright rectangle of light from the broken gateway, the pirates were assembling a gun. A very big one.

Holly sagged forward against the wall. Zach was right, they were done for. Suddenly, the enormity of her decision to fight hit home. What did she think she was trying to do? The captain had asked her to lead the Martians, to help them find food and water and escape the caverns. And what had she done? Started a war! People had been killed, for God's sake! And Zach, Toby and Sophie had almost been killed too. And all for . . . well, what exactly? Some trinkets?

The past mattered. The professor had taught her that. But the legacy of the Martians didn't live in their possessions; it lived in the Martians themselves. Perhaps if she hadn't been so fixated on finding out about her own past, she would have realised that. She covered her face with her hands. It was tender and swollen and aching. She shook her head. *What have I done?*

'Now is not the time to feel sorry for yourself. There'll be plenty of time for regret later.' The voice came from behind her. Holly looked around to find Claudia, one hand on the hilt of her pistol, the other holding a Martian sword.

'It's over,' said Holly. 'I will make a deal with Janus.'

'That would be a mistake. Janus will find a way to betray you.'

'But what else can I do?'

'I have an idea.'

Holly was suspicious. 'And the price?'

Claudia glanced at Zach before replying. 'Oh fuck it, we'll just waive the price for now.'

'What's the plan?' asked Zach.

'Betray him before he betrays you. I presume you keep the treasure in a locked room. Janus wants to see it, so let him and his partners see it. Then lock them in. With them separated from the rest of the pirates and unable to give orders, the coalition outside will quickly fall apart. It will take all of five minutes before they're fighting among themselves.'

'*That's* the plan?' scoffed Zach.

But Holly was nodding. Hurriedly, she conversed in Martian with the captain. He ran off to give orders.

'Okay,' said Holly, exhausted, 'let's finish this once and for all.'

Janus stood in the middle of the chamber surrounded by riches. He took a deep breath, puffing his chest out as if inhaling a sweet fragrance, and exhaled again in a low, slow sigh. Turning to an open box, he scooped up a handful of jewels and let them spill from between his fingers like granules of sand.

'You know, in a way, it's almost disappointing,' he said. 'Not the treasure, of course, but losing a certain way of life. I enjoyed what I did for a living.' He looked at Claudia and winked. 'But I'm sure I'll find something else to do.'

'This room and the adjacent two are yours, as per the deal,' said Claudia.

'But the more culturally important artefacts – the clothes, the scrolls, the maps, the sculptures and works of art – they stay here,' added Holly.

Janus bowed with mock solemnity. 'I wouldn't have it any other way.'

Holly, Patrice, Zach and Claudia had entered the chamber first, and as unobtrusively as possible, made their way to the far end, near to where they had concealed the rear exit behind a beautiful bronze partition. Some of Janus's minions stood guard at the top of the stairs. Holly had hoped to entice them down to the floor. The plan was to get them all into the room and then run out the rear door, sealing it behind them, while Captain Alarik and his guards blocked off the front by rolling boulders into the passage. All the treasures in the world wouldn't count for much when the pirates found themselves locked inside a vault without food or water.

But Janus wasn't stupid. He entered with half a dozen heavily armed pirates, stationing three at the entrance to the passage from the temple gateway and two at the door to the treasure rooms, while his personal bodyguard stood alongside him on the chamber floor.

Standing close to Zach, Holly's eyes darted to the main door. Janus caught Holly's glance. Instinctively, his hand went to the handle of the pistol by his side. He grunted sharply at the guards by the door. Bleary-eyed from gaping at the treasure, the guards responded sluggishly. 'Wake up!' Janus barked. They jumped as if they'd received an electric shock and tried to point their rifles in five directions at once.

Holly felt Zach tense beside her and from the corner of her eye she watched as his hand slid behind his back towards the pistol stuck in his trousers. She sensed, rather than saw, Claudia and Patrice tighten their grip on their own weapons. She glimpsed the eyes of the pirates narrow to slits as they raised their guns. For a heady moment, time and place were suspended . . .

'. . . do we have room for a couple of these little thingies? They would look really good on the mantlepiece of my apartment in . . .'

All heads turned as Sierra swanned in through an archway from an adjoining room. She was wearing a crown and a gold breastplate, and carrying an alabaster figurine. The crown was too big for her head and had slipped down rakishly to cover one eye.

'. . . New York – *arrrgh!*

Sierra dropped the figurine; it hit the floor and broke into several pieces. She lifted the crown above her eyes and looked around at the faces in the room. 'I can explain.'

'Explain what?' asked Jesse, before stopping dead a few steps behind her.

Unsure where to look, or how this additional element affected their respective ploys, the parties froze mid-draw.

'You?' said Holly, squinting at Jesse.

Jesse gave Holly a brief salute. Incredulous, Sierra looked back and forth between them. 'You two know each other?'

'He almost executed me when we were in Sicaria,' said Holly.

'*Almost*,' emphasized Jesse, wagging a finger.

'I knew she didn't escape on her own,' sneered Janus.

'Sorry, boss,' said Jesse sheepishly. He licked his lips. 'Look, clearly you people have issues to discuss. We don't want to intrude.' He reached for Sierra's hand.

Janus drew his gun. Claudia was a split second faster. But Jesse was quicker than both. The remaining participants followed as fast as their reflexes permitted. The exchange of gunfire was so rapid it sounded like hail on a tin roof.

The pirates at the top of the stairs went down first – no cover. Patrice took a bullet to the shoulder and fell to the floor. Multiple shots hit Janus's bodyguard, and he somersaulted backwards over a table full of crockery. A bullet struck Sierra in the chest and she fell into Jesse's arms. Zach took a bullet in his side a moment before Holly pushed him behind a trunk.

After firing a single shot, Janus ducked behind a statue of Patarka – goddess of home remedies – and continued firing from around her legs. Claudia, focused exclusively on Janus, poured a barrage of bullets into the statue until one leg fell off, at which point Janus ran ducking and weaving across the room to where Holly was trying to resuscitate Zach. Janus coiled an arm around her neck and dragged her to her feet.

'Please, let me help him. Please,' begged Holly.

But Janus choked her off, his thickly knotted arm tightening like a noose around her neck. Using Holly as a shield, he inched back towards the foot of the stairs.

Claudia ducked behind the partition. She crawled over to where Patrice lay moaning, holding a blood-soaked shoulder. 'Report,' she hissed.

'I've had worse,' said Patrice. 'Zach?'

Claudia could only see Zach's foot sticking out from behind a trunk. She crawled towards it and found her son unconscious and with a bloody graze along the side of his stomach, but otherwise unhurt. He'd probably hit his head when he fell. Claudia sighed in relief.

'You had to go and ruin it, didn't you, Claude?' Janus's voice boomed out from across the chamber.

Claudia risked a peek over the top of the trunk. Janus had made it to the centre of the room, Holly struggling weakly in his grip.

'Didn't you draw first?' Claudia asked, playing for time.

'Ah, maybe. I can't remember.' Janus shouted over his shoulder towards the stairs, 'Leroy? Spiro?'

A patter of gunfire sounded from the passage. There were several loud crashes and a couple of screams, and the gunfire ceased.

'I think that's the last we'll hear from Leroy and Spiro,' said Claudia. 'Not to mention your escape route.'

'It appears we have a conundrum,' said Janus.

Claudia reloaded her gun. 'Let the girl go now and you can go too.'

'I let her go when I get to the other side of the bridge. Or I can blow her brains out.'

Claudia risked another peek. Janus had rammed the barrel of his gun against Holly's temple. Red-faced and choking, she clawed at Janus's arm.

'She won't make it that far if you don't let her breathe.'

Reluctantly, Janus loosened his grip. Holly gasped for air.

'We have a deal then?' said Janus.

Claudia noticed a furtive movement to Janus's right. Jesse was sneaking around the edge of the room. A few seconds more and he would be behind Janus.

'Sure,' said Claudia. 'Let's discuss. Lower your gun.'

'Stand up, so I can see you've lowered yours.'

Claudia took a deep breath, counted to three, holstered her weapon and got to her feet.

Janus leered as he swung the barrel of his gun towards her. Jesse pounced on his back and the gun went off. The bullet zinged past Claudia's head, nicking her ear, and ricocheted around the chamber.

Janus grunted in fury. Releasing Holly, he plucked Jesse from his back and threw him to the floor. He raised a booted foot above Jesse's head. 'Traitorous little sh—'

Claudia shot him.

At first, the only effect on Janus was a look of mild surprise. He looked at the bullet hole in his chest and back at Claudia, then stumbled backwards a few steps and fell onto the grate in the centre of the room. The rusty iron bars gave way under his weight and Janus disappeared down the drain to land with a clang and a muffled wet thud somewhere below.

There was silence, apart from the occasional moan of pain. Claudia walked over to Jesse and Holly and helped them to their feet. Holly immediately ran to check on Zach.

Claudia sighed and turned to Jesse. 'How's your girl?'

A dazed Sierra popped up from behind a table, the crown still tilted at a crazy angle on her head, one finger absentmindedly tracing the bullet shell lodged in her breastplate.

'She'll live,' said Jesse. 'How's your boy?'

'Same. You should've told me you'd left Janus. You could've come work for me.'

Jesse shrugged. 'I was enjoying my independence.' He gestured at the treasure. 'Do we get to keep any of this?'

At that precise moment, the captain and a company of Martian guards burst in from the exit behind the partition. Alarik's sword was dripping with bright red blood.

Claudia pouted. 'Apparently not.'

Sierra had gingerly approached the drain. She leaned over and peered into the hole. 'Whaddya suppose . . .'

'Careful, sweetie,' said Jesse.

From the bottom of the shaft came a shuffling, snuffling noise, followed by a sharp gasp. Then a scream. Abruptly, the scream was cut off by a sickening crunch, like a wet tree branch snapping in two. There was a low gurgle, interspersed with more cracks and snaps and the occasional deeply satisfied growl.

Sierra wrapped her arms around her body and shivered. 'Cave troll.'

Chapter Twelve

Reconciliation

In the large foyer of the recently built Martian office of IMC Talent Management in Port Clarke, Sierra Garcia was giving a crowded press conference.

'It was incredible,' said Sierra, her voice rising in excitement. 'There I was, surrounded. Martians on one side and pirates on the other. I thought, I'm done for. No way I'm getting out of this one. After surviving a band of monstrous cave trolls and fighting off vicious pirates, this is it. Going down, guns blazing, fighting to protect the Martians—'

A reporter's hand shot up. 'Doesn't your father have a connection with the pirates?'

Sierra coughed. 'Well, you know, what does the word *connection* really mean?'

Ms Garcia, sitting next to Sierra, leaned in to the microphone and curtly said, 'Rumours about my ex-husband's involvement have been greatly exaggerated.'

'Anyway, as I was saying . . .' Sierra went on.

The sea of reporters hung on every word. The video was being live streamed all over Mars and Earth, as well as on

Ceres and the space stations in Earth orbit.

Standing at the back of the room with Holly, Zach watched the performance in slack-jawed wonder. 'Astonishing. How many cave trolls are in a band, do you think?'

'Six,' growled Holly.

'It should be you up there,' said Zach.

'I'll pass.'

Holly pulled the hoodie in closer around her face. Her green skin and bronze eyes made her easy to spot, and she hated running the gauntlet of journalists whenever she was in public.

'To the airport?' asked Zach.

'You go ahead. I need to stop somewhere first.'

Zach dithered in the doorway. 'Sure. Um, well, I guess I'll see you there.' He gave her an awkward smile.

Zach had been behaving funny for a while now. Holly wondered what it was all about, but then she realised she had forgotten something. She grabbed his shirt and kissed him on the lips. After ten long seconds, she released him and locked onto his eyes. 'Promise me when I get back, we'll do more of that.'

Zach blinked in confusion while his brain caught up. 'It's a deal.'

At Port Clarke Spaceport, the *Pointy End* was being refitted, refuelled and loaded with supplies for the Martians inhabiting the various encampments around the Well of Souls and the City of the Dead. It turned out that there were other pockets of pods hidden deep underground where Martians had survived the long sleep, with stashes of equipment, seeds, medicine, clothes and weapons too. The Martians had planned well, and as they awakened they had spread out and resettled some of the old cities around the Amalthea Basin.

The initial negotiations had been difficult. The Martians had lost so much, and finding their world crumbled to almost nothing and partially settled by interlopers from Earth had been a terrible shock – not to mention their anger over the battle with the pirates and the years of looting. But it helped that Mayor Garcia was a consummate diplomat, and that the Queen, arousing herself from her grief, adjusted quickly to the new conditions. They brokered an arrangement and drew borders, settled water rights and struck trade deals. In return for emergency supplies from Port Clarke, and Mayor Garcia returning the stolen artefacts (at least the ones she could recover), the Martians would sell a few trinkets, share the location of mineral deposits and aquifers, and help the Earthlings tap into that most precious resource of all: water.

It also helped that the Martians had a weapon that could turn everyone to stone.

Kebechet sat in the loading bay of the *Pointy End*. The robot was lounging up against the bulkhead with one leg jauntily sitting atop a pile of crates. Its green eyes swivelled down to watch Sophie as she furtively peeked out the back of the sand crawler before jumping to the floor.

'Ship, level three, please,' said Sophie, one hand hidden

behind her back.

The robot's arm swooped out and casually lifted Sophie to the top floor of the bay. Besides controlling Kebechet, Ship now had charge of the airship and the sand crawler – its empire was growing. Control of the airship had not been relinquished without argument, however. Claudia had reluctantly agreed only after she had failed to recruit more than a handful of crew. With the spoils of the pirate way of life drying up, she didn't have the money to pay them.

As Sophie alighted, she almost bumped into Claudia coming to supervise the loading of the cargo.

Claudia's eyes jumped from Sophie to the open door of the sand crawler. 'What were you doing in there?'

'Nothing,' replied Sophie and went to walk past, hand behind her back.

Claudia spun Sophie around and wrestled the pistol from her hand.

'How old are you again?'

Sophie stuck her chin out. 'Almost twelve.'

'Jesus. Go annoy your brother.'

Sophie left in a huff and went to find Toby. He was playing chess with Ezra in the crew lounge.

'Knight takes rook,' said Toby.

Ezra rubbed his forehead. He was losing to a child. Tentatively he lifted a pawn but dropped it again when he saw Toby's eyes widen in anticipation. He needed to get out of this.

'Have you finished your homework?'

Toby nodded without taking his eyes off the board. 'Yep, I did all the work Ms Garcia set me and then for fifty bucks I did Sierra's as well.'

'I'm not sure that's quite the point of homework, but . . .'

Sophie flounced in and plopped down heavily into an armchair. 'I'm bored,' she announced.

'Did you do *your* homework?' asked Ezra.

Sophie looked puzzled. 'What homework?'

Hmm. Ezra had never really thought of himself as parent material. Certainly, he hadn't been around much for his own son. But here were a couple of kids who could probably benefit from a little steering, and with Claudia too busy as usual trying to turn a profit on her latest change of circumstances, he did find himself at a loose end.

'They're dropping me back at my old airfield. Want to learn to fly?'

Sophie's eyes lit up. 'Yeaahh!'

'Wait, what? Isn't that dangerous?' asked Toby.

'Kiddo, after what you've been through, I'm sure you'll be able to handle it.' Ezra stood up and took Sophie's hand. 'Come on, the plane's in the forward cargo bay. Let's check it out.'

Sophie jumped out of her seat. 'Yeah, Toby. Come on. Let's learn to fly!'

Toby looked down at the chessboard. 'But what about our game?'

Ezra slapped Toby on the back so hard Toby's knee bumped the table and the chess pieces clattered to the floor. 'You're good, kid, but you fell into my trap. I'll explain your mistake when we get back.' And with that, he left the room, Sophie skipping by his side.

Toby stared at the pieces on the floor, nonplussed at first, but then his lips curved into a wry smile. He ran after them. 'Wait for me!'

Professor McGuire, now out of critical condition, had been moved to a private room in the recovery ward. Holly stood outside the large swing door and tried to find the right words. She stood there for a long time.

The professor was lying propped up in a bed by the window. He looked better than the last time she'd seen him. His skin had regained its colour and his blue eyes were clear, and even seemed to twinkle when he saw her. But he looked older and had lost a lot of weight.

'I just saw you on the news,' he said, smiling.

'Oh God. How bad was I?'

'It's a pity you aren't a princess. You'd make a wonderful spokesperson.'

Holly pulled up a chair and sat down. She was going to sit on the edge of the bed but found she couldn't.

'The Queen won't need any help in that regard. At first, she needed me to translate in the negotiations, but now she's mastered English. She speaks it better than I do.'

'I heard her speak. She's impressive.'

'She's a pain in the arse, but . . . she's been through a lot.'

The professor leaned forward. 'You need to help her, Holly. She doesn't know this world.'

Holly nodded. 'I know. I will.' She shifted awkwardly

in her chair. 'But first, I'm about to leave on another expedition. Captain Alarik gave me news about my mother. It was the deal I made with him in return for helping the Martians. He found a reference in the archives in the City to a woman who turned up at the palace asking for me. It's a long shot, but I may be able to find out what happened to her. Zach, Toby, Sophie and Ship are coming with me.'

The professor swallowed. 'I hope you find her.'

Holly couldn't meet his eyes and instead looked around the room. It was a pretty typical hospital room: sterile, smelling vaguely of disinfectant, and devoid of colour. There weren't any flowers, just some cards from some of his students. Holly was about to ask if he'd had many visitors but shut her mouth as soon as she opened it. Either way, the answer wouldn't reflect well on her.

'I'm so sorry,' she blurted out. 'I am *so, so* sorry.'

'No, no,' the professor replied quickly, 'you don't need to apologise.'

'I do. The things I did, the things I said. I really do.'

Professor McGuire shook his head emphatically. 'I should have told you the truth. I was going to – at the right time. But it never seemed to *be* the right time. And suddenly it was too late.'

Holly couldn't stop herself. The words tumbled out. 'I was so angry. I thought I'd lost the only part of my mother I ever had. And I blamed you for it, and you weren't really my father either, and then there was this mark on my back, and suddenly I was a Martian, and then a princess, and then not a princess, and then I turned green—'

'Stop. Please.' Wincing, the professor reached out and gripped her hand. 'It's okay, really.'

Holly placed one hand on top of his and wiped her tears away with the other. 'I am so sorry,' she said again, softly. 'Can you forgive me?'

'Already have,' he said. 'Can you forgive me?'

'Of course, I can.' She patted his hand and rubbed the last of her tears from her face. A long silence stretched out in front of them. Finally, Holly took out her handkerchief and blew her nose. 'Phew! I'm glad we're okay now.'

They talked and made plans. Professor McGuire had been appointed to head of department at the museum. His role in uncovering the Martians had boosted his profile, although this didn't come without some criticism. Before leaving, Holly would visit him and go through the archives to see if there was anything that might provide more clues about her mother. And she told him about Sierra, and Toby and Sophie, and Ship, and Zach too, of course – well, not too much about Zach.

Soon it was time to leave.

She stood at the door to the hospital room and waved goodbye. And in return, Professor McGuire managed an almost convincing smile. He put on a brave front, but Holly knew they weren't okay at all. She realised she had lost her father, and for that her heart ached – but she still had a friend, which is not the same thing, but not a terrible thing either.

She had regained the memory of her mother too. Before she had left the City to return to Port Clarke, the captain had uncovered another reference in the archives to a girl in a swimming costume found wandering by a canal.

So her dream wasn't a dream. It was something tiny, but real. She marvelled that something so small could matter so much. It made no sense, but it didn't have to. She would always have this one memory, and whether or not she discovered anything more about her mother, that would carry her.

As she left the hospital, she stood for a while on the front steps. In the sky, a spaceship was descending towards the spaceport on a column of smoke and orange flame. It was a settler ship, she could tell. She shook her head in wonder – more criminals, cultists, weirdos and immigrants of every stripe to join the riffraff already here.

A nurse saw her looking up into the sky and asked her what was so interesting.

'Dumb Martians,' said Holly.